The Editor

Michael Thurston is the Helen Means Professor of English at Smith College. His previous books include *Making Something Happen: American Political Poetry between the World Wars*, *The Underworld in Twentieth-Century Poetry*, and *Reading Postwar British and Irish Poetry* (with Nigel Alderman). He is the recipient of a National Endowment for the Humanities Fellowship and currently serves as Provost and Dean of the Faculty.

NORTON CRITICAL EDITIONS
MODERNIST & CONTEMPORARY ERAS

ANDERSON, WINESBURG, OHIO
AZUELA, THE UNDERDOGS
BURGESS, A CLOCKWORK ORANGE
CATHER, MY ÁNTONIA
CATHER, O PIONEERS!
CONRAD, HEART OF DARKNESS
CONRAD, LORD JIM
CONRAD, THE SECRET AGENT
CONRAD, THE SECRET SHARER AND OTHER STORIES
CUMMINGS, E. E. CUMMINGS: SELECTED WORKS
EIGHT MODERN PLAYS
ELIOT, THE WASTE LAND
FAULKNER, AS I LAY DYING
FAULKNER, THE SOUND AND THE FURY
FITZGERALD, THE GREAT GATSBY
FORD, THE GOOD SOLDIER
FORSTER, HOWARDS END
FORSTER, A PASSAGE TO INDIA
FREUD, CIVILIZATION AND ITS DISCONTENTS
FRIEDAN, THE FEMININE MYSTIQUE
HEMINGWAY, IN OUR TIME
HEMINGWAY, THE SUN ALSO RISES
JOHNSON, THE AUTOBIOGRAPHY OF AN EX-COLORED MAN
JOYCE, DUBLINERS
JOYCE, A PORTRAIT OF THE ARTIST AS A YOUNG MAN
KAFKA, KAFKA'S SELECTED STORIES
KAFKA, THE METAMORPHOSIS
LARSEN, PASSING
LARSEN, QUICKSAND
MANN, DEATH IN VENICE
MANSFIELD, KATHERINE MANSFIELD'S SELECTED STORIES
MODERN AFRICAN DRAMA
MODERN AND CONTEMPORARY IRISH DRAMA
PROUST, SWANN'S WAY
RHYS, WIDE SARGASSO SEA
RICH, ADRIENNE RICH: POETRY AND PROSE
SOYINKA, DEATH AND THE KING'S HORSEMAN
STEIN, THREE LIVES AND Q.E.D.
TOOMER, CANE
WATSON, THE DOUBLE HELIX
WHARTON, THE AGE OF INNOCENCE
WHARTON, ETHAN FROME
WHARTON, THE HOUSE OF MIRTH
WOOLF, JACOB'S ROOM
WOOLF, MRS. DALLOWAY
YEATS, YEATS'S POETRY, DRAMA, AND PROSE

A NORTON CRITICAL EDITION

Ernest Hemingway

THE SUN ALSO RISES

AUTHORITATIVE TEXT

BACKGROUNDS AND CONTEXTS

CRITICISM

Edited by

MICHAEL THURSTON
SMITH COLLEGE

W. W. NORTON & COMPANY
Independent Publishers Since 1923

W. W. Norton & Company has been independent since its founding in 1923, when William Warder Norton and Mary D. Herter Norton first published lectures delivered at the People's Institute, the adult education division of New York City's Cooper Union. The firm soon expanded its program beyond the Institute, publishing books by celebrated academics from America and abroad. By mid-century, the two major pillars of Norton's publishing program—trade books and college texts—were firmly established. In the 1950s, the Norton family transferred control of the company to its employees, and today—with a staff of five hundred and hundreds of trade, college, and professional titles published each year—W. W. Norton & Company stands as the largest and oldest publishing house owned wholly by its employees.

Printed in the United States of America

Book design by Antonina Krass
Manufacturing by Maple Press
Production Managers: Stephen Sajdak and Brenda Manzanedo

Library of Congress Cataloging-in-Publication Data

Names: Hemingway, Ernest, 1899–1961, author. | Thurston, Michael, 1965– editor.
Title: The sun also rises : authoritative text, backgrounds and contexts, criticism / Ernest Hemingway ; edited by Michael Thurston.
Description: First edition. | New York : W. W. Norton & Company, 2022. | Series: A Norton critical edition | Includes bibliographical references.
Identifiers: LCCN 2021005737 | **ISBN 9780393656008 (paperback)**
Subjects: LCSH: Ashley, Brett (Fictitious character)—Fiction. | Americans—Spain—Fiction. | Expatriation—Fiction. | Spain—History—Alfonso XIII, 1886–1931—Fiction. | Hemingway, Ernest, 1899–1961. Sun also rises.
Classification: LCC PS3515.E37 S8 2022 | DDC 813/.52—dc23
LC record available at https://lccn.loc.gov/2021005737

W. W. Norton & Company, Inc., 500 Fifth Avenue, New York, NY 10110-0017
wwnorton.com
W. W. Norton & Company Ltd., 15 Carlisle Street, London W1D 3BS

1 2 3 4 5 6 7 8 9 0

Contents

Introduction

In 1925, Ernest Hemingway was an ambitious young writer living with his wife and infant son in Paris. Supporting himself by writing for North American newspapers, he had also begun to build a reputation as an avant-garde prose stylist influenced by such modernist writers as Gertrude Stein, Sherwood Anderson, and Ezra Pound. He had published six striking prose vignettes in the *Little Review* (April 1923), perhaps the best known of the "little magazines" that incubated and circulated such important work as James Joyce's *Ulysses* and the poetry of Pound, T. S. Eliot, and Mina Loy. On the strength of these vignettes, he had been invited by Pound to contribute to a series of books Pound was producing with William Bird's Three Mountains Press in Paris. Hemingway published this book, *in our time*, in 1924. Enclosed in an elaborate, collaged cover and bearing typographical hallmarks of the avant-garde, this collection of eighteen short prose pieces—on war, bullfighting, and crime—established the young writer's signature style. Its sentences were affectless and ironically distant, enriched with auditory repetition that pushed the pieces toward the genre of the prose poem rather than the short story. At the same time, Hemingway was writing longer stories and trying to publish them not only in small magazines like *Transatlantic Review* (which he sometimes co-edited) or with small presses like Robert McAlmon's Contact Editions, but also in the mass-circulation magazines like *Collier's* and *Cosmopolitan*; these would pay substantially and enable him to make a living by writing fiction. In 1925, he combined such stories with the vignettes (now italicized "interchapters" that appeared between the stories) and brought out a collection, *In Our Time*, with Boni and Liveright, a press with one foot in the camp of modernist experiment and one in the popular book market. Garnering book jacket endorsements by important writers and critics, *In Our Time* shifted Hemingway from the adventurous and experimental cultural margins to the literary mainstream. But Hemingway's ambition required a novel.

That July, Hemingway began to write about his recent experience with a group of friends and acquaintances at Pamplona's San Fermin festival. He had been to the festival twice before and had developed both a fascination with and some expertise about the *corrida*, the bullfights that took place every afternoon over the festival's ten days. In 1925, he had spent the festival in the company of several friends: Donald Ogden Stewart, a playwright and humorist; Harold Loeb, a writer and editor of avant-garde magazines; British heiress Lady Duff Twysden and her fiancé, Pat Guthrie. Amid the festival's overheated and chaotic atmosphere, relationships frayed and conflicts emerged. Loeb had been involved in an affair with Twysden and his presence irritated both Guthrie and Hemingway, who nursed his own crush on her. Twysden and Guthrie were broke and could not pay their hotel bill, leaving Stewart to cover the expense for them. And Hemingway was annoyed that the festival had become a tourist attraction. Even the trout fishing near the Basque village of Burguete had been disappointing this time around, the streams clogged and fouled after loggers had clear-cut the surrounding forest. These conflicts and irritations proved strangely inspiring. Within two weeks of the festival's conclusion, Hemingway had started to write what would become *The Sun Also Rises*. By that September, he had finished a first draft, titling the novel *Fiesta*.

The completed first draft began by focusing on a young bullfighter. In the first longhand pages and even in the early beginnings of typed sheets, Hemingway described his main character's meeting with the matador in a hotel room. At first, Hemingway named his characters after the people he had been with in Pamplona. He even briefly called his first-person narrator "Hem." Soon, though, before he finished the first draft, he was more thoroughly transforming recollection into fiction, brainstorming "names for Duff," for example, and giving the history that brings "Elizabeth Neil/Brett Murray" to the name "generally used" by her friends: "Brett." On a skiing trip in Schruns, Austria, that winter, Hemingway set to work revising the novel. Other characters received new names now as well; Loeb disappeared to make way for Robert (originally Gerald) Cohn, Pat Guthrie became Mike Campbell, and Donald Ogden Stewart melded with Bill Smith, a friend of Hemingway's from Michigan, to become Bill Gorton. Hemingway changed the structure of the narrative as well, dropping the *medias res* opening (the meeting between Jake and the bullfighter who would become Pedro Romero) and focusing instead on the young woman who would be at the center of the novel's conflicts: "This is a novel about a lady. Her name is Lady Ashley and when the story begins she is living in Paris and it is Spring."[1]

Hemingway had struck early in the novel's composition on important features that remained consistent: its structure, its first-person

1. The galley proof of the opening chapter is included in Frederic Svoboda's *Hemingway and* The Sun Also Rises (Lawrence, KS: U of Kansas P, 1983), p. 131.

narrator, the device of Jake's wound, and the book's key themes. But while some passages from the first (handwritten) draft and the second (typed) draft made their way without profound change into the published novel, Hemingway heavily revised other sections of the novel as he worked in Schruns. The typescript, for example, includes several long passages in which Jake steps back from the action and makes statements about writing. Sometimes he wonders whether he is sufficient to the task of telling the story, sometimes he criticizes other writers and their work and even entire categories of writing, and sometimes he generalizes about what good writing requires. Hemingway cut almost all of this material in revision. In the typescript, Jake more than once spends a page or two hashing out his feelings about Brett and his understanding of these feelings. Here is an exemplary passage:

> And the conversation of all day kept coming back in a sort of regurgitation. I felt pretty well through with Brett. In life you tried to get along without criticizing the actions of other people but sometimes they offended you in spite of yourself. Brett had lost something. Since she had gone to San Sebastian with Cohn she seemed to have lost that quality in her that had never been touched before. All this talking now about her former lovers to make this seems quite ordinary. She was ashamed. ~~That was it.~~ Really ashamed. She had never been ashamed before. It made her vulgar where before she had been simply going by her own rules. She had wanted to kill off something in her and the killing had gotten out of her control. Well, she had killed it off in me. That was a good thing. I did not want to be in love with any woman. I did not want to have any grand passion that I could never do anything about. I was glad it was gone. The hell I was.[2]

Hemingway continues in this vein for three more paragraphs. In revision, though, he cut all of this, and most of the similar material throughout the novel. Some scenes that remained in the novel received scrupulous rewriting over several drafts as Hemingway worked to shape scenes, sharpening their thematic significance and heightening their emotional power. He sometimes achieved his aim by cutting sentences or paragraphs, but in some crucial scenes he rewrote individual sentences several times to get their tone and emphasis just right, to point with the language on the page at deeper meanings that he could then leave unspoken.

2. Typescript of *The Sun Also Rises*. Ernest Hemingway Papers, John F. Kennedy Library (MS 28, 198-2-1-2).

Even after the novel had been typeset, Hemingway continued to revise it. During the summer of 1926, Hemingway sent a carbon copy of his final typescript to F. Scott Fitzgerald. Fitzgerald's masterpiece, *The Great Gatsby*, had been published in 1925, and Hemingway had written to him about his own novel in progress, finally asking if Fitzgerald would read and comment on it. As he was checking the galley proofs, Hemingway received a ten-page letter from Fitzgerald, who recommended major changes, especially to the opening chapters. Throughout his early revisions, Hemingway had held on to a long opening that focused on Brett Ashley and her background and that included a good deal of information about the Montparnasse Quarter and its denizens. Fitzgerald urged him to cut this material:

> Anyhow I think parts of *Sun Also* are careless + ineffectual. As I said yestiday [*sic*] . . . I find in you the same tendency to envelope or (as it usually turns out) to *embalm* in mere wordiness an anecdote or joke thats [*sic*] casually appealed to you, that I find in myself in trying to preserve a piece of 'fine writing.' Your first chapter contains about 10 such things and it gives a feeling of condescending *casuallness* [*sic*].[3]

Fitzgerald found some of the early pages tonally wrong ("snobbish"), others "*merely recounted*," some effects "cheap" and others "flat." Hemingway cannot have enjoyed reading his friend's judgment on the first twenty pages: "Ernest, I can't tell you the sense of disappointment that beginning with its elephantine facetiousness gave me." Fitzgerald advised him to address the problems when correcting the proofs, to cut the first 7,500 words to 5,000, to pare away not only the background on Brett but also that on Cohn, and to delete "the worst of the *scenes*." The novel should begin, he argued, with Jake's meeting with the prostitute, Georgette.

Difficult as it might have been to read this critique, Hemingway took it very seriously. He followed most of Fitzgerald's recommendations, cutting not 2,500 but 3,500 words, reshaping, as he did so, not only the opening gambit (so that the novel would begin with Cohn rather than Brett) but also its tone. What had been sneering, glib, and superior became, in revision, more deeply ironic and more organically related to the novel's themes. In deleting so much of Brett's background, Hemingway also forced readers to understand her through scenes that dramatized her rather than narration that explained her, and in cutting so much of Jake's explicit judgment of other characters and of the Quarter's expatriate literary community, he enacted the virtues he had previously relied upon Jake to preach:

3. Quoted in Svoboda, see p. 194.

economy, rhythmic and energetic prose, scrupulous and significant description, rendering rather than telling.

The origins of *The Sun Also Rises* almost invite readers to treat the book as a *roman à clef*, a thinly fictionalized rehearsal of Hemingway's autobiography, a narrative whose characters are barely disguised versions of real-life people. This is one of several mistaken ways to read the novel. Some critics and many students since 1926 have spent their time wondering how similar Brett Ashley is to Duff Twysden, whether Harold Loeb had boxed at Princeton like Robert Cohn, and just how much of Bill Gorton's character came from the writer Donald Ogden Stewart and how much from Hemingway's Michigan friend, Bill Smith. They have been abetted in this not only by the memoirs of Hemingway's acquaintances and those acquaintances' comparisons of Hemingway's novel with their recollections, but also by work like Bertram Sarason's *Hemingway and the Sun Set*, which gathers episodes from these memoirs and undertakes its own comparisons. But as Frederic Svoboda's thorough analysis of Hemingway's composition and revision of the novel makes clear, "those sections of the first draft that were most literally true to what happened in Paris and Pamplona—those most closely journalistic or autobiographical—tended to be cut as Hemingway revised."[4] *The Sun Also Rises* is *not* a thinly fictionalized autobiography but is, instead, a carefully constructed novel that develops its questions of value, of masculinity, of ritual and its significance, through the machinery of literary form. While it is interesting to know that Hemingway borrowed for his characters aspects of his friends and took for his plot events he had lived through or witnessed, these subjects are best examined in light of the finished novel's elaboration of its themes. Readers' time will be better spent thinking about how several scenes between Brett and Jake Barnes hinge on vital questions of values, or how Cohn is set up by several characters as something of a scapegoat or how Hemingway plays on symbolic resonances of fishing and ritual in the key episode in which Jake and Bill go fishing together on the Irati river near Burguete (or how he flirts with homoerotic overtones in the scene). These are more productive foci of attention. The important question is not "How much is Mike Campbell like Pat Guthrie" but "How does Mike's combination of generosity and profligacy represent a way of understanding value?"

The same is true of the novel's early draft and original opening. Scholars have analyzed Hemingway's first plan for the novel's beginning: the introduction of Brett, the explicit address to the reader by

4. Svoboda, p. 9.

the narrator, the broad parody of the expatriate literary and artistic scene in Paris. They have noted areas of heavy revision in the novel's manuscript, pointing out, for example, that Hemingway originally intended to reproduce the long letter a young Black boxer sends to Bill Gorton after Bill had helped him out of a scrape in Vienna, or that Hemingway paid particularly careful attention to the precise itinerary when Bill and Jake walk around the Île Saint-Louis after dinner. Again, it can be interesting to see the process by which a writer, discovering his themes in the first draft of a novel, refines the action and the narration to heighten their felt presence in the finished work, but a reader's focus should be on that final product, the realization of the vision that guided those revisions.

The "Modern Criticism" section of this volume illustrates some useful and illuminating readings of *The Sun Also Rises*, examples of how the novel can be productively examined by emphasizing particular themes or elements of its form or by bringing to bear new critical methods as they emerge. In the remainder of this introduction, I will not rehearse the novel's reception history (an account of the ways the novel changes over time as new readers bring to it new approaches and new questions). I will focus, instead, on aspects of Hemingway's work that remain continuously present and important in the novel throughout the decades since its publication.

Chief among such things is the fact that *The Sun Also Rises* is a *modernist* novel. To describe the book as "modernist" is not simply to aver that it was written during the twentieth century; "modernist" is a conceptual, rather than a merely temporal, category. Modernism is the complex cultural phenomenon associated with the shocks of modernity in European and American life. As Stephen Kern demonstrates, over the course of the nineteenth century, and with ever great speed in the twentieth, humanity's fundamental relationships with time and space changed. For millennia, our movement across space was at the speed of horses or ships, the extent of most people's known part of the world was a few square miles, and immediate communication was possible only as far as a shout could reach (communication over great distances could take weeks or months).[5] In the early nineteenth century, though, railroads and steamships moved our bodies more quickly through space, their speeds increasing as their machinery was refined. Later, the telegraph allowed almost instantaneous communication across hundreds of miles. The internal combustion engine brought speedy travel to larger and larger numbers of people, and the telephone enabled not only ideas but also voices to exceed their former spatial limits. Technology

5. Stephen Kern, *The Culture of Time and Space, 1880–1918* (Cambridge: Harvard UP, 1983), p. 9.

produced these changes, and the speed of movement and communication contributed to new technologies in turn, hastening the industrialization and urbanization that were transforming communities, modes of work, and the foundations of personal identity.

For the intelligentsia, the fundamental physical changes that Kern notes were accompanied by profound challenges to basic assumptions about human beings. Charles Darwin's theories of evolution and natural selection shook the faith of many who had understood themselves as having been made by God in God's image. Karl Marx's theories of capitalism and the commodity shifted historical responsibility from the deliberate choices of individuals to the impersonal forces of economy and construed history as a long struggle between owners and alienated workers. Sigmund Freud's theories of the unconscious suggested that people were influenced by fears and desires they could not control because they could not directly recognize them. By the early twentieth century, the notion of a self-knowing and self-determining individual living in a world ordered by some combination of rational politics and divine providence was in deep crisis.

All of this technological innovation, intellectual ferment, and social change climaxed in the First World War and the devastation it wrought on European and American assumptions of order and meaning. Looking back over a century that saw ever greater industrial killing power used in total global warfare, that witnessed the bureaucratized slaughter of millions in the Holocaust, that suffered both the nuclear annihilation of cities and inescapable anxiety about the possible nuclear annihilation of all humanity, it can be difficult to recognize just how shocking and horrific the "Great War" was. That thousands of young men were mowed down in the first hours of a battle at the River Somme, in France, was horrible (British casualties alone on July 1, 1916, the first day of the battle, were 57,740). That hundreds of thousands of soldiers were bogged down in trench warfare along the front in France and Belgium was appalling. Worse still, the societies of Europe had chosen this path of self-destruction, and the absurd tactics and diplomatic failures came from an educated and supposedly intelligent elite.

Hemingway had first-hand knowledge of this war, its effects on both soldiers and civilians, and the absurdity of its causes, its conduct, and even its conclusion. As a volunteer ambulance driver on the Italian front, Hemingway not only witnessed combat but he was also severely wounded; on July 8, 1918, Austrian mortar fire left him with numerous shrapnel fragments in his legs. As a reporter working in Europe after the war, he saw the vanity and venality of national leaders meeting to work out the postwar settlement while their populations continued to suffer both violence and privation.

He also covered the small but intense armed conflicts that spun out in the Great War's aftermath, as small nations newly formed by the disintegration of old empires fought to maximize their territories and spheres of influence. The war that sputtered on between Greece and Turkey in the early 1920s would exemplify for him the meaninglessness of such skirmishing and the emptiness of justifications like patriotism or military glory.

To say that *The Sun Also Rises* is a modernist novel is at once to say that it engages the complex situation of modernity and the postwar world, and also to locate the novel in a set of artistic movements characterized by irony. For many writers and artists at work during and after the War, it was impossible to continue in dominant prewar forms and styles. These artists explored a variety of alternatives that ranged from the anti-art, intentional nonsense of Dada to the associational discontinuities of stream-of-consciousness narration (James Joyce's *Ulysses*, Virginia Woolf's *Mrs. Dalloway*), from the dreams and accidents of Surrealism to the gathering of fragments left after the shattering of societies and traditions (T. S. Eliot's *The Waste Land*, Ezra Pound's *Cantos*). These disparate methods were united by a stance toward prewar assumptions and conventions that we might best understand as ironic. Irony is the rhetorical trope or figure of speech in which we find a perceptible distance between what is said and what is meant. We are often most familiar with it in the form of sarcasm: "Lovely weather," for example, when an icy rain is pelting down on us. But irony is much broader than sarcasm. It includes the narrative repetition of a familiar story that revises or subverts the meaning of the original (as Joyce does when he constructs Leopold Bloom's day-long wandering in Dublin on the model of Odysseus's wandering after the Trojan War). It is visible and audible when Edna St. Vincent Millay casts her skepticism about romantic love in the form of the sonnet, which traditionally values romantic love. These two kinds of irony come together at the heart of *The Waste Land* (1922), when Eliot has the prophet, Tiresias, a crucial figure in Athenian tragedy and in the *Odyssey*, witness as fundamental universal truth a loveless seduction in a squalid London flat, the concluding stanzas not coincidentally forming an almost perfect Shakespearean sonnet.

Hemingway had gotten to know and like Ezra Pound when the two met in Paris. Pound influenced the younger writer's thinking about language and prose style. Through Pound and through *The Waste Land*'s immediate and powerful influence in the literary world, Hemingway also knew Eliot's poem, with its corrosively ironic deployment of the legend of the Holy Grail and the rituals of ancient fertility cults. As a regular at Sylvia Beach's Shakespeare and Company bookshop, which published *Ulysses* in 1922, Hemingway also knew Joyce's novel, in which the central institutions of Irish society and much of the European literary tradition came in for ironic treatment. Writing from his own experience, both on the front lines and as a journalist, and writing in the context of this modernist skepticism, Hemingway developed a prose style and an approach to narrative structure saturated in irony.

He performs this irony from the beginning of his career in fiction, in the six prose vignettes published as "In Our Time" in the April 1923 "Exiles" number of the *Little Review*. Here, readers encounter irony when Hemingway's narrator describes soldiers using a wrought-iron grating as a barricade and shooting enemy soldiers as they try to get over it: "absolutely perfect," "simply priceless," "absolutely topping," "frightfully put out." They can see it, too, in both the stories and "interchapters" of Hemingway's 1925 story collection, *In Our Time*, whether it takes the form of distance that allows them to realize the corruption of the narrator's father in "My Old Man" or the juxtaposition of Nick Adams carefully controlling himself in his environment in "Big Two-Hearted River" and Sam Cardinella losing control of himself in every way as he approaches the gallows in the "interchapter" that separates the two halves of that story.

When he came to write his first major novel (the earlier *Torrents of Spring* might be best considered an exercise in parody, itself a form of ironic citation), Hemingway brought his ironic convictions and constructions with him. The linguistic play of the early stories and vignettes continues here in much of Bill Gorton's speech. Early on, for example, Bill and Jake walk down boulevard Saint-Michel on their way to dinner:

> "Here's a taxidermist," Bill said. "Want to buy anything? Nice stuffed dog?"
> "Come on," I said. "You're pie-eyed."
> "Pretty nice stuffed dogs," Bill said. "Certainly brighten up your flat."
> "Come on."
> "Just one stuffed dog. I can take 'em or leave 'em alone. But listen, Jake. Just one stuffed dog."
> "Come on."
> "Mean everything in the world to you after you bought it. Simple exchange of values. You give them money. They give you a stuffed dog."
> "We'll get one on the way back."
> "All right. Have it your own way. Road to hell paved with unbought stuffed dogs. Not my fault." (54)

Jake's language, whether in dialogue or in his narration, is often, if more subtly, ironic. He introduces the prostitute, Georgette, to his acquaintances with the name of a popular singer. He ruefully acknowledges the humor (to others, at least) of his war injury. He skewers Cohn in a deft ironic reference to T. H. Hudson's romanticized travelogue, *The Purple Land*. He rejects Brett's attempt at consolation in the novel's last scene in a final line famous for its trenchant irony. And Hemingway builds irony into the very structure of his plot, from the love story between a sexually voracious woman and an emasculated man to the location of chaos and appetite in the context of a religious festival.

With its references (both explicit and implicit) to pilgrimage, ritual, and renewal, *The Sun Also Rises* also engages in an irony familiar to Hemingway and to many of his readers from Eliot's *The Waste Land*. In that poem, Eliot imagines the contemporary world as a living death as characters mechanically engage in meaningless relationships of power and desire. Through allusions, fragmentary quotations, and other references, Eliot suggests various possibilities of renewal: the Holy Grail might be discovered and the Fisher King addressed so that the land might be healed, or a god figure might be sacrificed to restore natural cycles of death and rebirth, or the transformative rituals of baptism and communion might offer salvation from the fallen world, or obedience to divine commandments might bring about the peace that passes understanding. The poem, though, fails to demonstrate the efficacy of any of these; indeed, the ironic references and juxtapositions strongly suggest that there is no way out of the wasteland, no way to bring the land back from its blasted, lifeless state.

Readers have long recognized similarities between *The Sun Also Rises* and *The Waste Land*. The two epigraphs Hemingway chose for his novel situate his narrative in a problem similar to Eliot's. A quotation from Gertrude Stein (whom Hemingway had also gotten to know in Paris and who also influenced his early prose) identifies Hemingway's generation as "lost," in need, perhaps, of the guidance offered by traditions of culture, society, or religion. A passage from the Old Testament book of *Ecclesiastes* points to the cycles of nature and their recognition in ritual, as if these might provide the necessary guidance. Some critics have found an opposition between the "meaningless" round of café and nightclub life in Paris and the rituals and values of the *corrida* at the heart of the San Fermin festival in Pamplona. Others have argued that Hemingway's precise descriptions of the routes that characters take and his careful mentioning of specific places they pass by allude to the pilgrims' way to Santiago de Compostela, a famous penitential journey that brings travelers to purification and renewed faith. And with the epigraphs' ideas in mind, it is difficult to miss the important moments of bathing in the novel, which take on the symbolic resonance of baptism, or of fishing, whose biblical significance is as palpable here as it is in "Big Two-Hearted River."

There are indeed ritual sacrifices, religious pilgrimages, baptisms, and Christ-like fishing and communion in the novel (as there are Grail and resurrection references in *The Waste Land*), but these references are ironic, and this irony subverts rather than suggests any sense that these practices can provide meaning, either for the novel's characters or for its readers. Indeed, such subversion of the sacramental is one of the most insistent patterns Hemingway constructs in *The Sun Also Rises*. As soon as the faint notion of the Eucharist appears when Jake and Bill enjoy eggs and wine for lunch on their fishing trip, its significance dissolves in the acidic exchange of jokes—about William Jennings Bryan, H. L. Mencken, American Catholic institutions, temperance activists, and the language of prayer itself. Neither the afición that Jake shares with Montoya nor the ritual sacrifice of the bullfight can withstand the corrosive desires of Brett Ashley or the decadence and commercialism that already infect the *corrida*. And Jake's attempts to cleanse himself, whether before, during, or after the festival in Pamplona, whether in a hotel bathroom or at the famous swimming beach of San Sebastian, find only short-lived renewal or rebirth as he is caught up once again in and by his love for Brett and her need for him. And though Brett promises during their final dinner together that she is turning over a new leaf, Jake can only do in the Madrid restaurant what he did when in painful proximity to Brett in Paris and Pamplona: drink too much.

In addition to irony, modernist writing is characterized by internal contradiction. Modernist novels and poems tend to be fragmented even when composed within the structure of a day or a ritual, and this fragmentation builds into the work moments of doubt and conflict that cannot be resolved into a single, coherent thematic paraphrase. It can seem, in *The Sun Also Rises*, as if we need not worry about such things; in the hands of the utterly competent and self-knowing Jake Barnes, who knows where he is going and how to get there, we are clearly on the road to sense and meaning. But notice how often Jake's expertise turns out to be insufficient, illusory, or inefficacious. Jake knows Brett, for example, and confidently explains her to Bill and even to Robert Cohn, but he does not know until much later that she has gone off to San Sebastian with Cohn. Jake is an expert on the *corrida*, able to interpret the action for his friends, he has achieved afición to the extent that Montoya acknowledges him as a member of the bullfight community, and he criticizes those who defile or degrade bullfighting either by decadent performance or by corrupting toreadors, but he abets precisely this corruption. Jake is articulate about values but abandons (or revises) his values at a crucial moment. And he bears contradiction within his very body, dedicating himself to (and basing his identity on) masculine pursuits while he is himself emasculated. If he seeks a kind of order through what we might see as prostheses for his missing phallus (the tennis racquet, the fishing pole, the matador's sword), the novel repeatedly narrates the dissolution of that order as a consequence of Jake's lack of the phallus as an organizing center. If on the one hand the emasculated Jake defines himself against the homosexuals with whom Brett arrives at the *bal masque* early in the novel, he implicitly identifies—through his desire for the androgynous-looking Brett, through the homosocial intimacy of his friendship with Bill, through his admiring detailed description of Romero—as someone whose desires might be quite like theirs.

Some readers, with Eliot in mind or merely looking for a clear set of structuring oppositions in the novel, draw overly stark contrasts between settings or characters. Paris and France, for them, represent fallenness, corruption, or meaninglessness, while Pamplona and Spain stand for redemption and meaning. Hemingway, though, does not set up such simple binaries. His Paris is at once the home of craven thrill seekers and deluded, failed artists and of the work that Jake finds sustaining, the friends he enjoys, the drinks and meals in which he takes pleasure. Pamplona is at once the locus of ritual and prayer and the hothouse atmosphere in which characters betray each other and their own best selves. Jake describes Spanish meals, waiters, and hotels disparagingly and their French counterparts with praise, though he also prizes the Hotel Montoya and the Café Iruña in Pamplona.

Easy oppositions among the characters fall apart just as easily under close examination. Following Brett's description of Count Mippipopolous as "one of us," some readers line up Jake, Brett, the Count, Bill, and maybe Mike Campbell on the side of proper values and set them against Robert Cohn, Braddocks, the Biarritz set (and maybe Mike Campbell), whose values are compromised. What, though, does "one of us" mean when Brett says it of the Count? Like Jake, Count Mippipopolous bears the scars of war wounds, and like Jake and Brett he enjoys nights out in the clubs and cabarets of Paris. At the same time, though, he is Jake's rival for Brett's romantic attention, one who clearly hopes to seduce her during their all-night party and early morning picnic. That he is disappointed in this might also link the Count to Jake, but this "us" cannot include Brett. The critic William Kerrigan long ago suggested that the Count, like Jake, is sexually impotent, so that the three characters share an important condition: the capacity to be in love (with each other) without the capacity to enact that love sexually (with each other).[6] But we might wonder whether the novel affirms this as a condition to which readers should aspire. The most obvious and thematically significant similarity between Jake and the Count is their shared sense that those things that one values must be earned or paid for and that it is important, therefore, really to know one's values so that one pays only for those things one really values. This sympathetic understanding might line the Count up with Jake and someone like Montoya, but, again, it seems to exclude Brett. More than this, there are other aspects of the Count that complicate his inclusion in any group that the novel offers as an affirmative "us." His experience—having participated in "seven wars and four revolutions," having received his arrow wounds while on a "business trip" in Abyssinia (where the Italian army was defeated in 1896), his postwar wealth as owner of a chain of American candy stores, and his conspicuous consumption of large cigars, old wine, and young women—and his appearance (large girth and fur coat) mark him as the very model of a war profiteer, one whose valued pleasures are bought not only at his own expense but also at the expense of those who suffer and die in war. Indeed, the Count's ostentatiously Greek name links him to the war that frames *In Our Time* and stands as perhaps Hemingway's most powerful example of war's meaningless savagery, the Greco-Turkish War of 1921.

Even Robert Cohn, the novel's (apparently) most obvious "them" character, complicates any easy binary. While Jake tends to set himself against Cohn, the opposition often collapses. The two men are linked by their love for Brett and also by their suffering when she goes off with Pedro Romero. When Mike calls Robert Cohn a "steer," comparing him to the geldings who receive the violence of newly arrived bulls, he unwittingly unites Cohn and Jake as emasculated males. While Jake narrates the novel and seems to be its protagonist, *The Sun Also Rises* opens not with information about Jake but with Jake's précis of Cohn's life, as if Robert were the novel's focal character. Cohn is a successful novelist where Jake is a reporter. He is athletic, physically accomplished, and able to consummate his relationship with Brett in ways that Jake cannot. And while we hear Jake make moral pronouncements (and are inclined to read these as Hemingway's own), Robert's actions evince a strong moral code as well. He defends himself both verbally and physically, he seems to lack the prejudice that infects even such sympathetic characters as Jake and Bill (both of whom make antisemitic comments about Cohn), and he attempts to set things right after he has acted violently

6. William Kerrigan, "Something Funny about Hemingway's Count." *American Literature* 46 (March 1974): 87–93.

(trying to shake hands with both Romero and Jake after he has punched them). When we step back from Jake's own biased judgment, Robert Cohn might seem as admirable a character as Jake himself. He certainly thwarts any attempt to see him only as Jake's foil.

In his representation of people and places in all of their moral complexity, and of the confusion that this complexity produces, Hemingway follows the lead of yet another modernist contemporary, Robert Frost, whose poems often confront readers with the illusion (or, better, the fiction) of a world that makes sense or can be made sense of. In "The Road Not Taken," for example, Frost *appears* to show a rational choice at a fork in the road that is at once literal and figurative, a choice that "has made all the difference." But the poem actually *shows* that the choice had no real basis (the two roads are "about the same") and so the "difference" might have no identifiable foundation either.

Similarly, Hemingway often *seems* to suggest through obvious alternatives that one might make a decision that enacts one's values, but actually *shows* that the alternatives were not so clear, that outcomes are overdetermined, and that values are hard to hold onto. Jake's response to Brett in the novel's last line should therefore be read not only as his rejoinder to her clearly false sense that they "could have had such a damned good time together" (unless we lean hard on that "damned"), but also as a reply to all of the stories people tell themselves about their values and their choices and the meaningfulness of life in the modern world: "Isn't it pretty to think so?"

Finally, is there nothing here but irony, fragmentation, and contradiction? It is hard to imagine that a novel so many readers have found inspiring offers nothing more positive to hang on to. While *The Sun Also Rises* does not provide the "code" of heroism, machismo, or moral behavior that some early critics claimed to find in Hemingway's work, it does offer, on every page, the model of its style, its repeated demonstration of Hemingway's mastery of the sentence. As the literary theorist Fredric Jameson argues, "one is wrong to say that Hemingway began by wishing to express or convey certain basic experiences; rather, he began by wishing to write a certain type of sentence, a kind of neutral *compte rendu* of external displacements."[7] Hemingway himself supports such a view when he writes, in *A Moveable Feast*, "All you have to do is write one true sentence. Write the truest sentence you know." By "true sentence," Hemingway means one in which the inherent distance between words and the things or actions or relationships those words name is as small as possible. Jameson goes on to say that Hemingway's stylistic achievement

7. Fredric Jameson, *Marxism and Form: Twentieth-Century Dialectical Theories of Literature* (Princeton: Princeton UP, 1974), p. 411.

makes the real action in his work: "the most essential event, the dominant category of experience for both writer and reader alike, is the process of writing" (411). What we enjoy in reading the sentences of *The Sun Also Rises* is something like what Jake enjoys in watching Romero's expert handling of the bull: not "grace under pressure," but consummate skill. And because our experience of the novel is an experience of sentence production as meaningful work, we are invited into a world that offers meaning not in codes of behavior or afición, but, instead, in assiduous attention at once to things, actions, and relationships and to the language in and through which we have access to them. We are invited to find meaning in the arduous achievement of technique. In this way, no character in the novel is a moral model; instead, the model is Hemingway, whose sentences powerfully convey the truth of the world's lack of moral guides.

A Note on the Text

The text of *The Sun Also Rises* here is based on the second edition, published by Scribner in 1927, which is the text the company has continued to republish in subsequent editions. I have silently corrected the small number of accents omitted from words in that edition and noted the one substantive emendation (Jake's introduction of Bill Gorton as "Bill Grundy" in Chapter IX).

The Text of
THE SUN ALSO RISES

THIS BOOK IS FOR HADLEY
AND FOR JOHN HADLEY NICANOR[1]

1. Elizabeth Hadley Richardson (1891–1979), Hemingway's first wife. They married in 1921 and lived together in Paris and Toronto until their divorce in 1927. John Hadley Nicanor Hemingway (1923–2000) was the couple's first son. He is named both for his mother and for the Spanish matador Nicanor Villalta (1897–1980), a favorite of Hemingway's.

"You are all a lost generation."

—Gertrude Stein in conversation[2]

"One generation passeth away, and another generation cometh; but the earth abideth forever. . . . The sun also ariseth, and the sun goeth down, and hasteth to the place where he arose. . . . The wind goeth toward the south, and turneth about unto the north; it whirleth about continually, and the wind returneth again according to his circuits. . . . All the rivers run into the sea; yet the sea is not full; unto the place from whence the rivers come, thither they return again."

—Ecclesiastes[3]

2. American poet and writer (1874–1946). Hemingway frequented Stein's residence and salon at 27, rue de Fleurus, while living in Paris in the early 1920s.
3. The passage is Ecclesiastes 1:3–7. In it, the Teacher (who identifies himself as King Solomon, though the book was not written by Solomon) meditates on the limits and complexities of life in an effort to teach wisdom. These opening verses focus on the cyclical character of existence. The ellipses do not appear in the King James Version, which Hemingway quotes, and seem intended to represent breaks between the verses.

Book I

Chapter I

Robert Cohn was once middleweight[1] boxing champion of Princeton. Do not think that I am very much impressed by that as a boxing title, but it meant a lot to Cohn. He cared nothing for boxing, in fact he disliked it, but he learned it painfully and thoroughly to counteract the feeling of inferiority and shyness he had felt on being treated as a Jew at Princeton.[2] There was a certain inner comfort in knowing he could knock down anybody who was snooty to him, although, being very shy and a thoroughly nice boy, he never fought except in the gym. He was Spider Kelly's[3] star pupil. Spider Kelly taught all his young gentlemen to box like featherweights, no matter whether they weighed one hundred and five or two hundred and five pounds. But it seemed to fit Cohn. He was really very fast. He was so good that Spider promptly overmatched him and got his nose permanently flattened. This increased Cohn's distaste for boxing, but it gave him a certain satisfaction of some strange sort, and it certainly improved his nose. In his last year at Princeton he read too much and took to wearing spectacles. I never met any one of his class who remembered him. They did not even remember that he was middleweight boxing champion.

I mistrust all frank and simple people, especially when their stories hold together, and I always had a suspicion that perhaps Robert Cohn had never been middleweight boxing champion, and that perhaps a horse had stepped on his face, or that maybe his mother had been frightened or seen something, or that he had, maybe, bumped into something as a young child, but I finally had somebody verify the story from Spider Kelly. Spider Kelly not only remembered Cohn. He had often wondered what had become of him.

Robert Cohn was a member, through his father, of one of the richest Jewish families in New York, and through his mother of one of

1. Middleweight boxers weigh between 154 and 160 pounds.
2. In the 1900s and 1910s, when Cohn would have been a student there, Princeton had the lowest number of Jewish students among the Ivy League universities, admitting only thirteen in 1909 where Harvard, for example, admitted seventy-one.
3. Tommy "Spider" Kelly (1867–1927), world-champion bantamweight boxer (1890–92).

the oldest. At the military school where he prepped for Princeton, and played a very good end on the football team, no one had made him race-conscious. No one had ever made him feel he was a Jew, and hence any different from anybody else, until he went to Princeton. He was a nice boy, a friendly boy, and very shy, and it made him bitter. He took it out in boxing, and he came out of Princeton with painful self-consciousness and the flattened nose, and was married by the first girl who was nice to him. He was married five years, had three children, lost most of the fifty thousand dollars[4] his father left him, the balance of the estate having gone to his mother, hardened into a rather unattractive mould under domestic unhappiness with a rich wife; and just when he had made up his mind to leave his wife she left him and went off with a miniature-painter. As he had been thinking for months about leaving his wife and had not done it because it would be too cruel to deprive her of himself, her departure was a very healthful shock.

The divorce was arranged and Robert Cohn went out to the Coast. In California he fell among literary people and, as he still had a little of the fifty thousand left, in a short time he was backing a review of the Arts.[5] The review commenced publication in Carmel, California, and finished in Provincetown, Massachusetts. By that time Cohn, who had been regarded purely as an angel,[6] and whose name had appeared on the editorial page merely as a member of the advisory board, had become the sole editor. It was his money and he discovered he liked the authority of editing. He was sorry when the magazine became too expensive and he had to give it up.

By that time, though, he had other things to worry about. He had been taken in hand by a lady who hoped to rise with the magazine. She was very forceful, and Cohn never had a chance of not being taken in hand. Also he was sure that he loved her. When this lady saw that the magazine was not going to rise, she became a little disgusted with Cohn and decided that she might as well get what there was to get while there was still something available, so she urged that they go to Europe, where Cohn could write. They came to Europe, where the lady had been educated, and stayed three years. During these three years, the first spent in travel, the last two in

4. While it is difficult to give precise equivalents, this amount would be roughly $840,000 today.
5. Harold Loeb, on whom Robert Cohn is loosely based, was co-owner of the Sunwise Turn bookstore in New York and co-publisher and co-editor of *Broom*, a little magazine devoted to the artistic and literary avant-garde. While *Broom* was published in New York, Hemingway here names, in Carmel, California, and Provincetown, Massachusetts, two well-known American arts colonies, the first associated with such writers as Mary Austin, Robinson Jeffers, and Upton Sinclair, the second with Eugene O'Neill and the Provincetown Players.
6. An anonymous donor and supporter, with no editorial role.

Paris, Robert Cohn had two friends, Braddocks and myself. Braddocks was his literary friend. I was his tennis friend.

The lady who had him, her name was Frances, found toward the end of the second year that her looks were going, and her attitude toward Robert changed from one of careless possession and exploitation to the absolute determination that he should marry her. During this time Robert's mother had settled an allowance on him, about three hundred dollars a month.[7] During two years and a half I do not believe that Robert Cohn looked at another woman. He was fairly happy, except that, like many people living in Europe, he would rather have been in America, and he had discovered writing. He wrote a novel, and it was not really such a bad novel as the critics later called it, although it was a very poor novel. He read many books, played bridge, played tennis, and boxed at a local gymnasium.

I first became aware of his lady's attitude toward him one night after the three of us had dined together. We had dined at l'Avenue's and afterward went to the Café de Versailles for coffee.[8] We had several *fines*[9] after the coffee, and I said I must be going. Cohn had been talking about the two of us going off somewhere on a weekend trip. He wanted to get out of town and get in a good walk. I suggested we fly to Strasbourg and walk up to Saint Odile,[1] or somewhere or other in Alsace. "I know a girl in Strasbourg who can show us the town," I said.

Somebody kicked me under the table. I thought it was accidental and went on: "She's been there two years and knows everything there is to know about the town. She's a swell girl."

I was kicked again under the table and, looking, saw Frances, Robert's lady, her chin lifting and her face hardening.

"Hell," I said, "why go to Strasbourg? We could go up to Bruges, or to the Ardennes."[2]

Cohn looked relieved. I was not kicked again. I said good-night and went out. Cohn said he wanted to buy a paper and would walk to the corner with me. "For God's sake," he said, "why did you say that about that girl in Strasbourg for? Didn't you see Frances?"

"No, why should I? If I know an American girl that lives in Strasbourg what the hell is it to Frances?"

7. About $4,500 per month today.
8. Lavenue (the correct spelling) was a restaurant located in rue du Départ, near the Gare Montparnasse. Café de Versailles was at 171, rue du Rennes, across the place de Rennes from Lavenue.
9. Brandies (French).
1. Mont Sainte-Odile, a peak in the Vosges Mountains of Alsace; *Strasbourg*: the capital of the Grand Est region of France and the largest city in the region of Alsace, near the German border.
2. A heavily forested region of rolling hills along the Moselle and Meuse River basins, covering area located in Belgium, Luxembourg, Germany, and France; *Bruges*: the capital and largest city of the Flemish region of Belgium, well known for its canals and churches (especially St. Salvator's Cathedral).

"It doesn't make any difference. Any girl. I couldn't go, that would be all."

"Don't be silly."

"You don't know Frances. Any girl at all. Didn't you see the way she looked?"

"Oh, well," I said, "let's go to Senlis."[3]

"Don't get sore."

"I'm not sore. Senlis is a good place and we can stay at the Grand Cerf and take a hike in the woods and come home."

"Good, that will be fine."

"Well, I'll see you to-morrow at the courts," I said.

"Good-night, Jake," he said, and started back to the café.

"You forgot to get your paper," I said.

"That's so." He walked with me up to the kiosque at the corner. "You are not sore, are you, Jake?" He turned with the paper in his hand.

"No, why should I be?"

"See you at tennis," he said. I watched him walk back to the café holding his paper. I rather liked him and evidently she led him quite a life.

Chapter II

That winter Robert Cohn went over to America with his novel, and it was accepted by a fairly good publisher. His going made an awful row I heard, and I think that was where Frances lost him, because several women were nice to him in New York, and when he came back he was quite changed. He was more enthusiastic about America than ever, and he was not so simple, and he was not so nice. The publishers had praised his novel pretty highly and it rather went to his head. Then several women had put themselves out to be nice to him, and his horizons had all shifted. For four years his horizon had been absolutely limited to his wife. For three years, or almost three years, he had never seen beyond Frances. I am sure he had never been in love in his life.

He had married on the rebound from the rotten time he had in college, and Frances took him on the rebound from his discovery that he had not been everything to his first wife. He was not in love yet but he realized that he was an attractive quantity to women, and that the fact of a woman caring for him and wanting to live with him was not simply a divine miracle. This changed him so that he was not so pleasant to have around. Also, playing for higher stakes than he could

3. A town about twenty miles north of Paris (so much closer to home than the other options Jake has offered), known for its cathedral and for the Bois du Saint-Hubert, a hunting forest nearby. The Grand Cerf was a hotel located near the center of Senlis.

afford in some rather steep bridge games with his New York connections, he had held cards and won several hundred dollars. It made him rather vain of his bridge game, and he talked several times of how a man could always make a living at bridge if he were ever forced to.

Then there was another thing. He had been reading W. H. Hudson. That sounds like an innocent occupation, but Cohn had read and reread "The Purple Land."[1] "The Purple Land" is a very sinister book if read too late in life. It recounts splendid imaginary amorous adventures of a perfect English gentleman in an intensely romantic land, the scenery of which is very well described. For a man to take it at thirty-four as a guide-book to what life holds is about as safe as it would be for a man of the same age to enter Wall Street direct from a French convent, equipped with a complete set of the more practical Alger books.[2] Cohn, I believe, took every word of "The Purple Land" as literally as though it had been an R. G. Dun report.[3] You understand me, he made some reservations, but on the whole the book to him was sound. It was all that was needed to set him off. I did not realize the extent to which it had set him off until one day he came into my office.

"Hello, Robert," I said. "Did you come in to cheer me up?"

"Would you like to go to South America, Jake?" he asked.

"No."

"Why not?"

"I don't know. I never wanted to go. Too expensive. You can see all the South Americans you want in Paris anyway."

"They're not the real South Americans."

"They look awfully real to me."

I had a boat train to catch with a week's mail stories, and only half of them written.[4]

"Do you know any dirt?" I asked.

"No."

"None of your exalted connections getting divorces?"

"No; listen, Jake. If I handled both our expenses, would you go to South America with me?"

1. William Henry Hudson (1841–1922) was an Argentina-born English writer and naturalist and a devotee of the Patagonia region. He was the author of several books, including *The Purple Land that England Lost: Adventures in the Banda Oriental, South America* (1885), later retitled *The Purple Land, Being One Richard Lamb's Adventures in the Banda Oriental, in South America, as told by Himself* (1904), a romantic adventure tale set among revolutionaries in Uruguay.
2. Horatio Alger (1832–1899), American author of numerous novels, most of which were "rags to riches" stories in which virtuous boys escaped poverty through hard work and luck; *Wall Street*: the center of finance in New York City, location of the headquarters of international banks and trading companies as well as the New York Stock Exchange.
3. The American firm R. G. Dun & Company (now Dun & Bradstreet) issued regular reports to subscribers on the creditworthiness of businesses, especially useful in decisions regarding the purchase or trade of stocks.
4. As a journalist, Jake must write and file by deadline stories he has covered for newspapers and/or a press association; the boat train was a train whose schedule was timed to coordinate with the departure of a boat (probably across the English Channel to England).

"Why me?"

"You can talk Spanish. And it would be more fun with two of us."

"No," I said, "I like this town and I go to Spain in the summertime."

"All my life I've wanted to go on a trip like that," Cohn said. He sat down. "I'll be too old before I can ever do it."

"Don't be a fool," I said. "You can go anywhere you want. You've got plenty of money."

"I know. But I can't get started."

"Cheer up," I said. "All countries look just like the moving pictures."

But I felt sorry for him. He had it badly.

"I can't stand it to think my life is going so fast and I'm not really living it."

"Nobody ever lives their life all the way up except bull-fighters."

"I'm not interested in bull-fighters. That's an abnormal life. I want to go back in the country in South America. We could have a great trip."

"Did you ever think about going to British East Africa[5] to shoot?"

"No, I wouldn't like that."

"I'd go there with you."

"No; that doesn't interest me."

"That's because you never read a book about it. Go on and read a book all full of love affairs with the beautiful shiny black princesses."

"I want to go to South America."

He had a hard, Jewish, stubborn streak.

"Come on down-stairs and have a drink."

"Aren't you working?"

"No," I said. We went down the stairs to the café on the ground floor. I had discovered that was the best way to get rid of friends. Once you had a drink all you had to say was: "Well, I've got to get back and get off some cables," and it was done.[6] It is very important to discover graceful exits like that in the newspaper business, where it is such an important part of the ethics that you should never seem to be working. Anyway, we went down-stairs to the bar and had a whiskey and soda. Cohn looked at the bottles in bins around the wall. "This is a good place," he said.

"There's a lot of liquor," I agreed.

"Listen, Jake," he leaned forward on the bar. "Don't you ever get the feeling that all your life is going by and you're not taking advantage of it? Do you realize you've lived nearly half the time you have to live already?"

5. Modern-day Kenya.
6. Telegrams.

"Yes, every once in a while."

"Do you know that in about thirty-five years more we'll be dead?"

"What the hell, Robert," I said. "What the hell."

"I'm serious."

"It's one thing I don't worry about," I said.

"You ought to."

"I've had plenty to worry about one time or other. I'm through worrying."

"Well, I want to go to South America."

"Listen, Robert, going to another country doesn't make any difference. I've tried all that. You can't get away from yourself by moving from one place to another. There's nothing to that."

"But you've never been to South America."

"South America hell! If you went there the way you feel now it would be exactly the same. This is a good town. Why don't you start living your life in Paris?"

"I'm sick of Paris, and I'm sick of the Quarter."[7]

"Stay away from the Quarter. Cruise around by yourself and see what happens to you."

"Nothing happens to me. I walked alone all one night and nothing happened except a bicycle cop stopped me and asked to see my papers."

"Wasn't the town nice at night?"

"I don't care for Paris."

So there you were. I was sorry for him, but it was not a thing you could do anything about, because right away you ran up against the two stubbornnesses: South America could fix it and he did not like Paris. He got the first idea out of a book, and I suppose the second came out of a book too.

"Well," I said, "I've got to go up-stairs and get off some cables."

"Do you really have to go?"

"Yes, I've got to get these cables off."

"Do you mind if I come up and sit around the office?"

"No, come on up."

He sat in the outer room and read the papers, and the Editor and Publisher and I worked hard for two hours. Then I sorted out the carbons, stamped on a by-line, put the stuff in a couple of big manila envelopes and rang for a boy to take them to the Gare St. Lazare.[8] I went out into the other room and there was Robert Cohn asleep in the big chair. He was asleep with his head on his arms. I did not like to wake him up, but I wanted to lock the office and shove off. I

7. The Montparnasse Quarter, an area in the fifteenth arrondissement of Paris, notable in the 1920s as a center of artistic and cultural life.

8. The second largest of Paris's six terminus railroad stations. Located on rue d'Amsterdam in the eighth arrondissement, it serves (now as in the 1920s) both the western suburbs of Paris and the mainline rail service to Normandy.

put my hand on his shoulder. He shook his head. "I can't do it," he said, and put his head deeper into his arms. "I can't do it. Nothing will make me do it."

"Robert," I said, and shook him by the shoulder. He looked up. He smiled and blinked.

"Did I talk out loud just then?"

"Something. But it wasn't clear."

"God, what a rotten dream!"

"Did the typewriter put you to sleep?"

"Guess so. I didn't sleep all last night."

"What was the matter?"

"Talking," he said.

I could picture it. I have a rotten habit of picturing the bedroom scenes of my friends. We went out to the Café Napolitain to have an *apéritif* and watch the evening crowd on the Boulevard.[9]

Chapter III

It was a warm spring night and I sat at a table on the terrace of the Napolitain after Robert had gone, watching it get dark and the electric signs come on, and the red and green stop-and-go traffic-signal, and the crowd going by, and the horse-cabs clippety-clopping along at the edge of the solid taxi traffic, and the *poules*[1] going by, singly and in pairs, looking for the evening meal. I watched a good-looking girl walk past the table and watched her go up the street and lost sight of her, and watched another, and then saw the first one coming back again. She went by once more and I caught her eye, and she came over and sat down at the table. The waiter came up.

"Well, what will you drink?" I asked.

"Pernod."[2]

"That's not good for little girls."

"Little girl yourself. Dites garçon, un pernod."[3]

"A pernod for me, too."

"What's the matter?" she asked. "Going on a party?"

"Sure. Aren't you?"

"I don't know. You never know in this town."

"Don't you like Paris?"

"No."

9. A popular café well known to tourists in the 1920s, Café Napolitain was located on boulevard des Capucines, near place de l'Opéra; *aperitif*: an alcoholic pre-dinner drink intended to stimulate the appetite.
1. Hens. (French). Here used as a term for "prostitutes."
2. A popular anise liqueur.
3. "Tell the waiter a Pernod (French)."

"Why don't you go somewhere else?"

"Isn't anywhere else."

"You're happy, all right."

"Happy, hell!"

Pernod is greenish imitation absinthe.[4] When you add water it turns milky. It tastes like licorice and it has a good uplift, but it drops you just as far. We sat and drank it, and the girl looked sullen.

"Well," I said, "are you going to buy me a dinner?"

She grinned and I saw why she made a point of not laughing. With her mouth closed she was a rather pretty girl. I paid for the saucers and we walked out to the street.[5] I hailed a horse-cab and the driver pulled up at the curb. Settled back in the slow, smoothly rolling *fiacre* we moved up the Avenue de l'Opéra,[6] passed the locked doors of the shops, their windows lighted, the Avenue broad and shiny and almost deserted. The cab passed the New York *Herald* bureau with the window full of clocks.[7]

"What are all the clocks for?" she asked.

"They show the hour all over America."

"Don't kid me."

We turned off the Avenue up the Rue des Pyramides, through the traffic of the Rue de Rivoli, and through a dark gate into the Tuileries.[8] She cuddled against me and I put my arm around her. She looked up to be kissed. She touched me with one hand and I put her hand away.

"Never mind."

"What's the matter? You sick?"[9]

"Yes."

"Everybody's sick. I'm sick, too."

We came out of the Tuileries into the light and crossed the Seine and then turned up the Rue des Saints Pères.[1]

4. A distilled spirit made from absinthe and (originally) *Artemisia absinthium* or "grand wormwood" as well as other herbs and flowers. Highly alcoholic, it was popular among (and came to be associated with) avant-garde writers and artists in Paris in the nineteenth century. The Pernod company had produced absinthe before the spirit was banned in France (and elsewhere in Europe and the United States) in 1915; after the ban, it produced instead the liqueur that Jake dismissively describes.
5. In Parisian cafés, waiters would bring each drink on a saucer so that the total bill could be easily calculated by counting the saucers at a table.
6. A major thoroughfare on the Right Bank of the Seine; *fiacre*: a small horse-drawn cab.
7. The New York *Herald* was an American newspaper whose international bureau office was located at 49 avenue de l'Opéra; the clocks showed the time in Paris and in the four American time zones.
8. The cab carries Jake and his companion along two major thoroughfares on the Right Bank before turning toward the River Seine and into the Tuileries, the large public garden located between the Louvre (to the east) and place de la Concorde (to the west) in the first arrondissement.
9. She asks whether Jake has a venereal disease.
1. The Seine is the river along which Paris is built and constitutes the major dividing line between the city's northern (or Right) bank and southern (Left) bank. Jake and his companion cross from Right to Left and then turn onto the Street of the Holy Fathers.

"You oughtn't to drink pernod if you're sick."

"You neither."

"It doesn't make any difference with me. It doesn't make any difference with a woman."

"What are you called?"

"Georgette. How are you called?"

"Jacob."

"That's a Flemish[2] name."

"American too."

"You're not Flamand?"

"No, American."

"Good, I detest Flamands."

By this time we were at the restaurant. I called to the *cocher*[3] to stop. We got out and Georgette did not like the looks of the place. "This is no great thing of a restaurant."

"No," I said. "Maybe you would rather go to Foyot's.[4] Why don't you keep the cab and go on?"

I had picked her up because of a vague sentimental idea that it would be nice to eat with some one. It was a long time since I had dined with a *poule*, and I had forgotten how dull it could be. We went into the restaurant, passed Madame Lavigne[5] at the desk and into a little room. Georgette cheered up a little under the food.

"It isn't bad here," she said. "It isn't chic, but the food is all right."

"Better than you eat in Liège."[6]

"Brussels,[7] you mean."

We had another bottle of wine and Georgette made a joke. She smiled and showed all her bad teeth, and we touched glasses.

"You're not a bad type," she said. "It's a shame you're sick. We get on well. What's the matter with you, anyway?"

"I got hurt in the war," I said.

"Oh, that dirty war."

We would probably have gone on and discussed the war and agreed that it was in reality a calamity for civilization, and perhaps would have been better avoided. I was bored enough. Just then from the other room some one called: "Barnes! I say, Barnes! Jacob Barnes!"

2. Dutch-derived language spoken in parts of Belgium, which comprises a region whose inhabitants speak Flemish and a region whose inhabitants speak French. There has been tension between the regions and populations for much of the country's history. Georgette "detest[s] Flamands," or Flemish speakers, because she is a French-speaking Belgian.
3. Coachman (French).
4. An exclusive restaurant on rue de Tournon, a place far too expensive for Georgette.
5. Lavigne's restaurant was on boulevard du Montparnasse. In *A Moveable Feast*, Hemingway writes that it was a favorite of his and Hadley's.
6. A major French-speaking city in Belgium.
7. The capital of Belgium; located in central Belgium, it is near both French- and Flemish-speaking regions.

"It's a friend calling me," I explained, and went out.

There was Braddocks at a big table with a party: Cohn, Frances Clyne, Mrs. Braddocks, several people I did not know.

"You're coming to the dance, aren't you?" Braddocks asked.

"What dance?"

"Why, the dancings. Don't you know we've revived them?" Mrs. Braddocks put in.

"You must come, Jake. We're all going," Frances said from the end of the table. She was tall and had a smile.

"Of course, he's coming," Braddocks said. "Come in and have coffee with us, Barnes."

"Right."

"And bring your friend," said Mrs. Braddocks laughing. She was a Canadian and had all their easy social graces.

"Thanks, we'll be in," I said. I went back to the small room.

"Who are your friends?" Georgette asked.

"Writers and artists."

"There are lots of those on this side of the river."

"Too many."

"I think so. Still, some of them make money."

"Oh, yes."

We finished the meal and the wine. "Come on," I said. "We're going to have coffee with the others."

Georgette opened her bag, made a few passes at her face as she looked in the little mirror, re-defined her lips with the lip-stick, and straightened her hat.

"Good," she said.

We went into the room full of people and Braddocks and the men at his table stood up.

"I wish to present my fiancée, Mademoiselle Georgette Leblanc," I said. Georgette smiled that wonderful smile, and we shook hands all round.

"Are you related to Georgette Leblanc,[8] the singer?" Mrs. Braddocks asked.

"Connais pas," Georgette answered.

"But you have the same name," Mrs. Braddocks insisted cordially.

"No," said Georgette. "Not at all. My name is Hobin."

"But Mr. Barnes introduced you as Mademoiselle Georgette Leblanc. Surely he did," insisted Mrs. Braddocks, who in the excitement of talking French was liable to have no idea what she was saying.

"He's a fool," Georgette said.

"Oh, it was a joke, then," Mrs. Braddocks said.

"Yes," said Georgette. "To laugh at."

8. French operatic soprano (1869–1941).

"Did you hear that, Henry?" Mrs. Braddocks called down the table to Braddocks. "Mr. Barnes introduced his fiancée as Mademoiselle Leblanc, and her name is actually Hobin."

"Of course, darling. Mademoiselle Hobin, I've known her for a very long time."

"Oh, Mademoiselle Hobin," Frances Clyne called, speaking French very rapidly and not seeming so proud and astonished as Mrs. Braddocks at its coming out really French. "Have you been in Paris long? Do you like it here? You love Paris, do you not?"

"Who's she?" Georgette turned to me. "Do I have to talk to her?"

She turned to Frances, sitting smiling, her hands folded, her head poised on her long neck, her lips pursed ready to start talking again.

"No, I don't like Paris. It's expensive and dirty."

"Really? I find it so extraordinarily clean. One of the cleanest cities in all Europe."

"I find it dirty."

"How strange! But perhaps you have not been here very long."

"I've been here long enough."

"But it does have nice people in it. One must grant that."

Georgette turned to me. "You have nice friends."

Frances was a little drunk and would have liked to have kept it up but the coffee came, and Lavigne with the liqueurs, and after that we all went out and started for Braddocks's dancing-club.

The dancing-club was a *bal musette* in the Rue de la Montagne Sainte Geneviève.[9] Five nights a week the working people of the Pantheon quarter[1] danced there. One night a week it was the dancing-club. On Monday nights it was closed. When we arrived it was quite empty, except for a policeman sitting near the door, the wife of the proprietor back of the zinc bar, and the proprietor himself. The daughter of the house came down-stairs as we went in. There were long benches, and tables ran across the room, and at the far end a dancing-floor.

"I wish people would come earlier," Braddocks said. The daughter came up and wanted to know what we would drink. The proprietor got up on a high stool beside the dancing-floor and began to play the accordion. He had a string of bells around one of his ankles and beat time with his foot as he played. Every one danced. It was hot and we came off the floor perspiring.

9. A street in the fifth arrondissement, on the Left Bank of the Seine. *bal musette*: a dance hall typically featuring music from the Auvergne region. The *musette* is a type of bagpipe from the region (usually made of goatskin); accordion was often played in these bars as well. Hemingway lived for a time over a *bal musette* (his first Paris apartment, at 74, rue du Cardinal Lemoine).

1. The Pantheon, originally the Church of Sainte-Genevieve, became, after the French Revolution, a secular mausoleum housing the remains of distinguished French citizens. The Pantheon quarter is the fifth arrondissment neighborhood around this building.

"My God," Georgette said. "What a box to sweat in!"

"It's hot."

"Hot, my God!"

"Take off your hat."

"That's a good idea."

Some one asked Georgette to dance, and I went over to the bar. It was really very hot and the accordion music was pleasant in the hot night. I drank a beer, standing in the doorway and getting the cool breath of wind from the street. Two taxis were coming down the steep street. They both stopped in front of the Bal. A crowd of young men, some in jerseys and some in their shirt-sleeves, got out. I could see their hands and newly washed, wavy hair in the light from the door. The policeman standing by the door looked at me and smiled. They came in.[2] As they went in, under the light I saw white hands, wavy hair, white faces, grimacing, gesturing, talking. With them was Brett. She looked very lovely and she was very much with them.

One of them saw Georgette and said: "I do declare. There is an actual harlot. I'm going to dance with her, Lett. You watch me."

The tall dark one, called Lett, said: "Don't you be rash."

The wavy blond one answered: "Don't you worry, dear." And with them was Brett.

I was very angry. Somehow they always made me angry. I know they are supposed to be amusing, and you should be tolerant, but I wanted to swing on one, any one, anything to shatter that superior, simpering composure. Instead, I walked down the street and had a beer at the bar at the next Bal. The beer was not good and I had a worse cognac to take the taste out of my mouth. When I came back to the Bal there was a crowd on the floor and Georgette was dancing with the tall blond youth, who danced big-hippily, carrying his head on one side, his eyes lifted as he danced. As soon as the music stopped another one of them asked her to dance. She had been taken up by them. I knew then that they would all dance with her. They are like that.

I sat down at a table. Cohn was sitting there. Frances was dancing. Mrs. Braddocks brought up somebody and introduced him as Robert Prentiss. He was from New York by way of Chicago, and was a rising new novelist. He had some sort of an English accent. I asked him to have a drink.

"Thanks so much," he said, "I've just had one."

"Have another."

"Thanks, I will then."

2. Hemingway's description suggests that the young men are homosexual. Jake's subsequent reaction confirms this.

We got the daughter of the house over and each had a *fine à l'eau*.[3]

"You're from Kansas City, they tell me," he said.

"Yes."

"Do you find Paris amusing?"

"Yes."

"Really?"

I was a little drunk. Not drunk in any positive sense but just enough to be careless.

"For God's sake," I said, "yes. Don't you?"

"Oh, how charmingly you get angry," he said. "I wish I had that faculty."

I got up and walked over toward the dancing-floor. Mrs. Braddocks followed me. "Don't be cross with Robert," she said. "He's still only a child, you know."

"I wasn't cross," I said. "I just thought perhaps I was going to throw up."

"Your fiancée is having a great success," Mrs. Braddocks looked out on the floor where Georgette was dancing in the arms of the tall, dark one, called Lett.

"Isn't she?" I said.

"Rather," said Mrs. Braddocks.

Cohn came up. "Come on, Jake," he said, "have a drink." We walked over to the bar. "What's the matter with you? You seem all worked up over something?"

"Nothing. This whole show makes me sick is all."

Brett came up to the bar.

"Hello, you chaps."

"Hello, Brett," I said. "Why aren't you tight?"[4]

"Never going to get tight any more. I say, give a chap a brandy and soda."

She stood holding the glass and I saw Robert Cohn looking at her. He looked a great deal as his compatriot must have looked when he saw the promised land.[5] Cohn, of course, was much younger. But he had that look of eager, deserving expectation.

Brett was damned good-looking. She wore a slipover jersey sweater and a tweed skirt, and her hair was brushed back like a boy's. She started all that. She was built with curves like the hull of a racing yacht, and you missed none of it with that wool jersey.

"It's a fine crowd you're with, Brett," I said.

"Aren't they lovely? And you, my dear. Where did you get it?"

3. Brandy and water (French).
4. Drunk.
5. Jake refers to Moses, who led the Israelites to the "promised land" of Canaan after the exodus from captivity in Egypt. Though he would not live to enter it, Moses is allowed by God to see the land from a mountaintop (Numbers 27:12).

"At the Napolitain."

"And have you had a lovely evening?"

"Oh, priceless," I said.

Brett laughed. "It's wrong of you, Jake. It's an insult to all of us. Look at Frances there, and Jo."

This for Cohn's benefit.

"It's in restraint of trade," Brett said. She laughed again.

"You're wonderfully sober," I said.

"Yes. Aren't I? And when one's with the crowd I'm with, one can drink in such safety, too."

The music started and Robert Cohn said: "Will you dance this with me, Lady Brett?"

Brett smiled at him. "I've promised to dance this with Jacob," she laughed. "You've a hell of a biblical name, Jake."

"How about the next?" asked Cohn.

"We're going," Brett said. "We've a date up at Montmartre."[6]

Dancing, I looked over Brett's shoulder and saw Cohn, standing at the bar, still watching her.

"You've made a new one there," I said to her.

"Don't talk about it. Poor chap. I never knew it till just now."

"Oh, well," I said. "I suppose you like to add them up."

"Don't talk like a fool."

"You do."

"Oh, well. What if I do?"

"Nothing," I said. We were dancing to the accordion and some one was playing the banjo. It was hot and I felt happy. We passed close to Georgette dancing with another one of them.

"What possessed you to bring her?"

"I don't know, I just brought her."

"You're getting damned romantic."

"No, bored."

"Now?"

"No, not now."

"Let's get out of here. She's well taken care of."

"Do you want to?"

"Would I ask you if I didn't want to?"

We left the floor and I took my coat off a hanger on the wall and put it on. Brett stood by the bar. Cohn was talking to her. I stopped at the bar and asked them for an envelope. The patronne[7] found

6. A large hill in the eighteenth arrondissement (on the Right Bank, in the northern area of Paris). It takes its name from the martyrdom of Saint Denis, the patron saint of the city. In the nineteenth century, it was known as the heart of bohemian culture, heavily associated with the artists who had studios in the area (including Monet, Renoir, Degas, and Van Gogh) and famous for its cafés, cabarets, and dance halls. By the 1920s, it was being superseded by Montparnasse, on the Left Bank, as a site of artistic and cultural ferment.

7. The female proprietor (or the wife of the male proprietor) of the *bal musette*.

one. I took a fifty-franc note[8] from my pocket, put it in the envelope, sealed it, and handed it to the patronne.

"If the girl I came with asks for me, will you give her this?" I said. "If she goes out with one of those gentlemen, will you save this for me?"

"C'est entendu, Monsieur,"[9] the patronne said. "You go now? So early?"

"Yes," I said.

We started out the door. Cohn was still talking to Brett. She said good night and took my arm. "Good night, Cohn," I said. Outside in the street we looked for a taxi.

"You're going to lose your fifty francs," Brett said.

"Oh, yes."

"No taxis."

"We could walk up to the Pantheon and get one."

"Come on and we'll get a drink in the pub next door and send for one."

"You wouldn't walk across the street."

"Not if I could help it."

We went into the next bar and I sent a waiter for a taxi.

"Well," I said, "we're out away from them."

We stood against the tall zinc bar and did not talk and looked at each other. The waiter came and said the taxi was outside. Brett pressed my hand hard. I gave the waiter a franc and we went out. "Where should I tell him?" I asked.

"Oh, tell him to drive around."

I told the driver to go to the Parc Monstsouris,[1] and got in, and slammed the door. Brett was leaning back in the corner, her eyes closed. I sat beside her. The cab started with a jerk.

"Oh, darling, I've been so miserable," Brett said.

Chapter IV

The taxi went up the hill, passed the lighted square, then on into the dark, still climbing, then levelled out onto a dark street behind St. Etienne du Mont, went smoothly down the asphalt, passed the trees and the standing bus at the Place de la Contrescarpe, then turned onto the cobbles of the Rue Mouffetard. There were lighted

8. Fifty francs in 1925 would have been worth between $1 and $2; in present-day terms, Jake leaves Georgette between $30 and $40, what she would normally have received for spending the whole night with him.
9. "That is understood, sir" (French).
1. A park about two miles from the Pantheon Quarter, on the south side of Paris (not near any obvious destination Jake and Brett would have, and so a way, as Brett says, simply to tell the driver "to drive around").

bars and late open shops on each side of the street. We were sitting apart and we jolted close together going down the old street. Brett's hat was off. Her head was back. I saw her face in the lights from the open shops, then it was dark, then I saw her face clearly as we came out on the Avenue des Gobelins.[1] The street was torn up and men were working on the car-tracks by the light of acetylene flares. Brett's face was white and the long line of her neck showed in the bright light of the flares. The street was dark again and I kissed her. Our lips were tight together and then she turned away and pressed against the corner of the seat, as far away as she could get. Her head was down.

"Don't touch me," she said. "Please don't touch me."

"What's the matter?"

"I can't stand it."

"Oh, Brett."

"You mustn't. You must know. I can't stand it, that's all. Oh, darling, please understand!"

"Don't you love me?"

"Love you? I simply turn all to jelly when you touch me."

"Isn't there anything we can do about it?"

She was sitting up now. My arm was around her and she was leaning back against me, and we were quite calm. She was looking into my eyes with that way she had of looking that made you wonder whether she really saw out of her own eyes. They would look on and on after every one else's eyes in the world would have stopped looking. She looked as though there were nothing on earth she would not look at like that, and really she was afraid of so many things.

"And there's not a damn thing we could do," I said.

"I don't know," she said. "I don't want to go through that hell again."

"We'd better keep away from each other."

"But, darling, I have to see you. It isn't all that you know."

"No, but it always gets to be."

"That's my fault. Don't we pay for all the things we do, though?"

She had been looking into my eyes all the time. Her eyes had different depths, sometimes they seemed perfectly flat. Now you could see all the way into them.

"When I think of the hell I've put chaps through. I'm paying for it all now."

"Don't talk like a fool," I said. "Besides, what happened to me is supposed to be funny.[2] I never think about it."

"Oh, no. I'll lay you don't."

1. Hemingway describes a route along mostly small Left Bank streets, up and down the hills of Montparnasse, which also takes Jake and Brett through darkness and light.
2. Jake has been wounded in the genitals and/or penis during the Great War.

"Well, let's shut up about it."

"I laughed about it too, myself, once." She wasn't looking at me. "A friend of my brother's came home that way from Mons.[3] It seemed like a hell of a joke. Chaps never know anything, do they?"

"No," I said. "Nobody ever knows anything."

I was pretty well through with the subject. At one time or another I had probably considered it from most of its various angles, including the one that certain injuries or imperfections are a subject of merriment while remaining quite serious for the person possessing them.

"It's funny," I said. "It's very funny. And it's a lot of fun, too, to be in love."

"Do you think so?" her eyes looked flat again.

"I don't mean fun that way. In a way it's an enjoyable feeling."

"No," she said. "I think it's hell on earth."

"It's good to see each other."

"No. I don't think it is."

"Don't you want to?"

"I have to."

We were sitting now like two strangers. On the right was the Parc Montsouris. The restaurant where they have the pool of live trout and where you can sit and look out over the park was closed and dark. The driver leaned his head around.

"Where do you want to go?" I asked. Brett turned her head away.

"Oh, go to the Select."[4]

"Café Select," I told the driver. "Boulevard Montparnasse." We drove straight down, turning around the Lion de Belfort[5] that guards the passing Montrouge trams. Brett looked straight ahead. On the Boulevard Raspail, with the lights of Montparnasse in sight, Brett said: "Would you mind very much if I asked you to do something?"

"Don't be silly."

"Kiss me just once more before we get there."

When the taxi stopped I got out and paid. Brett came out putting on her hat. She gave me her hand as she stepped down. Her hand was shaky. "I say, do I look too much of a mess?" She pulled her man's felt hat down and started in for the bar. Inside, against the bar and at tables, were most of the crowd who had been at the dance.

"Hello, you chaps," Brett said. "I'm going to have a drink."

3. Mons, Belgium, was the site of an important early battle of the First World War (August 23, 1914), in which the British Expeditionary Force was pressed by a determined German advance to retreat. The fourth of the six prose vignettes Hemingway published under the title "In Our Time" in the *Little Review* in April, 1923, was (only in this initial publication) titled "Mons."

4. The Café Select was (and is) located at 99, boulevard du Montparnasse, near the intersection of boulevard du Montparnasse and boulevard Raspail.

5. Sculpture by Bartholdi in the place Denfert-Rochereau, through which the cab passes on the way to the Café Select. Trams to and from Montrouge, a neighborhood on the southern edge of Paris, passed through this square.

"Oh, Brett! Brett!" the little Greek portrait-painter, who called himself a duke, and whom everybody called Zizi, pushed up to her. "I got something fine to tell you."

"Hello, Zizi," Brett said.

"I want you to meet a friend," Zizi said. A fat man came up.

"Count Mippipopolous, meet my friend Lady Ashley."

"How do you do?" said Brett.

"Well, does your Ladyship have a good time here in Paris?" asked Count Mippipopolous, who wore an elk's tooth on his watch-chain.

"Rather," said Brett.

"Paris is a fine town all right," said the count. "But I guess you have pretty big doings yourself over in London."

"Oh, yes," said Brett. "Enormous."

Braddocks called to me from a table. "Barnes," he said, "have a drink. That girl of yours got in a frightful row."

"What about?"

"Something the patronne's daughter said. A corking row. She was rather splendid, you know. Showed her yellow card and demanded the patronne's daughter's too.[6] I say it was a row."

"What finally happened?"

"Oh, some one took her home. Not a bad-looking girl. Wonderful command of the idiom. Do stay and have a drink."

"No," I said. "I must shove off. Seen Cohn?"

"He went home with Frances," Mrs. Braddocks put in.

"Poor chap, he looks awfully down," Braddocks said.

"I dare say he is," said Mrs. Braddocks.

"I have to shove off," I said. "Good night."

I said good night to Brett at the bar. The count was buying champagne. "Will you take a glass of wine with us, sir?" he asked.

"No. Thanks awfully. I have to go."

"Really going?" Brett asked.

"Yes," I said. "I've got a rotten headache."

"I'll see you to-morrow?"

"Come in at the office."

"Hardly."

"Well, where will I see you?"

"Anywhere around five o'clock."

"Make it the other side of town then."

"Good. I'll be at the Crillon[7] at five."

"Try and be there," I said.

"Don't worry," Brett said. "I've never let you down, have I?"

6. Registered prostitutes in Paris were required to carry a yellow health certification card; by requesting the patronne's daughter's, Georgette suggests that she, too, is a prostitute.
7. The Hotel Crillon, a luxury hotel on the place de la Concorde (on the Right Bank of the Seine).

"Heard from Mike?"

"Letter to-day."

"Good night, sir," said the count.

I went out onto the sidewalk and walked down toward the Boulevard St. Michel, passed the tables of the Rotonde, still crowded, looked across the street at the Dôme,[8] its tables running out to the edge of the pavement. Some one waved at me from a table, I did not see who it was and went on. I wanted to get home. The Boulevard Montparnasse was deserted. Lavigne's was closed tight, and they were stacking the tables outside the Closerie des Lilas.[9] I passed Ney's statue[1] standing among the new-leaved chestnut-trees in the arc-light. There was a faded purple wreath leaning against the base. I stopped and read the inscription: from the Bonapartist Groups, some date; I forget. He looked very fine, Marshal Ney in his top-boots, gesturing with his sword among the green new horse-chestnut leaves. My flat was just across the street, a little way down the Boulevard St. Michel.

There was a light in the concierge's room and I knocked on the door and she gave me my mail. I wished her good night and went up-stairs. There were two letters and some papers. I looked at them under the gas-light in the dining-room. The letters were from the States. One was a bank statement. It showed a balance of $2432.60. I got out my check-book and deducted four checks drawn since the first of the month, and discovered I had a balance of $1832.60.[2] I wrote this on the back of the statement. The other letter was a wedding announcement. Mr. and Mrs. Aloysius Kirby announce the marriage of their daughter Katherine—I knew neither the girl nor the man she was marrying. They must be circularizing the town. It was a funny name. I felt sure I could remember anybody with a name like Aloysius. It was a good Catholic name. There was a crest on the announcement. Like Zizi the Greek duke. And that count. The count was funny. Brett had a title, too. Lady Ashley. To hell with Brett. To hell with you, Lady Ashley.

I lit the lamp beside the bed, turned off the gas, and opened the wide windows. The bed was far back from the windows, and I sat with the windows open and undressed by the bed. Outside a night train, running on the street-car tracks, went by carrying vegetables to the markets. They were noisy at night when you could not sleep.

8. The Rotonde and Dôme were cafés frequented by the writers and artists of Montparnasse.
9. A brasserie that remains on boulevard du Montparnasse.
1. Michel Ney (1769–1815), French military commander during the Revolution and the Napoleonic wars, named a Marshal of France by Napoleon in 1804. Ney commanded a corps of the French Army during the invasion of Russia in 1812 and ordered a failed cavalry charge often named as a key to Napoleon's defeat at Waterloo in 1815. Executed by the French government after Napoleon's deposition in 1815, Ney was later honored as a hero of the French Empire.
2. Given the strength of the American dollar against the French franc and the low prices for accommodations and meals in Paris at this date, Jake's bank balance would enable him to live very comfortably.

Undressing, I looked at myself in the mirror of the big armoire beside the bed. That was a typically French way to furnish a room. Practical, too, I suppose. Of all the ways to be wounded. I suppose it was funny. I put on my pajamas and got into bed. I had the two bull-fight papers, and I took their wrappers off.[3] One was orange. The other yellow. They would both have the same news, so whichever I read first would spoil the other. *Le Toril* was the better paper, so I started to read it. I read it all the way through, including the Petite Correspondance and the Cornigrams. I blew out the lamp. Perhaps I would be able to sleep.

My head started to work. The old grievance. Well, it was a rotten way to be wounded and flying on a joke front like the Italian.[4] In the Italian hospital we were going to form a society. It had a funny name in Italian. I wonder what became of the others, the Italians. That was in the Ospedale Maggiore in Milano, Padiglione Ponte.[5] The next building was the Padiglione Zonda. There was a statue of Ponte, or maybe it was Zonda. That was where the liaison colonel came to visit me. That was funny. That was about the first funny thing. I was all bandaged up. But they had told him about it. Then he made that wonderful speech: "You, a foreigner, an Englishman" (any foreigner was an Englishman) "have given more than your life." What a speech! I would like to have it illuminated to hang in the office. He never laughed. He was putting himself in my place, I guess. "Che mala fortuna! Che mala fortuna!"[6]

I never used to realize it, I guess. I try and play it along and just not make trouble for people. Probably I never would have had any trouble if I hadn't run into Brett when they shipped me to England. I suppose she only wanted what she couldn't have. Well, people were that way. To hell with people. The Catholic Church had an awfully good way of handling all that. Good advice, anyway. Not to think about it. Oh, it was swell advice. Try and take it sometime. Try and take it.

I lay awake thinking and my mind jumping around. Then I couldn't keep away from it, and I started to think about Brett and all the rest of it went away. I was thinking about Brett and my mind stopped jumping around and started to go in sort of smooth waves. Then all of a sudden I started to cry. Then after a while it was better and I lay in bed and listened to the heavy trams go by and way down the street, and then I went to sleep.

3. The bullfight took various forms in Spain and the south of France, and was covered by multiple newspapers and magazines. *Le Toril* (The Bullpen) was a French bullfighting magazine.
4. The Italian front during the First World War was the area around the border between Italy and the Austro-Hungarian Empire. Hemingway himself was wounded in the legs by shrapnel while working as a Red Cross ambulance driver on the Italian front (July 8, 1918).
5. The Ospedale Maggiore in Milan, Italy, where Jake recalls being treated, was where Hemingway was treated after he was wounded. Padiglione Ponte and Padiglione Zonda refer to wings of the hospital. Each is named for a benefactor.
6. "What bad luck!" (Italian).

I woke up. There was a row going on outside. I listened and I thought I recognized a voice. I put on a dressing-gown and went to the door. The concierge was talking down-stairs.[7] She was very angry. I heard my name and called down the stairs.

"Is that you, Monsieur Barnes?" the concierge called.

"Yes. It's me."

"There's a species of woman here who's waked the whole street up. What kind of a dirty business at this time of night! She says she must see you. I've told her you're asleep."

Then I heard Brett's voice. Half asleep I had been sure it was Georgette. I don't know why. She could not have known my address.

"Will you send her up, please?"

Brett came up the stairs. I saw she was quite drunk. "Silly thing to do," she said. "Make an awful row. I say, you weren't asleep, were you?"

"What did you think I was doing?"

"Don't know. What time is it?"

I looked at the clock. It was half-past four. "Had no idea what hour it was," Brett said. "I say, can a chap sit down? Don't be cross, darling. Just left the count. He brought me here."

"What's he like?" I was getting brandy and soda and glasses.

"Just a little," said Brett. "Don't try and make me drunk. The count? Oh, rather. He's quite one of us."

"Is he a count?"

"Here's how. I rather think so, you know. Deserves to be, anyhow. Knows hell's own amount about people. Don't know where he got it all. Owns a chain of sweetshops in the States."

She sipped at her glass.

"Think he called it a chain. Something like that. Linked them all up. Told me a little about it. Damned interesting. He's one of us, though. Oh, quite. No doubt. One can always tell."

She took another drink.

"How do I buck on about all this? You don't mind, do you? He's putting up for Zizi, you know."

"Is Zizi really a duke, too?"

"I shouldn't wonder. Greek, you know. Rotten painter. I rather liked the count."

"Where did you go with him?"

"Oh, everywhere. He just brought me here now. Offered me ten thousand dollars to go to Biarritz[8] with him. How much is that in pounds?"

7. The concierge in Jake's apartment building would have been in charge of opening the building's main door for guests who did not have keys, and, as here, ensuring that the guests were indeed to be allowed in at such an odd hour.

8. A popular resort city on the Bay of Biscay in southern France.

"Around two thousand."

"Lot of money. I told him I couldn't do it. He was awfully nice about it. Told him I knew too many people in Biarritz."

Brett laughed.

"I say, you are slow on the up-take," she said. I had only sipped my brandy and soda. I took a long drink.

"That's better. Very funny," Brett said. "Then he wanted me to go to Cannes with him. Told him I knew too many people in Cannes. Monte Carlo.[9] Told him I knew too many people in Monte Carlo. Told him I knew too many people everywhere. Quite true, too. So I asked him to bring me here."

She looked at me, her hand on the table, her glass raised. "Don't look like that," she said. "Told him I was in love with you. True, too. Don't look like that. He was damn nice about it. Wants to drive us out to dinner to-morrow night. Like to go?"

"Why not?"

"I'd better go now."

"Why?"

"Just wanted to see you. Damned silly idea. Want to get dressed and come down? He's got the car just up the street."

"The count?"

"Himself. And a chauffeur in livery. Going to drive me around and have breakfast in the Bois.[1] Hampers. Got it all at Zelli's. Dozen bottles of Mumm's.[2] Tempt you?"

"I have to work in the morning," I said. "I'm too far behind you now to catch up and be any fun."

"Don't be an ass."

"Can't do it."

"Right. Send him a tender message?"

"Anything. Absolutely."

"Good night, darling."

"Don't be sentimental."

"You make me ill."

We kissed good night and Brett shivered. "I'd better go," she said. "Good night, darling."

"You don't have to go."

"Yes."

We kissed again on the stairs and as I called for the cordon the concierge muttered something behind her door. I went back upstairs and from the open window watched Brett walking up the street to

9. Two more famous resort cities on the coast of southern Europe, Cannes in France and Monte Carlo in the principality of Monaco.
1. The Bois de Boulogne, a large forested park on the outskirts of Paris.
2. One of the major vintners and dealers of Champagne. *Zelli's*: a cabaret in Montmartre, owned by the Italian-American Joe Zelli.

the big limousine drawn up to the curb under the arc-light. She got in and it started off. I turned around. On the table was an empty glass and a glass half-full of brandy and soda. I took them both out to the kitchen and poured the half-full glass down the sink. I turned off the gas in the dining-room, kicked off my slippers sitting on the bed, and got into bed. This was Brett, that I had felt like crying about. Then I thought of her walking up the street and stepping into the car, as I had last seen her, and of course in a little while I felt like hell again. It is awfully easy to be hard-boiled about everything in the daytime, but at night it is another thing.

Chapter V

In the morning I walked down the Boulevard to the Rue Soufflot[1] for coffee and brioche. It was a fine morning. The horse-chestnut trees in the Luxembourg gardens were in bloom. There was the pleasant early-morning feeling of a hot day. I read the papers with the coffee and then smoked a cigarette. The flower-women were coming up from the market and arranging their daily stock. Students went by going up to the law school, or down to the Sorbonne.[2] The Boulevard was busy with trams and people going to work. I got on an S bus and rode down to the Madeleine,[3] standing on the back platform. From the Madeleine I walked along the Boulevard des Capucines to the Opéra, and up to my office. I passed the man with the jumping frogs and the man with the boxer toys. I stepped aside to avoid walking into the thread with which his girl assistant manipulated the boxers. She was standing looking away, the thread in her folded hands. The man was urging two tourists to buy. Three more tourists had stopped and were watching. I walked on behind a man who was pushing a roller that printed the name CINZANO[4] on the sidewalk in damp letters. All along people were going to work. It felt pleasant to be going to work. I walked across the avenue and turned in to my office.

Up-stairs in the office I read the French morning papers, smoked, and then sat at the typewriter and got off a good morning's work. At eleven o'clock I went over to the Quai d'Orsay in a taxi and went

1. The boulevard Saint-Michel, where Jake's apartment is located, intersects with rue Soufflot at the edge of the Luxembourg Gardens.
2. The intellectual center of the University of Paris, one of the oldest parts of the university (founded in 1257) and the locus of theology and literature studies in the university system.
3. The Church of Saint Mary Magdalene in the eighth arrondissement. *S bus*: The S bus in Paris's bus system in the 1920s ran from rue Soufflot along boulevard Saint-Michel, boulevard Raspail, and boulevard Saint-Germain before crossing the Seine and traveling through place de la Concorde and rue Royale.
4. An Italian brand of vermouth; the roller printing the company's name on the pavement is a form of advertising.

in and sat with about a dozen correspondents, while the foreign-office mouthpiece, a young Nouvelle Revue Française[5] diplomat in horn-rimmed spectacles, talked and answered questions for half an hour. The President of the Council was in Lyons[6] making a speech, or, rather he was on his way back. Several people asked questions to hear themselves talk and there were a couple of questions asked by news service men who wanted to know the answers. There was no news. I shared a taxi back from the Quai d'Orsay with Woolsey and Krum.

"What do you do nights, Jake?" asked Krum. "I never see you around."

"Oh, I'm over in the Quarter."

"I'm coming over some night. The Dingo.[7] That's the great place, isn't it?"

"Yes. That, or this new dive, the Select."

"I've meant to get over," said Krum. "You know how it is, though, with a wife and kids."

"Playing any tennis?" Woolsey asked.

"Well, no," said Krum. "I can't say I've played any this year. I've tried to get away, but Sundays it's always rained, and the courts are so damned crowded."

"The Englishmen all have Saturday off," Woolsey said.

"Lucky beggars," said Krum. "Well, I'll tell you. Some day I'm not going to be working for an agency. Then I'll have plenty of time to get out in the country."

"That's the thing to do. Live out in the country and have a little car."

"I've been thinking some about getting a car next year."

I banged on the glass. The chauffeur stopped. "Here's my street," I said. "Come in and have a drink."

"Thanks, old man," Krum said. Woolsey shook his head. "I've got to file that line he got off this morning."

I put a two-franc piece in Krum's hand.

"You're crazy, Jake," he said. "This is on me."

"It's all on the office, anyway."

"Nope. I want to get it."

I waved good-bye. Krum put his head out. "See you at the lunch on Wednesday."

"You bet."

I went to the office in the elevator. Robert Cohn was waiting for me. "Hello, Jake," he said. "Going out to lunch?"

5. *Quai d'Orsay*: a quay that runs along the Left Bank in the seventh arrondissement. An influential and prestigious magazine of the arts and culture (founded in 1909).
6. Lyons (more typically Lyon) was France's second-largest city in 1925.
7. The Dingo Bar, 10, rue Delambre, in Montparnasse. In *A Moveable Feast*, Hemingway records first meeting F. Scott Fitzgerald at the Dingo in 1925.

"Yes. Let me see if there is anything new."

"Where will we eat?"

"Anywhere."

I was looking over my desk. "Where do you want to eat?"

"How about Vetzel's?[8] They've got good hors d'œuvres."

In the restaurant we ordered hors d'œuvres and beer. The sommelier brought the beer, tall, beaded on the outside of the steins, and cold. There were a dozen different dishes of hors d'œuvres.

"Have any fun last night?" I asked.

"No. I don't think so."

"How's the writing going?"

"Rotten. I can't get this second book going."

"That happens to everybody."

"Oh, I'm sure of that. It gets me worried, though."

"Thought any more about going to South America?"

"I mean that."

"Well, why don't you start off?"

"Frances."

"Well," I said, "take her with you."

"She wouldn't like it. That isn't the sort of thing she likes. She likes a lot of people around."

"Tell her to go to hell."

"I can't. I've got certain obligations to her."

He shoved the sliced cucumbers away and took a pickled herring.

"What do you know about Lady Brett Ashley, Jake?"

"Her name's Lady Ashley. Brett's her own name. She's a nice girl," I said. "She's getting a divorce and she's going to marry Mike Campbell. He's over in Scotland now. Why?"

"She's a remarkably attractive woman."

"Isn't she?"

"There's a certain quality about her, a certain fineness. She seems to be absolutely fine and straight."

"She's very nice."

"I don't know how to describe the quality," Cohn said. "I suppose it's breeding."

"You sound as though you liked her pretty well."

"I do. I shouldn't wonder if I were in love with her."

"She's a drunk," I said. "She's in love with Mike Campbell, and she's going to marry him. He's going to be rich as hell some day."

"I don't believe she'll ever marry him."

"Why not?"

8. Probably Wetzel's, a restaurant in rue Auber, near the location of Jake's office.

"I don't know. I just don't believe it. Have you known her a long time?"

"Yes," I said. "She was a V. A. D.[9] in a hospital I was in during the war."

"She must have been just a kid then."

"She's thirty-four now."

"When did she marry Ashley?"

"During the war. Her own true love had just kicked off with the dysentery."

"You talk sort of bitter."

"Sorry. I didn't mean to. I was just trying to give you the facts."

"I don't believe she would marry anybody she didn't love."

"Well," I said. "She's done it twice."

"I don't believe it."

"Well," I said, "don't ask me a lot of fool questions if you don't like the answers."

"I didn't ask you that."

"You asked me what I knew about Brett Ashley."

"I didn't ask you to insult her."

"Oh, go to hell."

He stood up from the table his face white, and stood there white and angry behind the little plates of hors d'œuvres.

"Sit down," I said. "Don't be a fool."

"You've got to take that back."

"Oh, cut out the prep-school stuff."

"Take it back."

"Sure. Anything. I never heard of Brett Ashley. How's that?"

"No. Not that. About me going to hell."

"Oh, don't go to hell," I said. "Stick around. We're just starting lunch."

Cohn smiled again and sat down. He seemed glad to sit down. What the hell would he have done if he hadn't sat down? "You say such damned insulting things, Jake."

"I'm sorry. I've got a nasty tongue. I never mean it when I say nasty things."

"I know it," Cohn said. "You're really about the best friend I have, Jake."

God help you, I thought. "Forget what I said," I said out loud. "I'm sorry."

"It's all right. It's fine. I was just sore for a minute."

"Good. Let's get something else to eat."

9. Voluntary Aid Detachment, hospital assistants in England during the First World War.

After we finished the lunch we walked up to the Café de la Paix[1] and had coffee. I could feel Cohn wanted to bring up Brett again, but I held him off it. We talked about one thing and another, and I left him to come to the office.

Chapter VI

At five o'clock I was in the Hotel Crillon waiting for Brett. She was not there, so I sat down and wrote some letters. They were not very good letters but I hoped their being on Crillon stationery would help them. Brett did not turn up, so about quarter to six I went down to the bar and had a Jack Rose[1] with George the barman. Brett had not been in the bar either, and so I looked for her up-stairs on my way out, and took a taxi to the Café Select. Crossing the Seine I saw a string of barges being towed empty down the current, riding high, the bargemen at the sweeps as they came toward the bridge. The river looked nice. It was always pleasant crossing bridges in Paris.

The taxi rounded the statue of the inventor of the semaphore[2] engaged in doing same, and turned up the Boulevard Raspail, and I sat back to let that part of the ride pass. The Boulevard Raspail always made dull riding. It was like a certain stretch on the P.L.M.[3] between Fontainebleau and Montereau that always made me feel bored and dead and dull until it was over. I suppose it is some association of ideas that makes those dead places in a journey. There are other streets in Paris as ugly as the Boulevard Raspail. It is a street I do not mind walking down at all. But I cannot stand to ride along it. Perhaps I had read something about it once. That was the way Robert Cohn was about all of Paris. I wondered where Cohn got that incapacity to enjoy Paris. Possibly from Mencken.[4] Mencken hates Paris, I believe. So many young men get their likes and dislikes from Mencken.

The taxi stopped in front of the Rotonde. No matter what café in Montparnasse you ask a taxi-driver to bring you to from the right

1. Café de la Paix is on boulevard des Capucines at place de l'Opéra, near the location of Jake's office. (*Paix* in French means "peace.")
1. A cocktail usually containing applejack (or apple brandy), grenadine, and lemon juice, shaken over ice and served in a chilled glass.
2. Claude Chappe (1763–1805) invented the semaphore code system; a bronze statue of Chappe stood at the intersection of boulevard Raspail and rue du Bac until its removal during the Nazi occupation of Paris.
3. The Paris-Lyon-Mediterranean railway, which departs from the Gare de Lyon, passing through the stretch (from Fontainebleau to Montereau) that Jake here characterizes as boring.
4. Henry Louis (H. L.) Mencken (1880–1956), American journalist, critic, and editor. He covered the Scopes "Monkey Trial" in Tennessee in 1925 and was renowned as a satirist and fierce critic of American parochialism. He wrote frequently for the *Smart Set* and in 1924 co-founded and edited (with George Jean Nathan) *The American Mercury*. Mencken negatively reviewed Hemingway's 1924 small-press *in our time*.

bank of the river, they always take you to the Rotonde. Ten years from now it will probably be the Dôme. It was near enough, anyway. I walked past the sad tables of the Rotonde to the Select. There were a few people inside at the bar, and outside, alone, sat Harvey Stone. He had a pile of saucers in front of him, and he needed a shave.

"Sit down," said Harvey, "I've been looking for you."

"What's the matter?"

"Nothing. Just looking for you."

"Been out to the races?"

"No. Not since Sunday."

"What do you hear from the States?"

"Nothing. Absolutely nothing."

"What's the matter?"

"I don't know. I'm through with them. I'm absolutely through with them."

He leaned forward and looked me in the eye.

"Do you want to know something, Jake?"

"Yes."

"I haven't had anything to eat for five days."

I figured rapidly back in my mind. It was three days ago that Harvey had won two hundred francs from me shaking poker dice in the New York Bar.[5]

"What's the matter?"

"No money. Money hasn't come," he paused. "I tell you it's strange, Jake. When I'm like this I just want to be alone. I want to stay in my own room. I'm like a cat."

I felt in my pocket.

"Would a hundred help you any, Harvey?"

"Yes."

"Come on. Let's go and eat."

"There's no hurry. Have a drink."

"Better eat."

"No. When I get like this I don't care whether I eat or not."

We had a drink. Harvey added my saucer to his own pile.

"Do you know Mencken, Harvey?"

"Yes. Why?"

"What's he like?"

"He's all right. He says some pretty funny things. Last time I had dinner with him we talked about Hoffenheimer.[6] 'The trouble is,' he said, 'he's a garter snapper.' That's not bad."

5. Harry's New York Bar was located on rue Daunou on the Right Bank of the Seine and was popular among American expatriates.
6. Hoffenheimer appears in the manuscript of *The Sun Also Rises* as Hergesheimer, Hemingway's reference to Joseph Hergesheimer, a novelist who was a friend of Mencken's and was listed as a leading American novelist in *The American Mercury* in 1924.

"That's not bad."

"He's through now," Harvey went on. "He's written about all the things he knows, and now he's on all the things he doesn't know."

"I guess he's all right," I said. "I just can't read him."

"Oh, nobody reads him now," Harvey said, "except the people that used to read the Alexander Hamilton Institute."[7]

"Well," I said. "That was a good thing, too."

"Sure," said Harvey. So we sat and thought deeply for a while.

"Have another port?"[8]

"All right," said Harvey.

"There comes Cohn," I said. Robert Cohn was crossing the street.

"That moron," said Harvey. Cohn came up to our table.

"Hello, you bums," he said.

"Hello, Robert," Harvey said. "I was just telling Jake here that you're a moron."

"What do you mean?"

"Tell us right off. Don't think. What would you rather do if you could do anything you wanted?"

Cohn started to consider.

"Don't think. Bring it right out."

"I don't know," Cohn said. "What's it all about, anyway?"

"I mean what would you rather do. What comes into your head first. No matter how silly it is."

"I don't know," Cohn said. "I think I'd rather play football again with what I know about handling myself, now."

"I misjudged you," Harvey said. "You're not a moron. You're only a case of arrested development."

"You're awfully funny, Harvey," Cohn said. "Some day somebody will push your face in."

Harvey Stone laughed. "You think so. They won't, though. Because it wouldn't make any difference to me. I'm not a fighter."

"It would make a difference to you if anybody did it."

"No, it wouldn't. That's where you make your big mistake. Because you're not intelligent."

"Cut it out about me."

"Sure," said Harvey. "It doesn't make any difference to me. You don't mean anything to me."

"Come on, Harvey," I said. "Have another porto."

"No," he said. "I'm going up the street and eat. See you later, Jake."

7. An organization for business education in New York City. Founded in 1909, the Institute closed in the 1980s.
8. Fortified sweet red wine (Jake later refers to it as "porto").

He walked out and up the street. I watched him crossing the street through the taxis, small, heavy, slowly sure of himself in the traffic.

"He always gets me sore," Cohn said. "I can't stand him."

"I like him," I said. "I'm fond of him. You don't want to get sore at him."

"I know it," Cohn said. "He just gets on my nerves."

"Write this afternoon?"

"No. I couldn't get it going. It's harder to do than my first book. I'm having a hard time handling it."

The sort of healthy conceit that he had when he returned from America early in the spring was gone. Then he had been sure of his work, only with these personal longings for adventure. Now the sureness was gone. Somehow I feel I have not shown Robert Cohn clearly. The reason is that until he fell in love with Brett, I never heard him make one remark that would, in any way, detach him from other people. He was nice to watch on the tennis-court, he had a good body, and he kept it in shape; he handled his cards well at bridge, and he had a funny sort of undergraduate quality about him. If he were in a crowd nothing he said stood out. He wore what used to be called polo shirts at school, and may be called that still, but he was not professionally youthful. I do not believe he thought about his clothes much. Externally he had been formed at Princeton. Internally he had been moulded by the two women who had trained him. He had a nice, boyish sort of cheerfulness that had never been trained out of him, and I probably have not brought it out. He loved to win at tennis. He probably loved to win as much as Lenglen,[9] for instance. On the other hand, he was not angry at being beaten. When he fell in love with Brett his tennis game went all to pieces. People beat him who had never had a chance with him. He was very nice about it.

Anyhow, we were sitting on the terrace of the Café Select, and Harvey Stone had just crossed the street.

"Come on up to the Lilas," I said.

"I have a date."

"What time?"

"Frances is coming here at seven-fifteen."

"There she is."

Frances Clyne was coming toward us from across the street. She was a very tall girl who walked with a great deal of movement. She waved and smiled. We watched her cross the street.

"Hello," she said, "I'm so glad you're here, Jake. I've been wanting to talk to you."

9. Suzanne Lenglen (1899–1938), French tennis player who won 241 titles, including thirty-one Championship titles during her career as an amateur and professional player.

"Hello, Frances," said Cohn. He smiled.

"Why, hello, Robert. Are you here?" She went on, talking rapidly. "I've had the darndest time. This one"—shaking her head at Cohn—"didn't come home for lunch."

"I wasn't supposed to."

"Oh, I know. But you didn't say anything about it to the cook. Then I had a date myself, and Paula wasn't at her office. I went to the Ritz and waited for her, and she never came, and of course I didn't have enough money to lunch at the Ritz——"[1]

"What did you do?"

"Oh, went out, of course." She spoke in a sort of imitation joyful manner. "I always keep my appointments. No one keeps theirs, nowadays. I ought to know better. How are you, Jake, anyway?"

"Fine."

"That was a fine girl you had at the dance, and then went off with that Brett one."

"Don't you like her?" Cohn asked.

"I think she's perfectly charming. Don't you?"

Cohn said nothing.

"Look, Jake. I want to talk with you. Would you come over with me to the Dôme? You'll stay here, won't you, Robert? Come on, Jake."

We crossed the Boulevard Montparnasse and sat down at a table. A boy came up with the *Paris Times*,[2] and I bought one and opened it.

"What's the matter, Frances?"

"Oh, nothing," she said, "except that he wants to leave me."

"How do you mean?"

"Oh, he told every one that we were going to be married, and I told my mother and every one, and now he doesn't want to do it."

"What's the matter?"

"He's decided he hasn't lived enough. I knew it would happen when he went to New York."

She looked up, very bright-eyed and trying to talk inconsequentially.

"I wouldn't marry him if he doesn't want to. Of course I wouldn't. I wouldn't marry him now for anything. But it does seem to me to be a little late now, after we've waited three years, and I've just gotten my divorce."

I said nothing.

"We were going to celebrate so, and instead we've just had scenes. It's so childish. We have dreadful scenes, and he cries and begs me to be reasonable, but he says he just can't do it."

"It's rotten luck."

1. Located at 15, place Vendôme (on the Right Bank), the Ritz was one of the most expensive and exclusive hotels in Paris.
2. A short-lived English-language newspaper, less well known and successful than its competitors, the International *Herald Tribune* and the Paris edition of the Chicago *Tribune*.

"I should say it is rotten luck. I've wasted two years and a half on him now. And I don't know now if any man will ever want to marry me. Two years ago I could have married anybody I wanted, down at Cannes. All the old ones that wanted to marry somebody chic and settle down were crazy about me. Now I don't think I could get anybody."

"Sure, you could marry anybody."

"No, I don't believe it. And I'm fond of him, too. And I'd like to have children. I always thought we'd have children."

She looked at me very brightly. "I never liked children much, but I don't want to think I'll never have them. I always thought I'd have them and then like them."

"He's got children."

"Oh, yes. He's got children, and he's got money, and he's got a rich mother, and he's written a book, and nobody will publish my stuff, nobody at all. It isn't bad, either. And I haven't got any money at all. I could have had alimony, but I got the divorce the quickest way."

She looked at me again very brightly.

"It isn't right. It's my own fault and it's not, too. I ought to have known better. And when I tell him he just cries and says he can't marry. Why can't he marry? I'd be a good wife. I'm easy to get along with. I leave him alone. It doesn't do any good."

"It's a rotten shame."

"Yes, it is a rotten shame. But there's no use talking about it, is there? Come on, let's go back to the café."

"And of course there isn't anything I can do."

"No. Just don't let him know I talked to you. I know what he wants." Now for the first time she dropped her bright, terribly cheerful manner. "He wants to go back to New York alone, and be there when his book comes out so when a lot of little chickens like it. That's what he wants."

"Maybe they won't like it. I don't think he's that way. Really."

"You don't know him like I do, Jake. That's what he wants to do. I know it. I know it. That's why he doesn't want to marry. He wants to have a big triumph this fall all by himself."

"Want to go back to the café?"

"Yes. Come on."

We got up from the table—they had never brought us a drink—and started across the street toward the Select, where Cohn sat smiling at us from behind the marble-topped table.

"Well, what are you smiling at?" Frances asked him. "Feel pretty happy?"

"I was smiling at you and Jake with your secrets."

"Oh, what I've told Jake isn't any secret. Everybody will know it soon enough. I only wanted to give Jake a decent version."

"What was it? About your going to England?"

"Yes, about my going to England. Oh, Jake! I forgot to tell you. I'm going to England."

"Isn't that fine!"

"Yes, that's the way it's done in the very best families. Robert's sending me. He's going to give me two hundred pounds and then I'm going to visit friends. Won't it be lovely? The friends don't know about it, yet."

She turned to Cohn and smiled at him. He was not smiling now.

"You were only going to give me a hundred pounds, weren't you, Robert? But I made him give me two hundred. He's really very generous. Aren't you, Robert?"

I do not know how people could say such terrible things to Robert Cohn. There are people to whom you could not say insulting things. They give you a feeling that the world would be destroyed, would actually be destroyed before your eyes, if you said certain things. But here was Cohn taking it all. Here it was, all going on right before me, and I did not even feel an impulse to try and stop it. And this was friendly joking to what went on later.

"How can you say such things, Frances?" Cohn interrupted.

"Listen to him. I'm going to England. I'm going to visit friends. Ever visit friends that didn't want you? Oh, they'll have to take me, all right. 'How do you do, my dear? Such a long time since we've seen you. And how is your dear mother?' Yes, how is my dear mother? She put all her money into French war bonds.[3] Yes, she did. Probably the only person in the world that did. 'And what about Robert?' or else very careful talking around Robert. 'You must be most careful not to mention him, my dear. Poor Frances has had a most unfortunate experience.' Won't it be fun, Robert? Don't you think it will be fun, Jake?"

She turned to me with that terribly bright smile. It was very satisfactory to her to have an audience for this.

"And where are you going to be, Robert? It's my own fault, all right. Perfectly my own fault. When I made you get rid of your little secretary on the magazine I ought to have known you'd get rid of me the same way. Jake doesn't know about that. Should I tell him?"

"Shut up, Frances, for God's sake."

"Yes, I'll tell him. Robert had a little secretary on the magazine. Just the sweetest little thing in the world, and he thought she was wonderful, and then I came along and he thought I was pretty wonderful, too. So I made him get rid of her, and he had brought her to Provincetown from Carmel when he moved the magazine, and he didn't even pay her fare back to the coast. All to please me. He thought I was pretty fine, then. Didn't you, Robert?

3. Investments in the French war effort. Though France was among the victorious nations after the First World War, the long-term struggles of the French economy, especially the low value of the franc against the U.S. dollar, made war bonds a poor investment.

"You mustn't misunderstand, Jake, it was absolutely platonic with the secretary. Not even platonic. Nothing at all, really. It was just that she was so nice. And he did that just to please me. Well, I suppose that we that live by the sword shall perish by the sword. Isn't that literary, though? You want to remember that for your next book, Robert.

"You know Robert is going to get material for a new book. Aren't you, Robert? That's why he's leaving me. He's decided I don't film well. You see, he was so busy all the time that we were living together, writing on this book, that he doesn't remember anything about us. So now he's going out and get some new material. Well, I hope he gets something frightfully interesting.

"Listen, Robert, dear. Let me tell you something. You won't mind, will you? Don't have scenes with your young ladies. Try not to. Because you can't have scenes without crying, and then you pity yourself so much you can't remember what the other person's said. You'll never be able to remember any conversations that way. Just try and be calm. I know it's awfully hard. But remember, it's for literature. We all ought to make sacrifices for literature. Look at me. I'm going to England without a protest. All for literature. We must all help young writers. Don't you think so, Jake? But you're not a young writer. Are you, Robert? You're thirty-four. Still, I suppose that is young for a great writer. Look at Hardy. Look at Anatole France.[4] He just died a little while ago. Robert doesn't think he's any good, though. Some of his French friends told him. He doesn't read French very well himself. He wasn't a good writer like you are, was he, Robert? Do you think he ever had to go and look for material? What do you suppose he said to his mistresses when he wouldn't marry them? I wonder if he cried, too? Oh, I've just thought of something." She put her gloved hand up to her lips. "I know the real reason why Robert won't marry me, Jake. It's just come to me. They've sent it to me in a vision in the Café Select. Isn't it mystic? Some day they'll put a tablet up. Like at Lourdes.[5] Do you want to hear, Robert? I'll tell you. It's so simple. I wonder why I never thought about it. Why, you see, Robert's always wanted to have a mistress, and if he doesn't marry me, why, then he's had one. She was his mistress for over two years. See how it is? And if he marries me, like he's always promised he would, that would be the end of all the romance. Don't you think that's bright of me to figure that out? It's true, too. Look at him and see if it's not. Where are you going, Jake?"

4. French poet, novelist, and journalist (1844–1924) who was awarded the Nobel Prize for Literature in 1921. Thomas Hardy (1840–1928), English novelist and poet, perhaps best known for his novels *Tess of the D'Urbervilles* and *Jude the Obscure*.

5. Town in southwestern France, in the foothills of the Pyrenees, best known as the site of Christian pilgrimage and religious tourism after a young local woman, Bernadette Soubirous, claimed to have had visions of the Virgin Mary in a grotto near the town.

"I've got to go in and see Harvey Stone a minute."

Cohn looked up as I went in. His face was white. Why did he sit there? Why did he keep on taking it like that?

As I stood against the bar looking out I could see them through the window. Frances was talking on to him, smiling brightly, looking into his face each time she asked: "Isn't it so, Robert?" Or maybe she did not ask that now. Perhaps she said something else. I told the barman I did not want anything to drink and went out through the side door. As I went out the door I looked back through the two thicknesses of glass and saw them sitting there. She was still talking to him. I went down a side street to the Boulevard Raspail. A taxi came along and I got in and gave the driver the address of my flat.

Chapter VII

As I started up the stairs the concierge knocked on the glass of the door of her lodge, and as I stopped she came out. She had some letters and a telegram.

"Here is the post. And there was a lady here to see you."

"Did she leave a card?"

"No. She was with a gentleman. It was the one who was here last night. In the end I find she is very nice."

"Was she with a friend of mine?"

"I don't know. He was never here before. He was very large. Very, very large. She was very nice. Very, very nice. Last night she was, perhaps, a little—" She put her head on one hand and rocked it up and down. "I'll speak perfectly frankly, Monsieur Barnes. Last night I found her not so gentille. Last night I formed another idea of her. But listen to what I tell you. She is très, très gentille.[1] She is of very good family. It is a thing you can see."

"They did not leave any word?"

"Yes. They said they would be back in an hour."

"Send them up when they come."

"Yes, Monsieur Barnes. And that lady, that lady there is some one. An eccentric, perhaps, but quelqu'un, quelqu'un!"[2]

The concierge, before she became a concierge, had owned a drink-selling concession at the Paris race-courses. Her life-work lay in the pelouse, but she kept an eye on the people of the pesage,[3] and she took

1. Very nice (French).
2. Somebody (French).
3. Weighing (French); *pelouse*: lawn (French). The distinction here is between the public facing side of the horse racing facility and the behind-the-scenes areas, between customers and horse owners.

great pride in telling me which of my guests were well brought up, which were of good family, who were sportsmen, a French word pronounced with the accent on the men. The only trouble was that people who did not fall into any of those three categories were very liable to be told there was no one home, chez Barnes. One of my friends, an extremely underfed-looking painter, who was obviously to Madame Duzinell neither well brought up, of good family, nor a sportsman, wrote me a letter asking if I could get him a pass to get by the concierge so he could come up and see me occasionally in the evenings.

I went up to the flat wondering what Brett had done to the concierge. The wire was a cable from Bill Gorton, saying he was arriving on the *France*.[4] I put the mail on the table, went back to the bedroom, undressed and had a shower. I was rubbing down when I heard the door-bell pull. I put on a bathrobe and slippers and went to the door. It was Brett. Back of her was the count. He was holding a great bunch of roses.

"Hello, darling," said Brett. "Aren't you going to let us in?"

"Come on. I was just bathing."

"Aren't you the fortunate man. Bathing."

"Only a shower. Sit down, Count Mippipopolous. What will you drink?"

"I don't know whether you like flowers, sir," the count said, "but I took the liberty of just bringing these roses."

"Here, give them to me." Brett took them. "Get me some water in this, Jake." I filled the big earthenware jug with water in the kitchen, and Brett put the roses in it, and placed them in the centre of the dining-room table.

"I say. We have had a day."

"You don't remember anything about a date with me at the Crillon?"

"No. Did we have one? I must have been blind."

"You were quite drunk, my dear," said the count.

"Wasn't I, though? And the count's been a brick, absolutely."

"You've got hell's own drag with the concierge now."

"I ought to have. Gave her two hundred francs."

"Don't be a damned fool."

"His," she said, and nodded at the count.

"I thought we ought to give her a little something for last night. It was very late."

"He's wonderful," Brett said. "He remembers everything that's happened."

"So do you, my dear."

4. A steamship.

"Fancy," said Brett. "Who'd want to? I say, Jake, do we get a drink?"

"You get it while I go in and dress. You know where it is."

"Rather."

While I dressed I heard Brett put down glasses and then a siphon, and then heard them talking. I dressed slowly, sitting on the bed. I felt tired and pretty rotten. Brett came in the room, a glass in her hand, and sat on the bed.

"What's the matter, darling? Do you feel rocky?"

She kissed me coolly on the forehead.

"Oh, Brett, I love you so much."

"Darling," she said. Then: "Do you want me to send him away?"

"No. He's nice."

"I'll send him away."

"No, don't."

"Yes, I'll send him away."

"You can't just like that."

"Can't I, though? You stay here. He's mad about me, I tell you." She was gone out of the room. I lay face down on the bed. I was having a bad time. I heard them talking but I did not listen. Brett came in and sat on the bed.

"Poor old darling." She stroked my head.

"What did you say to him?" I was lying with my face away from her. I did not want to see her.

"Sent him for champagne. He loves to go for champagne."

Then later: "Do you feel better, darling? Is the head any better?"

"It's better."

"Lie quiet. He's gone to the other side of town."

"Couldn't we live together, Brett? Couldn't we just live together?"

"I don't think so. I'd just *tromper*[5] you with everybody. You couldn't stand it."

"I stand it now."

"That would be different. It's my fault, Jake. It's the way I'm made."

"Couldn't we go off in the country for a while?"

"It wouldn't be any good. I'll go if you like. But I couldn't live quietly in the country. Not with my own true love."

"I know."

"Isn't it rotten? There isn't any use my telling you I love you."

"You know I love you."

"Let's not talk. Talking's all bilge. I'm going away from you, and then Michael's coming back."

"Why are you going away?"

"Better for you. Better for me."

5. Betray (French).

"When are you going?"

"Soon as I can."

"Where?"

"San Sebastian."[6]

"Can't we go together?"

"No. That would be a hell of an idea after we'd just talked it out."

"We never agreed."

"Oh, you know as well as I do. Don't be obstinate, darling."

"Oh, sure," I said. "I know you're right. I'm just low, and when I'm low I talk like a fool."

I sat up, leaned over, found my shoes beside the bed and put them on. I stood up.

"Don't look like that, darling."

"How do you want me to look?"

"Oh, don't be a fool. I'm going away to-morrow."

"To-morrow?"

"Yes. Didn't I say so? I am."

"Let's have a drink, then. The count will be back."

"Yes. He should be back. You know he's extraordinary about buying champagne. It means any amount to him."

We went into the dining-room. I took up the brandy bottle and poured Brett a drink and one for myself. There was a ring at the bell-pull. I went to the door and there was the count. Behind him was the chauffeur carrying a basket of champagne.

"Where should I have him put it, sir?" asked the count.

"In the kitchen," Brett said.

"Put it in there, Henry," the count motioned. "Now go down and get the ice." He stood looking after the basket inside the kitchen door. "I think you'll find that's very good wine," he said. "I know we don't get much of a chance to judge good wine in the States now, but I got this from a friend of mine that's in the business."[7]

"Oh, you always have some one in the trade," Brett said.

"This fellow raises the grapes. He's got thousands of acres of them."

"What's his name?" asked Brett. "Veuve Clicquot?"[8]

"No," said the count. "Mumm. He's a baron."

"Isn't it wonderful," said Brett. "We all have titles. Why haven't you a title, Jake?"

6. A coastal city on the Bay of Biscay, Spain, a renowned tourist site and resort.
7. Residents of the United States would have few opportunities (and no legal opportunities) to "judge good wine" because of the nationwide ban on the production, sale, and consumption of alcohol ("Prohibition") enacted by the Eighteenth Amendment to the Constitution and Congress' passage of the Volstead Act in 1920.
8. An expensive brand of champagne, like Mumm. The references here begin a passage characterized by wordplay (unusual for most of *The Sun Also Rises*) like that with which Hemingway experimented in the prose vignettes of *In Our Time*.

"I assure you, sir," the count put his hand on my arm. "It never does a man any good. Most of the time it costs you money."

"Oh, I don't know. It's damned useful sometimes," Brett said.

"I've never known it to do me any good."

"You haven't used it properly. I've had hell's own amount of credit on mine."

"Do sit down, count," I said. "Let me take that stick."

The count was looking at Brett across the table under the gas-light. She was smoking a cigarette and flicking the ashes on the rug. She saw me notice it. "I say, Jake, I don't want to ruin your rugs. Can't you give a chap an ash-tray?"

I found some ash-trays and spread them around. The chauffeur came up with a bucket full of salted ice. "Put two bottles in it, Henry," the count called.

"Anything else, sir?"

"No. Wait down in the car." He turned to Brett and to me. "We'll want to ride out to the Bois for dinner?"

"If you like," Brett said. "I couldn't eat a thing."

"I always like a good meal," said the count.

"Should I bring the wine in, sir?" asked the chauffeur.

"Yes. Bring it in, Henry," said the count. He took out a heavy pigskin cigar-case and offered it to me. "Like to try a real American cigar?"

"Thanks," I said. "I'll finish the cigarette."

He cut off the end of his cigar with a gold cutter he wore on one end of his watch-chain.

"I like a cigar to really draw," said the count. "Half the cigars you smoke don't draw."

He lit the cigar, puffed at it, looking across the table at Brett. "And when you're divorced, Lady Ashley, then you won't have a title."

"No. What a pity."

"No," said the count. "You don't need a title. You got class all over you."

"Thanks. Awfully decent of you."

"I'm not joking you," the count blew a cloud of smoke. "You got the most class of anybody I ever seen. You got it. That's all."

"Nice of you," said Brett. "Mummy would be pleased. Couldn't you write it out, and I'll send it in a letter to her."

"I'd tell her, too," said the count. "I'm not joking you. I never joke people. Joke people and you make enemies. That's what I always say."

"You're right," Brett said. "You're terribly right. I always joke people and I haven't a friend in the world. Except Jake here."

"You don't joke him."

"That's it."

"Do you, now?" asked the count. "Do you joke him?"

Brett looked at me and wrinkled up the corners of her eyes.

"No," she said. "I wouldn't joke him."

"See," said the count. "You don't joke him."

"This is a hell of a dull talk," Brett said. "How about some of that champagne?"

The count reached down and twirled the bottles in the shiny bucket. "It isn't cold, yet. You're always drinking, my dear. Why don't you just talk?"

"I've talked too ruddy much. I've talked myself all out to Jake."

"I should like to hear you really talk, my dear. When you talk to me you never finish your sentences at all."

"Leave 'em for you to finish. Let any one finish them as they like."

"It is a very interesting system," the count reached down and gave the bottles a twirl. "Still I would like to hear you talk some time."

"Isn't he a fool?" Brett asked.

"Now," the count brought up a bottle. "I think this is cool."

I brought a towel and he wiped the bottle dry and held it up. "I like to drink champagne from magnums. The wine is better but it would have been too hard to cool." He held the bottle, looking at it. I put out the glasses.

"I say. You might open it." Brett suggested.

"Yes, my dear. Now I'll open it."

It was amazing champagne.

"I say that is wine," Brett held up her glass. "We ought to toast something. 'Here's to royalty.'"

"This wine is too good for toast-drinking, my dear. You don't want to mix emotions up with a wine like that. You lose the taste."

Brett's glass was empty.

"You ought to write a book on wines, count," I said.

"Mr. Barnes," answered the count, "all I want out of wines is to enjoy them."

"Let's enjoy a little more of this," Brett pushed her glass forward. The count poured very carefully. "There, my dear. Now you enjoy that slowly, and then you can get drunk."

"Drunk? Drunk?"

"My dear, you are charming when you are drunk."

"Listen to the man."

"Mr. Barnes," the count poured my glass full. "She is the only lady I have ever known who was as charming when she was drunk as when she was sober."

"You haven't been around much, have you?"

"Yes, my dear. I have been around very much. I have been around a very great deal."

"Drink your wine," said Brett. "We've all been around. I dare say Jake here has seen as much as you have."

"My dear, I am sure Mr. Barnes has seen a lot. Don't think I don't think so, sir. I have seen a lot, too."

"Of course you have, my dear," Brett said. "I was only ragging."

"I have been in seven wars and four revolutions," the count said.

"Soldiering?" Brett asked.

"Sometimes, my dear. And I have got arrow wounds. Have you ever seen arrow wounds?"

"Let's have a look at them."

The count stood up, unbuttoned his vest, and opened his shirt. He pulled up the undershirt onto his chest and stood, his chest black, and big stomach muscles bulging under the light.

"You see them?"

Below the line where his ribs stopped were two raised white welts. "See on the back where they come out." Above the small of the back were the same two scars, raised as thick as a finger.

"I say. Those are something."

"Clean through."

The count was tucking in his shirt.

"Where did you get those?" I asked.

"In Abyssinia.[9] When I was twenty-one years old."

"What were you doing?" asked Brett. "Were you in the army?"

"I was on a business trip, my dear."

"I told you he was one of us. Didn't I?" Brett turned to me. "I love you, count. You're a darling."

"You make me very happy, my dear. But it isn't true."

"Don't be an ass."

"You see, Mr. Barnes, it is because I have lived very much that now I can enjoy everything so well. Don't you find it like that?"

"Yes. Absolutely."

"I know," said the count. "That is the secret. You must get to know the values."

"Doesn't anything ever happen to your values?" Brett asked.

"No. Not any more."

"Never fall in love?"

"Always," said the count. "I am always in love."

"What does that do to your values?"

"That, too, has got a place in my values."

"You haven't any values. You're dead, that's all."

"No, my dear. You're not right. I'm not dead at all."

We drank three bottles of the champagne and the count left the basket in my kitchen. We dined at a restaurant in the Bois. It was a good dinner. Food had an excellent place in the count's values. So

9. The Empire of Ethiopia, a kingdom that roughly comprised the northern half of the country of Ethiopia today.

did wine. The count was in fine form during the meal. So was Brett. It was a good party.

"Where would you like to go?" asked the count after dinner. We were the only people left in the restaurant. The two waiters were standing over against the door. They wanted to go home.

"We might go up on the hill," Brett said. "Haven't we had a splendid party?"

The count was beaming. He was very happy.

"You are very nice people," he said. He was smoking a cigar again. "Why don't you get married, you two?"

"We want to lead our own lives," I said.

"We have our careers," Brett said. "Come on. Let's get out of this."

"Have another brandy," the count said.

"Get it on the hill."

"No. Have it here where it is quiet."

"You and your quiet," said Brett. "What is it men feel about quiet?"

"We like it," said the count. "Like you like noise, my dear."

"All right," said Brett. "Let's have one."

"Sommelier!" the count called.

"Yes, sir."

"What is the oldest brandy you have?"

"Eighteen eleven, sir."

"Bring us a bottle."

"I say. Don't be ostentatious. Call him off, Jake."

"Listen, my dear. I get more value for my money in old brandy than in any other antiquities."

"Got many antiquities?"

"I got a houseful."

Finally we went up to Montmartre. Inside Zelli's it was crowded, smoky, and noisy. The music hit you as you went in. Brett and I danced. It was so crowded we could barely move. The nigger drummer[1] waved at Brett. We were caught in the jam, dancing in one place in front of him.

"Hahre you?"

"Great."

1. The history of this word and its usage in different communities and contexts is complex. It matters who is using the word, and about whom, and with what tone, and in what setting. In the 1920s, especially in predominantly Black or *some* interracial social settings (e.g., nightclubs in New York or Paris), the word *might* not carry the immediately harmful charge that it would in others, especially those in which the structural racism of American society more straightforwardly shapes the speech situation or when it is used with an obvious intention to insult or injure. Jake here seems to intend no insult. Nevertheless, the word's history imbues it with an inescapably racist significance, and his use of it to describe the drummer at the very least situates Jake in the web of racist assumption and stereotype from which the word is inextricable. He demonstrates here (as does Hemingway, in all likelihood) the casual and unthinking racism often characteristic of white Americans of most classes and cultural positions at the time.

"Thaats good."

He was all teeth and lips.

"He's a great friend of mine," Brett said. "Damn good drummer."

The music stopped and we started toward the table where the count sat. Then the music started again and we danced. I looked at the count. He was sitting at the table smoking a cigar. The music stopped again.

"Let's go over."

Brett started toward the table. The music started and again we danced, tight in the crowd.

"You are a rotten dancer, Jake. Michael's the best dancer I know."

"He's splendid."

"He's got his points."

"I like him," I said. "I'm damned fond of him."

"I'm going to marry him," Brett said. "Funny. I haven't thought about him for a week."

"Don't you write him?"

"Not I. Never write letters."

"I'll bet he writes to you."

"Rather. Damned good letters, too."

"When are you going to get married?"

"How do I know? As soon as we can get the divorce. Michael's trying to get his mother to put up for it."

"Could I help you?"

"Don't be an ass. Michael's people have loads of money."

The music stopped. We walked over to the table. The count stood up.

"Very nice," he said. "You looked very, very nice."

"Don't you dance, count?" I asked.

"No. I'm too old."

"Oh, come off it," Brett said.

"My dear. I would do it if I would enjoy it. I enjoy to watch you dance."

"Splendid," Brett said. "I'll dance again for you some time. I say. What about your little friend, Zizi?"

"Let me tell you. I support that boy, but I don't want to have him around."

"He is rather hard."

"You know I think that boy's got a future. But personally I don't want him around."

"Jake's rather the same way."

"He gives me the willies."

"Well," the count shrugged his shoulders. "About his future you can't ever tell. Anyhow, his father was a great friend of my father."

"Come on. Let's dance," Brett said.

We danced. It was crowded and close.

"Oh, darling," Brett said, "I'm so miserable."

I had that feeling of going through something that has all happened before. "You were happy a minute ago."

The drummer shouted: "You can't two time——"[2]

"It's all gone."

"What's the matter?"

"I don't know. I just feel terribly."

". . . . . ." the drummer chanted. Then turned to his sticks.

"Want to go?"

I had the feeling as in a nightmare of it all being something repeated, something I had been through and that now I must go through again.

". . . . . ." the drummer sang softly.

"Let's go," said Brett. "You don't mind."

". . . . . ." the drummer shouted and grinned at Brett.

"All right," I said. We got out from the crowd. Brett went to the dressing-room.

"Brett wants to go," I said to the count. He nodded. "Does she? That's fine. You take the car. I'm going to stay here for a while, Mr. Barnes."

We shook hands.

"It was a wonderful time," I said. "I wish you would let me get this." I took a note out of my pocket.

"Mr. Barnes, don't be ridiculous," the count said.

Brett came over with her wrap on. She kissed the count and put her hand on his shoulder to keep him from standing up. As we went out the door I looked back and there were three girls at his table. We got into the big car. Brett gave the chauffeur the address of her hotel.

"No, don't come up," she said at the hotel. She had rung and the door was unlatched.

"Really?"

"No. Please."

"Good night, Brett," I said. "I'm sorry you feel rotten."

"Good night, Jake. Good night, darling. I won't see you again." We kissed standing at the door. She pushed me away. We kissed again. "Oh, don't!" Brett said.

She turned quickly and went into the hotel. The chauffeur drove me around to my flat. I gave him twenty francs and he touched his cap and said: "Good night, sir," and drove off. I rang the bell. The door opened and I went up-stairs and went to bed.

2. The song the drummer sings here has been identified by Frederic Svoboda as "Aggravatin' Papa" (first recorded in 1923) and by H. R. Stoneback as "Cherry Picking Blues" (first recorded 1924). On the basis of this single line, an indisputable identification is impossible.

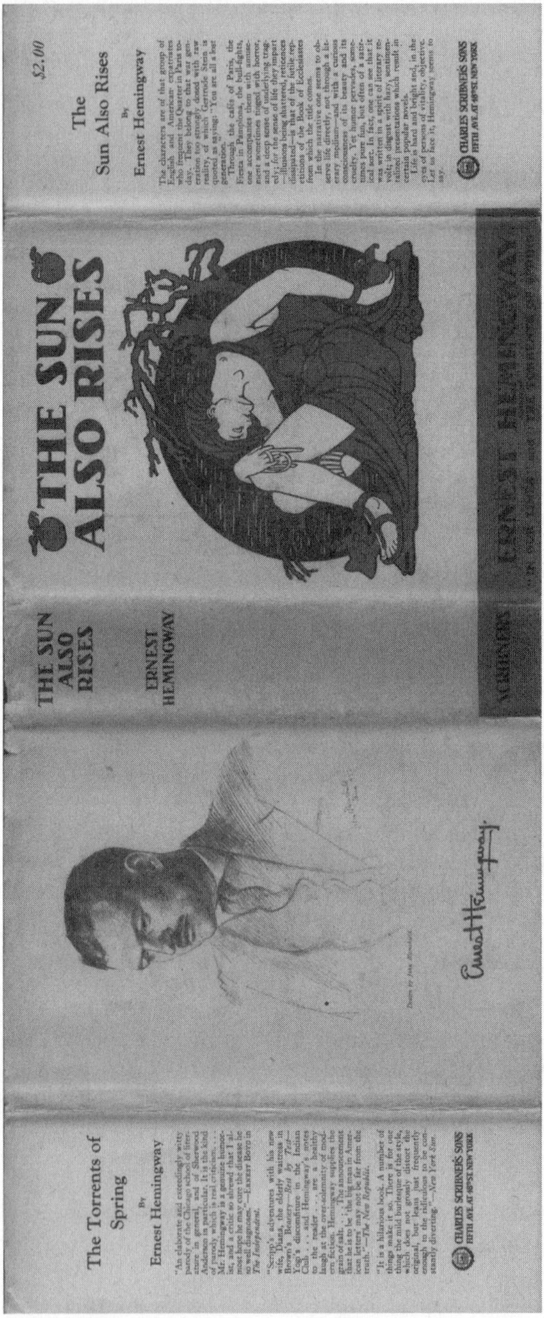

Dust jacket for the first edition of *The Sun Also Rises*. Courtesy of Mortimer Rare Book Collection, Smith College Special Collections, call no. PS3515.E37 S8 1926 copy 1.

Book II

Chapter VIII

I did not see Brett again until she came back from San Sebastian. One card came from her from there. It had a picture of the Concha,[1] and said: "Darling. Very quiet and healthy. Love to all the chaps. BRETT."

Nor did I see Robert Cohn again. I heard Frances had left for England and I had a note from Cohn saying he was going out in the country for a couple of weeks, he did not know where, but that he wanted to hold me to the fishing-trip in Spain we had talked about last winter. I could reach him always, he wrote, through his bankers.

Brett was gone, I was not bothered by Cohn's troubles, I rather enjoyed not having to play tennis, there was plenty of work to do, I went often to the races, dined with friends, and put in some extra time at the office getting things ahead so I could leave it in charge of my secretary when Bill Gorton and I should shove off to Spain the end of June. Bill Gorton arrived, put up a couple of days at the flat and went off to Vienna. He was very cheerful and said the States were wonderful. New York was wonderful. There had been a grand theatrical season and a whole crop of great young light heavyweights. Any one of them was a good prospect to grow up, put on weight and trim Dempsey.[2] Bill was very happy. He had made a lot of money on his last book, and was going to make a lot more. We had a good time while he was in Paris, and then he went off to Vienna. He was coming back in three weeks and we would leave for Spain to get in some fishing and go to the fiesta at Pamplona.[3] He wrote that Vienna was wonderful. Then a card from Budapest: "Jake, Budapest is wonderful." Then I got a wire: "Back on Monday."

Monday evening he turned up at the flat. I heard his taxi stop and went to the window and called to him; he waved and started up-stairs carrying his bags. I met him on the stairs, and took one of the bags.

1. Playa de la Concha, the premiere beach in the resort town of San Sebastian.
2. Jack Dempsey (1895–1983), heavyweight boxer and world champion from 1919–26.
3. The Festival of San Fermin, a week-long celebration in the city of Pamplona, Spain, dedicated to San Fermin, the patron saint of the province of Navarre. The festival occurs from July 6–14, includes processions, fireworks, and, most prominently, bullfights. It is the center of the action of Book II.

"Well," I said, "I hear you had a wonderful trip."

"Wonderful," he said. "Budapest is absolutely wonderful."

"How about Vienna?"

"Not so good, Jake. Not so good. It seemed better than it was."

"How do you mean?" I was getting glasses and a siphon.

"Tight, Jake. I was tight."

"That's strange. Better have a drink."

Bill rubbed his forehead. "Remarkable thing," he said. "Don't know how it happened. Suddenly it happened."

"Last long?"

"Four days, Jake. Lasted just four days."

"Where did you go?"

"Don't remember. Wrote you a post-card. Remember that perfectly."

"Do anything else?"

"Not so sure. Possible."

"Go on. Tell me about it."

"Can't remember. Tell you anything I could remember."

"Go on. Take that drink and remember."

"Might remember a little," Bill said. "Remember something about a prize-fight. Enormous Vienna prize-fight. Had a nigger in it. Remember the nigger perfectly."[4]

"Go on."

"Wonderful nigger. Looked like Tiger Flowers,[5] only four times as big. All of a sudden everybody started to throw things. Not me. Nigger'd just knocked local boy down. Nigger put up his glove. Wanted to make a speech. Awful noble-looking nigger. Started to make a speech. Then local white boy hit him. Then he knocked white boy cold. Then everybody commenced to throw chairs. Nigger went home with us in our car. Couldn't get his clothes. Wore my coat. Remember the whole thing now. Big sporting evening."

"What happened?"

"Loaned the nigger some clothes and went around with him to try and get his money. Claimed nigger owed them money on account of wrecking hall. Wonder who translated? Was it me?"

"Probably it wasn't you."

"You're right. Wasn't me at all. Was another fellow. Think we called him the local Harvard man. Remember him now. Studying music."

4. As in the scene with Jake and the drummer (p. 47, note 1), Bill seems to intend no cruelty or insult to the boxer he describes here, but his use of this word locates him in the racist discourse of assumption and stereotype prevalent among white Americans in the 1920s (and throughout American history). Like Jake, Bill demonstrates a now disturbing casual racism.

5. Theodore "Tiger" Flowers (1895–1927), renowned boxer and the first Black boxer to win the middleweight world championship (though he achieved this distinction after the publication of *The Sun Also Rises*).

"How'd you come out?"

"Not so good, Jake. Injustice everywhere. Promoter claimed nigger promised let local boy stay. Claimed nigger violated contract. Can't knock out Vienna boy in Vienna. 'My God, Mister Gorton,' said nigger, 'I didn't do nothing in there for forty minutes but try and let him stay. That white boy musta ruptured himself swinging at me. I never did hit him.'"

"Did you get any money?"

"No money, Jake. All we could get was nigger's clothes. Somebody took his watch, too. Splendid nigger. Big mistake to have come to Vienna. Not so good, Jake. Not so good."

"What became of the nigger?"

"Went back to Cologne.[6] Lives there. Married. Got a family. Going to write me a letter and send me the money I loaned him. Wonderful nigger. Hope I gave him the right address."

"You probably did."

"Well, anyway, let's eat," said Bill. "Unless you want me to tell you some more travel stories."

"Go on."

"Let's eat."

We went down-stairs and out onto the Boulevard St. Michel in the warm June evening.

"Where will we go?"

"Want to eat on the island?"[7]

"Sure."

We walked down the Boulevard. At the juncture of the Rue Denfert-Rochereau with the Boulevard is a statue of two men in flowing robes.[8]

"I know who they are." Bill eyed the monument. "Gentlemen who invented pharmacy. Don't try and fool me on Paris."

We went on.

"Here's a taxidermist's," Bill said. "Want to buy anything? Nice stuffed dog?"

"Come on," I said. "You're pie-eyed."

"Pretty nice stuffed dogs," Bill said. "Certainly brighten up your flat."

6. A major city on the Rhine River in Germany, near the borders of the Netherlands and Belgium. That the boxer lives in Cologne with his family means that he, like Jake, is an expatriate. In the novel's early manuscripts, the boxer has already repaid Bill and written to thank him; a long blank space is left for the letter itself (as if Hemingway intended to go back and write it later), and is followed by approving comments by Bill and Jake.

7. Île Saint-Louis, one of the Seine's two natural islands in Paris (fourth arrondissement). It is connected to both banks of the Seine by four bridges and to the other natural island, the Île de la Cité, by the Pont Saint-Louis.

8. At the intersection of boulevard Saint-Michel and rue Denfert-Rochereau is a bronze monument (erected 1900) to two French chemists, J. B. Caventou (1795–1877) and Pierre Pelletier (1788–1842), who isolated quinine, important for the treatment of malaria, in 1820.

"Come on."

"Just one stuffed dog. I can take 'em or leave 'em alone. But listen, Jake. Just one stuffed dog."

"Come on."

"Mean everything in the world to you after you bought it. Simple exchange of values. You give them money. They give you a stuffed dog."

"We'll get one on the way back."

"All right. Have it your own way. Road to hell paved with unbought stuffed dogs. Not my fault."

We went on.

"How'd you feel that way about dogs so sudden?"

"Always felt that way about dogs. Always been a great lover of stuffed animals."

We stopped and had a drink.

"Certainly like to drink," Bill said. "You ought to try it some times, Jake."

"You're about a hundred and forty-four ahead of me."

"Ought not to daunt you. Never be daunted. Secret of my success. Never been daunted. Never been daunted in public."

"Where were you drinking?"

"Stopped at the Crillon. George made me a couple of Jack Roses. George's a great man. Know the secret of his success? Never been daunted."

"You'll be daunted after about three more pernods."

"Not in public. If I begin to feel daunted I'll go off by myself. I'm like a cat that way."

"When did you see Harvey Stone?"

"At the Crillon. Harvey was just a little daunted. Hadn't eaten for three days. Doesn't eat any more. Just goes off like a cat. Pretty sad."

"He's all right."

"Splendid. Wish he wouldn't keep going off like a cat, though. Makes me nervous."

"What'll we do to-night?"

"Doesn't make any difference. Only let's not get daunted. Suppose they got any hard-boiled eggs here? If they had hard-boiled eggs here we wouldn't have to go all the way down to the island to eat."

"Nix," I said. "We're going to have a regular meal."

"Just a suggestion," said Bill. "Want to start now?"

"Come on."

We started on again down the Boulevard. A horse-cab passed us. Bill looked at it.

"See that horse-cab? Going to have that horse-cab stuffed for you for Christmas. Going to give all my friends stuffed animals. I'm a nature-writer."

A taxi passed, some one in it waved, then banged for the driver to stop. The taxi backed up to the curb. In it was Brett.

"Beautiful lady," said Bill. "Going to kidnap us."

"Hullo!" Brett said. "Hullo!"

"This is Bill Gorton. Lady Ashley."

Brett smiled at Bill. "I say I'm just back. Haven't bathed even. Michael comes in to-night."

"Good. Come on and eat with us, and we'll all go to meet him."

"Must clean myself."

"Oh, rot! Come on."

"Must bathe. He doesn't get in till nine."

"Come and have a drink, then, before you bathe."

"Might do that. Now you're not talking rot."

We got in the taxi. The driver looked around.

"Stop at the nearest bistro," I said.

"We might as well go to the Closerie," Brett said. "I can't drink these rotten brandies."

"Closerie des Lilas."

Brett turned to Bill.

"Have you been in this pestilential city long?"

"Just got in to-day from Budapest."

"How was Budapest?"

"Wonderful. Budapest was wonderful."

"Ask him about Vienna."

"Vienna," said Bill, "is a strange city."

"Very much like Paris," Brett smiled at him, wrinkling the corners of her eyes.

"Exactly," Bill said. "Very much like Paris at this moment."

"You have a good start."

Sitting out on the terrace of the Lilas Brett ordered a whiskey and soda, I took one, too, and Bill took another pernod.

"How are you, Jake?"

"Great," I said. "I've had a good time."

Brett looked at me. "I was a fool to go away," she said. "One's an ass to leave Paris."

"Did you have a good time?"

"Oh, all right. Interesting. Not frightfully amusing."

"See anybody?"

"No, hardly anybody. I never went out."

"Didn't you swim?"

"No. Didn't do a thing."

"Sounds like Vienna," Bill said.

Brett wrinkled up the corners of her eyes at him.

"So that's the way it was in Vienna."

"It was like everything in Vienna."

Brett smiled at him again.

"You've a nice friend, Jake."

"He's all right," I said. "He's a taxidermist."

"That was in another country," Bill said. "And besides all the animals were dead."[9]

"One more," Brett said, "and I must run. Do send the waiter for a taxi."

"There's a line of them. Right out in front."

"Good."

We had the drink and put Brett into her taxi.

"Mind you're at the Select around ten. Make him come. Michael will be there."

"We'll be there," Bill said. The taxi started and Brett waved.

"Quite a girl," Bill said. "She's damned nice. Who's Michael?"

"The man she's going to marry."

"Well, well," Bill said. "That's always just the stage I meet anybody. What'll I send them? Think they'd like a couple of stuffed race-horses?"

"We better eat."

"Is she really Lady something or other?" Bill asked in the taxi on our way down to the Ile Saint Louis.

"Oh, yes. In the stud-book and everything."

"Well, well."

We ate dinner at Madame Lecomte's restaurant on the far side of the island.[1] It was crowded with Americans and we had to stand up and wait for a place. Some one had put it in the American Women's Club list as a quaint restaurant on the Paris quais as yet untouched by Americans, so we had to wait forty-five minutes for a table. Bill had eaten at the restaurant in 1918, and right after the armistice, and Madame Lecomte made a great fuss over seeing him.

"Doesn't get us a table, though," Bill said. "Grand woman, though."

We had a good meal, a roast chicken, new green beans, mashed potatoes, a salad, and some apple-pie and cheese.

"You've got the world here all right," Bill said to Madame Lecomte. She raised her hand. "Oh, my God!"

"You'll be rich."

"I hope so."

After the coffee and a *fine* we got the bill, chalked up the same as ever on a slate, that was doubtless one of the "quaint" features, paid it, shook hands, and went out.

9. Bill here echoes the title of a story in Hemingway's *In Our Time* (1925).

1. Lecomte's restaurant was located on the quai d'Anjou, on the north or Right Bank side of the island, almost next door to the offices of both the *Transatlantic Review* (a magazine that Hemingway sometimes helped to edit with British author and editor Ford Madox Ford [1873–1939]) and Three Mountains Press, the small press run by American expatriate William Bird, publisher of Hemingway's *in our time* (1924).

"You never come here any more, Monsieur Barnes," Madame Lecomte said.

"Too many compatriots."

"Come at lunch-time. It's not crowded then."

"Good. I'll be down soon."

We walked along under the trees that grew out over the river on the Quai d'Orléans side of the island.[2] Across the river were the broken walls of old houses that were being torn down.

"They're going to cut a street through."

"They would," Bill said.

We walked on and circled the island. The river was dark and a bateau mouche[3] went by, all bright with lights, going fast and quiet up and out of sight under the bridge. Down the river was Notre Dame[4] squatting against the night sky. We crossed to the left bank of the Seine by the wooden foot-bridge from the Quai de Béthune, and stopped on the bridge and looked down the river at Notre Dame. Standing on the bridge the island looked dark, the houses were high against the sky, and the trees were shadows.

"It's pretty grand," Bill said. "God, I love to get back."

We leaned on the wooden rail of the bridge and looked up the river to the lights of the big bridges. Below the water was smooth and black. It made no sound against the piles of the bridge. A man and a girl passed us. They were walking with their arms around each other.

We crossed the bridge and walked up the Rue du Cardinal Lemoine.[5] It was steep walking, and we went all the way up to the Place de la Contrescarpe. The arc-light shone through the leaves of the trees in the square, and underneath the trees was an S bus ready to start. Music came out of the door of the Nègre Joyeux. Through the window of the Café des Amateurs[6] I saw the long zinc bar. Outside on the terrace working people were drinking. In the open kitchen of the Amateurs a girl was cooking potato-chips in oil. There was an iron pot of stew. The girl ladled some onto a plate for an old man who stood holding a bottle of red wine in one hand.

"Want to have a drink?"

"No," said Bill. "I don't need it."

We turned to the right off the Place de la Contrescarpe, walking along smooth narrow streets with high old houses on both sides.

2. On the south or Left Bank side of the island, across the island from the restaurant.
3. A large riverboat used for cruises up and down the Seine.
4. Cathedral of Notre-Dame de Paris (Our Lady of Paris), one of the most famous of the city's landmarks. Begun in 1160 and completed in 1260, it is an example of French Gothic architecture, notable for the rose window between its square front towers and for the flying buttresses at the rear (the side Jake and Bill would see from the bridge). *Quai de Béthune*: on the south side of the island.
5. The Left Bank street on which Hemingway first lived in Paris (1922–23).
6. The Nègre Joyeux and Café des Amateurs were located on the place de la Contrescarpe, at the top of rue du Cardinal Lemoine.

Some of the houses jutted out toward the street. Others were cut back. We came onto the Rue du Pot de Fer and followed it along until it brought us to the rigid north and south of the Rue Saint Jacques and then walked south, past Val de Grâce, set back behind the courtyard and the iron fence, to the Boulevard de Port Royal.[7]

"What do you want to do?" I asked. "Go up to the café and see Brett and Mike?"

"Why not?"

We walked along Port Royal until it became Montparnasse, and then on past the Lilas, Lavigne's, and all the little cafés, Damoy's, crossed the street to the Rotonde, past its lights and tables to the Select.

Michael came toward us from the tables. He was tanned and healthy-looking.

"Hel-lo, Jake," he said. "Hel-lo! Hel-lo! How are you, old lad?"

"You look very fit, Mike."

"Oh, I am. I'm frightfully fit. I've done nothing but walk. Walk all day long. One drink a day with my mother at tea."

Bill had gone into the bar. He was standing talking with Brett, who was sitting on a high stool, her legs crossed. She had no stockings on.

"It's good to see you, Jake," Michael said. "I'm a little tight you know. Amazing, isn't it? Did you see my nose?"

There was a patch of dried blood on the bridge of his nose.

"An old lady's bags did that," Mike said. "I reached up to help her with them and they fell on me."

Brett gestured at him from the bar with her cigarette-holder and wrinkled the corners of her eyes.

"An old lady," said Mike. "Her bags *fell* on me. Let's go in and see Brett. I say, she is a piece. You *are* a lovely lady, Brett. Where did you get that hat?"

"Chap bought it for me. Don't you like it?"

"It's a dreadful hat. Do get a good hat."

"Oh, we've so much money now," Brett said. "I say, haven't you met Bill yet? You *are* a lovely host, Jake."

She turned to Mike. "This is Bill Gorton. This drunkard is Mike Campbell. Mr. Campbell is an undischarged bankrupt."[8]

"Aren't I, though? You know I met my ex-partner yesterday in London. Chap who did me in."

7. Hemingway traces a route through the small streets of this Left Bank neighborhood as Jake and Bill make their way up Mont Sainte-Geneviève and into the quarter of Montparnasse.

8. Someone legally declared unable to pay outstanding debts. The property of a bankrupt is typically taken and disposed of in order to pay creditors. An undischarged bankrupt is such a person who is not granted an order of discharge by a court and is therefore disqualified from holding public office, directing a firm, or obtaining credit without telling a potential creditor of the undischarged status.

"What did he say?"

"Bought me a drink. I thought I might as well take it. I say, Brett, you *are* a lovely piece. Don't you think she's beautiful?"

"Beautiful. With this nose?"

"It's a lovely nose. Go on, point it at me. Isn't she a lovely piece?"

"Couldn't we have kept the man in Scotland?"

"I say, Brett, let's turn in early."

"Don't be indecent, Michael. Remember there are ladies at this bar."

"Isn't she a lovely piece? Don't you think so, Jake?"

"There's a fight to-night," Bill said. "Like to go?"

"Fight," said Mike. "Who's fighting?"

"Ledoux[9] and somebody."

"He's very good, Ledoux," Mike said. "I'd like to see it, rather"—he was making an effort to pull himself together—"but I can't go. I had a date with this thing here. I say, Brett, do get a new hat."

Brett pulled the felt hat down far over one eye and smiled out from under it. "You two run along to the fight. I'll have to be taking Mr. Campbell home directly."

"I'm not tight," Mike said. "Perhaps just a little. I say, Brett, you are a lovely piece."

"Go on to the fight," Brett said. "Mr. Campbell's getting difficult. What are these outbursts of affection, Michael?"

"I say, you are a lovely piece."

We said good night. "I'm sorry I can't go," Mike said. Brett laughed. I looked back from the door. Mike had one hand on the bar and was leaning toward Brett, talking. Brett was looking at him quite coolly, but the corners of her eyes were smiling.

Outside on the pavement I said: "Do you want to go to the fight?"

"Sure," said Bill. "If we don't have to walk."

"Mike was pretty excited about his girl friend," I said in the taxi.

"Well," said Bill. "You can't blame him such a hell of a lot."

Chapter IX

The Ledoux–Kid Francis fight was the night of the 20th of June.[1] It was a good fight. The morning after the fight I had a letter from Robert Cohn, written from Hendaye.[2] He was having a very quiet time, he said, bathing, playing some golf and much bridge. Hendaye

9. Charles Ledoux (1892–1967), French boxer, active in the bantamweight competition from 1909–26. As Jake will later clarify, the fight in question is the bout that Ledoux lost to Kid Francis (the Italian boxer Francesco Buonaugurio [1907–1943]) on June 9, 1925.
1. The fight was actually on June 9, 1925.
2. A resort town on the southwest French coast, near the Spanish border.

had a splendid beach, but he was anxious to start on the fishing-trip. When would I be down? If I would buy him a double-tapered line he would pay me when I came down.

That same morning I wrote Cohn from the office that Bill and I would leave Paris on the 25th unless I wired him otherwise, and would meet him at Bayonne,[3] where we could get a bus over the mountains to Pamplona. The same evening about seven o'clock I stopped in at the Select to see Michael and Brett. They were not there, and I went over to the Dingo. They were inside sitting at the bar.

"Hello, darling." Brett put out her hand.

"Hello, Jake," Mike said. "I understand I was tight last night."

"Weren't you, though," Brett said. "Disgraceful business."

"Look," said Mike, "when do you go down to Spain? Would you mind if we came down with you?"

"It would be grand."

"You wouldn't mind, really? I've been at Pamplona, you know. Brett's mad to go. You're sure we wouldn't just be a bloody nuisance?"

"Don't talk like a fool."

"I'm a little tight, you know. I wouldn't ask you like this if I weren't. You're sure you don't mind?"

"Oh, shut up, Michael," Brett said. "How can the man say he'd mind now? I'll ask him later."

"But you don't mind, do you?"

"Don't ask that again unless you want to make me sore. Bill and I go down on the morning of the 25th."

"By the way, where is Bill?" Brett asked.

"He's out at Chantilly[4] dining with some people."

"He's a good chap."

"Splendid chap," said Mike. "He is, you know."

"You don't remember him," Brett said.

"I do. Remember him perfectly. Look, Jake, we'll come down the night of the 25th. Brett can't get up in the morning."

"Indeed not!"

"If our money comes and you're sure you don't mind."

"It will come, all right. I'll see to that."

"Tell me what tackle to send for."

"Get two or three rods with reels, and lines, and some flies."

"I won't fish," Brett put in.

"Get two rods, then, and Bill won't have to buy one."

"Right," said Mike. "I'll send a wire to the keeper."

"Won't it be splendid," Brett said. "Spain! We *will* have fun."

"The 25th. When is that?"

3. A town in southwest France, in the Basque country and the foothills of the Pyrenees.
4. A town about twenty miles north-northeast of Paris.

"Saturday."

"We *will* have to get ready."

"I say," said Mike, "I'm going to the barber's."

"I must bathe," said Brett. "Walk up to the hotel with me, Jake. Be a good chap."

"We *have* got the loveliest hotel," Mike said. "I think it's a brothel!"

"We left our bags here at the Dingo when we got in, and they asked us at this hotel if we wanted a room for the afternoon only. Seemed frightfully pleased we were going to stay all night."

"*I* believe it's a brothel," Mike said. "And *I* should know."

"Oh, shut it and go and get your hair cut."

Mike went out. Brett and I sat on at the bar.

"Have another?"

"Might."

"I needed that," Brett said.

We walked up the Rue Delambre.[5]

"I haven't seen you since I've been back," Brett said.

"No."

"How *are* you, Jake?"

"Fine."

Brett looked at me. "I say," she said, "is Robert Cohn going on this trip?"

"Yes. Why?"

"Don't you think it will be a bit rough on him?"

"Why should it?"

"Who did you think I went down to San Sebastian with?"

"Congratulations," I said.

We walked along.

"What did you say that for?"

"I don't know. What would you like me to say?"

We walked along and turned a corner.

"He behaved rather well, too. He gets a little dull."

"Does he?"

"I rather thought it would be good for him."

"You might take up social service."

"Don't be nasty."

"I won't."

"Didn't you really know?"

"No," I said. "I guess I didn't think about it."

"Do you think it will be too rough on him?"

"That's up to him," I said. "Tell him you're coming. He can always not come."

"I'll write him and give him a chance to pull out of it."

5. A street in Paris's fourteenth arrondissement.

I did not see Brett again until the night of the 24th of June.

"Did you hear from Cohn?"

"Rather. He's keen about it."

"My God!"

"I thought it was rather odd myself."

"Says he can't wait to see me."

"Does he think you're coming alone?"

"No. I told him we were all coming down together. Michael and all."

"He's wonderful."

"Isn't he?"

They expected their money the next day. We arranged to meet at Pamplona. They would go directly to San Sebastian and take the train from there. We would all meet at the Montoya in Pamplona. If they did not turn up on Monday at the latest we would go on ahead up to Burguete[6] in the mountains, to start fishing. There was a bus to Burguete. I wrote out an itinerary so they could follow us.

Bill and I took the morning train from the Gare d'Orsay.[7] It was a lovely day, not too hot, and the country was beautiful from the start. We went back into the diner and had breakfast. Leaving the dining-car I asked the conductor for tickets for the first service.

"Nothing until the fifth."

"What's this?"

There were never more than two servings of lunch on that train, and always plenty of places for both of them.

"They're all reserved," the dining-car conductor said. "There will be a fifth service at three-thirty."

"This is serious," I said to Bill.

"Give him ten francs."

"Here," I said. "We want to eat in the first service."

The conductor put the ten francs in his pocket.

"Thank you," he said. "I would advise you gentlemen to get some sandwiches. All the places for the first four services were reserved at the office of the company."

"You'll go a long way, brother," Bill said to him in English. "I suppose if I'd given you five francs you would have advised us to jump off the train."

"*Comment*?"[8]

"Go to hell!" said Bill. "Get the sandwiches made and a bottle of wine. You tell him, Jake."

"And send it up to the next car." I described where we were.

6. A town in the Navarre region of northern Spain.
7. Railroad station where the Paris-Orléans railway terminated. It closed for mainline train service (though it remains open as a commuter rail and Metro station) in 1939. Trains left this station for southwestern France and Spain.
8. "What?" (French).

In our compartment were a man and his wife and their young son.

"I suppose you're Americans, aren't you?" the man asked. "Having a good trip?"

"Wonderful," said Bill.

"That's what you want to do. Travel while you're young. Mother and I always wanted to get over, but we had to wait a while."

"You could have come over ten years ago, if you'd wanted to," the wife said. "What you always said was: 'See America first!' I will say we've seen a good deal, take it one way and another."

"Say, there's plenty of Americans on this train," the husband said. "They've got seven cars of them from Dayton, Ohio. They've been on a pilgrimage to Rome, and now they're going down to Biarritz and Lourdes."

"So, that's what they are. Pilgrims. Goddam Puritans,"[9] Bill said.

"What part of the States you boys from?"

"Kansas City," I said. "He's from Chicago."

"You both going to Biarritz?"

"No. We're going fishing in Spain."

"Well, I never cared for it, myself. There's plenty that do out where I come from, though. We got some of the best fishing in the State of Montana. I've been out with the boys, but I never cared for it any."

"Mighty little fishing you did on them trips," his wife said.

He winked at us.

"You know how the ladies are. If there's a jug goes along, or a case of beer, they think it's hell and damnation."

"That's the way men are," his wife said to us. She smoothed her comfortable lap. "I voted against prohibition to please him, and because I like a little beer in the house, and then he talks that way. It's a wonder they ever find any one to marry them."

"Say," said Bill, "do you know that gang of Pilgrim Fathers have cornered the dining-car until half past three this afternoon?"

"How do you mean? They can't do a thing like that."

"You try and get seats."

"Well, mother, it looks as though we better go back and get another breakfast."

She stood up and straightened her dress.

"Will you boys keep an eye on our things? Come on, Hubert."

They all three went up to the wagon restaurant. A little while after they were gone a steward went through announcing the first service, and pilgrims, with their priests, commenced filing down the corridor.

9. As important sites associated with Catholicism, Biarritz and Lourdes would have attracted devout Christians (even the Protestants who made up the majority of Dayton's religious community), but probably not "Puritans." Bill jokingly selects the American connotation of "Pilgrims," as in "Pilgrim Fathers" below (rather than the Catholic or European significance) and slides from that to the synonymous "Puritans").

Our friend and his family did not come back. A waiter passed in the corridor with our sandwiches and the bottle of Chablis,[1] and we called him in.

"You're going to work to-day," I said.

He nodded his head. "They start now, at ten-thirty."

"When do we eat?"

"Huh! When do I eat?"

He left two glasses for the bottle, and we paid him for the sandwiches and tipped him.

"I'll get the plates," he said, "or bring them with you."

We ate the sandwiches and drank the Chablis and watched the country out of the window. The grain was just beginning to ripen and the fields were full of poppies. The pastureland was green, and there were fine trees, and sometimes big rivers and chateaux off in the trees.

At Tours[2] we got off and bought another bottle of wine, and when we got back in the compartment the gentleman from Montana and his wife and his son, Hubert, were sitting comfortably.

"Is there good swimming in Biarritz?" asked Hubert.

"That boy's just crazy till he can get in the water," his mother said. "It's pretty hard on youngsters travelling."

"There's good swimming," I said. "But it's dangerous when it's rough."

"Did you get a meal?" Bill asked.

"We sure did. We set right there when they started to come in, and they must have just thought we were in the party. One of the waiters said something to us in French, and then they just sent three of them back."

"They thought we were snappers, all right," the man said. "It certainly shows you the power of the Catholic Church. It's a pity you boys ain't Catholics. You could get a meal, then, all right."

"I am," I said. "That's what makes me so sore."

Finally at a quarter past four we had lunch. Bill had been rather difficult at the last. He buttonholed a priest who was coming back with one of the returning streams of pilgrims.

"When do us Protestants get a chance to eat, father?"

"I don't know anything about it. Haven't you got tickets?"

"It's enough to make a man join the Klan,"[3] Bill said. The priest looked back at him.

Inside the dining-car the waiters served the fifth successive table d'hôte meal. The waiter who served us was soaked through. His white jacket was purple under the arms.

1. A white wine from the northern part of Burgundy, France.
2. A city on the Loire River in central France.
3. The Ku Klux Klan is not only a white supremacist organization but also, especially in its 1920s incarnation, was virulently anti-Catholic.

"He must drink a lot of wine."

"Or wear purple undershirts."

"Let's ask him."

"No. He's too tired."

The train stopped for half an hour at Bordeaux[4] and we went out through the station for a little walk. There was not time to get in to the town. Afterward we passed through the Landes[5] and watched the sun set. There were wide fire-gaps cut through the pines, and you could look up them like avenues and see wooded hills way off. About seven-thirty we had dinner and watched the country through the open window in the diner. It was all sandy pine country full of heather. There were little clearings with houses in them, and once in a while we passed a sawmill. It got dark and we could feel the country hot and sandy and dark outside of the window, and about nine o'clock we got into Bayonne. The man and his wife and Hubert all shook hands with us. They were going on to La Négresse to change for Biarritz.[6]

"Well, I hope you have lots of luck," he said.

"Be careful about those bull-fights."

"Maybe we'll see you at Biarritz," Hubert said.

We got off with our bags and rod-cases and passed through the dark station and out to the lights and the line of cabs and hotel buses. There, standing with the hotel runners, was Robert Cohn. He did not see us at first. Then he started forward.

"Hello, Jake. Have a good trip?"

"Fine," I said. "This is Bill Gorton."[7]

"How are you?"

"Come on," said Robert. "I've got a cab." He was a little near-sighted. I had never noticed it before. He was looking at Bill, trying to make him out. He was shy, too.

"We'll go up to my hotel. It's all right. It's quite nice."

We got into the cab, and the cabman put the bags up on the seat beside him and climbed up and cracked his whip, and we drove over the dark bridge and into the town.

"I'm awfully glad to meet you," Robert said to Bill. "I've heard so much about you from Jake and I've read your books. Did you get my line, Jake?"

The cab stopped in front of the hotel and we all got out and went in. It was a nice hotel, and the people at the desk were very cheerful, and we each had a good small room.

4. A city in southwestern France.
5. A region of sandy soil and pine forests between Bordeaux and Bayonne.
6. La Negresse (without the accent that Hemingway incorrectly includes) is a railroad station outside Biarritz.
7. In the first edition, Jake introduces Bill as "Bill Grundy."

Hemingway with friends in Pamplona, 1925. From left: Hemingway, Harold Loeb, Duff Twysden, Hadley Richardson Hemingway, Donald Ogden Stewart, Pat Guthrie. Courtesy of the John F. Kennedy Library Archives.

Chapter X

In the morning it was bright, and they were sprinkling the streets of the town, and we all had breakfast in a café. Bayonne is a nice town. It is like a very clean Spanish town and it is on a big river. Already, so early in the morning, it was very hot on the bridge across the river. We walked out on the bridge and then took a walk through the town.

I was not at all sure Mike's rods would come from Scotland in time, so we hunted a tackle store and finally bought a rod for Bill up-stairs over a drygoods store. The man who sold the tackle was out, and we had to wait for him to come back. Finally he came in, and we bought a pretty good rod cheap, and two landing-nets.

We went out into the street again and took a look at the cathedral.[1] Cohn made some remark about it being a very good example of something or other, I forget what. It seemed like a nice cathedral, nice and dim, like Spanish churches. Then we went up past the old fort and out to the local Syndicat d'Initiative office,[2] where the bus was supposed to start from. There they told us the bus service did not start until the 1st of July. We found out at the tourist office what we ought to pay for a motor-car to Pamplona and hired one at a big garage just around the corner from the Municipal Theatre for four hundred francs. The car was to pick us up at the hotel in forty minutes, and we stopped at the café on the square where we had eaten breakfast, and had a beer. It was hot, but the town had a cool, fresh, early-morning smell and it was pleasant sitting in the café. A breeze started to blow, and you could feel that the air came from the sea. There were pigeons out in the square, and the houses were a yellow, sun-baked color, and I did not want to leave the café. But we had to go to the hotel to get our bags packed and pay the bill. We paid for the beers, we matched and I think Cohn paid, and went up to the hotel. It was only sixteen francs apiece for Bill and me, with ten per cent added for the service, and we had the bags sent down and waited for Robert Cohn. While we were waiting I saw a cockroach on the parquet floor that must have been at least three inches long. I pointed him out to Bill and then put my shoe on him. We agreed he must have just come in from the garden. It was really an awfully clean hotel.

Cohn came down, finally, and we all went out to the car. It was a big, closed car, with a driver in a white duster with blue collar and

1. The Cathédrale Sainte-Marie (earlier known as Notre-Dame de Bayonne), begun in 1140, was rebuilt after 1213 largely in the northern Gothic style.
2. Local office for tourists; *old fort*: the Citadelle Bayonne, added to Bayonne's fortifications in the 1670s.

cuffs, and we had him put the back of the car down. He piled in the bags and we started off up the street and out of the town. We passed some lovely gardens and had a good look back at the town, and then we were out in the country, green and rolling, and the road climbing all the time. We passed lots of Basques[3] with oxen, or cattle, hauling carts along the road, and nice farmhouses, low roofs, and all white-plastered. In the Basque country the land all looks very rich and green and the houses and villages look well-off and clean. Every village had a pelota[4] court and on some of them kids were playing in the hot sun. There were signs on the walls of the churches saying it was forbidden to play pelota against them, and the houses in the villages had red tiled roofs, and then the road turned off and commenced to climb and we were going way up close along a hillside, with a valley below and hills stretched off back toward the sea. You couldn't see the sea. It was too far away. You could see only hills and more hills, and you knew where the sea was.

We crossed the Spanish frontier. There was a little stream and a bridge, and Spanish carabineers, with patent-leather Bonaparte hats, and short guns on their backs, on one side, and on the other fat Frenchmen in képis[5] and mustaches. They only opened one bag and took the passports in and looked at them. There was a general store and inn on each side of the line. The chauffeur had to go in and fill out some papers about the car and we got out and went over to the stream to see if there were any trout. Bill tried to talk some Spanish to one of the carabineers, but it did not go very well. Robert Cohn asked, pointing with his finger, if there were any trout in the stream, and the carabineer said yes, but not many.

I asked him if he ever fished, and he said no, that he didn't care for it.

Just then an old man with long, sunburned hair and beard, and clothes that looked as though they were made of gunny-sacking, came striding up to the bridge. He was carrying a long staff, and he had a kid slung on his back, tied by the four legs, the head hanging down.

The carabineer waved him back with his sword. The man turned without saying anything, and started back up the white road into Spain.

3. An ethnic group (*Vasco* in Spanish) indigenous to the region that includes the western part of the Pyrenees and the coast of the Bay of Biscay (partly in southwestern France and partly in northwestern Spain). Basque is a language unrelated to French or Spanish and developed independently of the Indo-European family from which most European languages descended.
4. A Basque game played in a walled court with basket-like wooden racquets.
5. A short, cylindrical French military cap with a flat brim; *carabineer*: a soldier (here Spanish) armed with a carbine rifle; *Bonaparte hat*: a bicorne hat commonly associated with the nineteenth-century French emperor, worn here by the Spanish border guards or customs officers.

"What's the matter with the old one?" I asked.

"He hasn't got any passport."

I offered the guard a cigarette. He took it and thanked me.

"What will he do?" I asked.

The guard spat in the dust.

"Oh, he'll just wade across the stream."

"Do you have much smuggling?"

"Oh," he said, "they go through."

The chauffeur came out, folding up the papers and putting them in the inside pocket of his coat. We all got in the car and it started up the white dusty road into Spain. For a while the country was much as it had been; then, climbing all the time, we crossed the top of a Col,[6] the road winding back and forth on itself, and then it was really Spain. There were long brown mountains and a few pines and far-off forests of beech-trees on some of the mountainsides. The road went along the summit of the Col and then dropped down, and the driver had to honk, and slow up, and turn out to avoid running into two donkeys that were sleeping in the road. We came down out of the mountains and through an oak forest, and there were white cattle grazing in the forest. Down below there were grassy plains and clear streams, and then we crossed a stream and went through a gloomy little village, and started to climb again. We climbed up and up and crossed another high Col and turned along it, and the road ran down to the right, and we saw a whole new range of mountains off to the south, all brown and baked-looking and furrowed in strange shapes.

After a while we came out of the mountains, and there were trees along both sides of the road, and a stream and ripe fields of grain, and the road went on, very white and straight ahead, and then lifted to a little rise, and off on the left was a hill with an old castle, with buildings close around it and a field of grain going right up to the walls and shifting in the wind. I was up in front with the driver and I turned around. Robert Cohn was asleep, but Bill looked and nodded his head. Then we crossed a wide plain, and there was a big river off on the right shining in the sun from between the line of trees, and away off you could see the plateau of Pamplona rising out of the plain, and the walls of the city, and the great brown cathedral, and the broken skyline of the other churches. In back of the plateau were the mountains, and every way you looked there were other mountains, and ahead the road stretched out white across the plain going toward Pamplona.

We came into the town on the other side of the plateau, the road slanting up steeply and dustily with shade-trees on both sides, and

6. A gap in a mountain range, the low area between peaks.

then levelling out through the new part of town they are building up outside the old walls. We passed the bull-ring, high and white and concrete-looking in the sun, and then came into the big square by a side street and stopped in front of the Hotel Montoya.

The driver helped us down with the bags. There was a crowd of kids watching the car, and the square was hot, and the trees were green, and the flags hung on their staffs, and it was good to get out of the sun and under the shade of the arcade that runs all the way around the square. Montoya was glad to see us, and shook hands and gave us good rooms looking out on the square, and then we washed and cleaned up and went down-stairs in the dining-room for lunch. The driver stayed for lunch, too, and afterward we paid him and he started back to Bayonne.

There are two dining-rooms in the Montoya. One is up-stairs on the second floor and looks out on the square. The other is down one floor below the level of the square and has a door that opens on the back street that the bulls pass along when they run through the streets early in the morning on their way to the ring. It is always cool in the down-stairs dining-room and we had a very good lunch. The first meal in Spain was always a shock with the hors d'œuvres, an egg course, two meat courses, vegetables, salad, and dessert and fruit. You have to drink plenty of wine to get it all down. Robert Cohn tried to say he did not want any of the second meat course, but we would not interpret for him, and so the waitress brought him something else as a replacement, a plate of cold meats, I think. Cohn had been rather nervous ever since we had met at Bayonne. He did not know whether we knew Brett had been with him at San Sebastian, and it made him rather awkward.

"Well," I said, "Brett and Mike ought to get in to-night."

"I'm not sure they'll come," Cohn said.

"Why not?" Bill said. "Of course they'll come."

"They're always late," I said.

"I rather think they're not coming," Robert Cohn said.

He said it with an air of superior knowledge that irritated both of us.

"I'll bet you fifty pesetas[7] they're here to-night," Bill said. He always bets when he is angered, and so he usually bets foolishly.

"I'll take it," Cohn said. "Good. You remember it, Jake. Fifty pesetas."

"I'll remember it myself," Bill said. I saw he was angry and wanted to smooth him down.

7. In 1925, the Spanish peseta was worth just over 14 cents ($.14), so Bill bets the equivalent of $5.20. Given rough inflation figures in the intervening decades, the value of the bet would be in the neighborhood of $100 today.

"It's a sure thing they'll come," I said. "But maybe not tonight."

"Want to call it off?" Cohn asked.

"No. Why should I? Make it a hundred if you like."

"All right. I'll take that."

"That's enough," I said. "Or you'll have to make a book and give me some of it."

"I'm satisfied," Cohn said. He smiled. "You'll probably win it back at bridge, anyway."

"You haven't got it yet," Bill said.

We went out to walk around under the arcade to the Café Iruña for coffee.[8] Cohn said he was going over and get a shave.

"Say," Bill said to me, "have I got any chance on that bet?"

"You've got a rotten chance. They've never been on time anywhere. If their money doesn't come it's a cinch they won't get in tonight."

"I was sorry as soon as I opened my mouth. But I had to call him. He's all right, I guess, but where does he get this inside stuff? Mike and Brett fixed it up with us about coming down here."

I saw Cohn coming over across the square.

"Here he comes."

"Well, let him not get superior and Jewish."

"The barber shop's closed," Cohn said. "It's not open till four."

We had coffee at the Iruña, sitting in comfortable wicker chairs looking out from the cool of the arcade at the big square. After a while Bill went to write some letters and Cohn went over to the barber-shop. It was still closed, so he decided to go up to the hotel and get a bath, and I sat out in front of the café and then went for a walk in the town. It was very hot, but I kept on the shady side of the streets and went through the market and had a good time seeing the town again. I went to the Ayuntamiento[9] and found the old gentleman who subscribes for the bull-fight tickets for me every year, and he had gotten the money I sent him from Paris and renewed my subscriptions, so that was all set. He was the archivist, and all the archives of the town were in his office. That has nothing to do with the story. Anyway, his office had a green baize door and a big wooden door, and when I went out I left him sitting among the archives that covered all the walls, and I shut both the doors, and as I went out of the building into the street the porter stopped me to brush off my coat.

"You must have been in a motor-car," he said.

The back of the collar and the upper part of the shoulders were gray with dust.

8. Located on the Plaza del Castillo in Pamplona, The Café Iruña takes its name from the Basque for "Pamplona."

9. The city hall in Pamplona.

"From Bayonne."

"Well, well," he said. "I knew you were in a motor-car from the way the dust was." So I gave him two copper coins.

At the end of the street I saw the cathedral[1] and walked up toward it. The first time I ever saw it I thought the facade was ugly but I liked it now. I went inside. It was dim and dark and the pillars went high up, and there were people praying, and it smelt of incense, and there were some wonderful big windows. I knelt and started to pray and prayed for everybody I thought of, Brett and Mike and Bill and Robert Cohn and myself, and all the bull-fighters, separately for the ones I liked, and lumping all the rest, then I prayed for myself again, and while I was praying for myself I found I was getting sleepy, so I prayed that the bull-fights would be good, and that it would be a fine fiesta, and that we would get some fishing. I wondered if there was anything else I might pray for, and I thought I would like to have some money, so I prayed that I would make a lot of money, and then I started to think how I would make it, and thinking of making money reminded me of the count, and I started wondering about where he was, and regretting I hadn't seen him since that night in Montmartre, and about something funny Brett told me about him, and as all the time I was kneeling with my forehead on the wood in front of me, and was thinking of myself as praying, I was a little ashamed, and regretted that I was such a rotten Catholic, but realized there was nothing I could do about it, at least for a while, and maybe never, but that anyway it was a grand religion, and I only wished I felt religious and maybe I would the next time; and then I was out in the hot sun on the steps of the cathedral, and the forefingers and the thumb of my right hand were still damp, and I felt them dry in the sun.[2] The sunlight was hot and hard, and I crossed over beside some buildings, and walked back along side-streets to the hotel.

At dinner that night we found that Robert Cohn had taken a bath, had had a shave and a haircut and a shampoo, and something put on his hair afterward to make it stay down. He was nervous, and I did not try to help him any. The train was due in at nine o'clock from San Sebastian, and, if Brett and Mike were coming, they would be on it. At twenty minutes to nine we were not half through dinner. Robert Cohn got up from the table and said he would go to the station. I said I would go with him, just to devil him. Bill said he would be damned if he would leave his dinner. I said we would be right back.

1. Pamplona's Cathedral of Santa Maria was consecrated in 1127. The current Gothic structure was completed in the fifteenth century.
2. Jake's fingers are damp from the holy water into which he has dipped them before making the sign of the cross on his way out of the cathedral.

We walked to the station. I was enjoying Cohn's nervousness. I hoped Brett would be on the train. At the station the train was late, and we sat on a baggage-truck and waited outside in the dark. I have never seen a man in civil life as nervous as Robert Cohn—nor as eager. I was enjoying it. It was lousy to enjoy it, but I felt lousy. Cohn had a wonderful quality of bringing out the worst in anybody.

After a while we heard the train-whistle way off below on the other side of the plateau, and then we saw the headlight coming up the hill. We went inside the station and stood with a crowd of people just back of the gates, and the train came in and stopped, and everybody started coming out through the gates.

They were not in the crowd. We waited till everybody had gone through and out of the station and gotten into buses, or taken cabs, or were walking with their friends or relatives through the dark into the town.

"I knew they wouldn't come," Robert said. We were going back to the hotel.

"I thought they might," I said.

Bill was eating fruit when we came in and finishing a bottle of wine.

"Didn't come, eh?"

"No."

"Do you mind if I give you that hundred pesetas in the morning, Cohn?" Bill asked. "I haven't changed any money here yet."

"Oh, forget about it," Robert Cohn said. "Let's bet on something else. Can you bet on bull-fights?"

"You could," Bill said, "but you don't need to."

"It would be like betting on the war," I said. "You don't need any economic interest."

"I'm very curious to see them," Robert said.

Montoya came up to our table. He had a telegram in his hand. "It's for you." He handed it to me.

It read: "Stopped night San Sebastian."

"It's from them," I said. I put it in my pocket. Ordinarily I should have handed it over.

"They've stopped over in San Sebastian," I said. "Send their regards to you."

Why I felt that impulse to devil him I do not know. Of course I do know. I was blind, unforgivingly jealous of what had happened to him. The fact that I took it as a matter of course did not alter that any. I certainly did hate him. I do not think I ever really hated him until he had that little spell of superiority at lunch—that and when he went through all that barbering. So I put the telegram in my pocket. The telegram came to me, anyway.

"Well," I said. "We ought to pull out on the noon bus for Burguete. They can follow us if they get in to-morrow night."

There were only two trains up from San Sebastian, an early morning train and the one we had just met.

"That sounds like a good idea," Cohn said.

"The sooner we get on the stream the better."

"It's all one to me when we start," Bill said. "The sooner the better."

We sat in the Iruña for a while and had coffee and then took a little walk out to the bull-ring and across the field and under the trees at the edge of the cliff and looked down at the river in the dark, and I turned in early. Bill and Cohn stayed out in the café quite late, I believe, because I was asleep when they came in.

In the morning I bought three tickets for the bus to Burguete. It was scheduled to leave at two o'clock. There was nothing earlier. I was sitting over at the Iruña reading the papers when I saw Robert Cohn coming across the square. He came up to the table and sat down in one of the wicker chairs.

"This is a comfortable café," he said. "Did you have a good night, Jake?"

"I slept like a log."

"I didn't sleep very well. Bill and I were out late, too."

"Where were you?"

"Here. And after it shut we went over to that other café. The old man there speaks German and English."

"The Café Suizo."[3]

"That's it. He seems like a nice old fellow. I think it's a better café than this one."

"It's not so good in the daytime," I said. "Too hot. By the way, I got the bus tickets."

"I'm not going up to-day. You and Bill go on ahead."

"I've got your ticket."

"Give it to me. I'll get the money back."

"It's five pesetas."

Robert Cohn took out a silver five-peseta piece and gave it to me.

"I ought to stay," he said. "You see I'm afraid there's some sort of misunderstanding."

"Why," I said. "They may not come here for three or four days now if they start on parties at San Sebastian."

"That's just it," said Robert. "I'm afraid they expected to meet me at San Sebastian, and that's why they stopped over."

"What makes you think that?"

"Well, I wrote suggesting it to Brett."

3. Another café on Pamplona's Plaza del Castillo. (*Suizo* in Spanish means "Swiss.")

"Why in hell didn't you stay there and meet them, then?" I started to say, but I stopped. I thought that idea would come to him by itself, but I do not believe it ever did.

He was being confidential now and it was giving him pleasure to be able to talk with the understanding that I knew there was something between him and Brett.

"Well, Bill and I will go up right after lunch," I said.

"I wish I could go. We've been looking forward to this fishing all winter." He was being sentimental about it. "But I ought to stay. I really ought. As soon as they come I'll bring them right up."

"Let's find Bill."

"I want to go over to the barber-shop."

"See you at lunch."

I found Bill up in his room. He was shaving.

"Oh, yes, he told me all about it last night," Bill said. "He's a great little confider. He said he had a date with Brett at San Sebastian."

"The lying bastard!"

"Oh, no," said Bill. "Don't get sore. Don't get sore at this stage of the trip. How did you ever happen to know this fellow anyway?"

"Don't rub it in."

Bill looked around, half-shaved, and then went on talking into the mirror while he lathered his face.

"Didn't you send him with a letter to me in New York last winter? Thank God, I'm a travelling man. Haven't you got some more Jewish friends you could bring along?" He rubbed his chin with his thumb, looked at it, and then started scraping again.

"You've got some fine ones yourself."

"Oh, yes. I've got some darbs.[4] But not alongside of this Robert Cohn. The funny thing is he's nice, too. I like him. But he's just so awful."

"He can be damn nice."

"I know it. That's the terrible part."

I laughed.

"Yes. Go on and laugh," said Bill. "You weren't out with him last night until two o'clock."

"Was he very bad?"

"Awful. What's all this about him and Brett, anyway? Did she ever have anything to do with him?"

He raised his chin up and pulled it from side to side.

"Sure. She went down to San Sebastian with him."

"What a damn-fool thing to do. Why did she do that?"

"She wanted to get out of town and she can't go anywhere alone. She said she thought it would be good for him."

4. A darb is an excellent person or thing.

"What bloody-fool things people do. Why didn't she go off with some of her own people? Or you?"—he slurred that over—"or me? Why not me?" He looked at his face carefully in the glass, put a big dab of lather on each cheek-bone. "It's an honest face. It's a face any woman would be safe with."

"She'd never seen it."

"She should have. All women should see it. It's a face that ought to be thrown on every screen in the country. Every woman ought to be given a copy of this face as she leaves the altar. Mothers should tell their daughters about this face. My son"—he pointed the razor at me—"go west with this face and grow up with the country."

He ducked down to the bowl, rinsed his face with cold water, put on some alcohol, and then looked at himself carefully in the glass, pulling down his long upper lip.

"My God!" he said, "isn't it an awful face?"

He looked in the glass.

"And as for this Robert Cohn," Bill said, "he makes me sick, and he can go to hell, and I'm damn glad he's staying here so we won't have him fishing with us."

"You're damn right."

"We're going trout-fishing. We're going trout-fishing in the Irati River, and we're going to get tight now at lunch on the wine of the country, and then take a swell bus ride."

"Come on. Let's go over to the Iruña and start," I said.

Chapter XI

It was baking hot in the square when we came out after lunch with our bags and the rod-case to go to Burguete. People were on top of the bus, and others were climbing up a ladder. Bill went up and Robert sat beside Bill to save a place for me, and I went back in the hotel to get a couple of bottles of wine to take with us. When I came out the bus was crowded. Men and women were sitting on all the baggage and boxes on top, and the women all had their fans going in the sun. It certainly was hot. Robert climbed down and I fitted into the place he had saved on the one wooden seat that ran across the top.

Robert Cohn stood in the shade of the arcade waiting for us to start. A Basque with a big leather wine-bag in his lap lay across the top of the bus in front of our seat, leaning back against our legs. He offered the wine-skin to Bill and to me, and when I tipped it up to drink he imitated the sound of a klaxon motor-horn so well and so suddenly that I spilled some of the wine, and everybody laughed. He apologized and made me take another drink. He made the klaxon again a little later, and it fooled me the second time. He was very good at it. The Basques liked it. The man next to Bill was talking to him in Spanish and Bill was not getting it, so he offered the man one of the bottles of wine. The man waved it away. He said it was too hot and he had drunk too much at lunch. When Bill offered the bottle the second time he took a long drink, and then the bottle went all over that part of the bus. Every one took a drink very politely, and then they made us cork it up and put it away. They all wanted us to drink from their leather wine-bottles. They were peasants going up into the hills.

Finally, after a couple more false klaxons, the bus started, and Robert Cohn waved good-bye to us, and all the Basques waved good-bye to him. As soon as we started out on the road outside of town it was cool. It felt nice riding high up and close under the trees. The bus went quite fast and made a good breeze, and as we went out along the road with the dust powdering the trees and down the hill, we had a fine view, back through the trees, of the town rising up from the bluff above the river. The Basque lying against my knees pointed out the view with the neck of the wine-bottle, and winked at us. He nodded his head.

"Pretty nice, eh?"

"These Basques are swell people," Bill said.

The Basque lying against my legs was tanned the color of saddle-leather. He wore a black smock like all the rest. There were wrinkles in his tanned neck. He turned around and offered his wine-bag to Bill. Bill handed him one of our bottles. The Basque wagged a forefinger at him and handed the bottle back, slapping in the cork with the palm of his hand. He shoved the wine-bag up.

"Arriba! Arriba!" he said. "Lift it up."

Bill raised the wine-skin and let the stream of wine spurt out and into his mouth, his head tipped back. When he stopped drinking and tipped the leather bottle down a few drops ran down his chin.

"No! No!" several Basques said. "Not like that." One snatched the bottle away from the owner, who was himself about to give a demonstration. He was a young fellow and he held the wine-bottle at full arms' length and raised it high up, squeezing the leather bag with his hand so the stream of wine hissed into his mouth. He held the bag out there, the wine making a flat, hard trajectory into his mouth, and he kept on swallowing smoothly and regularly.

"Hey!" the owner of the bottle shouted. "Whose wine is that?"

The drinker waggled his little finger at him and smiled at us with his eyes. Then he bit the stream off sharp, made a quick lift with the wine-bag and lowered it down to the owner. He winked at us. The owner shook the wine-skin sadly.

We passed through a town and stopped in front of the posada,[1] and the driver took on several packages. Then we started on again, and outside the town the road commenced to mount. We were going through farming country with rocky hills that sloped down into the fields. The grain-fields went up the hillsides. Now as we went higher there was a wind blowing the grain. The road was white and dusty, and the dust rose under the wheels and hung in the air behind us. The road climbed up into the hills and left the rich grain-fields below. Now there were only patches of grain on the bare hillsides and on each side of the water-courses. We turned sharply out to the side of the road to give room to pass to a long string of six mules, following one after the other, hauling a high-hooded wagon loaded with freight. The wagon and the mules were covered with dust. Close behind was another string of mules and another wagon. This was loaded with lumber, and the arriero[2] driving the mules leaned back and put on the thick wooden brakes as we passed. Up here the country was quite barren and the hills were rocky and hard-baked clay furrowed by the rain.

We came around a curve into a town, and on both sides opened out a sudden green valley. A stream went through the centre of the town and fields of grapes touched the houses.

The bus stopped in front of a posada and many of the passengers got down, and a lot of the baggage was unstrapped from the roof from under the big tarpaulins and lifted down. Bill and I got down and went into the posada. There was a low, dark room with saddles and harness, and hay-forks made of white wood, and clusters of canvas rope-soled shoes and hams and slabs of bacon and white garlics and long sausages hanging from the roof. It was cool and dusky, and we stood in front of a long wooden counter with two women behind it serving drinks. Behind them were shelves stacked with supplies and goods.

We each had an aguardiente[3] and paid forty centimes for the two drinks. I gave the woman fifty centimes to make a tip, and she gave me back the copper piece, thinking I had misunderstood the price.

Two of our Basques came in and insisted on buying a drink. So they bought a drink and then we bought a drink, and then they slapped us on the back and bought another drink. Then we bought, and then we all went out into the sunlight and the heat, and climbed back on top of the bus. There was plenty of room now for every one to sit on the seat, and the Basque who had been lying on the tin

1. Inn or hotel (Spanish).
2. A muleteer (Spanish), one who transports goods with pack animals.
3. Could refer to an anise-derived spirit or to any clear spirit (e.g., brandy).

roof now sat between us. The woman who had been serving drinks came out wiping her hands on her apron and talked to somebody inside the bus. Then the driver came out swinging two flat leather mail-pouches and climbed up, and everybody waving we started off.

The road left the green valley at once, and we were up in the hills again. Bill and the wine-bottle Basque were having a conversation. A man leaned over from the other side of the seat and asked in English: "You're Americans?"

"Sure."

"I been there," he said. "Forty years ago."

He was an old man, as brown as the others, with the stubble of a white beard.

"How was it?"

"What you say?"

"How was America?"

"Oh, I was in California. It was fine."

"Why did you leave?"

"What you say?"

"Why did you come back here?"

"Oh! I come back to get married. I was going to go back but my wife she don't like to travel. Where you from?"

"Kansas City."

"I been there," he said. "I been in Chicago, St. Louis, Kansas City, Denver, Los Angeles, Salt Lake City."

He named them carefully.

"How long were you over?"

"Fifteen years. Then I come back and got married."

"Have a drink?"

"All right," he said. "You can't get this in America, eh?"

"There's plenty if you can pay for it."

"What you come over here for?"

"We're going to the fiesta at Pamplona."

"You like the bull-fights?"

"Sure. Don't you?"

"Yes," he said. "I guess I like them."

Then after a little:

"Where you go now?"

"Up to Burguete to fish."

"Well," he said, "I hope you catch something."

He shook hands and turned around to the back seat again. The other Basques had been impressed. He sat back comfortably and smiled at me when I turned around to look at the country. But the effort of talking American seemed to have tired him. He did not say anything after that.

The bus climbed steadily up the road. The country was barren and rocks stuck up through the clay. There was no grass beside the road. Looking back we could see the country spread out below. Far back the fields were squares of green and brown on the hillsides. Making the horizon were the brown mountains. They were strangely shaped. As we climbed higher the horizon kept changing. As the bus ground slowly up the road we could see other mountains coming up in the south. Then the road came over the crest, flattened out, and went into a forest. It was a forest of cork oaks, and the sun came through the trees in patches, and there were cattle grazing back in the trees. We went through the forest and the road came out and turned along a rise of land, and out ahead of us was a rolling green plain, with dark mountains beyond it. These were not like the brown, heat-baked mountains we had left behind. These were wooded and there were clouds coming down from them. The green plain stretched off. It was cut by fences and the white of the road showed through the trunks of a double line of trees that crossed the plain toward the north. As we came to the edge of the rise we saw the red roofs and white houses of Burguete ahead strung out on the plain, and away off on the shoulder of the first dark mountain was the gray metal-sheathed roof of the monastery of Roncesvalles.[4]

"There's Roncevaux," I said.

"Where?"

"Way off there where the mountain starts."

"It's cold up here," Bill said.

"It's high," I said. "It must be twelve hundred metres."

"It's awful cold," Bill said.

The bus levelled down onto the straight line of road that ran to Burguete. We passed a crossroads and crossed a bridge over a stream. The houses of Burguete were along both sides of the road. There were no side-streets. We passed the church and the school-yard, and the bus stopped. We got down and the driver handed down our bags and the rod-case. A carabineer in his cocked hat and yellow leather cross-straps came up.

"What's in there?" he pointed to the rod-case.

I opened it and showed him. He asked to see our fishing permits and I got them out. He looked at the date and then waved us on.

"Is that all right?" I asked.

"Yes. Of course."

4. Roncevaux (French), a village in Navarre, in northern Spain. It is the site of a battle fought in 778, during which the forces of Charlemagne (748–814, king of the Franks 800–814) were defeated by Basque warriors who attacked to avenge Charlemagne's destruction of the walls of Pamplona. The battle is the inspiration for the twelfth-century *Song of Roland*, which focuses on the heroism and death of the Frankish commander, Roland (d. 778).

We went up the street, past the whitewashed stone houses, families sitting in their doorways watching us, to the inn.

The fat woman who ran the inn came out from the kitchen and shook hands with us. She took off her spectacles, wiped them, and put them on again. It was cold in the inn and the wind was starting to blow outside. The woman sent a girl up-stairs with us to show the room. There were two beds, a washstand, a clothes-chest, and a big, framed steel-engraving of Nuestra Señora de Roncesvalles.[5] The wind was blowing against the shutters. The room was on the north side of the inn. We washed, put on sweaters, and came downstairs into the dining-room. It had a stone floor, low ceiling, and was oak-panelled. The shutters were all up and it was so cold you could see your breath.

"My God!" said Bill. "It can't be this cold to-morrow. I'm not going to wade a stream in this weather."

There was an upright piano in the far corner of the room beyond the wooden tables and Bill went over and started to play.

"I got to keep warm," he said.

I went out to find the woman and ask her how much the room and board was. She put her hands under her apron and looked away from me.

"Twelve pesetas."

"Why, we only paid that in Pamplona."

She did not say anything, just took off her glasses and wiped them on her apron.

"That's too much," I said. "We didn't pay more than that at a big hotel."

"We've put in a bathroom."

"Haven't you got anything cheaper?"

"Not in the summer. Now is the big season."

We were the only people in the inn. Well, I thought, it's only a few days.

"Is the wine included?"

"Oh, yes."

"Well," I said. "It's all right."

I went back to Bill. He blew his breath at me to show how cold it was, and went on playing. I sat at one of the tables and looked at the pictures on the wall. There was one panel of rabbits, dead, one of pheasants, also dead, and one panel of dead ducks. The panels were all dark and smoky-looking. There was a cupboard full of liqueur bottles. I looked at them all. Bill was still playing. "How

5. Our Lady of Roncesvalles (Spanish), a thirteenth-century Gothic statue of the Virgin Mary located in the Collegiate Church of Santa Maria, Roncesvalles.

about a hot rum punch?" he said. "This isn't going to keep me warm permanently."

I went out and told the woman what a rum punch was and how to make it. In a few minutes a girl brought a stone pitcher, steaming, into the room. Bill came over from the piano and we drank the hot punch and listened to the wind.

"There isn't too much rum in that."

I went over to the cupboard and brought the rum bottle and poured a half-tumblerful into the pitcher.

"Direct action," said Bill. "It beats legislation."

The girl came in and laid the table for supper.

"It blows like hell up here," Bill said.

The girl brought in a big bowl of hot vegetable soup and the wine. We had fried trout afterward and some sort of a stew and a big bowl full of wild strawberries. We did not lose money on the wine, and the girl was shy but nice about bringing it. The old woman looked in once and counted the empty bottles.

After supper we went up-stairs and smoked and read in bed to keep warm. Once in the night I woke and heard the wind blowing. It felt good to be warm and in bed.

Chapter XII

When I woke in the morning I went to the window and looked out. It had cleared and there were no clouds on the mountains. Outside under the window were some carts and an old diligence,[1] the wood of the roof cracked and split by the weather. It must have been left from the days before the motor-buses. A goat hopped up on one of the carts and then to the roof of the diligence. He jerked his head at the other goats below and when I waved at him he bounded down.

Bill was still sleeping, so I dressed, put on my shoes outside in the hall, and went down-stairs. No one was stirring down-stairs, so I unbolted the door and went out. It was cool outside in the early morning and the sun had not yet dried the dew that had come when the wind died down. I hunted around in the shed behind the inn and found a sort of mattock, and went down toward the stream to try and dig some worms for bait. The stream was clear and shallow but it did not look trouty. On the grassy bank where it was damp I drove the mattock into the earth and loosened a chunk of sod. There were worms underneath. They slid out of sight as I lifted the sod and I dug carefully and got a good many. Digging at the edge of the

1. A horse-drawn coach.

damp ground I filled two empty tobacco-tins with worms and sifted dirt onto them. The goats watched me dig.

When I went back into the inn the woman was down in the kitchen, and I asked her to get coffee for us, and that we wanted a lunch. Bill was awake and sitting on the edge of the bed.

"I saw you out of the window," he said. "Didn't want to interrupt you. What were you doing? Burying your money?"

"You lazy bum!"

"Been working for the common good? Splendid. I want you to do that every morning."

"Come on," I said. "Get up."

"What? Get up? I never get up."

He climbed into bed and pulled the sheet up to his chin.

"Try and argue me into getting up."

I went on looking for the tackle and putting it all together in the tackle-bag.

"Aren't you interested?" Bill asked.

"I'm going down and eat."

"Eat? Why didn't you say eat? I thought you just wanted me to get up for fun. Eat? Fine. Now you're reasonable. You go out and dig some more worms and I'll be right down."

"Oh, go to hell!"

"Work for the good of all." Bill stepped into his underclothes. "Show irony and pity."

I started out of the room with the tackle-bag, the nets, and the rod-case.

"Hey! come back!"

I put my head in the door.

"Aren't you going to show a little irony and pity?"

I thumbed my nose.

"That's not irony."

As I went down-stairs I heard Bill singing, "Irony and pity. When you're feeling . . . Oh, Give them Irony and Give them Pity. Oh, give them Irony. When they're feeling . . . Just a little irony. Just a little pity . . ." He kept on singing until he came down-stairs. The tune was: "The Bells are Ringing for Me and my Gal."[2] I was reading a week-old Spanish paper.

"What's all this irony and pity?"

"What? Don't you know about Irony and Pity?"

"No. Who got it up?"

2. A popular song recorded in 1917, music written by George W. Meyer, with lyrics by Edgar Leslie and E. Ray Goetz. Hemingway's ellipses invite readers to hear possible rhymes with "pity," including some that might not have been printable in 1925.

"Everybody. They're mad about it in New York. It's just like the Fratellinis[3] used to be."

The girl came in with the coffee and buttered toast. Or, rather, it was bread toasted and buttered.

"Ask her if she's got any jam," Bill said. "Be ironical with her."

"Have you got any jam?"

"That's not ironical. I wish I could talk Spanish."

The coffee was good and we drank it out of big bowls. The girl brought in a glass dish of raspberry jam.

"Thank you."

"Hey! that's not the way," Bill said. "Say something ironical. Make some crack about Primo de Rivera."[4]

"I could ask her what kind of a jam they think they've gotten into in the Riff."[5]

"Poor," said Bill. "Very poor. You can't do it. That's all. You don't understand irony. You have no pity. Say something pitiful."

"Robert Cohn."

"Not so bad. That's better. Now why is Cohn pitiful? Be ironic."

He took a big gulp of coffee.

"Aw, hell!" I said. "It's too early in the morning."

"There you go. And you claim you want to be a writer, too. You're only a newspaper man. An expatriated newspaper man. You ought to be ironical the minute you get out of bed. You ought to wake up with your mouth full of pity."

"Go on," I said. "Who did you get this stuff from?"

"Everybody. Don't you read? Don't you ever see anybody? You know what you are? You're an expatriate. Why don't you live in New York? Then you'd know these things. What do you want me to do? Come over here and tell you every year?"

"Take some more coffee," I said.

"Good. Coffee is good for you. It's the caffeine in it. Caffeine, we are here. Caffeine puts a man on her horse and a woman in his grave. You know what's the trouble with you? You're an expatriate. One of the worst type. Haven't you heard that? Nobody that ever left their own country ever wrote anything worth printing. Not even in the newspapers."

He drank the coffee.

3. A popular family of circus performers renowned in Europe and the United States during the 1910s and 1920s.
4. Miguel Primo de Rivera y Orbaneja (1870–1930), the prime minister of Spain from 1923 to 1930. Appointed prime minister by King Alfonso XIII (1836–1931; reigned 1902–1931) after he led a coup, Primo de Rivera was a staunchly conservative and authoritarian ruler.
5. A region in northern Morocco (also known as the Rif). In 1923, Berbers in the Riff rebelled against the Spanish colonial authority there, producing the "jam" Jake refers to when they drove the Spanish to their coastal redoubts.

"You're an expatriate. You've lost touch with the soil. You get precious. Fake European standards have ruined you. You drink yourself to death. You become obsessed by sex. You spend all your time talking, not working. You are an expatriate, see? You hang around cafés."[6]

"It sounds like a swell life," I said. "When do I work?"

"You don't work. One group claims women support you. Another group claims you're impotent."

"No," I said. "I just had an accident."

"Never mention that," Bill said. "That's the sort of thing that can't be spoken of. That's what you ought to work up into a mystery. Like Henry's bicycle."[7]

He had been going splendidly, but he stopped. I was afraid he thought he had hurt me with that crack about being impotent. I wanted to start him again.

"It wasn't a bicycle," I said. "He was riding horseback."

"I heard it was a tricycle."

"Well," I said. "A plane is sort of like a tricycle. The joystick works the same way."

"But you don't pedal it."

"No," I said, "I guess you don't pedal it."

"Let's lay off that," Bill said.

"All right. I was just standing up for the tricycle."

"I think he's a good writer, too," Bill said. "And you're a hell of a good guy. Anybody ever tell you were a good guy?"

"I'm not a good guy."

"Listen. You're a hell of a good guy, and I'm fonder of you than anybody on earth. I couldn't tell you that in New York. It'd mean I was a faggot.[8] That was what the Civil War was about. Abraham Lincoln was a faggot. He was in love with General Grant. So was Jefferson Davis. Lincoln just freed the slaves on a bet. The Dred Scott case was framed by the Anti-Saloon League.[9] Sex explains

6. Bill's ironic speech about expatriates here channels complaints that nativist writers like H. L. Mencken (1880–1956) frequently made about American writers and artists who moved to Europe and "lost touch" with American virtues and values.

7. Refers to an apocryphal story about the American expatriate writer Henry James (1843–1916), who was supposed to have suffered an injury to his groin in a bicycle accident and been rendered impotent. The typescript of *The Sun Also Rises* reads "Like Henry James's bicycle," but, as in the case of the change of Hergesheimer to Hoffenheimer (see Book I, chapter VI), Hemingway was persuaded to revise the reference.

8. As with some other derogatory language in the novel's dialogue and narration, this homophobic term was not understood in the 1920s to enact the verbal violence or dehumanization that have come to be associated with it. Nevertheless, Bill does intend his reference to homosexuality to carry a negative connotation. Like Jake when he sees Brett with gay men at the *bal masque*, Bill assumes a negative attitude toward homosexuality as he insists that the relationship between him and Jake is emphatically not based on desire or sexual attraction.

9. Bill's suggestion that the Civil War grew out of a gay love triangle between President Abraham Lincoln, United States General Ulysses S. Grant, and Confederate States of

it all. The Colonel's Lady and Judy O'Grady are Lesbians under their skin."[1]

He stopped.

"Want to hear some more?"

"Shoot," I said.

"I don't know any more. Tell you some more at lunch."

"Old Bill," I said.

"You bum!"

We packed the lunch and two bottles of wine in the rucksack, and Bill put it on. I carried the rod-case and the landing-nets slung over my back. We started up the road and then went across a meadow and found a path that crossed the fields and went toward the woods on the slope of the first hill. We walked across the fields on the sandy path. The fields were rolling and grassy and the grass was short from the sheep grazing. The cattle were up in the hills. We heard their bells in the woods.

The path crossed a stream on a foot-log. The log was surfaced off, and there was a sapling bent across for a rail. In the flat pool beside the stream tadpoles spotted the sand. We went up a steep bank and across the rolling fields. Looking back we saw Burguete, white houses and red roofs, and the white road with a truck going along it and the dust rising.

Beyond the fields we crossed another faster-flowing stream. A sandy road led down to the ford and beyond into the woods. The path crossed the stream on another foot-log below the ford, and joined the road, and we went into the woods.

It was a beech wood and the trees were very old. Their roots bulked above the ground and the branches were twisted. We walked on the road between the thick trunks of the old beeches and the sunlight came through the leaves in light patches on the grass. The trees were big, and the foliage was thick but it was not gloomy. There was no undergrowth, only the smooth grass, very green and fresh, and the big gray trees well spaced as though it were a park.

"This is country," Bill said.

The road went up a hill and we got into thick woods, and the road kept on climbing. Sometimes it dipped down but rose again steeply.

America President Jefferson Davis is, of course, tongue in cheek, an ironic commentary on the fashion, among some intellectuals influenced by the writing of Sigmund Freud (1856–1939), to reduce all kinds of phenomena to patterns of sexual desire ("Sex explains it all"). His explanation of the infamous Supreme Court decision in *Dred Scott v. Sandford* (1857) (which held that enslaved persons were not and could not be citizens entitled to sue whites who owned them) in terms of the Anti-Saloon League (an organization dedicated to "temperance," or the opposition to consuming alcoholic beverages, and a leading voice for prohibition in the early 1900s) is a swipe at American provincialism.

1. Bill revises the concluding line of Rudyard Kipling's (1865–1936) poem "The Ladies" (published in *Rudyard Kipling's Verse*, 1922): "The Colonel's Lady and Judy O'Grady are sisters under their skins!"

All the time we heard the cattle in the woods. Finally, the road came out on the top of the hills. We were on the top of the height of land that was the highest part of the range of wooded hills we had seen from Burguete. There were wild strawberries growing on the sunny side of the ridge in a little clearing in the trees.

Ahead the road came out of the forest and went along the shoulder of the ridge of hills. The hills ahead were not wooded, and there were great fields of yellow gorse. Way off we saw the steep bluffs, dark with trees and jutting with gray stone, that marked the course of the Irati River.[2]

"We have to follow this road along the ridge, cross these hills, go through the woods on the far hills, and come down to the Irati valley," I pointed out to Bill.

"That's a hell of a hike."

"It's too far to go and fish and come back the same day, comfortably."

"Comfortably. That's a nice word. We'll have to go like hell to get there and back and have any fishing at all."

It was a long walk and the country was very fine, but we were tired when we came down the steep road that led out of the wooded hills into the valley of the Río de la Fábrica.[3]

The road came out from the shadow of the woods into the hot sun. Ahead was a river-valley. Beyond the river was a steep hill. There was a field of buckwheat on the hill. We saw a white house under some trees on the hillside. It was very hot and we stopped under some trees beside a dam that crossed the river.

Bill put the pack against one of the trees and we jointed up the rods, put on the reels, tied on leaders, and got ready to fish.

"You're sure this thing has trout in it?" Bill asked.

"It's full of them."

"I'm going to fish a fly. You got any McGintys?"[4]

"There's some in there."

"You going to fish bait?"

"Yeah. I'm going to fish the dam here."

"Well, I'll take the fly-book, then." He tied on a fly. "Where'd I better go? Up or down?"

"Down is the best. They're plenty up above, too."

Bill went down the bank.

"Take a worm can."

2. A tributary of the Aragon River in northeastern Spain.

3. River of the factory (Spanish), a tributary stream of the Irati named for the firearms factory and the village that grew up around the factory in the nineteenth century.

4. A fly lure popular among trout fishermen from the late nineteenth and early twentieth centuries.

"No, I don't want one. If they won't take a fly I'll just flick it around."

Bill was down below watching the stream.

"Say," he called up against the noise of the dam. "How about putting the wine in that spring up the road?"

"All right," I shouted. Bill waved his hand and started down the stream. I found the two wine-bottles in the pack, and carried them up the road to where the water of a spring flowed out of an iron pipe. There was a board over the spring and I lifted it and, knocking the corks firmly into the bottles, lowered them down into the water. It was so cold my hand and wrist felt numbed. I put back the slab of wood, and hoped nobody would find the wine.

I got my rod that was leaning against the tree, took the bait-can and landing-net, and walked out onto the dam. It was built to provide a head of water for driving logs. The gate was up, and I sat on one of the squared timbers and watched the smooth apron of water before the river tumbled into the falls. In the white water at the foot of the dam it was deep. As I baited up, a trout shot up out of the white water into the falls and was carried down. Before I could finish baiting, another trout jumped at the falls, making the same lovely arc and disappearing into the water that was thundering down. I put on a good-sized sinker and dropped into the white water close to the edge of the timbers of the dam.

I did not feel the first trout strike. When I started to pull up I felt that I had one and brought him, fighting and bending the rod almost double, out of the boiling water at the foot of the falls, and swung him up and onto the dam. He was a good trout, and I banged his head against the timber so that he quivered out straight, and then slipped him into my bag.

While I had him on, several trout had jumped at the falls. As soon as I baited up and dropped in again I hooked another and brought him in the same way. In a little while I had six. They were all about the same size. I laid them out, side by side, all their heads pointing the same way, and looked at them. They were beautifully colored and firm and hard from the cold water. It was a hot day, so I slit them all and shucked out the insides, gills and all, and tossed them over across the river. I took the trout ashore, washed them in the cold, smoothly heavy water above the dam, and then picked some ferns and packed them all in the bag, three trout on a layer of ferns, then another layer of ferns, then three more trout, and then covered them with ferns. They looked nice in the ferns, and now the bag was bulky, and I put it in the shade of the tree.

It was very hot on the dam, so I put my worm-can in the shade with the bag, and got a book out of the pack and settled down under the tree to read until Bill should come up for lunch.

It was a little past noon and there was not much shade, but I sat against the trunk of two of the trees that grew together, and read. The book was something by A. E. W. Mason,[5] and I was reading a wonderful story about a man who had been frozen in the Alps and then fallen into a glacier and disappeared, and his bride was going to wait twenty-four years exactly for his body to come out on the moraine, while her true love waited too, and they were still waiting when Bill came up.

"Get any?" he asked. He had his rod and his bag and his net all in one hand, and he was sweating. I hadn't heard him come up, because of the noise from the dam.

"Six. What did you get?"

Bill sat down, opened up his bag, laid a big trout on the grass. He took out three more, each one a little bigger than the last, and laid them side by side in the shade from the tree. His face was sweaty and happy.

"How are yours?"

"Smaller."

"Let's see them."

"They're packed."

"How big are they really?"

"They're all about the size of your smallest."

"You're not holding out on me?"

"I wish I were."

"Get them all on worms?"

"Yes."

"You lazy bum!"

Bill put the trout in the bag and started for the river, swinging the open bag. He was wet from the waist down and I knew he must have been wading the stream.

I walked up the road and got out the two bottles of wine. They were cold. Moisture beaded on the bottles as I walked back to the trees. I spread the lunch on a newspaper, and uncorked one of the bottles and leaned the other against a tree. Bill came up drying his hands, his bag plump with ferns.

"Let's see that bottle," he said. He pulled the cork, and tipped up the bottle and drank. "Whew! That makes my eyes ache."

"Let's try it."

The wine was icy cold and tasted faintly rusty.

"That's not such filthy wine," Bill said.

"The cold helps it," I said.

5. Alfred Edward Woodley Mason (1865–1948), English author best known for *The Four Feathers*, his 1902 novel about cowardice during wartime. Jake describes Mason's story "The Crystal Trench," which appeared in his story collection *The Four Corners of the World* (1917).

We unwrapped the little parcels of lunch.

"Chicken."

"There's hard-boiled eggs."

"Find any salt?"

"First the egg," said Bill. "Then the chicken. Even Bryan[6] could see that."

"He's dead. I read it in the paper yesterday."

"No. Not really?"

"Yes. Bryan's dead."

Bill laid down the egg he was peeling.

"Gentlemen," he said, and unwrapped a drumstick from a piece of newspaper. "I reverse the order. For Bryan's sake. As a tribute to the Great Commoner. First the chicken; then the egg."

"Wonder what day God created the chicken?"

"Oh," said Bill, sucking the drumstick, "how should we know? We should not question. Our stay on earth is not for long. Let us rejoice and believe and give thanks."

"Eat an egg."

Bill gestured with the drumstick in one hand and the bottle of wine in the other.

"Let us rejoice in our blessings. Let us utilize the fowls of the air. Let us utilize the product of the vine. Will you utilize a little, brother?"

"After you, brother."

Bill took a long drink.

"Utilize a little, brother," he handed me the bottle. "Let us not doubt, brother. Let us not pry into the holy mysteries of the hencoop with simian fingers. Let us accept on faith and simply say—I want you to join with me in saying—What shall we say, brother?" He pointed the drumstick at me and went on. "Let me tell you. We will say, and I for one am proud to say—and I want you to say with me, on your knees, brother. Let no man be ashamed to kneel here in the great out-of-doors. Remember the woods were God's first temples. Let us kneel and say: 'Don't eat that, Lady—that's Mencken.'"

"Here," I said. "Utilize a little of this."

We uncorked the other bottle.

"What's the matter?" I said. "Didn't you like Bryan?"

6. William Jennings Bryan (1860–1925), an American politician from Nebraska. Known as "The Great Commoner," he ran for president three times as the nominee of the Democratic Party. After the end of his political career, Bryan became a spokesperson for fundamentalist Protestant Christianity and an opponent of the teaching of Charles Darwin's theory of evolution. In 1925, he participated in the Scopes "Monkey Trial" in Dayton, Tennessee, joining the prosecution of John Scopes for violation of a law that barred the teaching of evolution in Tennessee public schools. Bryan's death on July 26, 1925, does not fit with Jake's announcement, given the novel's timeline (Jake and Bill are fishing in late June, before Bryan died).

"I loved Bryan," said Bill. "We were like brothers."

"Where did you know him?"

"He and Mencken and I all went to Holy Cross[7] together."

"And Frankie Frisch."

"It's a lie. Frankie Frisch went to Fordham."[8]

"Well," I said, "I went to Loyola with Bishop Manning."[9]

"It's a lie," Bill said. "I went to Loyola with Bishop Manning myself."

"You're cock-eyed," I said.

"On wine?"

"Why not?"

"It's the humidity," Bill said. "They ought to take this damn humidity away."

"Have another shot."

"Is this all we've got?"

"Only the two bottles."

"Do you know what you are?" Bill looked at the bottle affectionately.

"No," I said.

"You're in the pay of the Anti-Saloon League."

"I went to Notre Dame with Wayne B. Wheeler."[1]

"It's a lie," said Bill. "I went to Austin Business College with Wayne B. Wheeler. He was class president."

"Well," I said, "the saloon must go."

"You're right there, old classmate," Bill said. "The saloon must go, and I will take it with me."

"You're cock-eyed."

"On wine?"

"On wine."

"Well, maybe I am."

"Want to take a nap?"

"All right."

We lay with our heads in the shade and looked up into the trees.

"You asleep?"

"No," Bill said. "I was thinking."

7. The College of the Holy Cross, a Jesuit university in Worcester, Massachusetts (founded 1843). Needless to say, neither Mencken nor Bill Gorton (nor Donald Ogden Stewart, on whom Bill was partially based) attended Holy Cross.

8. Frankie Frisch (1898–1973), second-baseman for the New York Giants and, starting in 1927, the St. Louis Cardinals. A graduate of Fordham University (a Jesuit university in the Bronx, New York, founded in 1841), he was nicknamed the Fordham Flash.

9. William T. Manning (1866–1949), Episcopal Bishop of New York City (1921–46). A graduate of the University of the South (Sewanee, Tennessee), he did not attend any of the several Jesuit Loyola universities (in Chicago or New Orleans or Maryland) in the United States.

1. A leading American prohibitionist (1869–1927), for many years the head of the Anti-Saloon League. He did not attend the University of Notre Dame (a Catholic university in South Bend, Indiana, founded in 1842). Nor did he attend Austin Business College; he graduated from Oberlin College, in Ohio.

I shut my eyes. It felt good lying on the ground.

"Say," Bill said, "what about this Brett business?"

"What about it?"

"Were you ever in love with her?"

"Sure."

"For how long?"

"Off and on for a hell of a long time."

"Oh, hell!" Bill said. "I'm sorry, fella."

"It's all right," I said. "I don't give a damn any more."

"Really?"

"Really. Only I'd a hell of a lot rather not talk about it."

"You aren't sore I asked you?"

"Why the hell should I be?"

"I'm going to sleep," Bill said. He put a newspaper over his face.

"Listen, Jake," he said, "are you really a Catholic?"

"Technically."

"What does that mean?"

"I don't know."

"All right, I'll go to sleep now," he said. "Don't keep me awake by talking so much."

I went to sleep, too. When I woke up Bill was packing the rucksack. It was late in the afternoon and the shadow from the trees was long and went out over the dam. I was stiff from sleeping on the ground.

"What did you do? Wake up?" Bill asked. "Why didn't you spend the night?" I stretched and rubbed my eyes.

"I had a lovely dream," Bill said. "I don't remember what it was about, but it was a lovely dream."

"I don't think I dreamt."

"You ought to dream," Bill said. "All our biggest business men have been dreamers. Look at Ford. Look at President Coolidge. Look at Rockefeller. Look at Jo Davidson."[2]

I disjointed my rod and Bill's and packed them in the rod-case. I put the reels in the tackle-bag. Bill had packed the rucksack and we put one of the trout-bags in. I carried the other.

"Well," said Bill, "have we got everything?"

"The worms."

"Your worms. Put them in there."

2. Bill lists four men not known for being "dreamers": industrialist, Henry Ford (1863–1947); President Calvin Coolidge (1872–1933); oil tycoon, John D. Rockefeller (1839–1937); and sculptor Jo Davidson (1883–1952). Hemingway had met Davidson in 1922, when the sculptor was in Genoa to work on portraits of statesmen gathered there for a conference, and Davidson produced a bronze portrait of Gertrude Stein (1874–1946), which Hemingway might have seen, in 1923.

He had the pack on his back and I put the worm-cans in one of the outside flap pockets.

"You got everything now?"

I looked around on the grass at the foot of the elm-trees.

"Yes."

We started up the road into the woods. It was a long walk home to Burguete, and it was dark when we came down across the fields to the road, and along the road between the houses of the town, their windows lighted, to the inn.

We stayed five days at Burguete and had good fishing. The nights were cold and the days were hot, and there was always a breeze even in the heat of the day. It was hot enough so that it felt good to wade in a cold stream, and the sun dried you when you came out and sat on the bank. We found a stream with a pool deep enough to swim in. In the evenings we played three-handed bridge with an Englishman named Harris, who had walked over from Saint Jean Pied de Port[3] and was stopping at the inn for the fishing. He was very pleasant and went with us twice to the Irati River. There was no word from Robert Cohn nor from Brett and Mike.

Chapter XIII

One morning I went down to breakfast and the Englishman, Harris, was already at the table. He was reading the paper through spectacles. He looked up and smiled.

"Good morning," he said. "Letter for you. I stopped at the post and they gave it me with mine."

The letter was at my place at the table, leaning against a coffee-cup. Harris was reading the paper again. I opened the letter. It had been forwarded from Pamplona. It was dated San Sebastian, Sunday:

Dear Jake,

We got here Friday, Brett passed out on the train, so brought her here for 3 days rest with old friends of ours. We go to Montoya Hotel Pamplona Tuesday, arriving at I don't know what hour. Will you send a note by the bus to tell us what to do to rejoin you all on Wednesday. All our love and sorry to be late, but Brett was really done in and will be quite all right by Tues. and is practically so now. I know her so well and try to look after her but it's not so easy. Love to all the chaps,

Michael.

3. A village in French Navarre, near the Pass of Roncevaux.

"What day of the week is it?" I asked Harris.

"Wednesday, I think. Yes, quite. Wednesday. Wonderful how one loses track of the days up here in the mountains."

"Yes. We've been here nearly a week."

"I hope you're not thinking of leaving?"

"Yes. We'll go in on the afternoon bus, I'm afraid."

"What a rotten business. I had hoped we'd all have another go at the Irati together."

"We have to go in to Pamplona. We're meeting people there."

"What rotten luck for me. We've had a jolly time here at Burguete."

"Come on in to Pamplona. We can play some bridge there, and there's going to be a damned fine fiesta."

"I'd like to. Awfully nice of you to ask me. I'd best stop on here, though. I've not much more time to fish."

"You want those big ones in the Irati."

"I say, I do, you know. They're enormous trout there."

"I'd like to try them once more."

"Do. Stop over another day. Be a good chap."

"We really have to get into town," I said.

"What a pity."

After breakfast Bill and I were sitting warming in the sun on a bench out in front of the inn and talking it over. I saw a girl coming up the road from the centre of the town. She stopped in front of us and took a telegram out of the leather wallet that hung against her skirt.

"Para ustedes[1]?"

I looked at it. The address was: "Barnes, Burguete."

"Yes. It's for us."

She brought out a book for me to sign, and I gave her a couple of coppers. The telegram was in Spanish:

VENGO JUEVES COHN[2]

I handed it to Bill.

"What does the word Cohn mean?" he asked.

"What a lousy telegram!" I said. "He could send ten words for the same price. 'I come Thursday'. That gives you a lot of dope, doesn't it?"

"It gives you all the dope that's of interest to Cohn."

"We're going in, anyway," I said. "There's no use trying to move Brett and Mike out here and back before the fiesta. Should we answer it?"

"We might as well," said Bill. "There's no need for us to be snooty."

1. "For you?" (Spanish).
2. I come Thursday (Spanish).

We walked up to the post-office and asked for a telegraph blank.

"What will we say?" Bill asked.

"'Arriving to-night.' That's enough."

We paid for the message and walked back to the inn. Harris was there and the three of us walked up to Roncesvalles. We went through the monastery.

"It's a remarkable place," Harris said, when we came out. "But you know I'm not much on those sort of places."

"Me either," Bill said.

"It's a remarkable place, though," Harris said. "I wouldn't not have seen it. I'd been intending coming up each day."

"It isn't the same as fishing, though, is it?" Bill asked. He liked Harris.

"I say not."

We were standing in front of the old chapel of the monastery.

"Isn't that a pub across the way?" Harris asked. "Or do my eyes deceive me?"

"It has the look of a pub," Bill said.

"It looks to me like a pub," I said.

"I say," said Harris, "let's utilize it." He had taken up utilizing from Bill.

We had a bottle of wine apiece. Harris would not let us pay.

He talked Spanish quite well, and the innkeeper would not take our money.

"I say. You don't know what it's meant to me to have you chaps up here."

"We've had a grand time, Harris."

Harris was a little tight.

"I say. Really you don't know how much it means. I've not had much fun since the war."

"We'll fish together again, some time. Don't you forget it, Harris."

"We must. We *have* had such a jolly good time."

"How about another bottle around?"

"Jolly good idea," said Harris.

"This is mine," said Bill. "Or we don't drink it."

"I wish you'd let me pay for it. It *does* give me pleasure, you know."

"This is going to give me pleasure," Bill said.

The innkeeper brought in the fourth bottle. We had kept the same glasses. Harris lifted his glass.

"I say. You know this does utilize well."

Bill slapped him on the back.

"Good old Harris."

"I say. You know my name isn't really Harris. It's Wilson-Harris. All one name. With a hyphen, you know."

"Good old Wilson-Harris," Bill said. "We call you Harris because we're so fond of you."

"I say, Barnes. You don't know what this all means to me."

"Come on and utilize another glass," I said.

"Barnes. Really, Barnes, you can't know. That's all."

"Drink up, Harris."

We walked back down the road from Roncesvalles with Harris between us. We had lunch at the inn and Harris went with us to the bus. He gave us his card, with his address in London and his club and his business address, and as we got on the bus he handed us each an envelope. I opened mine and there were a dozen flies in it. Harris had tied them himself. He tied all his own flies.

"I say, Harris—" I began.

"No, no!" he said. He was climbing down from the bus. "They're not first-rate flies at all. I only thought if you fished them some time it might remind you of what a good time we had."

The bus started. Harris stood in front of the post-office. He waved. As we started along the road he turned and walked back toward the inn.

"Say, wasn't that Harris nice?" Bill said.

"I think he really did have a good time."

"Harris? You bet he did."

"I wish he'd come into Pamplona."

"He wanted to fish."

"Yes. You couldn't tell how English would mix with each other, anyway."

"I suppose not."

We got into Pamplona late in the afternoon and the bus stopped in front of the Hotel Montoya. Out in the plaza they were stringing electric-light wires to light the plaza for the fiesta. A few kids came up when the bus stopped, and a customs officer for the town made all the people getting down from the bus open their bundles on the sidewalk. We went into the hotel and on the stairs I met Montoya. He shook hands with us, smiling in his embarrassed way.

"Your friends are here," he said.

"Mr. Campbell?"

"Yes. Mr. Cohn and Mr. Campbell and Lady Ashley."

He smiled as though there were something I would hear about.

"When did they get in?"

"Yesterday. I've saved you the rooms you had."

"That's fine. Did you give Mr. Campbell the room on the plaza?"

"Yes. All the rooms we looked at."

"Where are our friends now?"

"I think they went to the pelota."

"And how about the bulls?"

Montoya smiled. "To-night," he said. "To-night at seven o'clock they bring in the Villar bulls, and to-morrow come the Miuras.[3] Do you all go down?"

"Oh, yes. They've never seen a desencajonada."[4]

Montoya put his hand on my shoulder.

"I'll see you there."

He smiled again. He always smiled as though bull-fighting were a very special secret between the two of us; a rather shocking but really very deep secret that we knew about. He always smiled as though there were something lewd about the secret to outsiders, but that it was something that we understood. It would not do to expose it to people who would not understand.

"Your friend, is he aficionado,[5] too?" Montoya smiled at Bill.

"Yes. He came all the way from New York to see the San Fermines."

"Yes?" Montoya politely disbelieved. "But he's not aficionado like you."

He put his hand on my shoulder again embarrassedly.

"Yes," I said. "He's a real aficionado."

"But he's not aficionado like you are."

Afición means passion. An aficionado is one who is passionate about the bull-fights. All the good bull-fighters stayed at Montoya's hotel; that is, those with afición stayed there. The commercial bull-fighters stayed once, perhaps, and then did not come back. The good ones came each year. In Montoya's room were their photographs. The photographs were dedicated to Juanito Montoya or to his sister. The photographs of bull-fighters Montoya had really believed in were framed. Photographs of bull-fighters who had been without afición Montoya kept in a drawer of his desk. They often had the most flattering inscriptions. But they did not mean anything. One day Montoya took them all out and dropped them in the waste-basket. He did not want them around.

We often talked about bulls and bull-fighters. I had stopped at the Montoya for several years. We never talked for very long at a time. It was simply the pleasure of discovering what we each felt. Men would come in from distant towns and before they left Pamplona

3. Two breeds of bulls especially bred for fighting from the lineage of the Villar cattle ranch and the Miura cattle ranch in Seville. Hemingway writes about both breeds in *Death in the Afternoon*, singling out these breeds as "ideal bulls."

4. Literally "to take out of a box" (Spanish). Here, Jake refers to the *desencajonada del toros*, the release of the newly arrived bulls from their railroad cars into the paddock at Pamplona.

5. One with knowledge and enthusiasm for a subject or pastime (Spanish). As Jake says a few lines later, "an aficionado is one who is passionate about the bull-fights." The term has a deep significance for Montoya and Jake, signifying membership in a select community of knowledge and passion. Montoya recognizes their shared membership not only with this word but also with the gesture of putting his hand on Jake's shoulder.

stop and talk for a few minutes with Montoya about bulls. These men were aficionados. Those who were aficionados could always get rooms even when the hotel was full. Montoya introduced me to some of them. They were always very polite at first, and it amused them very much that I should be an American. Somehow it was taken for granted that an American could not have afición. He might simulate it or confuse it with excitement, but he could not really have it. When they saw that I had afición, and there was no password, no set questions that could bring it out, rather it was a sort of oral spiritual examination with the questions always a little on the defensive and never apparent, there was this same embarrassed putting the hand on the shoulder, or a "Buen hombre."[6] But nearly always there was the actual touching. It seemed as though they wanted to touch you to make it certain.

Montoya could forgive anything of a bull-fighter who had afición. He could forgive attacks of nerves, panic, bad unexplainable actions, all sorts of lapses. For one who had afición he could forgive anything. At once he forgave me all my friends. Without his ever saying anything they were simply a little something shameful between us, like the spilling open of the horses in bull-fighting.

Bill had gone up-stairs as we came in, and I found him washing and changing in his room.

"Well," he said, "talk a lot of Spanish?"

"He was telling me about the bulls coming in tonight."

"Let's find the gang and go down."

"All right. They'll probably be at the café."

"Have you got tickets?"

"Yes. I got them for all the unloadings."

"What's it like?" He was pulling his cheek before the glass, looking to see if there were unshaved patches under the line of the jaw.

"It's pretty good," I said. "They let the bulls out of the cages one at a time, and they have steers in the corral to receive them and keep them from fighting, and the bulls tear in at the steers and the steers run around like old maids trying to quiet them down."

"Do they ever gore the steers?"

"Sure. Sometimes they go right after them and kill them."

"Can't the steers do anything?"

"No. They're trying to make friends."

"What do they have them in for?"

"To quiet down the bulls and keep them from breaking their horns against the stone walls, or goring each other."

"Must be swell being a steer."

We went down the stairs and out of the door and walked across the square toward the café Iruña. There were two lonely looking

6. "Good man" (Spanish).

ticket-houses standing in the square. Their windows, marked SOL, SOL Y SOMBRA, and SOMBRA, were shut.[7] They would not open until the day before the fiesta.

Across the square the white wicker tables and chairs of the Iruña extended out beyond the Arcade to the edge of the street. I looked for Brett and Mike at the tables. There they were. Brett and Mike and Robert Cohn. Brett was wearing a Basque beret. So was Mike. Robert Cohn was bare-headed and wearing his spectacles. Brett saw us coming and waved. Her eyes crinkled up as we came up to the table.

"Hello, you chaps!" she called.

Brett was happy. Mike had a way of getting an intensity of feeling into shaking hands. Robert Cohn shook hands because we were back.

"Where the hell have you been?" I asked.

"I brought them up here," Cohn said.

"What rot," Brett said. "We'd have gotten here earlier if you hadn't come."

"You'd never have gotten here."

"What rot! You chaps are brown. Look at Bill."

"Did you get good fishing?" Mike asked. "We wanted to join you."

"It wasn't bad. We missed you."

"I wanted to come," Cohn said, "but I thought I ought to bring them."

"You bring us. What rot."

"Was it really good?" Mike asked. "Did you take many?"

"Some days we took a dozen apiece. There was an Englishman up there."

"Named Harris," Bill said. "Ever know him, Mike? He was in the war, too."

"Fortunate fellow," Mike said. "What times we had. How I wish those dear days were back."

"Don't be an ass."

"Were you in the war, Mike?" Cohn asked.

"Was I not."

"He was a very distinguished soldier," Brett said. "Tell them about the time your horse bolted down Piccadilly."

"I'll not. I've told that four times."

"You never told me," Robert Cohn said.

"I'll not tell that story. It reflects discredit on me."

"Tell them about your medals."

"I'll not. That story reflects great discredit on me."

"What story's that?"

7. Tickets are sold for different prices depending on whether the seats are in the sun (SOL), sun and shadow (SOL Y SOMBRA), or wholly shaded (SOMBRA).

"Brett will tell you. She tells all the stories that reflect discredit on me."

"Go on. Tell it, Brett."

"Should I?"

"I'll tell it myself."

"What medals have you got, Mike?"

"I haven't got any medals."

"You must have some."

"I suppose I've the usual medals. But I never sent in for them. One time there was this whopping big dinner and the Prince of Wales was to be there, and the cards said medals will be worn. So naturally I had no medals, and I stopped at my tailor's and he was impressed by the invitation, and I thought that's a good piece of business, and I said to him: 'You've got to fix me up with some medals.' He said: 'What medals, sir?' And I said: 'Oh, any medals. Just give me a few medals.' So he said: 'What medals *have* you, sir?' And I said: 'How should I know?' Did he think I spent all my time reading the bloody gazette? 'Just give me a good lot. Pick them out yourself.' So he got me some medals, you know, miniature medals, and handed me the box, and I put it in my pocket and forgot it. Well, I went to the dinner, and it was the night they'd shot Henry Wilson,[8] so the Prince didn't come and the King didn't come, and no one wore any medals, and all these coves were busy taking off their medals, and I had mine in my pocket."

He stopped for us to laugh.

"Is that all?"

"That's all. Perhaps I didn't tell it right."

"You didn't," said Brett. "But no matter."

We were all laughing.

"Ah, yes," said Mike. "I know now. It was a damn dull dinner, and I couldn't stick it, so I left. Later on in the evening I found the box in my pocket. What's this? I said. Medals? Bloody military medals? So I cut them all off their backing—you know, they put them on a strip—and gave them all around. Gave one to each girl. Form of souvenir. They thought I was hell's own shakes of a soldier. Give away medals in a night club. Dashing fellow."

"Tell the rest," Brett said.

"Don't you think that was funny?" Mike asked. We were all laughing. "It was. I swear it was. Any rate, my tailor wrote me and wanted

8. Sir Henry Wilson (1864–1922), British Field Marshal and Baronet who served as a senior staff officer in the British Army during the First World War. After the war, he was a Member of Parliament and adviser to the government of the newly formed Northern Ireland (after the partition of Ireland following the war of rebellion there in 1922). Wilson was shot to death by members of the Irish Republican Army (which had opposed the partition) on June 22, 1922, after unveiling a war memorial at London's Liverpool Street Station.

the medals back. Sent a man around. Kept on writing for months. Seems some chap had left them to be cleaned. Frightfully military cove. Set hell's own store by them." Mike paused. "Rotten luck for the tailor," he said.

"You don't mean it," Bill said. "I should think it would have been grand for the tailor."

"Frightfully good tailor. Never believe it to see me now," Mike said. "I used to pay him a hundred pounds a year just to keep him quiet. So he wouldn't send me any bills. Frightful blow to him when I went bankrupt. It was right after the medals. Gave his letters rather a bitter tone."

"How did you go bankrupt?" Bill asked.

"Two ways," Mike said. "Gradually and then suddenly."

"What brought it on?"

"Friends," said Mike. "I had a lot of friends. False friends. Then I had creditors, too. Probably had more creditors than anybody in England."

"Tell them about in the court," Brett said.

"I don't remember," Mike said. "I was just a little tight."

"Tight!" Brett exclaimed. "You were blind!"

"Extraordinary thing," Mike said. "Met my former partner the other day. Offered to buy me a drink."

"Tell them about your learned counsel," Brett said.

"I will not," Mike said. "My learned counsel was blind, too. I say this is a gloomy subject. Are we going down and see these bulls unloaded or not?"

"Let's go down."

We called the waiter, paid, and started to walk through the town. I started off walking with Brett, but Robert Cohn came up and joined her on the other side. The three of us walked along, past the Ayuntamiento with the banners hung from the balcony, down past the market and down past the steep street that led to the bridge across the Arga.[9] There were many people walking to go and see the bulls, and carriages drove down the hill and across the bridge, the drivers, the horses, and the whips rising above the walking people in the street. Across the bridge we turned up a road to the corrals. We passed a wine-shop with a sign in the window: Good Wine 30 Céntimos A Liter.

"That's where we'll go when funds get low," Brett said.

The woman standing in the door of the wine-shop looked at us as we passed. She called to some one in the house and three girls came to the window and stared. They were staring at Brett.

9. A tributary of the Aragon River that flows through Pamplona.

At the gate of the corrals two men took tickets from the people that went in. We went in through the gate. There were trees inside and a low, stone house. At the far end was the stone wall of the corrals, with apertures in the stone that were like loop-holes running all along the face of each corral. A ladder led up to the top of the wall, and people were climbing up the ladder and spreading down to stand on the walls that separated the two corrals. As we came up to the ladder, walking across the grass under the trees, we passed the big, gray painted cages with the bulls in them. There was one bull in each travelling-box. They had come by train from a bull-breeding ranch in Castile,[1] and had been unloaded off flat-cars at the station and brought up here to be let out of their cages into the corrals. Each cage was stencilled with the name and the brand of the bull-breeder.

We climbed up and found a place on the wall looking down into the corral. The stone walls were whitewashed, and there was straw on the ground and wooden feed-boxes and water-troughs set against the wall.

"Look up there," I said.

Beyond the river rose the plateau of the town. All along the old walls and ramparts people were standing. The three lines of fortifications made three black lines of people. Above the walls there were heads in the windows of the houses. At the far end of the plateau boys had climbed into the trees.

"They must think something is going to happen," Brett said.

"They want to see the bulls."

Mike and Bill were on the other wall across the pit of the corral. They waved to us. People who had come late were standing behind us, pressing against us when other people crowded them.

"Why don't they start?" Robert Cohn asked.

A single mule was hitched to one of the cages and dragged it up against the gate in the corral wall. The men shoved and lifted it with crowbars into position against the gate. Men were standing on the wall ready to pull up the gate of the corral and then the gate of the cage. At the other end of the corral a gate opened and two steers came in, swaying their heads and trotting, their lean flanks swinging. They stood together at the far end, their heads toward the gate where the bull would enter.

"They don't look happy," Brett said.

The men on top of the wall leaned back and pulled up the door of the corral. Then they pulled up the door of the cage.

1. Large region of central Spain that comprises the former kingdoms of Castile, Aragon, and Spain.

I leaned way over the wall and tried to see into the cage. It was dark. Some one rapped on the cage with an iron bar. Inside something seemed to explode. The bull, striking into the wood from side to side with his horns, made a great noise. Then I saw a dark muzzle and the shadow of horns, and then, with a clattering on the wood in the hollow box, the bull charged and came out into the corral, skidding with his forefeet in the straw as he stopped, his head up, the great hump of muscle on his neck swollen tight, his body muscles quivering as he looked up at the crowd on the stone walls. The two steers backed away against the wall, their heads sunken, their eyes watching the bull.

The bull saw them and charged. A man shouted from behind one of the boxes and slapped his hat against the planks, and the bull, before he reached the steer, turned, gathered himself and charged where the man had been, trying to reach him behind the planks with a half-dozen quick, searching drives with the right horn.

"My God, isn't he beautiful?" Brett said. We were looking right down on him.

"Look how he knows how to use his horns," I said. "He's got a left and a right just like a boxer."

"Not really?"

"You watch."

"It goes too fast."

"Wait. There'll be another one in a minute."

They had backed up another cage into the entrance. In the far corner a man, from behind one of the plank shelters, attracted the bull, and while the bull was facing away the gate was pulled up and a second bull came out into the corral.

He charged straight for the steers and two men ran out from behind the planks and shouted, to turn him. He did not change his direction and the men shouted: "Hah! Hah! Toro!"[2] and waved their arms; the two steers turned sideways to take the shock, and the bull drove into one of the steers.

"Don't look," I said to Brett. She was watching, fascinated.

"Fine," I said. "If it doesn't buck you."

"I saw it," she said. "I saw him shift from his left to his right horn."

"Damn good!"

The steer was down now, his neck stretched out, his head twisted, he lay the way he had fallen. Suddenly the bull left off and made for the other steer which had been standing at the far end, his head swinging, watching it all. The steer ran awkwardly and the bull caught him, hooked him lightly in the flank, and then turned away and looked up at the crowd on the walls, his crest of muscle rising.

2. Bull (Spanish).

The steer came up to him and made as though to nose at him and the bull hooked perfunctorily. The next time he nosed at the steer and then the two of them trotted over to the other bull.

When the next bull came out, all three, the two bulls and the steer, stood together, their heads side by side, their horns against the newcomer. In a few minutes the steer picked the new bull up, quieted him down, and made him one of the herd. When the last two bulls had been unloaded the herd were all together.

The steer who had been gored had gotten to his feet and stood against the stone wall. None of the bulls came near him, and he did not attempt to join the herd.

We climbed down from the wall with the crowd, and had a last look at the bulls through the loopholes in the wall of the corral. They were all quiet now, their heads down. We got a carriage outside and rode up to the café. Mike and Bill came in half an hour later. They had stopped on the way for several drinks.

We were sitting in the café.

"That's an extraordinary business," Brett said.

"Will those last ones fight as well as the first?" Robert Cohn asked. "They seemed to quiet down awfully fast."

"They all know each other," I said. "They're only dangerous when they're alone, or only two or three of them together."

"What do you mean, dangerous?" Bill said. "They all looked dangerous to me."

"They only want to kill when they're alone. Of course, if you went in there you'd probably detach one of them from the herd, and he'd be dangerous."

"That's too complicated," Bill said. "Don't you ever detach me from the herd, Mike."

"I say," Mike said, "they *were* fine bulls, weren't they? Did you see their horns?"

"Did I not," said Brett. "I had no idea what they were like."

"Did you see the one hit that steer?" Mike asked. "That was extraordinary."

"It's no life being a steer," Robert Cohn said.

"Don't you think so?" Mike said. "I would have thought you'd loved being a steer, Robert."

"What do you mean, Mike?"

"They lead such a quiet life. They never say anything and they're always hanging about so."

We were embarrassed. Bill laughed. Robert Cohn was angry. Mike went on talking.

"I should think you'd love it. You'd never have to say a word. Come on, Robert. Do say something. Don't just sit there."

"I said something, Mike. Don't you remember? About the steers."

"Oh, say something more. Say something funny. Can't you see we're all having a good time here?"

"Come off it, Michael. You're drunk," Brett said.

"I'm not drunk. I'm quite serious. *Is* Robert Cohn going to follow Brett around like a steer all the time?"

"Shut up, Michael. Try and show a little breeding."

"Breeding be damned. Who has any breeding, anyway, except the bulls? Aren't the bulls lovely? Don't you like them, Bill? Why don't you say something, Robert? Don't sit there looking like a bloody funeral. What if Brett did sleep with you? She's slept with lots of better people than you."

"Shut up," Cohn said. He stood up. "Shut up, Mike."

"Oh, don't stand up and act as though you were going to hit me. That won't make any difference to me. Tell me, Robert. Why do you follow Brett around like a poor bloody steer? Don't you know you're not wanted? I know when I'm not wanted. Why don't you know when you're not wanted? You came down to San Sebastian where you weren't wanted, and followed Brett around like a bloody steer. Do you think that's right?"

"Shut up. You're drunk."

"Perhaps I am drunk. Why aren't you drunk? Why don't you ever get drunk, Robert? You know you didn't have a good time at San Sebastian because none of our friends would invite you on any of the parties. You can't blame them hardly. Can you? I asked them to. They wouldn't do it. You can't blame them, now. Can you? Now, answer me. Can you blame them?"

"Go to hell, Mike."

"I can't blame them. Can you blame them? Why do you follow Brett around? Haven't you any manners? How do you think it makes *me* feel?"

"You're a splendid one to talk about manners," Brett said. "You've such lovely manners."

"Come on, Robert," Bill said.

"What do you follow her around for?"

Bill stood up and took hold of Cohn.

"Don't go," Mike said. "Robert Cohn's going to buy a drink."

Bill went off with Cohn. Cohn's face was sallow. Mike went on talking. I sat and listened for a while. Brett looked disgusted.

"I say, Michael, you might not be such a bloody ass," she interrupted. "I'm not saying he's not right, you know." She turned to me.

The emotion left Mike's voice. We were all friends together.

"I'm not so damn drunk as I sounded," he said.

"I know you're not," Brett said.

"We're none of us sober," I said.

"I didn't say anything I didn't mean."

"But you put it so badly," Brett laughed.

"He was an ass, though. He came down to San Sebastian where he damn well wasn't wanted. He hung around Brett and just *looked* at her. It made me damned well sick."

"He did behave very badly," Brett said.

"Mark you. Brett's had affairs with men before. She tells me all about everything. She gave me this chap Cohn's letters to read. I wouldn't read them."

"Damned noble of you."

"No, listen, Jake. Brett's gone off with men. But they weren't ever Jews, and they didn't come and hang about afterward."

"Damned good chaps," Brett said. "It's all rot to talk about it. Michael and I understand each other."

"She gave me Robert Cohn's letters. I wouldn't read them."

"You wouldn't read any letters, darling. You wouldn't read mine."

"I can't read letters," Mike said. "Funny, isn't it?"

"You can't read anything."

"No. You're wrong there. I read quite a bit. I read when I'm at home."

"You'll be writing next," Brett said. "Come on, Michael. Do buck up. You've got to go through with this thing now. He's here. Don't spoil the fiesta."

"Well, let him behave, then."

"He'll behave. I'll tell him."

"You tell him, Jake. Tell him either he must behave or get out."

"Yes," I said, "it would be nice for me to tell him."

"Look, Brett. Tell Jake what Robert calls you. That *is* perfect, you know."

"Oh, no. I can't."

"Go on. We're all friends. Aren't we all friends, Jake?"

"I can't tell him. It's too ridiculous."

"I'll tell him."

"You won't, Michael. Don't be an ass."

"He calls her Circe," Mike said. "He claims she turns men into swine.[3] Damn good. I wish I were one of these literary chaps."

"He'd be good, you know," Brett said. "He writes a good letter."

"I know," I said. "He wrote me from San Sebastian."

"That was nothing," Brett said. "He can write a damned amusing letter."

"She made me write that. She was supposed to be ill."

"I damned well was, too."

3. In Homer's *Odyssey*, Circe is an enchantress who keeps Odysseus and his men on her island in part by turning some of the men into swine.

"Come on," I said, "we must go in and eat."

"How should I meet Cohn?" Mike said.

"Just act as though nothing had happened."

"It's quite all right with me," Mike said. "I'm not embarrassed."

"If he says anything, just say you were tight."

"Quite. And the funny thing is I think I was tight."

"Come on," Brett said. "Are these poisonous things paid for? I must bathe before dinner."

We walked across the square. It was dark and all around the square were the lights from the cafés under the arcades. We walked across the gravel under the trees to the hotel.

They went up-stairs and I stopped to speak with Montoya.

"Well, how did you like the bulls?" he asked.

"Good. They were nice bulls."

"They're all right"—Montoya shook his head—"but they're not too good."

"What didn't you like about them?"

"I don't know. They just didn't give me the feeling that they were so good."

"I know what you mean."

"They're all right."

"Yes. They're all right."

"How did your friends like them?"

"Fine."

"Good," Montoya said.

I went up-stairs. Bill was in his room standing on the balcony looking out at the square. I stood beside him.

"Where's Cohn?"

"Up-stairs in his room."

"How does he feel?"

"Like hell, naturally. Mike was awful. He's terrible when he's tight."

"He wasn't so tight."

"The hell he wasn't. I know what we had before we came to the café."

"He sobered up afterward."

"Good. He was terrible. I don't like Cohn, God knows, and I think it was a silly trick for him to go down to San Sebastian, but nobody has any business to talk like Mike."

"How'd you like the bulls?"

"Grand. It's grand the way they bring them out."

"To-morrow come the Miuras."

"When does the fiesta start?"

"Day after to-morrow."

"We've got to keep Mike from getting so tight. That kind of stuff is terrible."

"We'd better get cleaned up for supper."

"Yes. That will be a pleasant meal."

"Won't it?"

As a matter of fact, supper was a pleasant meal. Brett wore a black, sleeveless evening dress. She looked quite beautiful. Mike acted as though nothing had happened. I had to go up and bring Robert Cohn down. He was reserved and formal, and his face was still taut and sallow, but he cheered up finally. He could not stop looking at Brett. It seemed to make him happy. It must have been pleasant for him to see her looking so lovely, and know he had been away with her and that every one knew it. They could not take that away from him. Bill was very funny. So was Michael. They were good together.

It was like certain dinners I remember from the war. There was much wine, an ignored tension, and a feeling of things coming that you could not prevent happening. Under the wine I lost the disgusted feeling and was happy. It seemed they were all such nice people.

Chapter XIV

I do not know what time I got to bed. I remember undressing, putting on a bathrobe, and standing out on the balcony. I knew I was quite drunk, and when I came in I put on the light over the head of the bed and started to read. I was reading a book by Turgenieff.[1] Probably I read the same two pages over several times. It was one of the stories in "A Sportsman's Sketches." I had read it before, but it seemed quite new. The country became very clear and the feeling of pressure in my head seemed to loosen. I was very drunk and I did not want to shut my eyes because the room would go round and round. If I kept on reading that feeling would pass.

I heard Brett and Robert Cohn come up the stairs. Cohn said good night outside the door and went on up to his room. I heard Brett go into the room next door. Mike was already in bed. He had come in with me an hour before. He woke as she came in, and they talked together. I heard them laugh. I turned off the light and tried to go to sleep. It was not necessary to read any more. I could shut my eyes without getting the wheeling sensation. But I could not sleep. There is no reason why because it is dark you should look at things differently from when it is light. The hell there isn't!

1. Ivan Sergeyevich Turgenev (1818–1883), Russian writer (of novels, poems, and short stories). His *Sportsman's Sketches* (1852) was the first of his books to bring him a wide readership. The collection of twenty-five stories is an early landmark in the Russian realist tradition, and Hemingway would often cite Turgenev as an influence on his own writing.

I figured that all out once, and for six months I never slept with the electric light off. That was another bright idea. To hell with women, anyway. To hell with you, Brett Ashley.

Women made such swell friends. Awfully swell. In the first place, you had to be in love with a woman to have a basis of friendship. I had been having Brett for a friend. I had not been thinking about her side of it. I had been getting something for nothing. That only delayed the presentation of the bill. The bill always came. That was one of the swell things you could count on.

I thought I had paid for everything. Not like the woman pays and pays and pays. No idea of retribution or punishment. Just exchange of values. You gave up something and got something else. Or you worked for something. You paid some way for everything that was any good. I paid my way into enough things that I liked, so that I had a good time. Either you paid by learning about them, or by experience, or by taking chances, or by money. Enjoying living was learning to get your money's worth and knowing when you had it. You could get your money's worth. The world was a good place to buy in. It seemed like a fine philosophy. In five years, I thought, it will seem just as silly as all the other fine philosophies I've had.

Perhaps that wasn't true, though. Perhaps as you went along you did learn something. I did not care what it was all about. All I wanted to know was how to live in it. Maybe if you found out how to live in it you learned from that what it was all about.

I wished Mike would not behave so terribly to Cohn, though. Mike was a bad drunk. Brett was a good drunk. Bill was a good drunk. Cohn was never drunk. Mike was unpleasant after he passed a certain point. I liked to see him hurt Cohn. I wished he would not do it, though, because afterward it made me disgusted at myself. That was morality; things that made you disgusted afterward. No, that must be immorality. That was a large statement. What a lot of bilge I could think up at night. What rot, I could hear Brett say it. What rot! When you were with the English you got into the habit of using English expressions in your thinking. The English spoken language—the upper classes, anyway—must have fewer words than the Eskimo.[2] Of course I didn't know anything about the Eskimo. Maybe the Eskimo was a fine language. Say the Cherokee. I didn't know anything about the Cherokee, either. The English talked with inflected phrases. One phrase to mean everything. I liked them, though. I liked the way they talked. Take Harris. Still Harris was not the upper classes.

I turned on the light again and read. I read the Turgenieff. I knew that now, reading it in the oversensitized state of my mind after much

2. "Inuit" has superseded "Eskimos" as the preferred term.

too much brandy, I would remember it somewhere, and afterward it would seem as though it had really happened to me. I would always have it. That was another good thing you paid for and then had. Some time along toward daylight I went to sleep.

The next two days in Pamplona were quiet, and there were no more rows. The town was getting ready for the fiesta. Workmen put up the gate-posts that were to shut off the side streets when the bulls were released from the corrals and came running through the streets in the morning on their way to the ring. The workmen dug holes and fitted in the timbers, each timber numbered for its regular place. Out on the plateau beyond the town employees of the bull-ring exercised picador horses, galloping them stiff-legged on the hard, sun-baked fields behind the bull-ring. The big gate of the bull-ring was open, and inside the amphitheatre was being swept. The ring was rolled and sprinkled, and carpenters replaced weakened or cracked planks in the barrera.[3] Standing at the edge of the smooth rolled sand you could look up in the empty stands and see old women sweeping out the boxes.

Outside, the fence that led from the last street of the town to the entrance of the bull-ring was already in place and made a long pen; the crowd would come running down with the bulls behind them on the morning of the day of the first bull-fight. Out across the plain, where the horse and cattle fair would be, some gypsies had camped under the trees. The wine and aguardiente sellers were putting up their booths. One booth advertised ANIS DEL TORO.[4] The cloth sign hung against the planks in the hot sun. In the big square that was the centre of the town there was no change yet. We sat in the white wicker chairs on the terrasse of the café and watched the motor-buses come in and unload peasants from the country coming in to the market, and we watched the buses fill up and start out with peasants sitting with their saddle-bags full of the things they had bought in the town. The tall gray motor-buses were the only life of the square except for the pigeons and the man with a hose who sprinkled the gravelled square and watered the streets.

In the evening was the paseo.[5] For an hour after dinner every one, all the good-looking girls, the officers from the garrison, all the fashionable people of the town, walked in the street on one side of the square while the café tables filled with the regular after-dinner crowd.

3. Wooden wall, often painted red, that separates the bullring from the spectators' seating area.
4. A liquor derived (like Pernod) from the licorice-flavored anise.
5. As Hemingway describes in the next sentence, the paseo is an informal evening procession of "fashionable people" around Pamplona's central square.

During the morning I usually sat in the café and read the Madrid papers and then walked in the town or out into the country. Sometimes Bill went along. Sometimes he wrote in his room. Robert Cohn spent the mornings studying Spanish or trying to get a shave at the barber-shop. Brett and Mike never got up until noon. We all had a vermouth[6] at the café. It was a quiet life and no one was drunk. I went to church a couple of times, once with Brett. She said she wanted to hear me go to confession, but I told her that not only was it impossible but it was not as interesting as it sounded, and, besides, it would be in a language she did not know. We met Cohn as we came out of church, and although it was obvious he had followed us, yet he was very pleasant and nice, and we all three went for a walk out to the gypsy camp, and Brett had her fortune told.

It was a good morning, there were high white clouds above the mountains. It had rained a little in the night and it was fresh and cool on the plateau, and there was a wonderful view. We all felt good and we felt healthy, and I felt quite friendly to Cohn. You could not be upset about anything on a day like that.

That was the last day before the fiesta.

6. A fortified wine flavored with herbs or other botanical compounds, often drunk as an aperitif.

Pamplona bullring during the *corrida*. Reprinted with permission of Getty Images.

Chapter XV

At noon of Sunday, the 6th of July, the fiesta exploded. There is no other way to describe it. People had been coming in all day from the country, but they were assimilated in the town and you did not notice them. The square was as quiet in the hot sun as on any other day. The peasants were in the outlying wine-shops. There they were drinking, getting ready for the fiesta. They had come in so recently from the plains and the hills that it was necessary that they make their shifting in values gradually. They could not start in paying café prices. They got their money's worth in the wine-shops. Money still had a definite value in hours worked and bushels of grain sold. Late in the fiesta it would not matter what they paid, nor where they bought.

Now on the day of the starting of the fiesta of San Fermin they had been in the wine-shops of the narrow streets of the town since early morning. Going down the streets in the morning on the way to mass in the cathedral, I heard them singing through the open doors of the shops. They were warming up. There were many people at the eleven o'clock mass. San Fermin is also a religious festival.

I walked down the hill from the cathedral and up the street to the café on the square. It was a little before noon. Robert Cohn and Bill were sitting at one of the tables. The marble-topped tables and the white wicker chairs were gone. They were replaced by cast-iron tables and severe folding chairs. The café was like a battleship stripped for action. Today the waiters did not leave you alone all morning to read without asking if you wanted to order something. A waiter came up as soon as I sat down.

"What are you drinking?" I asked Bill and Robert.

"Sherry," Cohn said.

"Jerez."[1] I said to the waiter.

Before the waiter brought the sherry the rocket that announced the fiesta went up in the square. It burst and there was a gray ball of smoke high up above the Theatre Gayarre,[2] across on the other side of the plaza. The ball of smoke hung in the sky like a shrapnel burst, and as I watched, another rocket came up to it, trickling smoke in the bright sunlight. I saw the bright flash as it burst and another little cloud of smoke appeared. By the time the second rocket had burst there were so many people in the arcade, that had been empty a minute before, that the waiter, holding the bottle high up

1. Sherry (Spanish).
2. Originally the Teatro Principal de Pamplona, this theater was named in 1903 for the tenor Julián Gayarre.

over his head, could hardly get through the crowd to our table. People were coming into the square from all sides, and down the street we heard the pipes and the fifes and the drums coming. They were playing the *riau-riau*[3] music, the pipes shrill and the drums pounding, and behind them came the men and boys dancing. When the fifers stopped they all crouched down in the street, and when the reed-pipes and the fifes shrilled, and the flat, dry, hollow drums tapped it out again, they all went up in the air dancing. In the crowd you saw only the heads and shoulders of the dancers going up and down.

In the square a man, bent over, was playing on a reed-pipe, and a crowd of children were following him shouting, and pulling at his clothes. He came out of the square, the children following him, and piped them past the café and down a side street. We saw his blank pockmarked face as he went by, piping, the children close behind him shouting and pulling at him.

"He must be the village idiot," Bill said. "My God! look at that!"

Down the street came dancers. The street was solid with dancers, all men. They were all dancing in time behind their own fifers and drummers. They were a club of some sort, and all wore workmen's blue smocks, and red handkerchiefs around their necks, and carried a great banner on two poles. The banner danced up and down with them as they came down surrounded by the crowd.

"Hurray for Wine! Hurray for the Foreigners!" was painted on the banner.

"Where are the foreigners?" Robert Cohn asked.

"We're the foreigners," Bill said.

All the time rockets were going up. The café tables were all full now. The square was emptying of people and the crowd was filling the cafés.

"Where's Brett and Mike?" Bill asked.

"I'll go and get them," Cohn said.

"Bring them here."

The fiesta was really started. It kept up day and night for seven days. The dancing kept up, the drinking kept up, the noise went on. The things that happened could only have happened during a fiesta. Everything became quite unreal finally and it seemed as though nothing could have any consequences. It seemed out of place to think of consequences during the fiesta. All during the fiesta you had the feeling, even when it was quiet, that you had to shout any remark to make it heard. It was the same feeling about any action. It was a fiesta and it went on for seven days.

3. Part of the religious and civic Festival of San Fermin. On the first day of the festival, members of Pamplona's city council parade from City Hall to the Chapel dedicated to San Fermin, accompanied by musicians and dancers.

That afternoon was the big religious procession. San Fermin was translated from one church to another. In the procession were all the dignitaries, civil and religious. We could not see them because the crowd was too great. Ahead of the formal procession and behind it danced the *riau-riau* dancers. There was one mass of yellow shirts dancing up and down in the crowd. All we could see of the procession through the closely pressed people that crowded all the side streets and curbs were the great giants, cigar-store Indians, thirty feet high, Moors, a King and Queen, whirling and waltzing solemnly to the *riau-riau*.

They were all standing outside the chapel where San Fermin and the dignitaries had passed in, leaving a guard of soldiers, the giants, with the men who danced in them standing beside their resting frames, and the dwarfs moving with their whacking bladders through the crowd. We started inside and there was a smell of incense and people filing back into the church, but Brett was stopped just inside the door because she had no hat, so we went out again and along the street that ran back from the chapel into town. The street was lined on both sides with people keeping their place at the curb for the return of the procession. Some dancers formed a circle around Brett and started to dance. They wore big wreaths of white garlics around their necks. They took Bill and me by the arms and put us in the circle. Bill started to dance, too. They were all chanting. Brett wanted to dance but they did not want her to. They wanted her as an image to dance around. When the song ended with the sharp *riau-riau!* they rushed us into a wine-shop.

We stood at the counter. They had Brett seated on a wine-cask. It was dark in the wine-shop and full of men singing, hard-voiced singing. Back of the counter they drew the wine from casks. I put down money for the wine, but one of the men picked it up and put it back in my pocket.

"I want a leather wine-bottle," Bill said.

"There's a place down the street," I said. "I'll go get a couple."

The dancers did not want me to go out. Three of them were sitting on the high wine-cask beside Brett, teaching her to drink out of the wine-skins. They had hung a wreath of garlics around her neck. Some one insisted on giving her a glass. Somebody was teaching Bill a song. Singing it into his ear. Beating time on Bill's back.

I explained to them that I would be back. Outside in the street I went down the street looking for the shop that made leather wine-bottles. The crowd was packed on the sidewalks and many of the shops were shuttered, and I could not find it. I walked as far as the church, looking on both sides of the street. Then I asked a man and he took me by the arm and led me to it. The shutters were up but the door was open.

Inside it smelled of fresh tanned leather and hot tar. A man was stencilling completed wine-skins. They hung from the roof in bunches. He took one down, blew it up, screwed the nozzle tight, and then jumped on it.

"See! It doesn't leak."

"I want another one, too. A big one."

He took down a big one that would hold a gallon or more, from the roof. He blew it up, his cheeks puffing ahead of the wine-skin, and stood on the bota holding on to a chair.

"What are you going to do? Sell them in Bayonne?"

"No. Drink out of them."

He slapped me on the back.

"Good man. Eight pesetas for the two. The lowest price."

The man who was stencilling the new ones and tossing them into a pile stopped.

"It's true," he said. "Eight pesetas is cheap."

I paid and went out and along the street back to the wine-shop. It was darker than ever inside and very crowded. I did not see Brett and Bill, and some one said they were in the back room. At the counter the girl filled the two wine-skins for me. One held two litres. The other held five litres. Filling them both cost three pesetas sixty céntimos. Some one at the counter, that I had never seen before, tried to pay for the wine, but I finally paid for it myself. The man who had wanted to pay then bought me a drink. He would not let me buy one in return, but said he would take a rinse of the mouth from the new wine-bag. He tipped the big five-litre bag up and squeezed it so the wine hissed against the back of his throat.

"All right," he said, and handed back the bag.

In the back room Brett and Bill were sitting on barrels surrounded by the dancers. Everybody had his arms on everybody else's shoulders, and they were all singing. Mike was sitting at a table with several men in their shirt-sleeves, eating from a bowl of tuna fish, chopped onions and vinegar. They were all drinking wine and mopping up the oil and vinegar with pieces of bread.

"Hello, Jake. Hello!" Mike called. "Come here. I want you to meet my friends. We're all having an hors d'œuvre."

I was introduced to the people at the table. They supplied their names to Mike and sent for a fork for me.

"Stop eating their dinner, Michael," Brett shouted from the wine-barrels.

"I don't want to eat up your meal," I said when some one handed me a fork.

"Eat," he said. "What do you think it's here for?"

I unscrewed the nozzle of the big wine-bottle and handed it around. Every one took a drink, tipping the wine-skin at arm's length.

Outside, above the singing, we could hear the music of the procession going by.

"Isn't that the procession?" Mike asked.

"Nada,"[4] some one said. "It's nothing. Drink up. Lift the bottle."

"Where did they find you?" I asked Mike.

"Some one brought me here," Mike said. "They said you were here."

"Where's Cohn?"

"He's passed out," Brett called. "They've put him away somewhere."

"Where is he?"

"I don't know."

"How should we know," Bill said. "I think he's dead."

"He's not dead," Mike said. "I know he's not dead. He's just passed out on Anís del Mono."[5]

As he said Anís del Mono one of the men at the table looked up, brought out a bottle from inside his smock, and handed it to me.

"No," I said. "No, thanks!"

"Yes. Yes. Arriba![6] Up with the bottle!"

I took a drink. It tasted of licorice and warmed all the way. I could feel it warming in my stomach.

"Where the hell is Cohn?"

"I don't know," Mike said. "I'll ask. Where is the drunken comrade?" he asked in Spanish.

"You want to see him?"

"Yes," I said.

"Not me," said Mike. "This gent."

The Anís del Mono man wiped his mouth and stood up.

"Come on."

In a back room Robert Cohn was sleeping quietly on some wine-casks. It was almost too dark to see his face. They had covered him with a coat and another coat was folded under his head. Around his neck and on his chest was a big wreath of twisted garlics.

"Let him sleep," the man whispered. "He's all right."

Two hours later Cohn appeared. He came into the front room still with the wreath of garlics around his neck. The Spaniards shouted when he came in. Cohn wiped his eyes and grinned.

"I must have been sleeping," he said.

"Oh, not at all," Brett said.

"You were only dead," Bill said.

"Aren't we going to go and have some supper?" Cohn asked.

"Do you want to eat?"

4. Nothing (Spanish).
5. A brand of anise liqueur.
6. Literally "Up!" (Spanish); here also with the sense of "Go, get on with it!"

"Yes. Why not? I'm hungry."

"Eat those garlics, Robert, Mike said. "I say. Do eat those garlics."

Cohn stood there. His sleep had made him quite all right.

"Do let's go and eat," Brett said. "I must get a bath."

"Come on," Bill said. "Let's translate Brett to the hotel."

We said good-bye to many people and shook hands with many people and went out. Outside it was dark.

"What time is it do you suppose?" Cohn asked.

"It's to-morrow," Mike said. "You've been asleep two days."

"No," said Cohn, "what time is it?"

"It's ten o'clock."

"What a lot we've drunk."

"You mean what a lot *we've* drunk. You went to sleep."

Going down the dark streets to the hotel we saw the sky-rockets going up in the square. Down the side streets that led to the square we saw the square solid with people, those in the centre all dancing.

It was a big meal at the hotel. It was the first meal of the prices being doubled for the fiesta, and there were several new courses. After the dinner we were out in the town. I remember resolving that I would stay up all night to watch the bulls go through the streets at six o'clock in the morning, and being so sleepy that I went to bed around four o'clock. The others stayed up.

My own room was locked and I could not find the key, so I went up-stairs and slept on one of the beds in Cohn's room. The fiesta was going on outside in the night, but I was too sleepy for it to keep me awake. When I woke it was the sound of the rocket exploding that announced the release of the bulls from the corrals at the edge of town. They would race through the streets and out to the bull-ring. I had been sleeping heavily and I woke feeling I was too late. I put on a coat of Cohn's and went out on the balcony. Down below the narrow street was empty. All the balconies were crowded with people. Suddenly a crowd came down the street. They were all running, packed close together. They passed along and up the street toward the bull-ring and behind them came more men running faster, and then some stragglers who were really running. Behind them was a little bare space, and then the bulls galloping, tossing their heads up and down. It all went out of sight around the corner. One man fell, rolled to the gutter, and lay quiet. But the bulls went right on and did not notice him. They were all running together.

After they went out of sight a great roar came from the bull-ring. It kept on. Then finally the pop of the rocket that meant the bulls had gotten through the people in the ring and into the corrals. I went back in the room and got into bed. I had been standing on the stone balcony in bare feet. I knew our crowd must have all been out at the bull-ring. Back in bed, I went to sleep.

Cohn woke me when he came in. He started to undress and went over and closed the window because the people on the balcony of the house just across the street were looking in.

"Did you see the show?" I asked.

"Yes. We were all there."

"Anybody get hurt?"

"One of the bulls got into the crowd in the ring and tossed six or eight people."

"How did Brett like it?"

"It was all so sudden there wasn't any time for it to bother anybody."

"I wish I'd been up."

"We didn't know where you were. We went to your room but it was locked."

"Where did you stay up?"

"We danced at some club."

"I got sleepy," I said.

"My gosh! I'm sleepy now," Cohn said. "Doesn't this thing ever stop?"

"Not for a week."

Bill opened the door and put his head in.

"Where were you, Jake?"

"I saw them go through from the balcony. How was it?"

"Grand."

"Where you going?"

"To sleep."

No one was up before noon. We ate at tables set out under the arcade. The town was full of people. We had to wait for a table. After lunch we went over to the Iruña. It had filled up, and as the time for the bull-fight came it got fuller, and the tables were crowded closer. There was a close, crowded hum that came every day before the bull-fight. The café did not make this same noise at any other time, no matter how crowded it was. This hum went on, and we were in it and a part of it.

I had taken six seats for all the fights. Three of them were barreras, the first row at the ring-side, and three were sobrepuertas, seats with wooden backs, half-way up the amphitheatre. Mike thought Brett had best sit high up for her first time, and Cohn wanted to sit with them. Bill and I were going to sit in the barreras, and I gave the extra ticket to a waiter to sell. Bill said something to Cohn about what to do and how to look so he would not mind the horses.[7] Bill had seen one season of bull-fights.

7. In the bullfight, the bull is encouraged to charge at horses ridden by picadors (riders armed with a long spear). As the bull gores the horse, the picador digs into the bull's

"I'm not worried about how I'll stand it. I'm only afraid I may be bored," Cohn said.

"You think so?"

"Don't look at the horses, after the bull hits them," I said to Brett. "Watch the charge and see the picador try and keep the bull off, but then don't look again until the horse is dead if it's been hit."

"I'm a little nervy about it," Brett said. "I'm worried whether I'll be able to go through with it all right."

"You'll be all right. There's nothing but that horse part that will bother you, and they're only in for a few minutes with each bull. Just don't watch when it's bad."

"She'll be all right," Mike said. "I'll look after her."

"I don't think you'll be bored," Bill said.

"I'm going over to the hotel to get the glasses and the wine-skin," I said. "See you back here. Don't get cock-eyed."

"I'll come along," Bill said. Brett smiled at us.

We walked around through the arcade to avoid the heat of the square.

"That Cohn gets me," Bill said. "He's got this Jewish superiority so strong that he thinks the only emotion he'll get out of the fight will be being bored."

"We'll watch him with the glasses," I said.

"Oh, to hell with him!"

"He spends a lot of time there."

"I want him to stay there."

In the hotel on the stairs we met Montoya.

"Come on," said Montoya. "Do you want to meet Pedro Romero?"

"Fine," said Bill. "Let's go see him."

We followed Montoya up a flight and down the corridor.

"He's in room number eight," Montoya explained. "He's getting dressed for the bull-fight."

Montoya knocked on the door and opened it. It was a gloomy room with a little light coming in from the window on the narrow street. There were two beds separated by a monastic partition. The electric light was on. The boy stood very straight and unsmiling in his bull-fighting clothes. His jacket hung over the back of a chair. They were just finishing winding his sash. His black hair shone under the electric light. He wore a white linen shirt and the sword-handler finished his sash and stood up and stepped back. Pedro Romero nodded, seeming very far away and dignified when we shook hands. Montoya said something about what great aficionados we were, and

---

shoulders with the pic, or spear, wounding and weakening the shoulder muscles so that the bull tires and will not be able to hold its head upright when facing the matador. The horses are often disemboweled in the process.

that we wanted to wish him luck. Romero listened very seriously. Then he turned to me. He was the best-looking boy I have ever seen.

"You go to the bull-fight," he said in English.

"You know English," I said, feeling like an idiot.

"No," he answered, and smiled.

One of three men who had been sitting on the beds came up and asked us if we spoke French. "Would you like me to interpret for you? Is there anything you would like to ask Pedro Romero?"

We thanked him. What was there that you would like to ask? The boy was nineteen years old, alone except for his sword-handler, and the three hangers-on, and the bull-fight was to commence in twenty minutes. We wished him "Mucha suerte,"[8] shook hands, and went out. He was standing, straight and handsome and altogether by himself, alone in the room with the hangers-on as we shut the door.

"He's a fine boy, don't you think so?" Montoya asked.

"He's a good-looking kid," I said.

"He looks like a torero,"[9] Montoya said. "He has the type."

"He's a fine boy."

"We'll see how he is in the ring," Montoya said.

We found the big leather wine-bottle leaning against the wall in my room, took it and the field-glasses, locked the door, and went down-stairs.

It was a good bull-fight. Bill and I were very excited about Pedro Romero. Montoya was sitting about ten places away. After Romero had killed his first bull Montoya caught my eye and nodded his head. This was a real one. There had not been a real one for a long time. Of the other two matadors, one was very fair and the other was passable. But there was no comparison with Romero, although neither of his bulls was much.

Several times during the bull-fight I looked up at Mike and Brett and Cohn, with the glasses. They seemed to be all right. Brett did not look upset. All three were leaning forward on the concrete railing in front of them.

"Let me take the glasses," Bill said.

"Does Cohn look bored?" I asked.

"That kike!"[1]

Outside the ring, after the bull-fight was over, you could not move in the crowd. We could not make our way through but had to be moved with the whole thing, slowly, as a glacier, back to town. We had

8. "Good luck" (Spanish).
9. Bullfighter (Spanish).
1. This offensive slur for a Jewish person dates from the 1880s and is thought by some linguists to derive from the Yiddish word *kikel* ("circle"). Bill here takes an even more directly insulting tone than usual in the casually antisemitic way in which he (and other characters) deride Robert Cohn on the basis of and in terms of his Jewishness.

that disturbed emotional feeling that always comes after a bull-fight, and the feeling of elation that comes after a good bull-fight. The fiesta was going on. The drums pounded and the pipe music was shrill, and everywhere the flow of the crowd was broken by patches of dancers. The dancers were in a crowd, so you did not see the intricate play of the feet. All you saw was the heads and shoulders going up and down, up and down. Finally, we got out of the crowd and made for the café. The waiter saved chairs for the others, and we each ordered an absinthe and watched the crowd in the square and the dancers.

"What do you suppose that dance is?" Bill asked.

"It's a sort of jota."[2]

"They're not all the same," Bill said. "They dance differently to all the different tunes."

"It's swell dancing."

In front of us on a clear part of the street a company of boys were dancing. The steps were very intricate and their faces were intent and concentrated. They all looked down while they danced. Their rope-soled shoes tapped and spatted on the pavement. The toes touched. The heels touched. The balls of the feet touched. Then the music broke wildly and the step was finished and they were all dancing on up the street.

"Here come the gentry," Bill said.

They were crossing the street.

"Hello, men," I said.

"Hello, gents!" said Brett. "You saved us seats? How nice."

"I say," Mike said, "that Romero what'shisname is somebody. Am I wrong?"

"Oh, isn't he lovely," Brett said. "And those green trousers."

"Brett never took her eyes off them."

"I say, I must borrow your glasses to-morrow."

"How did it go?"

"Wonderfully! Simply perfect. I say, it is a spectacle!"

"How about the horses?"

"I couldn't help looking at them."

"She couldn't take her eyes off them," Mike said. "She's an extraordinary wench."

"They do have some rather awful things happen to them," Brett said. "I couldn't look away, though."

"Did you feel all right?"

"I didn't feel badly at all."

"Robert Cohn did," Mike put in. "You were quite green, Robert."

"The first horse did bother me," Cohn said.

2. A folk dance of northern Spain.

"You weren't bored, were you?" asked Bill.

Cohn laughed.

"No. I wasn't bored. I wish you'd forgive me that."

"It's all right," Bill said, "so long as you weren't bored."

"He didn't look bored," Mike said. "I thought he was going to be sick."

"I never felt that bad. It was just for a minute."

"I thought he was going to be sick. You weren't bored, were you, Robert?"

"Let up on that, Mike. I said I was sorry I said it."

"He was, you know. He was positively green."

"Oh, shove it along, Michael."

"You mustn't ever get bored at your first bull-fight, Robert," Mike said. "It might make such a mess."

"Oh, shove it along, Michael," Brett said.

"He said Brett was a sadist," Mike said. "Brett's not a sadist. She's just a lovely, healthy wench."

"Are you a sadist, Brett?" I asked.

"Hope not."

"He said Brett was a sadist just because she has a good, healthy stomach."

"Won't be healthy long."

Bill got Mike started on something else than Cohn. The waiter brought the absinthe glasses.

"Did you really like it?" Bill asked Cohn.

"No, I can't say I liked it. I think it's a wonderful show."

"Gad, yes! What a spectacle!" Brett said.

"I wish they didn't have the horse part," Cohn said.

"They're not important," Bill said. "After a while you never notice anything disgusting."

"It is a bit strong just at the start," Brett said. "There's a dreadful moment for me just when the bull starts for the horse."

"The bulls were fine," Cohn said.

"They were very good," Mike said.

"I want to sit down below, next time." Brett drank from her glass of absinthe.

"She wants to see the bull-fighters close by," Mike said.

"They are something," Brett said. "That Romero lad is just a child."

"He's a damned good-looking boy," I said. "When we were up in his room I never saw a better-looking kid."

"How old do you suppose he is?"

"Nineteen or twenty."

"Just imagine it."

The bull-fight on the second day was much better than on the first. Brett sat between Mike and me at the barrera, and Bill and Cohn went up above. Romero was the whole show. I do not think Brett saw any other bull-fighter. No one else did either, except the hard-shelled technicians. It was all Romero. There were two other matadors, but they did not count. I sat beside Brett and explained to Brett what it was all about. I told her about watching the bull, not the horse, when the bulls charged the picadors, and got her to watching the picador place the point of his pic so that she saw what it was all about, so that it became more something that was going on with a definite end, and less of a spectacle with unexplained horrors. I had her watch how Romero took the bull away from a fallen horse with his cape, and how he held him with the cape and turned him, smoothly and suavely, never wasting the bull. She saw how Romero avoided every brusque movement and saved his bulls for the last when he wanted them, not winded and discomposed but smoothly worn down. She saw how close Romero always worked to the bull, and I pointed out to her the tricks the other bull-fighters used to make it look as though they were working closely. She saw why she liked Romero's cape-work and why she did not like the others.

Romero never made any contortions, always it was straight and pure and natural in line. The others twisted themselves like corkscrews, their elbows raised, and leaned against the flanks of the bull after his horns had passed, to give a faked look of danger. Afterward, all that was faked turned bad and gave an unpleasant feeling. Romero's bull-fighting gave real emotion, because he kept the absolute purity of line in his movements and always quietly and calmly let the horns pass him close each time. He did not have to emphasize their closeness. Brett saw how something that was beautiful done close to the bull was ridiculous if it were done a little way off. I told her how since the death of Joselito[3] all the bull-fighters had been developing a technique that simulated this appearance of danger in order to give a fake emotional feeling, while the bull-fighter was really safe. Romero had the old thing, the holding of his purity of line through the maximum of exposure, while he dominated the bull by making him realize he was unattainable, while he prepared him for the killing.

"I've never seen him do an awkward thing," Brett said.

"You won't until he gets frightened," I said.

"He'll never be frightened," Mike said. "He knows too damned much."

"He knew everything when he started. The others can't ever learn what he was born with."

3. Nickname of the matador José Gómez Ortega (1895–1920), a prodigious and popular bullfighter widely seen as one of the great toreadors of bullfighting's "Golden Age" in the 1910s. He was killed in the ring at the age of twenty-five.

"And God, what looks," Brett said.

"I believe, you know, that she's falling in love with this bull-fighter chap," Mike said.

"I wouldn't be surprised."

"Be a good chap, Jake. Don't tell her anything more about him. Tell her how they beat their old mothers."

"Tell me what drunks they are."

"Oh, frightful," Mike said. "Drunk all day and spend all their time beating their poor old mothers."

"He looks that way," Brett said.

"Doesn't he?" I said.

They had hitched the mules to the dead bull and then the whips cracked, the men ran, and the mules, straining forward, their legs pushing, broke into a gallop, and the bull, one horn up, his head on its side, swept a swath smoothly across the sand and out the red gate.

"This next is the last one."

"Not really," Brett said. She leaned forward on the barrera. Romero waved his picadors to their places, then stood, his cape against his chest, looking across the ring to where the bull would come out.

After it was over we went out and were pressed tight in the crowd.

"These bull-fights are hell on one," Brett said. "I'm limp as a rag."

"Oh, you'll get a drink," Mike said.

The next day Pedro Romero did not fight. It was Miura bulls, and a very bad bull-fight. The next day there was no bull-fight scheduled. But all day and all night the fiesta kept on.

Chapter XVI

In the morning it was raining. A fog had come over the mountains from the sea. You could not see the tops of the mountains. The plateau was dull and gloomy, and the shapes of the trees and the houses were changed. I walked out beyond the town to look at the weather. The bad weather was coming over the mountains from the sea.

The flags in the square hung wet from the white poles and the banners were wet and hung damp against the front of the houses, and in between the steady drizzle the rain came down and drove every one under the arcades and made pools of water in the square, and the streets wet and dark and deserted; yet the fiesta kept up without any pause. It was only driven under cover.

The covered seats of the bull-ring had been crowded with people sitting out of the rain watching the concourse of Basque and Navarrais dancers and singers, and afterward the Val Carlos dancers in their costumes danced down the street in the rain, the drums sounding hollow and damp, and the chiefs of the bands riding ahead on their big, heavy-footed horses, their costumes wet, the horses' coats wet in the rain.[1] The crowd was in the cafés and the dancers came in, too, and sat, their tight-wound white legs under the tables, shaking the water from their belled caps, and spreading their red and purple jackets over the chairs to dry. It was raining hard outside.

I left the crowd in the café and went over to the hotel to get shaved for dinner. I was shaving in my room when there was a knock on the door.

"Come in," I called.

Montoya walked in.

"How are you?" he said.

"Fine," I said.

"No bulls to-day."

"No," I said, "nothing but rain."

"Where are your friends?"

"Over at the Iruña."

Montoya smiled his embarrassed smile.

"Look," he said. "Do you know the American ambassador?"

"Yes," I said. "Everybody knows the American ambassador."[2]

"He's here in town, now."

"Yes," I said. "Everybody's seen them."

"I've seen them, too," Montoya said. He didn't say anything. I went on shaving.

"Sit down," I said. "Let me send for a drink."

"No, I have to go."

I finished shaving and put my face down into the bowl and washed it with cold water. Montoya was standing there looking more embarrassed.

"Look," he said. "I've just had a message from them at the Grand Hotel that they want Pedro Romero and Marcial Lalanda to come over for coffee to-night after dinner."

"Well," I said, "it can't hurt Marcial any."

"Marcial has been in San Sebastian all day. He drove over in a car this morning with Márquez. I don't think they'll be back to-night."

Montoya stood embarrassed. He wanted me to say something.

"Don't give Romero the message," I said.

"You think so?"

1. Groups performing folk dances of the Basque people of the Pyrenees and the Kingdom of Navarre (the region of Spain that includes Pamplona). Val Carlos dancers are from Valcarlos, about eight miles north of the monastery of Roncesvalles, near the French border (its name means Valley of Charlemagne).
2. Alexander Pollock Moore (1867–1930), the American ambassador to Spain at the time of the novel's action.

"Absolutely."

Montoya was very pleased.

"I wanted to ask you because you were an American," he said.

"That's what I'd do."

"Look," said Montoya. "People take a boy like that. They don't know what he's worth. They don't know what he means. Any foreigner can flatter him. They start this Grand Hotel business, and in one year they're through."

"Like Algabeño,"[3] I said.

"Yes, like Algabeño."

"They're a fine lot," I said. "There's one American woman down here now that collects bull-fighters."

"I know. They only want the young ones."

"Yes," I said. "The old ones get fat."

"Or crazy like Gallo."[4]

"Well," I said, "it's easy. All you have to do is not give him the message."

"He's such a fine boy," said Montoya. "He ought to stay with his own people. He shouldn't mix in that stuff."

"Won't you have a drink?" I asked.

"No," said Montoya, "I have to go." He went out.

I went down-stairs and out the door and took a walk around through the arcades around the square. It was still raining. I looked in at the Iruña for the gang and they were not there, so I walked on around the square and back to the hotel. They were eating dinner in the down-stairs dining-room.

They were well ahead of me and it was no use trying to catch them. Bill was buying shoe-shines for Mike. Bootblacks opened the street door and each one Bill called over and started to work on Mike.

"This is the eleventh time my boots have been polished," Mike said. "I say, Bill is an ass."

The bootblacks had evidently spread the report. Another came in.

"Limpia botas?"[5] he said to Bill.

"No," said Bill. "For this Señor."

The bootblack knelt down beside the one at work and started on Mike's free shoe that shone already in the electric light.

"Bill's a yell of laughter," Mike said.

I was drinking red wine, and so far behind them that I felt a little uncomfortable about all this shoe-shining. I looked around the room. At the next table was Pedro Romero. He stood up when I nodded,

3. José o García Carranza (1902–1936), the bullfighter known as Algabeño.
4. Rafael Gómez Ortega (1882–1960), the bullfighter known as Gallo and the older brother of Joselito.
5. "Shine your boots?" (Spanish).

and asked me to come over and meet a friend. His table was beside ours, almost touching. I met the friend, a Madrid bull-fight critic, a little man with a drawn face. I told Romero how much I liked his work, and he was very pleased. We talked Spanish and the critic knew a little French. I reached to our table for my wine-bottle, but the critic took my arm. Romero laughed.

"Drink here," he said in English.

He was very bashful about his English, but he was really very pleased with it, and as we went on talking he brought out words he was not sure of, and asked me about them. He was anxious to know the English for *corrida de toros*, the exact translation. Bull-fight he was suspicious of. I explained that bull-fight in Spanish was the *lidia* of a *toro*. The Spanish word *corrida* means in English the running of bulls—the French translation is *course des taureaux*. The critic put that in. There is no Spanish word for bull-fight.

Pedro Romero said he had learned a little English in Gibraltar. He was born in Ronda. That is not far above Gibraltar. He started bull-fighting in Málaga[6] in the bull-fighting school there. He had only been at it three years. The bull-fight critic joked him about the number of *Malagueño* expressions he used. He was nineteen years old, he said. His older brother was with him as a banderillero, but he did not live in this hotel. He lived in a smaller hotel with the other people who worked for Romero. He asked me how many times I had seen him in the ring. I told him only three. It was really only two, but I did not want to explain after I had made the mistake.

"Where did you see me the other time? In Madrid?"

"Yes," I lied. I had read the accounts of his two appearances in Madrid in the bull-fight papers, so I was all right.

"The first or the second time?"

"The first."

"I was very bad," he said. "The second time I was better. You remember?" He turned to the critic.

He was not at all embarrassed. He talked of his work as something altogether apart from himself. There was nothing conceited or braggartly about him.

"I like it very much that you like my work," he said. "But you haven't seen it yet. To-morrow, if I get a good bull, I will try and show it to you."

When he said this he smiled, anxious that neither the bull-fight critic nor I would think he was boasting.

6. A coastal city in Andalusia, southern Spain. *Malagueño* expressions are dialect or colloquial expressions from that region.

"I am anxious to see it," the critic said. "I would like to be convinced."

"He doesn't like my work much." Romero turned to me. He was serious.

The critic explained that he liked it very much, but that so far it had been incomplete.

"Wait till to-morrow, if a good one comes out."

"Have you seen the bulls for to-morrow?" the critic asked me.

"Yes. I saw them unloaded."

Pedro Romero leaned forward.

"What did you think of them?"

"Very nice," I said. "About twenty-six arrobas.[7] Very short horns. Haven't you seen them?"

"Oh, yes," said Romero.

"They won't weigh twenty-six arrobas," said the critic.

"No," said Romero.

"They've got bananas for horns," the critic said.

"You call them bananas?" asked Romero. He turned to me and smiled. "*You* wouldn't call them bananas?"

"No," I said. "They're horns all right."

"They're very short," said Pedro Romero. "Very, very short. Still, they aren't bananas."

"I say, Jake," Brett called from the next table, "you *have* deserted us."

"Just temporarily," I said. "We're talking bulls."

"You *are* superior."

"Tell him that bulls have no balls," Mike shouted. He was drunk.

Romero looked at me inquiringly.

"Drunk," I said. "Borracho! Muy borracho!"[8]

"You might introduce your friends," Brett said. She had not stopped looking at Pedro Romero. I asked them if they would like to have coffee with us. They both stood up. Romero's face was very brown. He had very nice manners.

I introduced them all around and they started to sit down, but there was not enough room, so we all moved over to the big table by the wall to have coffee. Mike ordered a bottle of Fundador[9] and glasses for everybody. There was a lot of drunken talking.

"Tell him I think writing is lousy," Bill said. "Go on, tell him. Tell him I'm ashamed of being a writer."

Pedro Romero was sitting beside Brett and listening to her.

7. A unit of weight in Spain; one arroba weighs around twenty-five pounds.
8. "Drunk! Very drunk!" (Spanish).
9. One of the oldest amontillado brandies. Fundador means "founder".

"Go on. Tell him!" Bill said.

Romero looked up smiling.

"This gentleman," I said, "is a writer."

Romero was impressed. "This other one, too," I said, pointing at Cohn.

"He looks like Villalta,"[1] Romero said, looking at Bill. "Rafael, doesn't he look like Villalta?"

"I can't see it," the critic said.

"Really," Romero said in Spanish. "He looks a lot like Villalta. What does the drunken one do?"

"Nothing."

"Is that why he drinks?"

"No. He's waiting to marry this lady."

"Tell him bulls have no balls!" Mike shouted, very drunk, from the other end of the table.

"What does he say?"

"He's drunk."

"Jake," Mike called. "Tell him bulls have no balls!"

"You understand?" I said.

"Yes."

I was sure he didn't, so it was all right.

"Tell him Brett wants to see him put on those green pants."

"Pipe down, Mike."

"Tell him Brett is dying to know how he can get into those pants."

"Pipe down."

During this Romero was fingering his glass and talking with Brett. Brett was talking French and he was talking Spanish and a little English, and laughing.

Bill was filling the glasses.

"Tell him Brett wants to come into——"

"Oh, pipe down, Mike, for Christ's sake!"

Romero looked up smiling. "Pipe down! I know that," he said.

Just then Montoya came into the room. He started to smile at me, then he saw Pedro Romero with a big glass of cognac in his hand, sitting laughing between me and a woman with bare shoulders, at a table full of drunks. He did not even nod.

Montoya went out of the room. Mike was on his feet proposing a toast. "Let's all drink to—" he began. "Pedro Romero," I said. Everybody stood up. Romero took it very seriously, and we touched glasses and drank it down, I rushing it a little because Mike was trying to make it clear that that was not at all what he was going to drink to. But it went off all right, and Pedro Romero shook hands with every one and he and the critic went out together.

1. Nicanor Villalta (see note to Dedication, p. 2).

"My God! he's a lovely boy," Brett said. "And how I would love to see him get into those clothes. He must use a shoe-horn."

"I started to tell him," Mike began. "And Jake kept interrupting me. Why do you interrupt me? Do you think you talk Spanish better than I do?"

"Oh, shut up, Mike! Nobody interrupted you."

"No, I'd like to get this settled." He turned away from me. "Do you think you amount to something, Cohn? Do you think you belong here among us? People who are out to have a good time? For God's sake don't be so noisy, Cohn!"

"Oh, cut it out, Mike," Cohn said.

"Do you think Brett wants you here? Do you think you add to the party? Why don't you say something?"

"I said all I had to say the other night, Mike."

"I'm not one of you literary chaps." Mike stood shakily and leaned against the table. "I'm not clever. But I do know when I'm not wanted. Why don't you see when you're not wanted, Cohn? Go away. Go away, for God's sake. Take that sad Jewish face away. Don't you think I'm right?"

He looked at us.

"Sure," I said. "Let's all go over to the Iruña."

"No. Don't you think I'm right? I love that woman."

"Oh, don't start that again. Do shove it along, Michael," Brett said.

"Don't you think I'm right, Jake?"

Cohn still sat at the table. His face had the sallow, yellow look it got when he was insulted, but somehow he seemed to be enjoying it. The childish, drunken heroics of it. It was his affair with a lady of title.

"Jake," Mike said. He was almost crying. "You know I'm right. Listen, you!" He turned to Cohn: "Go away! Go away now!"

"But I won't go, Mike," said Cohn.

"Then I'll make you!" Mike started toward him around the table. Cohn stood up and took off his glasses. He stood waiting, his face sallow, his hands fairly low, proudly and firmly waiting for the assault, ready to do battle for his lady love.

I grabbed Mike. "Come on to the café," I said. "You can't hit him here in the hotel."

"Good!" said Mike. "Good idea!"

We started off. I looked back as Mike stumbled up the stairs and saw Cohn putting his glasses on again. Bill was sitting at the table pouring another glass of Fundador. Brett was sitting looking straight ahead at nothing.

Outside on the square it had stopped raining and the moon was trying to get through the clouds. There was a wind blowing. The military band was playing and the crowd was massed on the far side of the square where the fireworks specialist and his son were trying to send up fire balloons. A balloon would start up jerkily, on a great bias, and be torn by the wind or blown against the houses of the square. Some fell into the crowd. The magnesium flared and the fireworks exploded and chased about in the crowd. There was no one dancing in the square. The gravel was too wet.

Brett came out with Bill and joined us. We stood in the crowd and watched Don Manuel Orquito, the fireworks king, standing on a little platform, carefully starting the balloons with sticks, standing above the heads of the crowd to launch the balloons off into the wind. The wind brought them all down, and Don Manuel Orquito's face was sweaty in the light of his complicated fireworks that fell into the crowd and charged and chased, sputtering and cracking, between the legs of the people. The people shouted as each new luminous paper bubble careened, caught fire, and fell.

"They're razzing Don Manuel," Bill said.

"How do you know he's Don Manuel?" Brett said.

"His name's on the programme. Don Manuel Orquito, the pirotécnico of esta ciudad."[2]

"Globos iluminados,"[3] Mike said. "A collection of globos iluminados. That's what the paper said."

The wind blew the band music away.

"I say, I wish one would go up," Brett said. "That Don Manuel chap is furious."

"He's probably worked for weeks fixing them to go off, spelling out 'Hail to San Fermin,'" Bill said.

"Globos iluminados," Mike said. "A bunch of bloody globos iluminados."

"Come on," said Brett. "We can't stand here."

"Her ladyship wants a drink," Mike said.

"How you know things," Brett said.

Inside, the café was crowded and very noisy. No one noticed us come in. We could not find a table. There was a great noise going on.

"Come on, let's get out of here," Bill said.

Outside the paseo was going on under the arcade. There were some English and Americans from Biarritz in sport clothes scattered at the tables. Some of the women stared at the people going by with lorgnons.[4] We had acquired, at some time, a friend of Bill's from Biarritz. She was staying with another girl at the Grand Hotel. The other girl had a headache and had gone to bed.

2. Fireworks expert of this city (Spanish).
3. Illuminated globes/balls (Spanish).
4. Opera glasses (French).

"Here's the pub," Mike said. It was the Bar Milano, a small, tough bar where you could get food and where they danced in the back room. We all sat down at a table and ordered a bottle of Fundador. The bar was not full. There was nothing going on.

"This is a hell of a place," Bill said.

"It's too early."

"Let's take the bottle and come back later," Bill said. "I don't want to sit here on a night like this."

"Let's go and look at the English," Mike said. "I love to look at the English."

"They're awful," Bill said. "Where did they all come from?"

"They come from Biarritz," Mike said. "They come to see the last day of the quaint little Spanish fiesta."

"I'll festa them," Bill said.

"You're an extraordinarily beautiful girl." Mike turned to Bill's friend. "When did you come here?"

"Come off it, Michael."

"I say, she *is* a lovely girl. Where have I been? Where have I been looking all this while? You're a lovely thing. *Have* we met? Come along with me and Bill. We're going to festa the English."

"I'll festa them," Bill said. "What the hell are they doing at this fiesta?"

"Come on," Mike said. "Just us three. We're going to festa the bloody English. I hope you're not English? I'm Scotch. I hate the English. I'm going to festa them. Come on, Bill."

Through the window we saw them, all three arm in arm, going toward the café. Rockets were going up in the square.

"I'm going to sit here," Brett said.

"I'll stay with you," Cohn said.

"Oh, don't!" Brett said. "For God's sake, go off somewhere. Can't you see Jake and I want to talk?"

"I didn't," Cohn said. "I thought I'd sit here because I felt a little tight."

"What a hell of a reason for sitting with any one. If you're tight, go to bed. Go on to bed."

"Was I rude enough to him?" Brett asked. Cohn was gone. "My God! I'm so sick of him!"

"He doesn't add much to the gaiety."

"He depresses me so."

"He's behaved very badly."

"Damned badly. He had a chance to behave so well."

"He's probably waiting just outside the door now."

"Yes. He would. You know I do know how he feels. He can't believe it didn't mean anything."

"I know."

"Nobody else would behave as badly. Oh, I'm so sick of the whole thing. And Michael. Michael's been lovely, too."

"It's been damned hard on Mike."

"Yes. But he didn't need to be a swine."

"Everybody behaves badly," I said. "Give them the proper chance."

"You wouldn't behave badly." Brett looked at me.

"I'd be as big an ass as Cohn," I said.

"Darling, don't let's talk a lot of rot."

"All right. Talk about anything you like."

"Don't be difficult. You're the only person I've got, and I feel rather awful to-night."

"You've got Mike."

"Yes, Mike. Hasn't he been pretty?"

"Well," I said, "it's been damned hard on Mike, having Cohn around and seeing him with you."

"Don't I know it, darling? Please don't make me feel any worse than I do."

Brett was nervous as I had never seen her before. She kept looking away from mc and looking ahead at the wall.

"Want to go for a walk?"

"Yes. Come on."

I corked up the Fundador bottle and gave it to the bartender.

"Let's have one more drink of that," Brett said. "My nerves are rotten."

We each drank a glass of the smooth amontillado brandy.

"Come on," said Brett.

As we came out the door I saw Cohn walk out from under the arcade.

"He *was* there," Brett said.

"He can't be away from you."

"Poor devil!"

"I'm not sorry for him. I hate him, myself."

"I hate him, too," she shivered. "I hate his damned suffering."

We walked arm in arm down the side street away from the crowd and the lights of the square. The street was dark and wet, and we walked along it to the fortifications at the edge of town. We passed wine-shops with light coming out from their doors onto the black, wet street, and sudden bursts of music.

"Want to go in?"

"No."

We walked out across the wet grass and onto the stone wall of the fortifications. I spread a newspaper on the stone and Brett sat down. Across the plain it was dark, and we could see the mountains. The wind was high up and took the clouds across the moon. Below us were the dark pits of the fortifications. Behind were the trees and the shadow of the cathedral, and the town silhouetted against the moon.

"Don't feel bad," I said.

"I feel like hell," Brett said. "Don't let's talk."

We looked out at the plain. The long lines of trees were dark in the moonlight. There were the lights of a car on the road climbing the mountain. Up on the top of the mountain we saw the lights of the fort. Below to the left was the river. It was high from the rain, and black and smooth. Trees were dark along the banks. We sat and looked out. Brett stared straight ahead. Suddenly she shivered.

"It's cold."

"Want to walk back?"

"Through the park."

We climbed down. It was clouding over again. In the park it was dark under the trees.

"Do you still love me, Jake?"

"Yes," I said.

"Because I'm a goner," Brett said.

"How?"

"I'm a goner. I'm mad about the Romero boy. I'm in love with him, I think."

"I wouldn't be if I were you."

"I can't help it. I'm a goner. It's tearing me all up inside."

"Don't do it."

"I can't help it. I've never been able to help anything."

"You ought to stop it."

"How can I stop it? I can't stop things. Feel that?"

Her hand was trembling.

"I'm like that all through."

"You oughtn't to do it."

"I can't help it. I'm a goner now, anyway. Don't you see the difference?"

"No."

"I've got to do something. I've got to do something I really want to do. I've lost my self-respect."

"You don't have to do that."

"Oh, darling, don't be difficult. What do you think it's meant to have that damned Jew about, and Mike the way he's acted?"

"Sure."

"I can't just stay tight all the time."

"No."

"Oh, darling, please stay by me. Please stay by me and see me through this."

"Sure."

"I don't say it's right. It is right though for me. God knows, I've never felt such a bitch."

"What do you want me to do?"

"Come on," Brett said. "Let's go and find him."

Together we walked down the gravel path in the park in the dark, under the trees and then out from under the trees and past the gate into the street that led into town.

Pedro Romero was in the café. He was at a table with other bull-fighters and bull-fight critics. They were smoking cigars. When we came in they looked up. Romero smiled and bowed. We sat down at a table half-way down the room.

"Ask him to come over and have a drink."

"Not yet. He'll come over."

"I can't look at him."

"He's nice to look at," I said.

"I've always done just what I wanted."

"I know."

"I do feel such a bitch."

"Well," I said.

"My God!" said Brett, "the things a woman goes through."

"Yes?"

"Oh, I do feel such a bitch."

I looked across at the table. Pedro Romero smiled. He said something to the other people at his table, and stood up. He came over to our table. I stood up and we shook hands.

"Won't you have a drink?"

"You must have a drink with me," he said. He seated himself, asking Brett's permission without saying anything. He had very nice manners. But he kept on smoking his cigar. It went well with his face.

"You like cigars?" I asked.

"Oh, yes. I always smoke cigars."

It was part of his system of authority. It made him seem older. I noticed his skin. It was clear and smooth and very brown. There was a triangular scar on his cheek-bone. I saw he was watching Brett. He felt there was something between them. He must have felt it when Brett gave him her hand. He was being very careful. I think he was sure, but he did not want to make any mistake.

"You fight to-morrow?" I said.

"Yes," he said. "Algabeño was hurt to-day in Madrid. Did you hear?"

"No," I said. "Badly?"

He shook his head.

"Nothing. Here," he showed his hand. Brett reached out and spread the fingers apart.

"Oh!" he said in English, "you tell fortunes?"

"Sometimes. Do you mind?"

"No. I like it." He spread his hand flat on the table. "Tell me I live for always, and be a millionaire."

He was still very polite, but he was surer of himself. "Look," he said, "do you see any bulls in my hand?"

He laughed. His hand was very fine and the wrist was small.

"There are thousands of bulls," Brett said. She was not at all nervous now. She looked lovely.

"Good," Romero laughed. "At a thousand duros[5] apiece," he said to me in Spanish. "Tell me some more."

"It's a good hand," Brett said. "I think he'll live a long time."

"Say it to me. Not to your friend."

"I said you'd live a long time."

"I know it," Romero said. "I'm never going to die."

I tapped with my finger-tips on the table. Romero saw it. He shook his head.

"No. Don't do that. The bulls are my best friends."

I translated to Brett.

"You kill your friends?" she asked.

"Always," he said in English, and laughed. "So they don't kill me." He looked at her across the table.

"You know English well."

"Yes," he said. "Pretty well, sometimes. But I must not let anybody know. It would be very bad, a torero who speaks English."

"Why?" asked Brett.

"It would be bad. The people would not like it. Not yet."

"Why not?"

"They would not like it. Bull-fighters are not like that."

"What are bull-fighters like?"

He laughed and tipped his hat down over his eyes and changed the angle of his cigar and the expression of his face.

"Like at the table," he said. I glanced over. He had mimicked exactly the expression of Nacional. He smiled, his face natural again. "No. I must forget English."

"Don't forget it, yet," Brett said.

"No?"

"No."

"All right."

He laughed again.

"I would like a hat like that," Brett said.

"Good. I'll get you one."

"Right. See that you do."

"I will. I'll get you one to-night."

5. A colloquialism for peso duro, a unit of Spanish currency equal to five pesetas.

I stood up. Romero rose, too.

"Sit down," I said. "I must go and find our friends and bring them here."

He looked at me. It was a final look to ask if it were understood. It was understood all right.

"Sit down," Brett said to him. "You must teach me Spanish."

He sat down and looked at her across the table. I went out. The hard-eyed people at the bull-fighter table watched me go. It was not pleasant. When I came back and looked in the café, twenty minutes later, Brett and Pedro Romero were gone. The coffee-glasses and our three empty cognac-glasses were on the table. A waiter came with a cloth and picked up the glasses and mopped off the table.

Chapter XVII

Outside the Bar Milano I found Bill and Mike and Edna. Edna was the girl's name.

"We've been thrown out," Edna said.

"By the police," said Mike. "There's some people in there that don't like me."

"I've kept them out of four fights," Edna said. "You've got to help me."

Bill's face was red.

"Come back in, Edna," he said. "Go on in there and dance with Mike."

"It's silly," Edna said. "There'll just be another row."

"Damned Biarritz swine," Bill said.

"Come on," Mike said. "After all, it's a pub. They can't occupy a whole pub."

"Good old Mike," Bill said. "Damned English swine come here and insult Mike and try and spoil the fiesta."

"They're so bloody," Mike said. "I hate the English."

"They can't insult Mike," Bill said. "Mike is a swell fellow. They can't insult Mike. I won't stand it. Who cares if he is a damn bankrupt?" His voice broke.

"Who cares?" Mike said. "I don't care. Jake doesn't care. Do *you* care?"

"No," Edna said. "Are you a bankrupt?"

"Of course I am. You don't care, do you, Bill?"

Bill put his arm around Mike's shoulder.

"I wish to hell I was a bankrupt. I'd show those bastards."

"They're just English," Mike said. "It never makes any difference what the English say."

"The dirty swine," Bill said. "I'm going to clean them out."

"Bill," Edna looked at me. "Please don't go in again, Bill. They're so stupid."

"That's it," said Mike. "They're stupid. I knew that was what it was."

"They can't say things like that about Mike," Bill said.

"Do you know them?" I asked Mike.

"No. I never saw them. They say they know me."

"I won't stand it," Bill said.

"Come on. Let's go over to the Suizo," I said.

"They're a bunch of Edna's friends from Biarritz," Bill said.

"They're simply stupid," Edna said.

"One of them's Charley Blackman, from Chicago," Bill said.

"I was never in Chicago," Mike said.

Edna started to laugh and could not stop.

"Take me away from here," she said, "you bankrupts."

"What kind of a row was it?" I asked Edna. We were walking across the square to the Suizo. Bill was gone.

"I don't know what happened, but some one had the police called to keep Mike out of the back room. There were some people that had known Mike at Cannes. What's the matter with Mike?"

"Probably he owes them money," I said. "That's what people usually get bitter about."

In front of the ticket-booths out in the square there were two lines of people waiting. They were sitting on chairs or crouched on the ground with blankets and newspapers around them. They were waiting for the wickets to open in the morning to buy tickets for the bull-fight. The night was clearing and the moon was out. Some of the people in the line were sleeping.

At the Café Suizo we had just sat down and ordered Fundador when Robert Cohn came up.

"Where's Brett?" he asked.

"I don't know."

"She was with you."

"She must have gone to bed."

"She's not."

"I don't know where she is."

His face was sallow under the light. He was standing up.

"Tell me where she is."

"Sit down," I said. "I don't know where she is."

"The hell you don't!"

"You can shut your face."

"Tell me where Brett is."

"I'll not tell you a damn thing."

"You know where she is."

"If I did I wouldn't tell you."

"Oh, go to hell, Cohn," Mike called from the table. "Brett's gone off with the bull-fighter chap. They're on their honeymoon."

"You shut up."

"Oh, go to hell!" Mike said languidly.

"Is that where she is?" Cohn turned to me.

"Go to hell!"

"She was with you. Is that where she is?"

"Go to hell!"

"I'll make you tell me"—he stepped forward—"you damned pimp."

I swung at him and he ducked. I saw his face duck sideways in the light. He hit me and I sat down on the pavement. As I started to get on my feet he hit me twice. I went down backward under a table. I tried to get up and felt I did not have any legs. I felt I must get on my feet and try and hit him. Mike helped me up. Some one poured a carafe of water on my head. Mike had an arm around me, and I found I was sitting on a chair. Mike was pulling at my ears.

"I say, you were cold," Mike said.

"Where the hell were you?"

"Oh, I was around."

"You didn't want to mix in it?"

"He knocked Mike down, too," Edna said.

"He didn't knock me out," Mike said. "I just lay there."

"Does this happen every night at your fiestas?" Edna asked. "Wasn't that Mr. Cohn?"

"I'm all right," I said. "My head's a little wobbly."

There were several waiters and a crowd of people standing around.

"Vaya!" said Mike. "Get away. Go on."

The waiters moved the people away.

"It was quite a thing to watch," Edna said. "He must be a boxer."

"He is."

"I wish Bill had been here," Edna said. "I'd like to have seen Bill knocked down, too. I've always wanted to see Bill knocked down. He's so big."

"I was hoping he would knock down a waiter," Mike said, "and get arrested. I'd like to see Mr. Robert Cohn in jail."

"No," I said.

"Oh, no," said Edna. "You don't mean that."

"I do, though," Mike said. "I'm not one of these chaps likes being knocked about. I never play games, even."

Mike took a drink.

"I never liked to hunt, you know. There was always the danger of having a horse fall on you. How do you feel, Jake?"

"All right."

"You're nice," Edna said to Mike. "Are you really a bankrupt?"

"I'm a tremendous bankrupt," Mike said. "I owe money to everybody. Don't you owe any money?"

"Tons."

"I owe everybody money," Mike said. "I borrowed a hundred pesetas from Montoya to-night."

"The hell you did," I said.

"I'll pay it back," Mike said. "I always pay everything back."

"That's why you're a bankrupt, isn't it?" Edna said.

I stood up. I had heard them talking from a long way away. It all seemed like some bad play.

"I'm going over to the hotel," I said. Then I heard them talking about me.

"Is he all right?" Edna asked.

"We'd better walk with him."

"I'm all right," I said. "Don't come. I'll see you all later."

I walked away from the café. They were sitting at the table. I looked back at them and at the empty tables. There was a waiter sitting at one of the tables with his head in his hands.

Walking across the square to the hotel everything looked new and changed. I had never seen the trees before. I had never seen the flagpoles before, nor the front of the theatre. It was all different. I felt as I felt once coming home from an out-of-town football game. I was carrying a suitcase with my football things in it, and I walked up the street from the station in the town I had lived in all my life and it was all new. They were raking the lawns and burning leaves in the road, and I stopped for a long time and watched. It was all strange. Then I went on, and my feet seemed to be a long way off, and everything seemed to come from a long way off, and I could hear my feet walking a great distance away. I had been kicked in the head early in the game. It was like that crossing the square. It was like that going up the stairs in the hotel. Going up the stairs took a long time, and I had the feeling that I was carrying my suitcase. There was a light in the room. Bill came out and met me in the hall.

"Say," he said, "go up and see Cohn. He's been in a jam, and he's asking for you."

"The hell with him."

"Go on. Go on up and see him."

I did not want to climb another flight of stairs.

"What are you looking at me that way for?"

"I'm not looking at you. Go on up and see Cohn. He's in bad shape."

"You were drunk a little while ago," I said.

"I'm drunk now," Bill said. "But you go up and see Cohn. He wants to see you."

"All right," I said. It was just a matter of climbing more stairs. I went on up the stairs carrying my phantom suitcase. I walked down the hall to Cohn's room. The door was shut and I knocked.

"Who is it?"

"Barnes."

"Come in, Jake."

I opened the door and went in, and set down my suitcase. There was no light in the room. Cohn was lying, face down, on the bed in the dark.

"Hello, Jake."

"Don't call me Jake."

I stood by the door. It was just like this that I had come home. Now it was a hot bath that I needed. A deep, hot bath, to lie back in.

"Where's the bathroom?" I asked.

Cohn was crying. There he was, face down on the bed, crying. He had on a white polo shirt, the kind he'd worn at Princeton.

"I'm sorry, Jake. Please forgive me."

"Forgive you, hell."

"Please forgive me, Jake."

I did not say anything. I stood there by the door.

"I was crazy. You must see how it was."

"Oh, that's all right."

"I couldn't stand it about Brett."

"You called me a pimp."

I did not care. I wanted a hot bath. I wanted a hot bath in deep water.

"I know. Please don't remember it. I was crazy."

"That's all right."

He was crying. His voice was funny. He lay there in his white shirt on the bed in the dark. His polo shirt.

"I'm going away in the morning."

He was crying without making any noise.

"I just couldn't stand it about Brett. I've been through hell, Jake. It's been simply hell. When I met her down here Brett treated me as though I were a perfect stranger. I just couldn't stand it. We lived together at San Sebastian. I suppose you know it. I can't stand it any more."

He lay there on the bed.

"Well," I said, "I'm going to take a bath."

"You were the only friend I had, and I loved Brett so."

"Well," I said, "so long."

"I guess it isn't any use," he said. "I guess it isn't any damn use."

"What?"

"Everything. Please say you forgive me, Jake."

"Sure," I said. "It's all right."

"I felt so terribly. I've been through such hell, Jake. Now everything's gone. Everything."

"Well," I said, "so long. I've got to go."

He rolled over, sat on the edge of the bed, and then stood up.

"So long, Jake," he said. "You'll shake hands, won't you?"

"Sure. Why not?"

We shook hands. In the dark I could not see his face very well.

"Well," I said, "see you in the morning."

"I'm going away in the morning."

"Oh, yes," I said.

I went out. Cohn was standing in the door of the room.

"Are you all right, Jake?" he asked.

"Oh, yes," I said. "I'm all right."

I could not find the bathroom. After a while I found it. There was a deep stone tub. I turned on the taps and the water would not run. I sat down on the edge of the bath-tub. When I got up to go I found I had taken off my shoes. I hunted for them and found them and carried them down-stairs. I found my room and went inside and undressed and got into bed.

I woke with a headache and the noise of the bands going by in the street. I remembered I had promised to take Bill's friend Edna to see the bulls go through the street and into the ring. I dressed and went down-stairs and out into the cold early morning. People were crossing the square, hurrying toward the bull-ring. Across the square were the two lines of men in front of the ticket-booths. They were still waiting for the tickets to go on sale at seven o'clock. I hurried across the street to the café. The waiter told me that my friends had been there and gone.

"How many were they?"

"Two gentlemen and a lady."

That was all right. Bill and Mike were with Edna. She had been afraid last night they would pass out. That was why I was to be sure to take her. I drank the coffee and hurried with the other people toward the bull-ring. I was not groggy now. There was only a bad headache. Everything looked sharp and clear, and the town smelt of the early morning.

The stretch of ground from the edge of the town to the bull-ring was muddy. There was a crowd all along the fence that led to the ring, and the outside balconies and the top of the bull-ring were solid with people. I heard the rocket and I knew I could not get into the ring in time to see the bulls come in, so I shoved through the crowd to the fence. I was pushed close against the planks of the fence. Between the two fences of the runway the police were clearing the crowd along. They walked or trotted on into the bull-ring. Then people commenced to come running. A drunk slipped and fell. Two policemen grabbed him and rushed him over to the fence. The crowd were running fast now. There was a great shout from the crowd, and putting my head through between the boards I saw the bulls just coming out of the street into the long running pen. They were going fast and gaining on the crowd. Just then another drunk started out from the fence with a blouse in his hands. He wanted to do cape-work with the bulls. The two policemen tore out, collared him, one hit him with a club, and they dragged him against the fence and stood flattened out against the fence as the last of the crowd and the bulls went by. There were so many people running ahead of the bulls that the mass thickened and slowed up going through the gate into the ring, and as the bulls passed, galloping together, heavy, muddy-sided, horns swinging, one shot ahead, caught a man in the running crowd in the back and lifted him in the air. Both the man's arms were by his sides, his head went back as the horn went in, and the bull lifted him and then dropped him. The bull picked another man running in front, but the man disappeared into the crowd, and the crowd was through the gate and into the ring with the bulls behind them. The red door of the ring went shut, the crowd on the outside balconies of the bull-ring were pressing through to the inside, there was a shout, then another shout.

The man who had been gored lay face down in the trampled mud. People climbed over the fence, and I could not see the man because the crowd was so thick around him. From inside the ring came the shouts. Each shout meant a charge by some bull into the crowd. You could tell by the degree of intensity in the shout how bad a thing it was that was happening. Then the rocket went up that meant the steers had gotten the bulls out of the ring and into the corrals. I left the fence and started back toward the town.

Back in the town I went to the café to have a second coffee and some buttered toast. The waiters were sweeping out the café and mopping off the tables. One came over and took my order.

"Anything happen at the encierro?"[1]

"I didn't see it all. One man was badly cogido."[2]

"Where?"

"Here." I put one hand on the small of my back and the other on my chest, where it looked as though the horn must have come through. The waiter nodded his head and swept the crumbs from the table with his cloth.

"Badly cogido," he said. "All for sport. All for pleasure."

1. Literally "confinement" (Spanish). The term as used here names the famous "running of the bulls" through the streets of Pamplona (from their pens to the bullring) every morning during the Festival of San Fermin.
2. Literally "caught" (Spanish), here meaning caught (or gored) on the horns of a bull.

He went away and came back with the long-handled coffee and milk pots. He poured the milk and coffee. It came out of the long spouts in two streams into the big cup. The waiter nodded his head.

"Badly cogido through the back," he said. He put the pots down on the table and sat down in the chair at the table. "A big horn wound. All for fun. Just for fun. What do you think of that?"

"I don't know."

"That's it. All for fun. Fun, you understand."

"You're not an aficionado?"

"Me? What are bulls? Animals. Brute animals." He stood up and put his hand on the small of his back. "Right through the back. A cornada right through the back. For fun—you understand."

He shook his head and walked away, carrying the coffee-pots. Two men were going by in the street. The waiter shouted to them. They were grave-looking. One shook his head. "Muerto!" he called.

The waiter nodded his head. The two men went on. They were on some errand. The waiter came over to my table.

"You hear? Muerto. Dead. He's dead. With a horn through him. All for morning fun. Es muy flamenco."[3]

"It's bad."

"Not for me," the waiter said. "No fun in that for me."

Later in the day we learned that the man who was killed was named Vicente Gironés, and came from near Tafalla.[4] The next day in the paper we read that he was twenty-eight years old, and had a farm, a wife, and two children. He had continued to come to the fiesta each year after he was married. The next day his wife came in from Tafalla to be with the body, and the day after there was a service in the chapel of San Fermin, and the coffin was carried to the railway-station by members of the dancing and drinking society of Tafalla. The drums marched ahead, and there was music on the fifes, and behind the men who carried the coffin walked the wife and two children. . . . Behind them marched all the members of the dancing and drinking societies of Pamplona, Estella, Tafalla, and Sangüesa who could stay over for the funeral. The coffin was loaded into the baggage-car of the train, and the widow and the two children rode, sitting, all three together, in an open third-class railway-carriage. The train started with a jerk, and then ran smoothly, going down grade around the edge of the plateau and out into the fields of grain that blew in the wind on the plain on the way to Tafalla.

The bull who killed Vicente Gironés was named Bocanegra,[5] was Number 118 of the bull-breeding establishment of Sanchez Taberno,

3. "It's very flamenco," (Spanish), meaning (ironically) something like "It's quite a party."
4. The identity and background of this victim are fictional; no one was killed during the *encierro* in Pamplona in 1925.
5. Black mouth (Spanish).

and was killed by Pedro Romero as the third bull of that same afternoon. His ear was cut by popular acclamation and given to Pedro Romero, who, in turn, gave it to Brett, who wrapped it in a handkerchief belonging to myself, and left both ear and handkerchief, along with a number of Muratti[6] cigarette-stubs, shoved far back in the drawer of the bed-table that stood beside her bed in the Hotel Montoya, in Pamplona.

Back in the hotel, the night watchman was sitting on a bench inside the door. He had been there all night and was very sleepy. He stood up as I came in. Three of the waitresses came in at the same time. They had been to the morning show at the bull-ring. They went upstairs laughing. I followed them up-stairs and went into my room. I took off my shoes and lay down on the bed. The window was open onto the balcony and the sunlight was bright in the room. I did not feel sleepy. It must have been half past three o'clock when I had gone to bed and the bands had waked me at six. My jaw was sore on both sides. I felt it with my thumb and fingers. That damn Cohn. He should have hit somebody the first time he was insulted, and then gone away. He was so sure that Brett loved him. He was going to stay, and true love would conquer all. Some one knocked on the door.

"Come in."

It was Bill and Mike. They sat down on the bed.

"Some encierro," Bill said. "Some encierro."

"I say, weren't you there?" Mike asked. "Ring for some beer, Bill."

"What a morning!" Bill said. He mopped off his face. "My God! what a morning! And here's old Jake. Old Jake, the human punching-bag."

"What happened inside?"

"Good God!" Bill said, "what happened, Mike?"

"There were these bulls coming in," Mike said. "Just ahead of them was the crowd, and some chap tripped and brought the whole lot of them down."

"And the bulls all came in right over them," Bill said.

"I heard them yell."

"That was Edna," Bill said.

"Chaps kept coming out and waving their shirts."

"One bull went along the barrera and hooked everybody over."

"They took about twenty chaps to the infirmary," Mike said.

"What a morning!" Bill said. "The damn police kept arresting chaps that wanted to go and commit suicide with the bulls."

"The steers took them in, in the end," Mike said.

"It took about an hour."

6. A cigarette brand whose headquarters in the 1920s were in London and Berlin.

"It was really about a quarter of an hour," Mike objected.

"Oh, go to hell," Bill said. "You've been in the war. It was two hours and a half for me."

"Where's that beer?" Mike asked.

"What did you do with the lovely Edna?"

"We took her home just now. She's gone to bed."

"How did she like it?"

"Fine. We told her it was just like that every morning."

"She was impressed," Mike said.

"She wanted us to go down in the ring, too," Bill said. "She likes action."

"I said it wouldn't be fair to my creditors," Mike said.

"What a morning," Bill said. "And what a night!"

"How's your jaw, Jake?" Mike asked.

"Sore," I said.

Bill laughed.

"Why didn't you hit him with a chair?"

"You can talk," Mike said. "He'd have knocked you out, too. I never saw him hit me. I rather think I saw him just before, and then quite suddenly I was sitting down in the street, and Jake was lying under a table."

"Where did he go afterward?" I asked.

"Here she is," Mike said. "Here's the beautiful lady with the beer."

The chambermaid put the tray with the beer-bottles and glasses down on the table.

"Now bring up three more bottles," Mike said.

"Where did Cohn go after he hit me?" I asked Bill.

"Don't you know about that?" Mike was opening a beer-bottle. He poured the beer into one of the glasses, holding the glass close to the bottle.

"Really?" Bill asked.

"Why he went in and found Brett and the bull-fighter chap in the bull-fighter's room, and then he massacred the poor, bloody bull-fighter."

"No."

"Yes."

"What a night!" Bill said.

"He nearly killed the poor, bloody bull-fighter. Then Cohn wanted to take Brett away. Wanted to make an honest woman of her, I imagine. Damned touching scene."

He took a long drink of the beer.

"He is an ass."

"What happened?"

"Brett gave him what for. She told him off. I think she was rather good."

"I'll bet she was," Bill said.

"Then Cohn broke down and cried, and wanted to shake hands with the bull-fighter fellow. He wanted to shake hands with Brett, too."

"I know. He shook hands with me."

"Did he? Well, they weren't having any of it. The bull-fighter fellow was rather good. He didn't say much, but he kept getting up and getting knocked down again. Cohn couldn't knock him out. It must have been damned funny."

"Where did you hear all this?"

"Brett. I saw her this morning."

"What happened finally?"

"It seems the bull-fighter fellow was sitting on the bed. He'd been knocked down about fifteen times, and he wanted to fight some more. Brett held him and wouldn't let him get up. He was weak, but Brett couldn't hold him, and he got up. Then Cohn said he wouldn't hit him again. Said he couldn't do it. Said it would be wicked. So the bull-fighter chap sort of rather staggered over to him. Cohn went back against the wall.

"'So you won't hit me?'

"'No,' said Cohn. 'I'd be ashamed to.'

"So the bull-fighter fellow hit him just as hard as he could in the face, and then sat down on the floor. He couldn't get up, Brett said. Cohn wanted to pick him up and carry him to the bed. He said if Cohn helped him he'd kill him, and he'd kill him anyway this morning if Cohn wasn't out of town. Cohn was crying, and Brett had told him off, and he wanted to shake hands. I've told you that before."

"Tell the rest," Bill said.

"It seems the bull-fighter chap was sitting on the floor. He was waiting to get strength enough to get up and hit Cohn again. Brett wasn't having any shaking hands, and Cohn was crying and telling her how much he loved her, and she was telling him not to be a ruddy ass. Then Cohn leaned down to shake hands with the bull-fighter fellow. No hard feelings, you know. All for forgiveness. And the bull-fighter chap hit him in the face again."

"That's quite a kid," Bill said.

"He ruined Cohn," Mike said. "You know I don't think Cohn will ever want to knock people about again."

"When did you see Brett?"

"This morning. She came in to get some things. She's looking after this Romero lad."

He poured out another bottle of beer.

"Brett's rather cut up. But she loves looking after people. That's how we came to go off together. She was looking after me."

"I know," I said.

"I'm rather drunk," Mike said. "I think I'll *stay* rather drunk. This is all awfully amusing, but it's not too pleasant. It's not too pleasant for me."

He drank off the beer.

"I gave Brett what for, you know. I said if she would go about with Jews and bull-fighters and such people, she must expect trouble." He leaned forward. "I say, Jake, do you mind if I drink that bottle of yours? She'll bring you another one."

"Please," I said. "I wasn't drinking it, anyway."

Mike started to open the bottle. "Would you mind opening it?" I pressed up the wire fastener and poured it for him.

"You know," Mike went on, "Brett was rather good. She's always rather good. I gave her a fearful hiding about Jews and bull-fighters, and all those sort of people, and do you know what she said: 'Yes. I've had such a hell of a happy life with the British aristocracy!'"

He took a drink.

"That was rather good. Ashley, chap she got the title from, was a sailor, you know. Ninth baronet. When he came home he wouldn't sleep in a bed. Always made Brett sleep on the floor. Finally, when he got really bad, he used to tell her he'd kill her. Always slept with a loaded service revolver. Brett used to take the shells out when he'd gone to sleep. She hasn't had an absolutely happy life, Brett. Damned shame, too. She enjoys things so."

He stood up. His hand was shaky.

"I'm going in the room. Try and get a little sleep."

He smiled.

"We go too long without sleep in these fiestas. I'm going to start now and get plenty of sleep. Damn bad thing not to get sleep. Makes you frightfully nervy."

"We'll see you at noon at the Iruña," Bill said.

Mike went out the door. We heard him in the next room.

He rang the bell and the chambermaid came and knocked at the door.

"Bring up half a dozen bottles of beer and a bottle of Fundador," Mike told her.

"Sí, Señorito."

"I'm going to bed," Bill said. "Poor old Mike. I had a hell of a row about him last night."

"Where? At that Milano place?"

"Yes. There was a fellow there that had helped pay Brett and Mike out of Cannes, once. He was damned nasty."

"I know the story."

"I didn't. Nobody ought to have a right to say things about Mike."

"That's what makes it bad."

"They oughtn't to have any right. I wish to hell they didn't have any right. I'm going to bed."

"Was anybody killed in the ring?"

"I don't think so. Just badly hurt."

"A man was killed outside in the runway."

"Was there?" said Bill.

Chapter XVIII

At noon we were all at the café. It was crowded. We were eating shrimps and drinking beer. The town was crowded. Every street was full. Big motor-cars from Biarritz and San Sebastian kept driving up and parking around the square. They brought people for the bull-fight. Sight-seeing cars came up, too. There was one with twenty-five Englishwomen in it. They sat in the big, white car and looked through their glasses at the fiesta. The dancers were all quite drunk. It was the last day of the fiesta.

The fiesta was solid and unbroken, but the motor-cars and tourist-cars made little islands of onlookers. When the cars emptied, the onlookers were absorbed into the crowd. You did not see them again except as sport clothes, odd-looking at a table among the closely packed peasants in black smocks. The fiesta absorbed even the Biarritz English so that you did not see them unless you passed close to a table. All the time there was music in the street. The drums kept on pounding and the pipes were going. Inside the cafés men with their hands gripping the table, or on each other's shoulders, were singing the hard-voiced singing.

"Here comes Brett," Bill said.

I looked and saw her coming through the crowd in the square, walking, her head up, as though the fiesta were being staged in her honor, and she found it pleasant and amusing.

"Hello, you chaps!" she said. "I say, I *have* a thirst."

"Get another big beer," Bill said to the waiter.

"Shrimps?"

"Is Cohn gone?" Brett asked.

"Yes," Bill said. "He hired a car."

The beer came. Brett started to lift the glass mug and her hand shook. She saw it and smiled, and leaned forward and took a long sip.

"Good beer."

"Very good," I said. I was nervous about Mike. I did not think he had slept. He must have been drinking all the time, but he seemed to be under control.

"I heard Cohn had hurt you, Jake," Brett said.

"No. Knocked me out. That was all."

"I say, he did hurt Pedro Romero," Brett said. "He hurt him most badly."

"How is he?"

"He'll be all right. He won't go out of the room."

"Does he look badly?"

"Very. He was really hurt. I told him I wanted to pop out and see you chaps for a minute."

"Is he going to fight?"

"Rather. I'm going with you, if you don't mind."

"How's your boy friend?" Mike asked. He had not listened to anything that Brett had said.

"Brett's got a bull-fighter," he said. "She had a Jew named Cohn, but he turned out badly."

Brett stood up.

"I am not going to listen to that sort of rot from you, Michael."

"How's your boy friend?"

"Damned well," Brett said. "Watch him this afternoon."

"Brett's got a bull-fighter," Mike said. "A beautiful, bloody bull-fighter."

"Would you mind walking over with me? I want to talk to you, Jake."

"Tell him all about your bull-fighter," Mike said. "Oh, to hell with your bull-fighter!" He tipped the table so that all the beers and the dish of shrimps went over in a crash.

"Come on," Brett said. "Let's get out of this."

In the crowd crossing the square I said: "How is it?"

"I'm not going to see him after lunch until the fight. His people come in and dress him. They're very angry about me, he says."

Brett was radiant. She was happy. The sun was out and the day was bright.

"I feel altogether changed," Brett said. "You've no idea, Jake."

"Anything you want me to do?"

"No, just go to the fight with me."

"We'll see you at lunch?"

"No. I'm eating with him."

We were standing under the arcade at the door of the hotel. They were carrying tables out and setting them up under the arcade.

"Want to take a turn out to the park?" Brett asked. "I don't want to go up yet. I fancy he's sleeping."

We walked along past the theatre and out of the square and along through the barracks of the fair, moving with the crowd between the lines of booths. We came out on a cross-street that led to the Paseo de Sarasate.[1] We could see the crowd walking there, all the fashionably dressed people. They were making the turn at the upper end of the park.

"Don't let's go there," Brett said. "I don't want staring at just now."

We stood in the sunlight. It was hot and good after the rain and the clouds from the sea.

"I hope the wind goes down," Brett said. "It's very bad for him."

"So do I."

"He says the bulls are all right."

"They're good."

"Is that San Fermin's?"[2]

Brett looked at the yellow wall of the chapel.

"Yes. Where the show started on Sunday."

"Let's go in. Do you mind? I'd rather like to pray a little for him or something."

We went in through the heavy leather door that moved very lightly. It was dark inside. Many people were praying. You saw them as your eyes adjusted themselves to the half-light. We knelt at one of the long wooden benches. After a little I felt Brett stiffen beside me, and saw she was looking straight ahead.

"Come on," she whispered throatily. "Let's get out of here. Makes me damned nervous."

Outside in the hot brightness of the street Brett looked up at the tree-tops in the wind. The praying had not been much of a success.

"Don't know why I get so nervy in church," Brett said. "Never does me any good."

We walked along.

"I'm damned bad for a religious atmosphere," Brett said. "I've the wrong type of face.

"You know," Brett said, "I'm not worried about him at all. I just feel happy about him."

"Good."

"I wish the wind would drop, though."

"It's liable to go down by five o'clock."

"Let's hope."

"You might pray," I laughed.

1. A boulevard in Pamplona that leads to the Palacio de Navarra, the seat of provincial government.
2. Brett means the Church of San Lorenzo, in which the San Fermín Chapel is located.

"Never does me any good. I've never gotten anything I prayed for. Have you?"

"Oh, yes."

"Oh, rot," said Brett. "Maybe it works for some people, though you don't look very religious, Jake."

"I'm pretty religious."

"Oh, rot," said Brett. "Don't start proselyting to-day. To-day's going to be bad enough as it is."

It was the first time I had seen her in the old happy, careless way since before she went off with Cohn. We were back again in front of the hotel. All the tables were set now, and already several were filled with people eating.

"Do look after Mike," Brett said. "Don't let him get too bad."

"Your frients haff gone up-stairs," the German maître d'hôtel said in English. He was a continual eavesdropper. Brett turned to him:

"Thank you, so much. Have you anything else to say?"

"No, *ma'am.*"

"Good," said Brett.

"Save us a table for three," I said to the German. He smiled his dirty little pink-and-white smile.

"Iss madam eating here?"

"No," Brett said.

"Den I think a tabul for two will be enuff."

"Don't talk to him," Brett said. "Mike must have been in bad shape," she said on the stairs. We passed Montoya on the stairs. He bowed and did not smile.

"I'll see you at the café," Brett said. "Thank you, so much, Jake."

We had stopped at the floor our rooms were on. She went straight down the hall and into Romero's room. She did not knock. She simply opened the door, went in, and closed it behind her.

I stood in front of the door of Mike's room and knocked. There was no answer. I tried the knob and it opened. Inside the room was in great disorder. All the bags were opened and clothing was strewn around. There were empty bottles beside the bed. Mike lay on the bed looking like a death mask of himself. He opened his eyes and looked at me.

"Hello, Jake," he said very slowly. "I'm getting a lit tle sleep. I've want ed a lit tle sleep for a long time."

"Let me cover you over."

"No. I'm quite warm."

"Don't go. I have n't got ten to sleep yet."

"You'll sleep, Mike. Don't worry, boy."

"Brett's got a bull-fighter," Mike said. "But her Jew has gone away."

He turned his head and looked at me.

"Damned good thing, what?"

"Yes. Now go to sleep, Mike. You ought to get some sleep."

"I'm just start ing. I'm go ing to get a lit tle sleep."

He shut his eyes. I went out of the room and turned the door to quietly. Bill was in my room reading the paper.

"See Mike?"

"Yes."

"Let's go and eat."

"I won't eat down-stairs with that German head waiter. He was damned snotty when I was getting Mike up-stairs."

"He was snotty to us, too."

"Let's go out and eat in the town."

We went down the stairs. On the stairs we passed a girl coming up with a covered tray.

"There goes Brett's lunch," Bill said.

"And the kid's," I said.

Outside on the terrace under the arcade the German head waiter came up. His red cheeks were shiny. He was being polite.

"I haff a tabul for two for you gentlemen," he said.

"Go sit at it," Bill said. We went on out across the street.

We ate at a restaurant in a side street off the square. They were all men eating in the restaurant. It was full of smoke and drinking and singing. The food was good and so was the wine. We did not talk much. Afterward we went to the café and watched the fiesta come to the boiling-point. Brett came over soon after lunch. She said she had looked in the room and that Mike was asleep.

When the fiesta boiled over and toward the bull-ring we went with the crowd. Brett sat at the ringside between Bill and me. Directly below us was the callejon, the passageway between the stands and the red fence of the barrera. Behind us the concrete stands filled solidly. Out in front, beyond the red fence, the sand of the ring was smooth-rolled and yellow. It looked a little heavy from the rain, but it was dry in the sun and firm and smooth. The sword-handlers and bull-ring servants came down the callejon carrying on their shoulders the wicker baskets of fighting capes and muletas.[3] They were bloodstained and compactly folded and packed in the baskets. The sword-handlers opened the heavy leather sword-cases so the red wrapped hilts of the sheaf of swords showed as the leather case leaned against the fence. They unfolded the dark-stained red

3. A small red cape affixed to a stick or baton, used by a matador to guide the bull through turns during the bullfight. *Callejon:* Literally "alley" (Spanish), the passageway between the barrera and the seating area of the bullring.

flannel of the muletas and fixed batons in them to spread the stuff and give the matador something to hold. Brett watched it all. She was absorbed in the professional details.

"He's his name stencilled on all the capes and muletas," she said. "Why do they call them muletas?"

"I don't know."

"I wonder if they ever launder them."

"I don't think so. It might spoil the color."

"The blood must stiffen them," Bill said.

"Funny," Brett said. "How one doesn't mind the blood."

Below in the narrow passage of the callejon the sword-handlers arranged everything. All the seats were full. Above, all the boxes were full. There was not an empty seat except in the President's box. When he came in the fight would start. Across the smooth sand, in the high doorway that led into the corrals, the bull-fighters were standing, their arms furled in their capes, talking, waiting for the signal to march in across the arena. Brett was watching them with the glasses.

"Here, would you like to look?"

I looked through the glasses and saw the three matadors. Romero was in the centre, Belmonte on his left, Marcial on his right. Back of them were their people, and behind the banderilleros, back in the passageway and in the open space of the corral, I saw the picadors.[4] Romero was wearing a black suit. His tricornered hat was low down over his eyes. I could not see his face clearly under the hat, but it looked badly marked. He was looking straight ahead. Marcial was smoking a cigarette guardedly, holding it in his hand. Belmonte looked ahead, his face wan and yellow, his long wolf jaw out. He was looking at nothing. Neither he nor Romero seemed to have anything in common with the others. They were all alone. The President came in; there was handclapping above us in the grand stand, and I handed the glasses to Brett. There was applause. The music started. Brett looked through the glasses.

"Here, take them," she said.

Through the glasses I saw Belmonte speak to Romero. Marcial straightened up and dropped his cigarette, and, looking straight ahead, their heads back, their free arms swinging, the three matadors walked out. Behind them came all the procession, opening out, all striding in step, all the capes furled, everybody with free arms swinging, and behind rode the picadors, their pics rising like lances. Behind all came the two trains of mules and the bull-ring servants.

4. Banderilleros and picadors are participants in the *corrida*. *Banderillas* are decorated barbed darts stabbed into the neck and shoulders of the bull to begin to weaken the muscles that let the bull hold its head up. On picadors see p. 119, note 7.

The matadors bowed, holding their hats on, before the President's box, and then came over to the barrera below us. Pedro Romero took off his heavy gold-brocaded cape and handed it over the fence to his sword-handler. He said something to the sword-handler. Close below us we saw Romero's lips were puffed, both eyes were discolored. His face was discolored and swollen. The sword-handler took the cape, looked up at Brett, and came over to us and handed up the cape.

"Spread it out in front of you," I said.

Brett leaned forward. The cape was heavy and smoothly stiff with gold. The sword-handler looked back, shook his head, and said something. A man beside me leaned over toward Brett.

"He doesn't want you to spread it," he said. "You should fold it and keep it in your lap."

Brett folded the heavy cape.

Romero did not look up at us. He was speaking to Belmonte. Belmonte had sent his formal cape over to some friends. He looked across at them and smiled, his wolf smile that was only with the mouth. Romero leaned over the barrera and asked for the water-jug. The sword-handler brought it and Romero poured water over the percale of his fighting-cape, and then scuffed the lower folds in the sand with his slippered foot.

"What's that for?" Brett asked.

"To give it weight in the wind."

"His face looks bad," Bill said.

"He feels very badly," Brett said. "He should be in bed."

The first bull was Belmonte's. Belmonte was very good. But because he got thirty thousand pesetas and people had stayed in line all night to buy tickets to see him, the crowd demanded that he should be more than very good. Belmonte's great attraction is working close to the bull. In bull-fighting they speak of the terrain of the bull and the terrain of the bull-fighter. As long as a bull-fighter stays in his own terrain he is comparatively safe. Each time he enters into the terrain of the bull he is in great danger. Belmonte, in his best days, worked always in the terrain of the bull. This way he gave the sensation of coming tragedy. People went to the corrida to see Belmonte, to be given tragic sensations, and perhaps to see the death of Belmonte. Fifteen years ago they said if you wanted to see Belmonte you should go quickly, while he was still alive. Since then he has killed more than a thousand bulls. When he retired the legend grew up about how his bull-fighting had been, and when he came out of retirement the public were disappointed because no real man could work as close to the bulls as Belmonte was supposed to have done, not, of course, even Belmonte.

Also Belmonte imposed conditions and insisted that his bulls should not be too large, nor too dangerously armed with horns, and so the element that was necessary to give the sensation of tragedy was not there, and the public, who wanted three times as much from Belmonte, who was sick with a fistula, as Belmonte had ever been able to give, felt defrauded and cheated, and Belmonte's jaw came further out in contempt, and his face turned yellower, and he moved with greater difficulty as his pain increased, and finally the crowd were actively against him, and he was utterly contemptuous and indifferent. He had meant to have a great afternoon, and instead it was an afternoon of sneers, shouted insults, and finally a volley of cushions and pieces of bread and vegetables, thrown down at him in the plaza where he had had his greatest triumphs. His jaw only went further out. Sometimes he turned to smile that toothed, long-jawed, lipless smile when he was called something particularly insulting, and always the pain that any movement produced grew stronger and stronger, until finally his yellow face was parchment color, and after his second bull was dead and the throwing of bread and cushions was over, after he had saluted the President with the same wolf-jawed smile and contemptuous eyes, and handed his sword over the barrera to be wiped, and put back in its case, he passed through into the callejón and leaned on the barrera below us, his head on his arms, not seeing, not hearing anything, only going through his pain. When he looked up, finally, he asked for a drink of water. He swallowed a little, rinsed his mouth, spat the water, took his cape, and went back into the ring.

Because they were against Belmonte the public were for Romero. From the moment he left the barrera and went toward the bull they applauded him. Belmonte watched Romero, too, watched him always without seeming to. He paid no attention to Marcial. Marcial was the sort of thing he knew all about. He had come out of retirement to compete with Marcial, knowing it was a competition gained in advance. He had expected to compete with Marcial and the other stars of the decadence of bull-fighting, and he knew that the sincerity of his own bull-fighting would be so set off by the false aesthetics of the bull-fighters of the decadent period that he would only have to be in the ring. His return from retirement had been spoiled by Romero. Romero did always, smoothly, calmly, and beautifully, what he, Belmonte, could only bring himself to do now sometimes. The crowd felt it, even the people from Biarritz, even the American ambassador saw it, finally. It was a competition that Belmonte would not enter because it would lead only to a bad horn wound or death. Belmonte was no longer well enough. He no longer had his greatest moments in the bull-ring. He was not sure that there were any great moments. Things were not the same and now life only came in flashes. He had flashes of the old greatness with his bulls, but they were not of value because he had discounted them in advance when he had picked the bulls out for their safety, getting out of a motor and leaning on a fence, looking over at the herd on the ranch of his friend the bull-breeder. So he had two small, manageable bulls without much horns, and when he felt the greatness again coming, just a little of it through the pain that was always with him, it had been discounted and sold in advance, and it did not give him a good feeling. It was the greatness, but it did not make bull-fighting wonderful to him any more.

Pedro Romero had the greatness. He loved bull-fighting, and I think he loved the bulls, and I think he loved Brett. Everything of which he could control the locality he did in front of her all that afternoon. Never once did he look up. He made it stronger that way, and did it for himself, too, as well as for her. Because he did not look up to ask if it pleased he did it all for himself inside, and it strengthened him, and yet he did it for her, too. But he did not do it for her at any loss to himself. He gained by it all through the afternoon.

His first "quite"[5] was directly below us. The three matadors take the bull in turn after each charge he makes at a picador. Belmonte was the first. Marcial was the second. Then came Romero. The three of them were standing at the left of the horse. The picador, his hat down over his eyes, the shaft of his pic angling sharply toward the bull, kicked in the spurs and held them and with the reins in his left hand walked the horse forward toward the bull. The bull was watching. Seemingly he watched the white horse, but really he watched the triangular steel point of the pic. Romero, watching, saw the bull start to turn his head. He did not want to charge. Romero flicked his cape so the color caught the bull's eye. The bull charged with the reflex, charged, and found not the flash of color but a white horse, and a man leaned far over the horse, shot the steel point of the long hickory shaft into the hump of muscle on the bull's shoulder, and pulled his horse sideways as he pivoted on the pic, making a wound, enforcing the iron into the bull's shoulder, making him bleed for Belmonte.

The bull did not insist under the iron. He did not really want to get at the horse. He turned and the group broke apart and Romero was taking him out with his cape. He took him out softly and smoothly, and then stopped and, standing squarely in front of the bull, offered him the cape. The bull's tail went up and he charged, and Romero moved his arms ahead of the bull, wheeling, his feet firmed. The dampened, mud-weighted cape swung open and full as a sail fills, and Romero pivoted with it just ahead of the bull. At the end of the pass they were facing each other again. Romero smiled. The bull

5. The matador's act of drawing the bull away (from a picador's horse, e.g.) with the action of his cape.

wanted it again, and Romero's cape filled again, this time on the other side. Each time he let the bull pass so close that the man and the bull and the cape that filled and pivoted ahead of the bull were all one sharply etched mass. It was all so slow and so controlled. It was as though he were rocking the bull to sleep. He made four veronicas[6] like that, and finished with a half-veronica that turned his back on the bull and came away toward the applause, his hand on his hip, his cape on his arm, and the bull watching his back going away.

In his own bulls he was perfect. His first bull did not see well. After the first two passes with the cape Romero knew exactly how bad the vision was impaired. He worked accordingly. It was not brilliant bull-fighting. It was only perfect bull-fighting. The crowd wanted the bull changed. They made a great row. Nothing very fine could happen with a bull that could not see the lures, but the President would not order him replaced.

"Why don't they change him?" Brett asked.

"They've paid for him. They don't want to lose their money."

"It's hardly fair to Romero."

"Watch how he handles a bull that can't see the color."

"It's the sort of thing I don't like to see."

It was not nice to watch if you cared anything about the person who was doing it. With the bull who could not see the colors of the capes, or the scarlet flannel of the muleta, Romero had to make the bull consent with his body. He had to get so close that the bull saw his body, and would start for it, and then shift the bull's charge to the flannel and finish out the pass in the classic manner. The Biarritz crowd did not like it. They thought Romero was afraid, and that was why he gave that little sidestep each time as he transferred the bull's charge from his own body to the flannel. They preferred Belmonte's imitation of himself or Marcial's imitation of Belmonte. There were three of them in the row behind us.

"What's he afraid of the bull for? The bull's so dumb he only goes after the cloth."

"He's just a young bull-fighter. He hasn't learned it yet."

"But I thought he was fine with the cape before."

"Probably he's nervous now."

Out in the centre of the ring, all alone, Romero was going on with the same thing, getting so close that the bull could see him plainly, offering the body, offering it again a little closer, the bull watching dully, then so close that the bull thought he had him, offering again and finally drawing the charge and then, just before the horns came,

6. A pass with the bull in which the matador holds the cape with both hands. It is named for Saint Veronica, who offered a cloth to Jesus so that he could wipe the sweat and blood from his face as he made his way to his Crucifixion.

giving the bull the red cloth to follow with that little, almost imperceptible, jerk that so offended the critical judgment of the Biarritz bull-fight experts.

"He's going to kill now," I said to Brett. "The bull's still strong. He wouldn't wear himself out."

Out in the centre of the ring Romero profiled in front of the bull, drew the sword out from the folds of the muleta, rose on his toes, and sighted along the blade. The bull charged as Romero charged. Romero's left hand dropped the muleta over the bull's muzzle to blind him, his left shoulder went forward between the horns as the sword went in, and for just an instant he and the bull were one, Romero way out over the bull, the right arm extended high up to where the hilt of the sword had gone in between the bull's shoulders. Then the figure was broken. There was a little jolt as Romero came clear, and then he was standing, one hand up, facing the bull, his shirt ripped out from under his sleeve, the white blowing in the wind, and the bull, the red sword hilt tight between his shoulders, his head going down and his legs settling.

"There he goes," Bill said.

Romero was close enough so the bull could see him. His hand still up, he spoke to the bull. The bull gathered himself, then his head went forward and he went over slowly, then all over, suddenly, four feet in the air.

They handed the sword to Romero, and carrying it blade down, the muleta in his other hand, he walked over to in front of the President's box, bowed, straightened, and came over to the barrera and handed over the sword and muleta.

"Bad one," said the sword-handler.

"He made me sweat," said Romero. He wiped off his face. The sword-handler handed him the water-jug. Romero wiped his lips. It hurt him to drink out of the jug. He did not look up at us.

Marcial had a big day. They were still applauding him when Romero's last bull came in. It was the bull that had sprinted out and killed the man in the morning running.

During Romero's first bull his hurt face had been very noticeable. Everything he did showed it. All the concentration of the awkwardly delicate working with the bull that could not see well brought it out. The fight with Cohn had not touched his spirit but his face had been smashed and his body hurt. He was wiping all that out now. Each thing that he did with this bull wiped that out a little cleaner. It was a good bull, a big bull, and with horns, and it turned and recharged easily and surely. He was what Romero wanted in bulls.

When he had finished his work with the muleta and was ready to kill, the crowd made him go on. They did not want the bull killed yet, they did not want it to be over. Romero went on. It was like a course in bull-fighting. All the passes he linked up, all completed, all slow, templed and smooth. There were no tricks and no mystifications. There was no brusqueness. And each pass as it reached the summit gave you a sudden ache inside. The crowd did not want it ever to be finished.

The bull was squared on all four feet to be killed, and Romero killed directly below us. He killed not as he had been forced to by the last bull, but as he wanted to. He profiled directly in front of the bull, drew the sword out of the folds of the muleta and sighted along the blade. The bull watched him. Romero spoke to the bull and tapped one of his feet. The bull charged and Romero waited for the charge, the muleta held low, sighting along the blade, his feet firm. Then without taking a step forward, he became one with the bull, the sword was in high between the shoulders, the bull had followed the low-swung flannel, that disappeared as Romero lurched clear to the left, and it was over. The bull tried to go forward, his legs commenced to settle, he swung from side to side, hesitated, then went down on his knees, and Romero's older brother leaned forward behind him and drove a short knife into the bull's neck at the base of the horns. The first time he missed. He drove the knife in again, and the bull went over, twitching and rigid. Romero's brother, holding the bull's horn in one hand, the knife in the other, looked up at the President's box. Handkerchiefs were waving all over the bull-ring. The President looked down from the box and waved his handkerchief. The brother cut the notched black ear from the dead bull and trotted over with it to Romero. The bull lay heavy and black on the sand, his tongue out. Boys were running toward him from all parts of the arena, making a little circle around him. They were starting to dance around the bull.

Romero took the ear from his brother and held it up toward the President. The President bowed and Romero, running to get ahead of the crowd, came toward us. He leaned up against the barrera and gave the ear to Brett. He nodded his head and smiled. The crowd were all about him. Brett held down the cape.

"You liked it?" Romero called.

Brett did not say anything. They looked at each other and smiled. Brett had the ear in her hand.

"Don't get bloody," Romero said, and grinned. The crowd wanted him. Several boys shouted at Brett. The crowd was the boys, the dancers, and the drunks. Romero turned and tried to get through the crowd. They were all around him trying to lift him and put him on their shoulders. He fought and twisted away, and started running, in the midst of them, toward the exit. He did not want to be carried on people's shoulders. But they held him and lifted him. It was uncomfortable and his legs were spraddled and his body was very sore. They were lifting him and all running toward the gate. He had his hand on somebody's shoulder. He looked around at us apologetically. The crowd, running, went out the gate with him.

We all three went back to the hotel. Brett went upstairs. Bill and I sat in the down-stairs dining-room and ate some hard-boiled eggs and drank several bottles of beer. Belmonte came down in his street clothes with his manager and two other men. They sat at the next table and ate. Belmonte ate very little. They were leaving on the seven o'clock train for Barcelona. Belmonte wore a blue-striped shirt and a dark suit, and ate soft-boiled eggs. The others ate a big meal. Belmonte did not talk. He only answered questions.

Bill was tired after the bull-fight. So was I. We both took a bull-fight very hard. We sat and ate the eggs and I watched Belmonte and the people at his table. The men with him were tough-looking and businesslike.

"Come on over to the café," Bill said. "I want an absinthe."

It was the last day of the fiesta. Outside it was beginning to be cloudy again. The square was full of people and the fireworks experts were making up their set pieces for the night and covering them over with beech branches. Boys were watching. We passed stands of rockets with long bamboo stems. Outside the café there was a great crowd. The music and the dancing were going on. The giants and the dwarfs were passing.

"Where's Edna?" I asked Bill.

"I don't know."

We watched the beginning of the evening of the last night of the fiesta. The absinthe made everything seem better. I drank it without sugar in the dripping glass, and it was pleasantly bitter.

"I feel sorry about Cohn," Bill said. "He had an awful time."

"Oh, to hell with Cohn," I said.

"Where do you suppose he went?"

"Up to Paris."

"What do you suppose he'll do?"

"Oh, to hell with him."

"What do you suppose he'll do?"

"Pick up with his old girl, probably."

"Who was his old girl?"

"Somebody named Frances."

We had another absinthe.

"When do you go back?" I asked.

"To-morrow."

After a little while Bill said: "Well, it was a swell fiesta."

"Yes," I said; "something doing all the time."

"You wouldn't believe it. It's like a wonderful nightmare."

"Sure," I said. "I'd believe anything. Including nightmares."

"What's the matter? Feel low?"

"Low as hell."

"Have another absinthe. Here, waiter! Another absinthe for this señor."

"I feel like hell," I said.

"Drink that," said Bill. "Drink it slow."

It was beginning to get dark. The fiesta was going on. I began to feel drunk but I did not feel any better.

"How do you feel?"

"I feel like hell."

"Have another?"

"It won't do any good."

"Try it. You can't tell; maybe this is the one that gets it. Hey, waiter! Another absinthe for this señor!"

I poured the water directly into it and stirred it instead of letting it drip. Bill put in a lump of ice. I stirred the ice around with a spoon in the brownish, cloudy mixture.

"How is it?"

"Fine."

"Don't drink it fast that way. It will make you sick."

I set down the glass. I had not meant to drink it fast.

"I feel tight."

"You ought to."

"That's what you wanted, wasn't it?"

"Sure. Get tight. Get over your damn depression."

"Well, I'm tight. Is that what you want?"

"Sit down."

"I won't sit down," I said. "I'm going over to the hotel."

I was very drunk. I was drunker than I ever remembered having been. At the hotel I went up-stairs. Brett's door was open. I put my head in the room. Mike was sitting on the bed. He waved a bottle.

"Jake," he said. "Come in, Jake."

I went in and sat down. The room was unstable unless I looked at some fixed point.

"Brett, you know. She's gone off with the bull-fighter chap."

"No."

"Yes. She looked for you to say good-bye. They went on the seven o'clock train."

"Did they?"

"Bad thing to do," Mike said. "She shouldn't have done it."

"No."

"Have a drink? Wait while I ring for some beer."

"I'm drunk," I said. "I'm going in and lie down."

"Are you blind? I was blind myself."

"Yes," I said, "I'm blind."

"Well, bung-o," Mike said. "Get some sleep, old Jake."

I went out the door and into my own room and lay on the bed. The bed went sailing off and I sat up in bed and looked at the wall to make it stop. Outside in the square the fiesta was going on. It did not mean anything. Later Bill and Mike came in to get me to go down and eat with them. I pretended to be asleep.

"He's asleep. Better let him alone."

"He's blind as a tick," Mike said. They went out.

I got up and went to the balcony and looked out at the dancing in the square. The world was not wheeling any more. It was just very clear and bright, and inclined to blur at the edges. I washed, brushed my hair. I looked strange to myself in the glass, and went down-stairs to the dining-room.

"Here he is!" said Bill. "Good old Jake! I knew you wouldn't pass out."

"Hello, you old drunk," Mike said.

"I got hungry and woke up."

"Eat some soup," Bill said.

The three of us sat at the table, and it seemed as though about six people were missing.

Book III

Chapter XIX

In the morning it was all over. The fiesta was finished. I woke about nine o'clock, had a bath, dressed, and went down-stairs. The square was empty and there were no people on the streets. A few children were picking up rocket-sticks in the square. The cafés were just opening and the waiters were carrying out the comfortable white wicker chairs and arranging them around the marble-topped tables in the shade of the arcade. They were sweeping the streets and sprinkling them with a hose.

I sat in one of the wicker chairs and leaned back comfortably. The waiter was in no hurry to come. The white-paper announcements of the unloading of the bulls and the big schedules of special trains were still up on the pillars of the arcade. A waiter wearing a blue apron came out with a bucket of water and a cloth, and commenced to tear down the notices, pulling the paper off in strips and washing and rubbing away the paper that stuck to the stone. The fiesta was over.

I drank a coffee and after a while Bill came over. I watched him come walking across the square. He sat down at the table and ordered a coffee.

"Well," he said, "it's all over."

"Yes," I said. "When do you go?"

"I don't know. We better get a car, I think. Aren't you going back to Paris?"

"No. I can stay away another week. I think I'll go to San Sebastian."

"I want to get back."

"What's Mike going to do?"

"He's going to Saint Jean de Luz."[1]

"Let's get a car and all go as far as Bayonne. You can get the train up from there to-night."

"Good. Let's go after lunch."

1. A fishing village on the southwest coast of France (at the mouth of the Nivelle River), about a fifteen-minute drive from Biarritz.

"All right. I'll get the car."

We had lunch and paid the bill. Montoya did not come near us. One of the maids brought the bill. The car was outside. The chauffeur piled and strapped the bags on top of the car and put them in beside him in the front seat and we got in. The car went out of the square, along through the side streets, out under the trees and down the hill and away from Pamplona. It did not seem like a very long ride. Mike had a bottle of Fundador. I only took a couple of drinks. We came over the mountains and out of Spain and down the white roads and through the overfoliaged, wet, green, Basque country, and finally into Bayonne. We left Bill's baggage at the station, and he bought a ticket to Paris. His train left at seven-ten. We came out of the station. The car was standing out in front.

"What shall we do about the car?" Bill asked.

"Oh, bother the car," Mike said. "Let's just keep the car with us."

"All right," Bill said. "Where shall we go?"

"Let's go to Biarritz and have a drink."

"Old Mike the spender," Bill said.

We drove in to Biarritz and left the car outside a very Ritz place. We went into the bar and sat on high stools and drank a whiskey and soda.

"That drink's mine," Mike said.

"Let's roll for it."

So we rolled poker dice out of a deep leather dice-cup. Bill was out first roll. Mike lost to me and handed the bartender a hundred-franc note. The whiskeys were twelve francs apiece. We had another round and Mike lost again. Each time he gave the bartender a good tip. In a room off the bar there was a good jazz band playing. It was a pleasant bar. We had another round. I went out on the first roll with four kings. Bill and Mike rolled. Mike won the first roll with four jacks. Bill won the second. On the final roll Mike had three kings and let them stay. He handed the dice-cup to Bill. Bill rattled them and rolled, and there were three kings, an ace, and a queen.

"It's yours, Mike," Bill said. "Old Mike, the gambler."

"I'm so sorry," Mike said. "I can't get it."

"What's the matter?"

"I've no money," Mike said. "I'm stony.[2] I've just twenty francs. Here, take twenty francs."

Bill's face sort of changed.

"I just had enough to pay Montoya. Damned lucky to have it, too."

"I'll cash you a check," Bill said.

"That's damned nice of you, but you see I can't write checks."

"What are you going to do for money?"

2. A slang term for "broke."

"Oh, some will come through. I've two weeks allowance should be here. I can live on tick[3] at this pub in Saint Jean."

"What do you want to do about the car?" Bill asked me. "Do you want to keep it on?"

"It doesn't make any difference. Seems sort of idiotic."

"Come on, let's have another drink," Mike said.

"Fine. This one is on me," Bill said. "Has Brett any money?" He turned to Mike.

"I shouldn't think so. She put up most of what I gave to old Montoya."

"She hasn't any money with her?" I asked.

"I shouldn't think so. She never has any money. She gets five hundred quid[4] a year and pays three hundred and fifty of it in interest to Jews."

"I suppose they get it at the source," said Bill.

"Quite. They're not really Jews. We just call them Jews.[5] They're Scotsmen, I believe."

"Hasn't she any at all with her?" I asked.

"I hardly think so. She gave it all to me when she left."

"Well," Bill said, "we might as well have another drink."

"Damned good idea," Mike said. "One never gets anywhere by discussing finances."

"No," said Bill. Bill and I rolled for the next two rounds. Bill lost and paid. We went out to the car.

"Anywhere you'd like to go, Mike?" Bill asked.

"Let's take a drive. It might do my credit good. Let's drive about a little."

"Fine. I'd like to see the coast. Let's drive down toward Hendaye."

"I haven't any credit along the coast."

"You can't ever tell," said Bill.

We drove out along the coast road. There was the green of the headlands, the white, red-roofed villas, patches of forest, and the ocean very blue with the tide out and the water curling far out along the beach. We drove through Saint Jean de Luz and passed through villages farther down the coast. Back of the rolling country we were going through we saw the mountains we had come over from Pamplona. The road went on ahead. Bill looked at his watch. It was time

3. Slang for "on credit."
4. Slang for the pound sterling. Brett's income of 500 pounds would have been worth just over $2730 at the time (an amount equivalent to around $39,000 today).
5. Mike here plays on a fundamental antisemitic stereotype that associates Jews with moneylending and, especially, with sharp or swindling practices regarding money. His concession that the finance professionals he is talking about are Scots rather than Jews deploys a stereotype about the thrift of Scottish people, but this does nothing to reduce the casual antisemitism that characterizes his attitudes toward Jews (and those of other characters) throughout the novel.

for us to go back. He knocked on the glass and told the driver to turn around. The driver backed the car out into the grass to turn it. In back of us were the woods, below a stretch of meadow, then the sea.

At the hotel where Mike was going to stay in Saint Jean we stopped the car and he got out. The chauffeur carried in his bags. Mike stood by the side of the car.

"Good-bye, you chaps," Mike said. "It was a damned fine fiesta."

"So long, Mike," Bill said.

"I'll see you around," I said.

"Don't worry about money," Mike said. "You can pay for the car, Jake, and I'll send you my share."

"So long, Mike."

"So long, you chaps. You've been damned nice."

We all shook hands. We waved from the car to Mike. He stood in the road watching. We got to Bayonne just before the train left. A porter carried Bill's bags in from the consigne. I went as far as the inner gate to the tracks.

"So long, fella," Bill said.

"So long, kid!"

"It was swell. I've had a swell time."

"Will you be in Paris?"

"No, I have to sail on the 17th. So long, fella!"

"So long, old kid!"

He went in through the gate to the train. The porter went ahead with the bags. I watched the train pull out. Bill was at one of the windows. The window passed, the rest of the train passed, and the tracks were empty. I went outside to the car.

"How much do we owe you?" I asked the driver. The price to Bayonne had been fixed at a hundred and fifty pesetas.

"Two hundred pesetas."

"How much more will it be if you drive me to San Sebastian on your way back?"

"Fifty pesetas."

"Don't kid me."

"Thirty-five pesetas."

"It's not worth it," I said. "Drive me to the Hotel Panier Fleuri."[6]

At the hotel I paid the driver and gave him a tip. The car was powdered with dust. I rubbed the rod-case through the dust. It seemed the last thing that connected me with Spain and the fiesta. The driver put the car in gear and went down the street. I watched it turn off to take the road to Spain. I went into the hotel and they gave me a room. It was the same room I had slept in when Bill and Cohn

6. Located near the cathedral, in the old town section of Bayonne. Jake says he stayed here on the way *to* Spain as well (see chapter IX).

and I were in Bayonne. That seemed a very long time ago. I washed, changed my shirt, and went out in the town.

At a newspaper kiosque I bought a copy of the New York *Herald* and sat in a café to read it. It felt strange to be in France again. There was a safe, suburban feeling. I wished I had gone up to Paris with Bill, except that Paris would have meant more fiesta-ing. I was through with fiestas for a while. It would be quiet in San Sebastian. The season does not open there until August. I could get a good hotel room and read and swim. There was a fine beach there. There were wonderful trees along the promenade above the beach, and there were many children sent down with their nurses before the season opened. In the evening there would be band concerts under the trees across from the Café Marinas. I could sit in the Marinas and listen.

"How does one eat inside?" I asked the waiter. Inside the café was a restaurant.

"Well. Very well. One eats very well."

"Good."

I went in and ate dinner. It was a big meal for France but it seemed very carefully apportioned after Spain. I drank a bottle of wine for company. It was a Château Margaux.[7] It was pleasant to be drinking slowly and to be tasting the wine and to be drinking alone. A bottle of wine was good company. Afterward I had coffee. The waiter recommended a Basque liqueur called Izarra. He brought in the bottle and poured a liqueur-glass full. He said Izarra was made of the flowers of the Pyrenees. The veritable flowers of the Pyrenees. It looked like hair-oil and smelled like Italian *strega*.[8] I told him to take the flowers of the Pyrenees away and bring me a *vieux marc*.[9] The *marc* was good. I had a second *marc* after the coffee.

The waiter seemed a little offended about the flowers of the Pyrenees, so I overtipped him. That made him happy. It felt comfortable to be in a country where it is so simple to make people happy. You can never tell whether a Spanish waiter will thank you. Everything is on such a clear financial basis in France. It is the simplest country to live in. No one makes things complicated by becoming your friend for any obscure reason. If you want people to like you you have only to spend a little money. I spent a little money and the waiter liked me. He appreciated my valuable qualities. He would be glad to see me back. I would dine there again some time and he would be glad to see me, and would want me at his table. It would be a sincere liking because it would have a sound basis. I was back in France.

7. A famous winery in Bordeaux, known for very fine (and expensive) wines.
8. An herbal liqueur, like Izarra, made from plants common in the Italian alps rather than the Pyrenees.
9. An "old *marc*" (French), a brandy made from the skins, stems, and seeds of grapes that are left over after the process of making wine.

Next morning I tipped every one a little too much at the hotel to make more friends, and left on the morning train for San Sebastian. At the station I did not tip the porter more than I should because I did not think I would ever see him again. I only wanted a few good French friends in Bayonne to make me welcome in case I should come back there again. I knew that if they remembered me their friendship would be loyal.

At Irún[1] we had to change trains and show passports. I hated to leave France. Life was so simple in France. I felt I was a fool to be going back into Spain. In Spain you could not tell about anything. I felt like a fool to be going back into it, but I stood in line with my passport, opened my bags for the customs, bought a ticket, went through a gate, climbed onto the train, and after forty minutes and eight tunnels I was at San Sebastian.

Even on a hot day San Sebastian has a certain early-morning quality. The trees seem as though their leaves were never quite dry. The streets feel as though they had just been sprinkled. It is always cool and shady on certain streets on the hottest day. I went to a hotel in the town where I had stopped before, and they gave me a room with a balcony that opened out above the roofs of the town. There was a green mountainside beyond the roofs.

I unpacked my bags and stacked my books on the table beside the head of the bed, put out my shaving things, hung up some clothes in the big armoire, and made up a bundle for the laundry. Then I took a shower in the bathroom and went down to lunch. Spain had not changed to summer-time, so I was early. I set my watch again. I had recovered an hour by coming to San Sebastian.

As I went into the dining-room the concierge brought me a police bulletin to fill out. I signed it and asked him for two telegraph forms, and wrote a message to the Hotel Montoya, telling them to forward all mail and telegrams for me to this address. I calculated how many days I would be in San Sebastian and then wrote out a wire to the office asking them to hold mail, but forward all wires for me to San Sebastian for six days. Then I went in and had lunch.

After lunch I went up to my room, read a while, and went to sleep. When I woke it was half past four. I found my swimming-suit, wrapped it with a comb in a towel, and went down-stairs and walked up the street to the Concha. The tide was about half-way out. The beach was smooth and firm, and the sand yellow. I went into a bathing-cabin, undressed, put on my suit, and walked across the smooth sand to the sea. The sand was warm under bare feet. There were quite a few people in the water and on the beach. Out beyond where the headlands of the Concha almost met to form the harbor

1. A Basque town on the French-Spanish border.

there was a white line of breakers and the open sea. Although the tide was going out, there were a few slow rollers. They came in like undulations in the water, gathered weight of water, and then broke smoothly on the warm sand. I waded out. The water was cold. As a roller came I dove, swam out under water, and came to the surface with all the chill gone. I swam out to the raft, pulled myself up, and lay on the hot planks. A boy and girl were at the other end. The girl had undone the top strap of her bathing-suit and was browning her back. The boy lay face downward on the raft and talked to her. She laughed at things he said, and turned her brown back in the sun. I lay on the raft in the sun until I was dry. Then I tried several dives. I dove deep once, swimming down to the bottom. I swam with my eyes open and it was green and dark. The raft made a dark shadow. I came out of the water beside the raft, pulled up, dove once more, holding it for length, and then swam ashore. I lay on the beach until I was dry, then went into the bathing-cabin, took off my suit, sloshed myself with fresh water, and rubbed dry.

I walked around the harbor under the trees to the casino, and then up one of the cool streets to the Café Marinas.[2] There was an orchestra playing inside the café and I sat out on the terrace and enjoyed the fresh coolness in the hot day, and had a glass of lemon-juice and shaved ice and then a long whiskey and soda. I sat in front of the Marinas for a long time and read and watched the people, and listened to the music.

Later when it began to get dark, I walked around the harbor and out along the promenade, and finally back to the hotel for supper. There was a bicycle-race on, the Tour du Pays Basque,[3] and the riders were stopping that night in San Sebastian. In the dining-room, at one side, there was a long table of bicycle-riders, eating with their trainers and managers. They were all French and Belgians, and paid close attention to their meal, but they were having a good time. At the head of the table were two good-looking French girls, with much Rue du Faubourg Montmartre chic. I could not make out whom they belonged to. They all spoke in slang at the long table and there were many private jokes and some jokes at the far end that were not repeated when the girls asked to hear them. The next morning at five o'clock the race resumed with the last lap, San Sebastian-Bilbao. The bicycle-riders drank much wine, and were burned and browned by the sun. They did not take the race seriously except among themselves. They had raced among themselves so often that it did not

2. The Café Marina (not Marinas) was located near the casino in San Sebastian.

3. A multi-stage bicycle race that is still held. The riders described here would just have completed the Pamplona-San Sebastian stage (around 270 kilometers, or 168 miles) and would be completing the San Sebastian Bilbao leg (as Jake notes) the next day (a distance of around 170 kilometers, or 105 miles).

make much difference who won. Especially in a foreign country. The money could be arranged.

The man who had a matter of two minutes lead in the race had an attack of boils, which were very painful. He sat on the small of his back. His neck was very red and the blond hairs were sunburned. The other riders joked him about his boils. He tapped on the table with his fork.

"Listen," he said, "to-morrow my nose is so tight on the handle-bars that the only thing touches those boils is a lovely breeze."

One of the girls looked at him down the table, and he grinned and turned red. The Spaniards, they said, did not know how to pedal.

I had coffee out on the terrasse with the team manager of one of the big bicycle manufacturers. He said it had been a very pleasant race, and would have been worth watching if Bottechia had not abandoned it at Pamplona. The dust had been bad, but in Spain the roads were better than in France. Bicycle road-racing was the only sport in the world, he said. Had I ever followed the Tour de France? Only in the papers. The Tour de France was the greatest sporting event in the world. Following and organizing the road races had made him know France. Few people know France. All spring and all summer and all fall he spent on the road with bicycle road-racers. Look at the number of motor-cars now that followed the riders from town to town in a road race. It was a rich country and more *sportif*[4] every year. It would be the most *sportif* country in the world. It was bicycle road-racing did it. That and football. He knew France. *La France Sportive.* He knew road-racing. We had a cognac. After all, though, it wasn't bad to get back to Paris. There is only one Paname.[5] In all the world, that is. Paris is the town the most *sportif* in the world. Did I know the *Chope de Nègre*?[6] Did I not. I would see him there some time. I certainly would. We would drink another *fine* together. We certainly would. They started at six o'clock less a quarter in the morning. Would I be up for the depart? I would certainly try to. Would I like him to call me? It was very interesting. I would leave a call at the desk. He would not mind calling me. I could not let him take the trouble. I would leave a call at the desk. We said good-bye until the next morning.

In the morning when I awoke the bicycle-riders and their following cars had been on the road for three hours. I had coffee and the

4. Athletic, sporty (French).
5. A French nickname for Paris. According to John Leland, the name originated among prisoners on the French penal colony, Devil's Island, because Panama was where one headed upon escaping the island (on the way back to Paris).
6. The *Chope du Nègre* (not "de") was a sports tavern located at 13, rue du Faubourg, Montmartre.

papers in bed and then dressed and took my bathing-suit down to the beach. Everything was fresh and cool and damp in the early morning. Nurses in uniform and in peasant costume walked under the trees with children. The Spanish children were beautiful. Some bootblacks sat together under a tree talking to a soldier. The soldier had only one arm. The tide was in and there was a good breeze and a surf on the beach.

I undressed in one of the bath-cabins, crossed the narrow line of beach and went into the water. I swam out, trying to swim through the rollers, but having to dive sometimes. Then in the quiet water I turned and floated. Floating I saw only the sky, and felt the drop and lift of the swells. I swam back to the surf and coasted in, face down, on a big roller, then turned and swam, trying to keep in the trough and not have a wave break over me. It made me tired, swimming in the trough, and I turned and swam out to the raft. The water was buoyant and cold. It felt as though you could never sink. I swam slowly, it seemed like a long swim with the high tide, and then pulled up on the raft and sat, dripping, on the boards that were becoming hot in the sun. I looked around at the bay, the old town, the casino, the line of trees along the promenade, and the big hotels with their white porches and gold-lettered names. Off on the right, almost closing the harbor, was a green hill with a castle. The raft rocked with the motion of the water. On the other side of the narrow gap that led into the open sea was another high headland. I thought I would like to swim across the bay but I was afraid of cramp.

I sat in the sun and watched the bathers on the beach. They looked very small. After a while I stood up, gripped with my toes on the edge of the raft as it tipped with my weight, and dove cleanly and deeply, to come up through the lightening water, blew the salt water out of my head, and swam slowly and steadily in to shore.

After I was dressed and had paid for the bath-cabin, I walked back to the hotel. The bicycle-racers had left several copies of *L'Auto*[7] around, and I gathered them up in the reading-room and took them out and sat in an easy chair in the sun to read about and catch up on French sporting life. While I was sitting there the concierge came out with a blue envelope in his hand.

"A telegram for you, sir."

I poked my finger along under the fold that was fastened down, spread it open, and read it. It had been forwarded from Paris:

> COULD YOU COME HOTEL MONTANA MADRID AM RATHER IN TROUBLE BRETT.

7. A French sports magazine whose editor was instrumental in the creation of the Tour de France in the early twentieth century.

I tipped the concierge and read the message again. A postman was coming along the sidewalk. He turned into the hotel. He had a big moustache and looked very military. He came out of the hotel again. The concierge was just behind him.

"Here's another telegram for you, sir."

"Thank you," I said.

I opened it. It was forwarded from Pamplona.

> COULD YOU COME HOTEL MONTANA MADRID AM RATHER IN TROUBLE BRETT.

The concierge stood there waiting for another tip, probably.

"What time is there a train for Madrid?"

"It left at nine this morning. There is a slow train at eleven, and the Sud Express[8] at ten to-night."

"Get me a berth on the Sud Express. Do you want the money now?"

"Just as you wish," he said. "I will have it put on the bill."

"Do that."

Well, that meant San Sebastian all shot to hell. I suppose, vaguely, I had expected something of the sort. I saw the concierge standing in the doorway.

"Bring me a telegram form, please."

He brought it and I took out my fountain-pen and printed:

> LADY ASHLEY HOTEL MONTANA MADRID ARRIVING SUD EXPRESS TOMORROW LOVE JAKE.

That seemed to handle it. That was it. Send a girl off with one man. Introduce her to another to go off with him. Now go and bring her back. And sign the wire with love. That was it all right. I went in to lunch.

I did not sleep much that night on the Sud Express. In the morning I had breakfast in the dining-car and watched the rock and pine country between Avila and Escorial. I saw the Escorial[9] out of the window, gray and long and cold in the sun, and did not give a damn about it. I saw Madrid come up over the plain, a compact white sky-line on the top of a little cliff away off across the sun-hardened country.

The Norte station in Madrid is the end of the line. All trains finish there. They don't go on anywhere. Outside were cabs and taxis and a line of hotel runners. It was like a country town. I took a taxi and we climbed up through the gardens, by the empty palace and the unfinished church on the edge of the cliff, and on up until we

8. A fast train whose route runs from Paris to Gibraltar via Bordeaux and Madrid.
9. The Royal Site of San Lorenzo de El Escorial, the historical residence of the King of Spain, located about forty-five kilometers (or twenty-eight miles) northwest of Madrid.

were in the high, hot, modern town. The taxi coasted down a smooth street to the Puerta del Sol, and then through the traffic and out into the Carrera San Jerónimo.[1] All the shops had their awnings down against the heat. The windows on the sunny side of the street were shuttered. The taxi stopped at the curb. I saw the sign HOTEL MONTANA on the second floor. The taxi-driver carried the bags in and left them by the elevator. I could not make the elevator work, so I walked up. On the second floor up was a cut brass sign: HOTEL MONTANA. I rang and no one came to the door. I rang again and a maid with a sullen face opened the door.

"Is Lady Ashley here?" I asked.

She looked at me dully.

"Is an Englishwoman here?"

She turned and called some one inside. A very fat woman came to the door. Her hair was gray and stiffly oiled in scallops around her face. She was short and commanding.

"Muy buenas,"[2] I said. "Is there an Englishwoman here? I would like to see this English lady."

"Muy buenas. Yes, there is a female English. Certainly you can see her if she wishes to see you."

"She wishes to see me."

"The chica[3] will ask her."

"It is very hot."

"It is very hot in the summer in Madrid."

"And how cold in winter."

"Yes, it is very cold in winter."

Did I want to stay myself in person in the Hotel Montana?

Of that as yet I was undecided, but it would give me pleasure if my bags were brought up from the ground floor in order that they might not be stolen. Nothing was ever stolen in the Hotel Montana. In other fondas,[4] yes. Not here. No. The personages of this establishment were rigidly selectioned. I was happy to hear it. Nevertheless I would welcome the upbringal[5] of my bags.

The maid came in and said that the female English wanted to see the male English now, at once.

"Good," I said. "You see. It is as I said."

1. Street of Saint Jerome, a thoroughfare in central Madrid. *Puerta del Sol* (Gate of the Sun): a major public square in Madrid, located where one of the gates had stood in the old city wall. It is the location of the starting point (Kilometer Zero) for the network of Spanish roads that radiate out from Madrid.
2. "Very good" (Spanish), here intended as a greeting.
3. Girl or young woman (Spanish).
4. Small and inexpensive boarding houses or taverns providing lodging (Spanish).
5. Throughout this passage, Hemingway plays the collision of languages or dialects for humorous effect.

"Clearly."

I followed the maid's back down a long, dark corridor. At the end she knocked on a door.

"Hello," said Brett. "Is it you, Jake?"

"It's me."

"Come in. Come in."

I opened the door. The maid closed it after me. Brett was in bed. She had just been brushing her hair and held the brush in her hand. The room was in that disorder produced only by those who have always had servants.

"Darling!" Brett said.

I went over to the bed and put my arms around her. She kissed me, and while she kissed me I could feel she was thinking of something else. She was trembling in my arms. She felt very small.

"Darling! I've had such a hell of a time."

"Tell me about it."

"Nothing to tell. He only left yesterday. I made him go."

"Why didn't you keep him?"

"I don't know. It isn't the sort of thing one does. I don't think I hurt him any."

"You were probably damn good for him."

"He shouldn't be living with any one. I realized that right away."

"No."

"Oh, hell!" she said, "let's not talk about it. Let's never talk about it."

"All right."

"It was rather a knock his being ashamed of me. He was ashamed of me for a while, you know."

"No."

"Oh, yes. They ragged him about me at the café, I guess. He wanted me to grow my hair out. Me, with long hair. I'd look so like hell."

"It's funny."

"He said it would make me more womanly. I'd look a fright."

"What happened?"

"Oh, he got over that. He wasn't ashamed of me long."

"What was it about being in trouble?"

"I didn't know whether I could make him go, and I didn't have a sou[6] to go away and leave him. He tried to give me a lot of money, you know. I told him I had scads of it. He knew that was a lie. I couldn't take his money, you know."

"No."

"Oh, let's not talk about it. There were some funny things, though. Do give me a cigarette."

6. A French coin (long out of circulation by 1925). Brett here means something like "without a farthing" or "without a penny."

I lit the cigarette.

"He learned his English as a waiter in Gib."[7]

"Yes."

"He wanted to marry me, finally."

"Really?"

"Of course. I can't even marry Mike."

"Maybe he thought that would make him Lord Ashley."

"No. It wasn't that. He really wanted to marry me. So I couldn't go away from him, he said. He wanted to make it sure I could never go away from him. After I'd gotten more womanly, of course."

"You ought to feel set up."

"I do. I'm all right again. He's wiped out that damned Cohn."

"Good."

"You know I'd have lived with him if I hadn't seen it was bad for him. We got along damned well."

"Outside of your personal appearance."

"Oh, he'd have gotten used to that."

She put out the cigarette.

"I'm thirty-four, you know. I'm not going to be one of these bitches that ruins children."

"No."

"I'm not going to be that way. I feel rather good, you know. I feel rather set up."

"Good."

She looked away. I thought she was looking for another cigarette. Then I saw she was crying. I could feel her crying. Shaking and crying. She wouldn't look up. I put my arms around her.

"Don't let's ever talk about it. Please don't let's ever talk about it."

"Dear Brett."

"I'm going back to Mike." I could feel her crying as I held her close. "He's so damned nice and he's so awful. He's my sort of thing."

She would not look up. I stroked her hair. I could feel her shaking.

"I won't be one of those bitches," she said. "But, oh, Jake, please let's never talk about it."

We left the Hotel Montana. The woman who ran the hotel would not let me pay the bill. The bill had been paid.

"Oh, well. Let it go," Brett said. "It doesn't matter now."

We rode in a taxi down to the Palace Hotel,[8] left the bags, arranged for berths on the Sud Express for the night, and went into the bar of the hotel for a cocktail. We sat on high stools at the bar while the barman shook the Martinis[9] in a large nickelled shaker.

7. Abbreviation for Gibraltar, the tiny (2.5 square-mile) British territory at the southern tip of the Iberian Peninsula.
8. A luxury hotel in central Madrid, open since 1912.
9. A cocktail consisting of gin and dry or white vermouth.

"It's funny what a wonderful gentility you get in the bar of a big hotel," I said.

"Barmen and jockeys are the only people who are polite any more."

"No matter how vulgar a hotel is, the bar is always nice."

"It's odd."

"Bartenders have always been fine."

"You know," Brett said, "it's quite true. He is only nineteen. Isn't it amazing?"

We touched the two glasses as they stood side by side on the bar. They were coldly beaded. Outside the curtained window was the summer heat of Madrid.

"I like an olive in a Martini," I said to the barman.

"Right you are, sir. There you are."

"Thanks."

"I should have asked, you know."

The barman went far enough up the bar so that he would not hear our conversation. Brett had sipped from the Martini as it stood, on the wood. Then she picked it up. Her hand was steady enough to lift it after that first sip.

"It's good. Isn't it a nice bar?"

"They're all nice bars."

"You know I didn't believe it at first. He was born in 1905. I was in school in Paris, then. Think of that."

"Anything you want me to think about it?"

"Don't be an ass. *Would* you buy a lady a drink?"

"We'll have two more Martinis."

"As they were before, sir?"

"They were very good." Brett smiled at him.

"Thank you, ma'am."

"Well, bung-o," Brett said.

"Bung-o!"

"You know," Brett said, "he'd only been with two women before. He never cared about anything but bull-fighting."

"He's got plenty of time."

"I don't know. He thinks it was me. Not the show in general."

"Well, it was you."

"Yes. It was me."

"I thought you weren't going to ever talk about it."

"How can I help it?"

"You'll lose it if you talk about it."

"I just talk around it. You know I feel rather damned good, Jake."

"You should."

"You know it makes one feel rather good deciding not to be a bitch."

"Yes."

"It's sort of what we have instead of God."

"Some people have God," I said. "Quite a lot."

"He never worked very well with me."

"Should we have another Martini?"

The barman shook up two more Martinis and poured them out into fresh glasses.

"Where will we have lunch?" I asked Brett. The bar was cool. You could feel the heat outside through the window.

"Here?" asked Brett.

"It's rotten here in the hotel. Do you know a place called Botín's?"[1] I asked the barman.

"Yes, sir. Would you like to have me write out the address?"

"Thank you."

We lunched up-stairs at Botín's. It is one of the best restaurants in the world. We had roast young suckling pig and drank *rioja alta*.[2] Brett did not eat much. She never ate much. I ate a very big meal and drank three bottles of *rioja alta*.

"How do you feel, Jake?" Brett asked. "My God! what a meal you've eaten."

"I feel fine. Do you want a dessert?"

"Lord, no."

Brett was smoking.

"You like to eat, don't you?" she said.

"Yes," I said. "I like to do a lot of things."

"What do you like to do?"

"Oh," I said, "I like to do a lot of things. Don't you want a dessert?"

"You asked me that once," Brett said.

"Yes," I said. "So I did. Let's have another bottle of *rioja alta*."

"It's very good."

"You haven't drunk much of it," I said.

"I have. You haven't seen."

"Let's get two bottles," I said. The bottles came. I poured a little in my glass, then a glass for Brett, then filled my glass. We touched glasses.

"Bung-o!" Brett said. I drank my glass and poured out another. Brett put her hand on my arm.

"Don't get drunk, Jake," she said. "You don't have to."

"How do you know?"

"Don't," she said. "You'll be all right."

1. El Sobrino de Botín, a Madrid restaurant founded in 1725 and famous for its suckling pig.
2. A red wine from the Rioja region in Spain.

"I'm not getting drunk," I said. "I'm just drinking a little wine. I like to drink wine."

"Don't get drunk," she said. "Jake, don't get drunk."

"Want to go for a ride?" I said. "Want to ride through the town?"

"Right," Brett said. "I haven't seen Madrid. I should see Madrid."

"I'll finish this," I said.

Down-stairs we came out through the first-floor dining-room to the street. A waiter went for a taxi. It was hot and bright. Up the street was a little square with trees and grass where there were taxis parked. A taxi came up the street, the waiter hanging out at the side. I tipped him and told the driver where to drive, and got in beside Brett. The driver started up the street. I settled back. Brett moved close to me. We sat close against each other. I put my arm around her and she rested against me comfortably. It was very hot and bright, and the houses looked sharply white. We turned out onto the Gran Vía.[3]

"Oh, Jake," Brett said, "we could have had such a damned good time together."

Ahead was a mounted policeman in khaki directing traffic. He raised his baton. The car slowed suddenly pressing Brett against me.

"Yes," I said. "Isn't it pretty to think so?"

THE END

3. The Great Way, a thoroughfare in central Madrid, running from the Calle de Alcalá to Plaza de España.

BACKGROUNDS AND CONTEXTS

Biographical and Autobiographical Background

This section begins with excerpts from autobiographies by two important acquaintances of Hemingway: Harold Loeb and Sylvia Beach. Each of these offers a portrait of Hemingway as the young writer scrambling to make a style and a reputation in Paris during 1922–24. Loeb's is particularly interesting in the context of *The Sun Also Rises* because he was the model for Robert Cohn. Beach was the owner of the Shakespeare and Company Bookshop in Paris, which Hemingway frequented during his years in the city.

SYLVIA BEACH

My Best Customer†

A customer we liked, one who gave us no trouble, was that young man you saw almost every morning over there in a corner at Shakespeare and Company, reading the magazines or Captain Marryat or some other book. This was Ernest Hemingway, who turned up in Paris, as I remember, late in 1921. My "best customer," he called himself, a title that no one disputed with him. Great was our esteem for a customer who was not only a regular visitor, but spent money on books, a trait very pleasing to the proprietor of a small book business.

However, he would have endeared himself to me just as much if he hadn't spent a penny in my establishment. I felt the warmest friendship for Ernest Hemingway from the day we met.

Sherwood Anderson, in Chicago, had given his "young friends Mr. and Mrs. Ernest Hemingway" a letter of introduction to me.[1] I have it still, and it reads as follows:

† From *Shakespeare and Company* (New York: Harcourt, Brace and Company, 1956), pp. 77–83. Copyright © 1959 by Sylvia Beach and renewed 1987 by Frederic Beach Dennis. Reprinted by permission of Mariner Books, an imprint of HarperCollins Publishers. All rights reserved. Notes are by the editor of this Norton Critical Edition.

1. Sherwood Anderson (1876–1941) American short story writer and novelist.

> I am writing this note to make you acquainted with my friend Ernest Hemingway, who with Mrs. Hemingway is going to Paris to live, and will ask him to drop it in the mails when he arrives there.
>
> Mr. Hemingway is an American writer instinctively in touch with everything worth while going on here and I know you will find both Mr. and Mrs. Hemingway delightful people to know. . . .

But the Hemingways and I had known each other for some time before they remembered to produce Anderson's letter. Hemingway just walked in one day.

I looked up and saw a tall, dark young fellow with a small mustache, and heard him say, in a deep, deep voice, that he was Ernest Hemingway. I invited him to sit down, and, drawing him out, I learned that he was from Chicago originally. I also learned that he had spent two years in a military hospital, getting back the use of his leg. What had happened to his leg? Well, he told me apologetically, like a boy confessing he had been in a scrap, he had got wounded in the knee, fighting in Italy. Would I care to see it? Of course I would. So business at Shakespeare and Company was suspended while he removed his shoe and sock, and showed me the dreadful scars covering his leg and foot. The knee was the worst hurt, but the foot seemed to have been badly injured, too, from a burst of shrapnel, he said. In the hospital, they had thought he was done for, there was even some question of administering the last sacraments. But this was changed, with his feeble consent, to baptism—"just in case they were right."

So Hemingway was baptized. Baptized or not—and I am going to say this whether Hemingway shoots me or not—I have always felt that he was a deeply religious man. Hemingway was a great pal of Joyce's,[2] and Joyce remarked to me one day that he thought it was a mistake, Hemingway's thinking himself such a tough fellow and McAlmon trying to pass himself off as the sensitive type.[3] It was the other way round, he thought. So Joyce found you out, Hemingway!

Hemingway confided to me that before he was out of high school, when he was still "a boy in short pants," his father had died suddenly and in tragic circumstances, leaving him a gun as a sole legacy. He found himself the head of a family, his mother and brothers and sister dependent on him. He had to leave school and begin making

2. James Joyce (1882–1941), Irish writer, author of *Ulysses* (1922), which Beach published through Shakespeare and Company.
3. Robert McAlmon (1895–1956) American author and publisher of Contact Editions, which published Hemingway's *Three Stories and Ten Poems* (1924).

a living. He earned his first money in a boxing match, but, from what I gathered, didn't linger in this career. He spoke rather bitterly of his boyhood.

He didn't tell me much about his life after he left school. He earned his living at various jobs, including newspaper work, I believe, then went over to Canada and enlisted in the armed forces. He was so young he had to fake his age to be accepted.

Hemingway was a widely educated young man, who knew many countries and several languages; and he had learned it all at first hand, not in universities. He seemed to me to have gone a great deal farther and faster than any of the young writers I knew. In spite of a certain boyishness, he was exceptionally wise and self-reliant. In Paris, Hemingway had a job as sports correspondent for the Toronto *Star*. No doubt he was already trying his hand at writing fiction.

He brought his young wife, Hadley, to see me. She was an attractive, delightfully jolly person. Of course I took them both around to see Adrienne Monnier.[4] Hemingway's knowledge of French was remarkable, and he managed somehow to find time to read all the French publications as well as ours.

* * *

A much more exciting event awaited us. I had had the impression for some time that Hemingway was working hard on some stories. He told me one day he had finished one, and asked if Adrienne and I would care to hear it. Eagerly we attended this event. * * *

So Hemingway read us one of the stories from *In Our Time*. We were impressed by his originality, his very personal style, his skillful workmanship, his tidiness, his storyteller's gift and sense of the dramatic, his power to create—well, I could go on, but as Adrienne summed him up: "Hemingway has the true writer's temperament" ("*le tempérament authentique d'écrivain*").[5]

Of course, today Hemingway is the acknowledged daddy of modern fiction. You can't open a novel or a short story in France, or in England or Germany or Italy or anywhere else, without noticing that Hemingway has passed that way. He has landed in schoolbooks, which is more fun for the children than they have as a rule and very lucky for them!

Though the question who has influenced such and such a writer has never bothered me, and the adult writer doesn't stay awake at night to wonder who has influenced him, I do think Hemingway readers should know who taught him to write: it was Ernest Hemingway.

4. French bookseller and publisher (1892–1955).
5. The authentic temperament of the writer (French).

And, like all authentic writers, he knew that to make it "good," as he called it, you had to work.

* * *

Hemingway was serious and competent in whatever he did, even when he went in for the care of an infant. After a brief visit to Canada, Hadley and Hemingway came back bringing another "best customer," John Hadley Hemingway. Dropping in one morning and seeing him giving the baby his bath, I was amazed at his deft handling of Bumby. Hemingway *père* was justly proud, and asked me if I didn't think he had a future as a nursemaid.

Bumby was frequenting Shakespeare and Company before he could walk. Holding his son carefully, though sometimes upside down, Hemingway went on reading the latest periodicals, which required some technique, I must say. As for Bumby, anything was all right as long as he was with his adored Papa. His first steps were to what he called "Sylver Beach's." I can see them, father and son, coming along hand in hand up the street. Bumby, hoisted on a high stool, observed his old man gravely, never showing any impatience, waiting to be lifted from his high perch at last; it must have seemed a long wait sometimes. Then I would watch the two of them as they set off, not for home, since they had to keep out of Hadley's way till the housekeeping was done, but to the bistrot around the corner; there, seated at a table, their drinks before them—Bumby's was a grenadine—they went over all the questions of the day.

Everybody at that time had been in Spain, and varied were the impressions. Gertrude Stein and Alice B. Toklas had found it very amusing.[6] Others had gone to a bullfight, been shocked, and come away before the end. The bullfight had been written up from the moral and the sexual point of view, and as a bright-colored sport, picturesque and all that. The Spanish themselves usually found anything foreigners said about *los toros* bewildering and, besides, technically unsound.

Hemingway, unlike the others, set out to learn and to write about the bulls in his usual serious, competent manner. So we have, in *Death in the Afternoon*, a complete treatise on bull-fighting, one that my Spanish friends, the most difficult to please, have acknowledged as excellent. And some of Hemingway's finest writing is in this book.

Good writers are so rare that if I were a critic, I would only try to point out what I think makes them reliable and enjoyable. For how can anyone explain the mystery of creation?

6. Gertrude Stein (1874–1946), American avant-garde writer who lived in Paris after 1903. Alice B. Toklas (1877–1967), American writer who lived with Stein from 1907 to 1946.

Hemingway can take any amount of criticism—from himself; he is his own severest critic, but, like all his fellow-writers, he is hypersensitive to the criticism of others. It's true that some critics are terribly expert in sticking the sharp penpoint into the victim and are delighted when he squirms. Wyndham Lewis[7] succeeded in making Joyce squirm. And his article on Hemingway entitled "The Dumb Ox," which the subject of it picked up in my bookshop, I regret to say, roused him to such anger that he punched the heads off three dozen tulips, a birthday gift. As a result, the vase upset its contents over the books, after which Hemingway sat down at my desk and wrote a check payable to Sylvia Beach for a sum that covered the damage twice over.

As a bookseller and librarian, I paid more attention to titles perhaps than others who simply rush past the threshold of a book without ringing the bell. I think Hemingway's titles should be awarded first prize in any contest. Each of them is a poem, and their mysterious power over readers contributes to Hemingway's success. His titles have a life of their own, and they have enriched the American vocabulary.

HAROLD LOEB

From The Way It Was[†]

* * *

When I ran into Ernest at the Dôme, I suggested that we have dinner together, and we arranged to meet at Le Nègre de Toulouse. He would bring his wife and I would come with Lily.

Hadley, Hem's wife, had red hair and an easy smile. Lily took to her at once. We had lobster *à l' Améicaine*, two bottles of Pouilly-Fuissé, and a Brie. Hem talked a lot about Ford,[1] at whose office party we had met. He was not a hero worshiper.

The next day we visited the Hemingways at their apartment on rue Notre Dame des Champs. They had an infant son named Bumby who had been trained to put up his fists and assume a ferocious expression. I had the feeling that Bumby's expression was not as ferocious as his father would have liked. Hem spoke of prizefights and boxing. I told him I liked tennis and we made a date to play when the courts dried.

7. English writer, critic, and painter (1882–1957). Lewis published a critique of Hemingway, "The Dumb Ox," in *The American Review* (June 1934).

† From *The Way It Was* (New York: Criterion, 1959), pp. 193–94, 216–20. Reprinted with permission of the author's estate. Notes are by the editor of this Norton Critical Edition.

1. Ford Madox Ford (1873–1939), English author and editor with whom Hemingway worked for a short time on the *Transatlantic Review* magazine.

It was perhaps a week later that we got in several sets on the public courts near the prison where the guillotine was kept. Ernest's game was not too good. He was hindered by a trick knee and a bad eye, relics of wounds he had received in Italy while serving with the Red Cross; but he tried so hard and got such pleasure out of a successful shot that it was good fun notwithstanding. The game was even better the next day when Paul Fisher, a tall young architect, and Bill Bullett joined us in doubles.

The more I saw of Ernest the more I liked him. I admired his combination of toughness and sensitiveness, his love of sport and his dedication to writing. I had long suspected that one reason for the scarcity of good writers in the United States was the popular impression—for which Oscar Wilde[2] and his lily were in part responsible—that artists were not quite virile. It was a good sign that men like Hemingway were taking up writing.

* * *

Montparnasse was beautiful that September. Although I got nowhere on my second book, I did not fret much now that *Doodab*[3] had a publisher. And my tennis was steadily getting better: soon I would be giving Paul Fisher a battle.

And I enjoyed boxing with Hem, although I never lost a slight feeling of trepidation. Hem was some forty pounds heavier than I, but he did not fully exert his strength, and on that basis I could hold my own.

One day I was able to get in my left jab when a shift in Hem's eyes signaled that a punch was coming. This checked his blows. It was a pleasant feeling, but I felt that the ground was treacherous: one hot afternoon, for no apparent reason, Hem let go on Paul Fisher. Paul got pretty well battered; Hem explained that he had just felt like "blasting hell out of him." I had no illusions about being able to fend off Hem should he ever feel like "blasting hell" out of me.

Hem and I made plans for skiing that winter in Austria, trout fishing in the spring on a very special Spanish river, and then going on to the bullfights in Pamplona. Nothing, in Hem's opinion, quite equaled bullfighting.

I was willing to be shown, though from what I understood, bullfights were more slaughter than fight. And, too, I looked forward to being on my own for a little while. And I would be: Lily declared that life was cruel enough, and she wasn't going out of her way to watch brutality and suffering.

2. Irish playwright and poet (1854–1900), renowned for his wit and his dandyish style.
3. Loeb's first novel, published by Boni & Liveright in 1925.

In October, Hem and I went to Senlis. Lily did not come along, and Hadley had to stay with the baby. We strolled around the lichenous walls, the dark, still moats, and the shaded streets of the town where Hugh Capet was proclaimed King just thirteen years before the world was supposed to reach its end. Everything we did seemed so pleasant and free and easy.

Suddenly things changed between us. It happened during a poker game in a hotel room. I seldom enjoyed poker, even when five or six were playing, but for some reason the two of us started to play and didn't stop playing.

I could not stop winning. I got the cards I needed nearly every time, and it soon became embarrassing. Hem could not spare the money, yet he would not stop. Then he started writing IOU's. I didn't want his money, and I certainly didn't want his IOU's, but the pile before me, consisting of money, matches, and IOU's, grew bigger and bigger.

Finally Hem wrote out an IOU for one hundred francs and raised me. I called and broke a pair of aces to try for an inside straight, hoping that Hem would win for a change. He did. I drew an ace and lost the pot.

Thereafter nothing worked right for me. Slowly, then faster and faster, my pile dwindled. At first I was pleased, then indifferent. In due course I began to be concerned.

I tried to avoid further loss by playing cautiously; that didn't work either. When my strong hands weren't topped, they weren't even called; and when I folded a poor hand, I lost the ante.

A little less than even, I suggested stopping but Hem would have none of it. When my money was gone, I got up from the table. Hem wanted to continue, even tried to shame me into going on. A shadow seemed to come between us. Dame Luck, I felt, disliked ingratitude as much as Hemingway disliked defeat.

Afterward our relationship was subtly different. I was aware for the first time that I was not immune to his displeasure, although this awareness seemed to make no difference. We continued to spend a lot of time together without friction. I enjoyed being with him, relishing his spontaneity, his zest for living, as much as ever.

* * *

Later I wondered if the distinction of Hem's writing was due in part to his ability to immerse himself in an experience. Unlike Burke, Coates, Aragon, and most of the prose writers published in *Broom*,[4] Hem in his stories did not describe unusual happenings,

4. Loeb edited *Broom*, a modernist "little magazine," with Arthur Kreymborg and Lola Ridge, from 1921 to 1923.

odd emotions, or strange characters. Hem wrote about ordinary things, the ordinary things that had happened to him; for he knew that every event, if looked at closely, was unlike anything that had ever happened before. He tried to tell just what had happened: precision was his criterion rather than beauty or virtue. Thus, fishing as described by Hem was an unprecedented experience, even if one had been casting flies all his life. And his special quality—his ability to evoke a scene or a moment so that it was as real or more real to the reader than an actual happening—had universal appeal.

Yet his stories kept coming back from publishers. True, *The Double Dealer* in New Orleans had taken one or two, and Bob McAlmon and William Bird were getting out a small paper-bound collection, but these paid little or no money. And Hem's money problem was serious because Ford's *transatlantic review* might end any day.

I gave much thought as to why Hem was getting nowhere. It was hardly surprising that the subject of his writing should eventually come up. It did one rainy night at L'Avenue on Boulevard Montparnasse where we'd gone to eat oysters. First we had a dozen Marennes and drank two bottles of Pouilly-Fuissé. Then, with good if somewhat alcoholic intentions, I offered what was intended to be a constructive criticism. No doubt the acceptance of my novel by a leading publisher made me a little more confident of my critical judgment than I had previously been.

"What you've got to do," I suggested, "is bring in women. People like to read about women and violence. You've got plenty of violence in your stories. Now all you need is women."

"Women?" Hem asked.

"It's your good luck to have married happily right off the bat. It must be wonderful. But a happily married man misses so much."

"Such as what?"

"Oh," I said, "such as misery."

Hem's face went stiff and dark. I realized I had said the wrong thing, but did not suppose my offense was serious. Yet the corners of Hem's mouth were retracted, exposing his teeth.

"So I haven't had misery," he said. "So that's what you think."

I smiled hopefully. I did not intend to argue about his misery. I liked to argue about things which I thought I knew about—certain abstractions, for example. But Hem would not argue about abstractions: they were "balls" to him.

"How about another bottle," I suggested, pouring the dregs of our bottle. "It's still raining. To hell with misery!"

Hem's anger had vanished, and creases dented his forehead. Finally he repeated, "You think I haven't had misery—that I'm just a Midwestern——?"

"Just thought you were a little luckier than some," I said.

But he was not listening. He was describing a girl. She was an English girl who had served in the Red Cross in Italy. She had taken care of him when he was brought to the hospital. They had fallen in love. It hadn't worked out. She had left him, gone away. But he still couldn't rid himself of her memory. In short words—Hem didn't like the long ones—he described her hair, her breasts, her body. He described the parts of this haunting girl with an explicitness . . .

I was quite convinced. Of nothing was I more convinced than that Hem had suffered because of this girl. I toyed with my wine glass, not knowing what to say. Hem had floundered in the depths. It was something else that had kept women from his stories, not inexperience.

"Sure," I said. "I should have known. There's nothing tougher. And no one worth a damn escapes it."

Hem kept on talking.

Composition and Revision

Hemingway's novel originally began with two chapters about Brett Ashley and the milieu of the Montparnasse Quarter. Only at the end of these chapters does the current first sentence of the novel appear. As late as the galley proof stage (the last moment before publication, when the pages have been typeset), the novel began "This is a novel about a lady. Her name is Lady Ashley and when the story begins she is living in Paris and it is Spring." The first chapter narrated detailed back-stories of Brett Ashley and Mike Campbell, including the impact the Great War had on both, the experiences of Brett's marriage to Ashley, and the different effects that drinking produces on each of them. The portraits emphasize both characters' boredom and hollow social lives, and Hemingway's style in this chapter is characterized by repetition of both individual words and syntactic structures. The portrait of Mike illustrates both the substance and style of the chapter:

> Mike was a charming companion, one of the most charming. He was nice and he was weak and he had a certain very hard gentleness in him that could not be touched and that never disappeared until liquor dissolved him entirely (quoted in Svoboda, *Hemingway and* The Sun Also Rises: *The Crafting of a Style*, 132).

Hemingway's language and sentences here show the strong influence of Gertrude Stein, and they resemble those of the "interchapters" of *In Our Time*. The second chapter introduces two key elements. First, Hemingway draws explicit attention to the first-person narration ("I did not want to tell this story in the first person but I find that I must"). The chapter provides more sustained history of Jake Barnes than appears in the published novel, including something of a professional résumé paragraph about Jake's experience as a newspaperman. Hemingway then introduces the Montparnasse Quarter as something of a character. Just as he does with Brett, Mike, and Jake, he provides a sketch of the Quarter ("more a state of mind than a geographical area") and its denizens (loafers, artists, drunks). Finally, the chapter concludes with a version of an anecdote that Hemingway would later include in *A Moveable Feast*, his posthumously published book of Paris reminiscences. In the galleys of *The Sun Also Rises*, Jake's acquaintance, Braddocks, snubs someone he says is the English writer Hilaire Belloc, but who turns out to be the demimonde figure, Aleister Crowley; in his final revisions, Hemingway cut these opening chapters. An excerpt from Fitzgerald's letter is included here. In addition, Hemingway's letter to Maxwell Perkins, his editor at Scribner, is included. The letter mentions Hemingway's intention to revise the book in proofs, cutting the opening fifteen pages to begin where the novel now does, and answers Scribner's concerned query about a reference to Henry James in the dialogue between Jake Barnes and Bill Gorton during their fishing trip in Spain.

F. SCOTT FITZGERALD

[Letter Recommending Revisions to the Novel's Opening]†

Dear Ernest: Nowadays when almost everyone is a genius, at least for awhile, the temptation for the bogus to profit is no greater than the temptation for the good man to relax (in one mysterious way or another)—not realizing the transitory quality of his glory because he forgets that it rests on the frail shoulders of professional enthusiasts. This should frighten all of us into a lust for anything honest that people have to say about our work. I've taken what proved to be excellent advice (On The B. + Damned) from Bunny Wilson who never wrote a novel (on Gatsby—change of many thousand wds) from Max Perkins who never considered writing one, and on T. S. of Paradise from Katherine [*sic*] Tighe (you don't know her) who had probably never read a novel before.[1]

[This is beginning to sound like my own current work which resolves itself into laborious + sententious preliminaries].

Anyhow I think parts of *Sun Also* are careless + ineffectual. As I said yestiday (and, as I recollect, in trying to get you to cut the 1st part of 50 Grand)[2] I find in you the same tendency to envelope or (as it usually turns out) to *embalm* in mere wordiness an anecdote or joke thats casually appealed to you, that I find in myself in trying to preserve a piece of "fine writing." Your first chapter contains about 10 such things and it gives a feeling of condescending *casuallness*

P. 1. "highly moral story"

"Brett said" (O. Henry stuff)

† From *Hemingway and* The Sun Also Rises: *The Crafting of a Style* (Lawrence, KS: U of Kansas P, 1983), pp. 137–40. Copyright © 1980 by F. Scott Fitzgerald Smith, reprinted by permission of Eleanor Lanahan, Eleanor Blake Hazard and Christopher T. Byrne. Notes are by the editor of this Norton Critical Edition.

1. Fitzgerald refers here to his novels *The Beautiful and the Damned* (Scribner's, 1922), *The Great Gatsby* (Scribner's, 1925), and *This Side of Paradise* (Scribner's, 1920). Bunny is Edmund Wilson (1895–1972), American literary critic. Maxwell Perkins (1884–1947), American editor. Katharine Tighe (1896–1974), childhood friend of Fitzgerald.
2. A short story that Hemingway published in the *Atlantic Monthly* in 1927 (and collected in *Men Without Women*, 1927).

"much too expensive"

"something or other" (if you don't want to tell, why waste wds. saying it. See P. 23—"9 or 14" and "or how many years it was since 19xx" when it would take two words to say That's what youd kid in anyone else as mere "style"—mere horseshit I can't find this latter but anyhow you've not only got to write well yourself but you've also got to *not-do* to do what anyone can do and I think that there are about 24 sneers, superiorities and nose-thumbings-at-nothing that mar the whole narrative up to p. 29 where (after a false start on the introduction of Cohn) it really gets going. And to preserve these perverse and willfull non-essentials you're [*sic*] done a lot of writing that *honestly* reminded me of Michael Arlen[3]

[You know the very fact that people have committed themselves to you will make them watch you like a cat. + if they don't like it creap [*sic*] away like one]

For example.

Pps. 1 + 2. Snobbish (not in itself but because of the history of English Aristocrats in the war, set down so verbosely so uncritically, so exteriorly and yet so obviously inspired from within, is *shopworn.*) You had the same problem that I had with my Rich Boy, previously debauched by Chambers ect. Either bring more thot to it with the realization that that ground has already raised its wheat + weeds or cut it down to seven sentences. It hasn't even your rhythym and the fact that may be "true" is utterly immaterial.

That biography from you, who allways believed in the superiority (the preferability) of the *imagined* to the *seen not to say to the merely recounted.*

P. 3 "Beautifully engraved shares"

(Beautifully engraved 1886 irony) All this is O.K. but so glib *when* its glib + *so* profuse.

P. 5 Painters are no longer *real* in prose. They must be minimized. [This is not done by making them schlptors, backhouse wall-experts or miniature painters]

P. 8. "highly moral urges" "because I believe its a good story" If this paragraph isn't maladroit then I'm a rewrite man for Dr. Cadman.

P. 9. Somehow its not good. I can't quite put my hand on it—it has a ring of "This is a true story ect."

P. 10. "Quarter being a state of mine ect." This is in all guide books. I haven't read Basil Swoon's but I have fifty francs to lose. [About this time I can hear you say "Jesus this guy thinks Im lousy. + he can

3. British novelist and playwright (1895–1956), author of *The Green Hat* (1924), which influenced Hemingway's characterization of Brett Ashley.

stick it up his ass for all I give a Gd Dm for his 'critisism'." But remember this is a new departure for you, and that I think your stuff is great. You were the first American I wanted to meet in Europe—and the last. (This latter clause is simply to balance the sentence. It doesn't seem to make sense tho I have pawed at it for several minutes. Its like the age of the French women.

P. 14 (+therabout) as I said yesterday I think this anecdote is flat as hell without naming Ford[4] which would be cheap.

It's flat because you end with mention of Allister Crowly. [*sic*] If he's nobody it's nothing. If he's somebody, it's cheap. This is a novel. Also I'd cut out mention of H. Stearns earlier.

Why not cut the inessentials in Cohens biography? His first marriage is of no importance. When so many people can write well+the competition is so heavy I can't imagine how you could have done these first 20 pps. so casually. You can't *play* with peoples attention—a good man who has the power of arresting attention at will must be especially careful.

From here. Or rather from p. 30 I began to like the novel but Ernest I can't tell you the sense of disappointment that beginning with its elephantine facetiousness gave me. Please do what you can about it in proof. Its 7500 words—you could reduce it to 5000. And my advice is not to do it by mere pareing but to take out the worst of the *scenes*.

I've decided not to pick at anything else because I wasn't at all inspired to pick when reading it. I was much too excited. Besides This is probably a heavy dose. That novel's damn good. The central theme is marred somewhere but hell! unless you're writing your life history where you have an inevitable pendulum to swing you true (Harding metaphor), who can bring it entirely off? And what critic can trace whether the fault lies in a possible insufficient thinking out, in the biteing off of more than you eventually cared to chew in the impotent theme or in the elusiveness of the lady character herself. My theory always was that she dramatized herself in terms of Arlen's dramatization of somebody's dramatizing of Stephen McKenna's dramatization of the last girl in Well's *Tono Bungay*—who's original probably liked more things about Beatrix Esmond that [*sic*] about Jane Austin's Elizabeth (to whom we owe the manners of so many of our wives.)[5]

4. Ford Madox Ford (1873–1939), British novelist and critic.
5. H. G. Wells (1866–1946), British novelist whose novel *Tono Bungay* was published in 1909. Beatrix Esmond, a character in the novel *The History of Henry Esmond* (1852), by British novelist William Makepeace Thackeray (1811–1863). Elizabeth Bennet is a central character in *Pride and Prejudice* (1813), by British novelist Jane Austen (1775–1817).

Appropos of your foreward about the Latin quarter—suppose you had begun your stories with phrases like: "Spain is a peculiar place—ect" or "Michigan is interesting to two classes—the fisherman + the drummer."

Pps 64 + 65 with a bit of work should tell all that need be known about *Brett's* past.

(Small point) "Dysemtry" instead of "killed" is a clichê to avoid a clichê. It stands out. I suppose it can't be helped. I suppose all the 75,000000 Europeans who died between 1914–1918 will always be among the 10,000,000 who were killed in the war.

God! The bottom of p. 77 Jusque the top p. 78 are wonderful, I go crazy when people aren't always at their best. This isn't picked out—I just happened on it.

The heart of my critisism beats somewhere apon p. 87. I think you can't change it, though. I felt the lack of some crazy torturing tentativeness or security—horror, all at once, that she'd feel—and he'd feel—maybe I'm crazy. He isn't *like an impotent man. He's like a man in a sort of moral chastity belt.*

Oh, well. It's fine, from Chap V on, anyhow, in spite of that—which fact is merely a proof of its brilliance.

Station Z. W. X. square says good night. Good night all.

ERNEST HEMINGWAY

Letter to Maxwell Perkins, Juan-les-Pins, France, June 5, 1926†

Dear Mr. Perkins:

I was very glad to get your letter and hear that you liked The Sun a.r. Scott claims to too. We are here temporarily quarantined with whooping cough. I went to Madrid and my wife came down here with the child and nurse expecting to join me in a week in Madrid. Himself developed the whooping on arriving here so after 3 weeks in Madrid I came on here, and we will be here another 3 weeks and then take up our Spanish trip.

† From *Ernest Hemingway: Selected Letters*, ed. Carlos Baker (New York: Charles Scribner's Sons, 1981), pp. 208–09. Unless otherwise indicated, notes are by the editor of the original work.

As to addresses: Care Guaranty Trust Co. of N.Y., 1, Rue des Italiens, Paris, is the best permanent address. I will keep them informed by wire of my address in Spain and they have an excellent mail forwarding service.

Between July 6 and July 13—inclusive—I will be at the Hotel Quintana, Pamplona (Navarra), SPAIN if you should want to reach me by cable.

It would be better not to try and hit that address with mail.

That is the only address I am sure of but will keep the Guaranty Trust exactly informed. They will re-wire all cables and re-forward letters with no delay.

I believe that, in the proofs, I will start the book at what is now page 16 in the Mss. There is nothing in those first sixteen pages that does not come out, or is explained, or re-stated in the rest of the book—or is unnecessary to state. I think it will move much faster from the start that way. Scott agrees with me. He suggested various things in it to cut out—in those first chapters—which I have never liked—but I think it is better to just lop that off and he agrees. He will probably write you what he thinks about it—the book in general. He said he was very excited by it.

As for the Henry James thing—I haven't the second part of the Ms. here—it is over at Scott's—so I can't recall the wording. But I believe that it is a reference to some accident that is generally known to have happened to Henry James in his youth.[1] To me Henry James is as historical a name as Byron, Keats, or any other great writer about whose life, personal and literary, books have been written. I do not believe that the reference is sneering, or if it is, it is not the writer who is sneering as the writer does not appear in this book. Henry James is dead and left no descendants to be hurt, nor any wife, and therefore I feel that he is as dead as he will ever be. I wish I had the ms. here to see exactly what it said. If Henry James never had an accident of that sort I should think it would be libelous to say he had no matter how long he were dead. But if he did I do not see how it can affect him—now he is dead. As I recall Gorton and Barnes are talking humourously around the subject of Barnes' mutilation and to them Henry James is not a man to be insulted or protected from insult but simply an historical example. I remember there was something about an airplane and a bicycle—but that had nothing to do with James and was simply a non-sequitor. Scott said he saw nothing off-color about it.

Until the proofs come I do not want to think about the book as I am trying to write some stories and I want to see the proofs,

1. See Book II, chapter XII, note 7 [*Editor*].

when they come, from as new and removed a viewpoint as possible.

Up till now I have heard nothing about a story called—An Alpine Idyll—that I mailed to you sometime the first week in May. Did you ever receive it? I have another copy which I will send if you did not. In Madrid I wrote three stories ranging from 1400 to 3,000 words. I haven't had them re-typed and sent on as I was waiting word about The Alpine Idyll.[2]

What is the news about Torrents?[3] Have any copies been mailed to me as yet?

Could you send me a check for $200.[4] in a registered letter to the Guaranty Trust Co. address? It was very pleasant to get your letter and learn that you liked the book.

Yours very sincerely,
Ernest Hemingway

2. Refused by *Scribner's Magazine*, "Alpine Idyll" first appeared in *American Caravan*, ed. Van Wyck Brooks (New York, 1927). The stories composed in one day in Madrid were "The Killers," "Ten Indians," and "Today Is Friday." But EH had a start on them before going to Spain.
3. *Torrents of Spring*, a parodic novel Hemingway published with Scribner's in 1926 [*Editor*].
4. Worth about $3,000 today [*Editor*].

Letters

Hemingway was a frequent and voluble writer of letters to friends and acquaintances. Included here are four letters: two to Harold Loeb, with whom Hemingway had traveled to Pamplona, one to Gertrude Stein and Alice B. Toklas, whom Hemingway had come to know in Paris, and one to Jane Heap, co-editor of the *Little Review*, an arts magazine in which Hemingway had published the first six prose pieces of what would eventually become *In Our Time*. In these letters, Hemingway describes events on the trip to Pamplona that inspired some of the action in the novel. The two to Loeb are illuminating because Loeb is supposed to be the model for Robert Cohn; those to Stein and Toklas and to Heap give a sense of the intensity of Hemingway's work on the book, the speed with which he composed it in the aftermath of the trip.

ERNEST HEMINGWAY

To Harold Loeb, June 21, [1925][†]

June 21, Sunday.

Dear Harold:

My son of a bitching editor[1] has double X ed me and is arriving tomorrow—I.E. Monday June 22nd—So we cant get off till Wednesday morning or Thursday night.

I'll wire you. Pat and Duff are coming too.[2] Pat has sent off to Scotland for rods and Duff to England for Funds. As far as I know Duff is not bringing any fairies with her. You might arrange to have

† From *The Letters of Ernest Hemingway* Vol. 2, eds. Sandra Spanier, Albert J. DeFazio III, and Robert W. Trogdon (New York: Cambridge UP, 2013), pp. 353–54, 359–61, 282–85. Unless otherwise indicated, notes are by the editors of the original work.

1. Perhaps Leon Fleischman, Boni & Liveright's European representative.
2. Patrick (Pat) Stirling Guthrie (1895–1932) and Duff Twysden (née Mary Duff Stirling Byrom, 1893–1938), as well as Loeb, joined EH's group at the 1925 Fiesta of San Fermin in Pamplona. What EH did not know when writing to Loeb was that Loeb and Duff would spend a week together in Saint-Jean-de-Luz beforehand, which led to tensions in the group that EH would evoke in *SAR*. Twysden served as the prototype for the character Brett Ashley and Guthrie for Mike Campbell, her dissipated Scottish fiancé.

a band of local fairies meet her at the train carrying a Daisy chain so that the transition from the quarter will not be too sudden.

I have been having a swell time with Don Stewart[3] here and feel like a million seeds. Don will be at Pamplona and so will Bob Benchley.[4] Pamplona's going to be damned good. I feel like hell at every day that is lopped off our fishing—but we will get a good week anyway. Hadley and I have been very tight and having a swell time. I havent felt as good since we came back from Austria. See you soon.

Hadley sends her love.

Yours,
Ernest

Will get your line.

Will write a note to Pauline[5] about your mail. Is there anything else we can do. Go see Krebs Friend about fishing.

The 1st 15 page installment of my bull fight story are in this mos. Querschnitt.[6]

Yrs.
E

Bob McAlmon writes about going to the theater with Kitty in London. I've already written and sent the money for the Pamplona tickets. Paul Fisher may be coming. There is a swell program.

No other news I think. I've been having a hell of a swell time and feel like working. Christ I wish this bludy editor wasnt coming. Ive had hell getting them rooms during the Grand Semaine.[7]

To Harold Loeb, [ca. July 12, 1925]

Dear Harold—

I was terribly tight and nasty to you last night and I ~~hope you can~~ dont want you to go away with that nasty insulting lousiness as the last thing of the fiestas. I wish I could wipe out all the mean-ness and I suppose I cant but this is to let you know that I'm thoroly

3. Donald Ogden Stewart (1894–1980), American writer and humorist [*Editor*].
4. Robert Benchley (1889–1945), American writer, columnist, and humorist [*Editor*].
5. In March 1925, EH had met Pauline Pfeiffer (1895–1951), contributor and assistant to the editor of Paris *Vogue*, at a party hosted by Kitty Cannell. EH and Pauline would be married in 1927.
6. EH's "Stierkampf" appeared in two parts in the June and July 1925 issues of *Der Querschnitt*.
7. The annual *Grand Semaine*, a series of three major horse races in June (beginning with the Grand Steeplechase race at Auteuil and ending with the Grand Prix de Paris at Longchamp), was a high point of the Paris social season. The "Big Week" was June 21–28, 1925.

ashamed of the way I acted and the stinking, unjust uncalled for things I said.

So long and good luck to you and I hope we'll see you soon and well.

Yours Ernest.

To Gertrude Stein and Alice B. Toklas, July [16], 1925

July 15 1925[1]
Hotel Aguilar
Carrera San Jeronimo, 37
Madrid.

Dear Friends—

We have had a fine time and no bad hot weather and seen Belmonte cogida-ed, and he is not so bad, and had a bull dedicated to us and Hadley got the ear given to her and wrapped it up in a handkerchief which, thank God was Don Stewarts. I tell her she ought to throw it away or cut it up into pieces and send them in letters to her friends in St. Louis but she wont let it go and it is doing very nicely.

Madrid is nice now and we have good rooms and pensione for 10 pesetas a day. They have re-built and re-hung the Prado—probably on Bob McAlmon's complaint and it is very fine. Hadley is there now and I'm going down when I finish this. Last night we went to a nocturnal and this afternoon is the Big Corrida de la Prensa with Freg—Villalta, Litri and Niño de la Palma. The last two are the great new phenomenons and Niño mano a mano with Belmonte made Belmonte look cheap. He did everything Belmonte did and did it better—kidding him—all the adornos and desplantes and all.

Then he stepped out all by himself without any tricks—suave, templando with the cape, smooth and slow—splendid banderillos and started with 5 naturales with the muleta—beautiful complete faena all linked up and then killed perfectly.

He comes from Ronda and everybody in Spain is crazy about him—except of course those that can't stand him. But they were lined up all night before his first appearance in Madrid. We've seen him 4 times and will see him 4 more at Valencia. His giving Hadley his cape to hold etc. is quite efficacious at keeping her from worrying about Bumby. He is in great shape Marie writes and plays with all the kids and talks more all the time.

1. EH apparently misdated the letter. The annual Corrida de la Prensa of Madrid, which he writes he and Hadley would attend that afternoon, took place on 16 July 1925.

How is the proof coming and have you been fishing?

We found our best stream which was full of trout last year ruined by logging and running logs down—all the pools cleaned out—trout killed. We go to Valencia on the 21st and will be there till the 2nd of August at Poste Restante. Travelling 3rd class it hasnt been expensive and is very funny. Coming down from Pamplona there was a kid whose father raised wine near Tafalla and he was bringing big sample jugs down to Madrid to sell wine and of course every body was offering drinks to everybody else and he got inspired and opened jug after jug and 3 compartments including 2 priests and 4 Guardia Civil got very tight including unfortunately myself and I either lost or gave away our tickets and became worried or as worried as I could get as we got near Madrid but the Guardia Civil got us through all right with no tickets at all. It was the best party almost I've ever been on. Spaniards are the only people. Hadley and the priests talked Latin. It was very fine.

Love to you from us both,
Always yours
Hemingway.

To Jane Heap, [ca. August 23, 1925]

Sunday—afternoon

Dear Jane—

Thanks for writing me. I've looked around for you and havent been able to find you. Have been working all the time. Still am. I've got about a months more work and then will leave it alone and this winter will type it all out and go over it finally doing that. It is a hell of a fine novel. Written very simply and full of things happening and people and places and exciting as hell and no autobiographical 1st novel stuff. I think it will be a knock out and will let these bastards who say yes he can write very beautiful little paragraphs know where they get off at. I've tried to write a hell of a good story about people without faking, preciosity or horseshit. Everybody knows life is a tragic show ie born here—die there. Everybody dies, Everybody gets bitched. Also—and we havent had this since the great ones—life is funny. Conversations among people worth bothering to write about are often funny. Damn funny. Do you ever get that in Sherwoods stories? Huh? No. That's the defect of all Am. writers. Sherwood ~~has~~ doesnt have it when he talks. He talks funny as hell. When he starts to write it's all wiped out. Like takeing your pen in hand. In Modern Eng. writers it is always the Author making delicate fun of his characters. That's awful. Never any funny people. Never do they make any good cracks. Well wait for this one. I'm not going to show it to anyone until it is done. I dont want all my great literary friends giving me good advice. Want it to have all its defects.

Eliots Criterion coupled me (complimentarily) with Kenneth Burke.[1] Saw that yest. Well after this comes out I dont think they will anymore. Not that it makes any difference. Only that while it tears hell out of you and you cant sleep and you work all the time it is fun to write a hell of really swell big book and know that you are definitely through with a hell of a lot of disappointed gents who instead of trying to push you because they think you were going to be one of them will now commence to knock you and hate you.

Gee isnt this a wonderful line of Blah? I've never read anything worse. I ought to tear it up and start over again. Will leave it in if you'll promise never to use it against me just to give a sample of what awful stuff a fellow can write when he's tired and needs some one to praise him and not having anyone starts in to praise himself. Ulyses is a splendid book and Making of Americans is a great book but I've just read—about 3 mo. back—Constance Garnett's translation of War and Peace.[2] That guy has at least 400 pages her of 1500 some that are as good as the very best In Our Time. That gave me considerable jolt. That was when I stopped being satisfied with perfect small ones.

Anyway what I started to write you was that Boni and Liveright are bringing out the stories 1st Oct. Have sent me jacket etc. and I've seen the book advertized. They have an option on my next 3 books—said option to lapse if they refuse any one book

[*Middle portion of MS page torn away*][3]

So I cant very well talk business yet. Nobody is going to get this novel without a 1,000 dollar advance. That's what I'm going to want for it in the spring. I've worked a hell of a long time for love and now when I've got something I know is valuable I'm not going to give it away. The bigger advance a publisher makes on a good book the

1. In a review critical of the most recent numbers of H. L. Mencken's *American Mercury*, British poet and critic Sir Herbert Edward Read (1893–1968) wrote: "Mr. Mencken is the enemy of humbug, but he is not particularly the friend of genius. He has his own code of safety, which would admit, say, Mr. Vachel Lindsay, but would exclude, say, Mr. Hemingway or Mr. Kenneth Burke" (*Criterion* 3, no. 12 [July 1925], 598–99). Burke (1897–1993), American writer and literary critic, had published *The White Oxen and Other Stories* (1924) and a translation of Thomas Mann's *Death in Venice* (1925), and had assisted in editing the little magazines *Broom* and *Secession*. He later became a regular contributor to the *Dial* and other magazines and published his influential work of rhetorical criticism, *Counter-Statement*, in 1931.
2. Constance Black Garnett (1861–1946), prolific British translator who introduced British and American readers to a number of works of Russian literature, including Tolstoy's *War and Peace* (London: Heinemann, 1904).
3. The middle portion of the letter's second page is torn away, apparently an intentional edit by EH. He numbered the top portion of that page with a circled numeral 2, and the remaining lower portion with a circled numeral 3, concluding the letter on the verso of the lower portion.

more they have to push it and the more money both you and they make in the end.

You see I can't talk business now but I would like very much to meet your friend and I wish you would bring him around. Because you cant ever tell what might happen.

Come on in as soon as you can because we want to see you. We are being kicked out and will probably go to the Mts. in Oct. Austria. I want to take a hiking trip through the Mts. down into Italy when we get through with this.

What kind of summer have you had? That's a grand letter head. We are going to U.SA in Spring. Stay until winter then probably live in Madrid or Mex. City. Paris is getting all shot to hell. Not like the old days. It is grand for Gertrude Stein with a rent of probably 2 or 3000 francs a year but we cant stand the strain and damned unpleasantness of moving and being moved. Would rather travel than move. We'll look for you next week. If you come and I'm not there leave a note for when you will be back.

Best from Hadley, Yours Always—

Hem

On Postwar Paris and Expatriates

Book I draws on Hemingway's experience as an American expatriate living in Paris in the early 1920s. In this section, the excerpt by Frederick J. Hoffman provides information both about the motivations of many expatriate writers and artists as they left the United States for Paris and about such concrete factors as the relative costs of goods and services in Paris and New York in the early 1920s. The excerpt from Malcolm Cowley's *Exile's Return* is an account of life in Paris by a contemporary of Hemingway's, a writer and intellectual who also chose to leave the United States and live and work in Paris. It is evocative of the atmosphere of cultural ferment in and around Montparnasse and the Latin Quarter.

FREDERICK J. HOFFMAN

The Expatriate†

"After all everybody, that is, everybody who writes," said Gertrude Stein in *Paris France* (1940), "is interested in living inside themselves in order to tell what is inside themselves. That is why writers have to have two countries, the one where they belong and the one in which they live really. The second one is romantic, it is separate from themselves, it is not real but it is really there."

* * *

The expatriated Americans, such as those described in Hemingway's *The Sun Also Rises*, lived, ate, drank, made love, and tried or pretended to write, on the Left Bank (the Fifth and Sixth Arrondissements). It was Greenwich Village on a very large scale with the Village's attractions extended and more varied. There was the same mixture of the genuine and struggling artist with the eccentric, the wastrel, the opportunist, and the egomaniac. On the compact

† From *The Twenties: American Writing in the Postwar Decade* (New York: Free Press, 1949), pp. 43–49. Unless otherwise indicated, notes are by the editor of this Norton Critical Edition.

little streets off the boulevard Saint Michel and the boulevard Saint Germain were the small, inexpensive hotels where rooms might be rented for very little in American money (like the Hotel du Caveau on the rue de la Huchette, described in Elliott Paul's[1] *The Last Time I Saw Paris*). Here scores of American expatriates stayed during the 1920s—wrote, painted, or merely lived. Almost all the bars and cafés described in *The Sun Also Rises* were in the Quarter; others; like the Café du Dôme, had over many decades of bohemian life established reputations as gathering places for artists and writers.

Americans who worked, as distinguished from those who came chiefly to spend money they had brought with them, went to the Place de l'Opéra on the Right Bank to do their daily stint in the Paris offices of American newspapers; or they stayed in their small, cheap rooms and worked at translations; or they turned out articles and essays for American commercial magazines; or, in the much less certain economy of haphazard patronage and amateur business enterprise, they attempted to make a go of the little magazines. In studio apartments they gathered to talk, searching for some vagrant clue to "the word" in its various and significant disguises. Among these informal salons were the apartments of Ford Madox Ford and Stella Bowen, of Bill and Mary Widney ("where one was always likely to find some of the *transition* crowd or the monocled Tristan Tzara, founder of dada, and a young French surrealist or two"), the home of Professor Bernard Faÿ of the Sorbonne, and the salon of Nathalie Barney in the rue Jacob.[2]

The favorable rate of exchange brought over many of the writers and editors of little magazines, who moved from one place to another in the hope of finding better and better values for their American money: Berlin, where one's dollar was worth twenty times its value in other places; Vienna, where the first issue of Gorham Munson's *Secession*, twenty-two leaves in all and printed on excellent paper, cost twenty dollars to produce; Rome, where the more ambitious and lavish *Broom* of Alfred Kreymborg and Harold Loeb cost five hundred dollars an issue, including payment to contributors.[3] In Paris,

1. American journalist and writer (1891–1958).
2. Ford Madox Ford (1873–1939), English novelist and critic. Stella Bowen (1893–1947), Australian writer and artist. Bill and Mary Widney, wealthy American expatriates whose Paris apartment served as an informal salon, especially for Surrealist writers and artists. Tristan Tzara (1896–1963), Romanian poet and artist, a central figure in the Dada anti-art movement of the 1910s and 1920s. Bernard Faÿ (1893–1978), French historian, known for anti-Masonic and antisemitic views; though an official in the Vichy government of France during the Second World War, Faÿ sheltered Gertrude Stein and Alice B. Toklas. Natalie Clifford Barney (1876–1972), American novelist and playwright who lived for many years as an expatriate in Paris.
3. Gorham Munson (1896–1969), American literary critic, founder and co-editor of *Secession*, a literary magazine published 1922–24. Alfred Kreymborg (1883–1966), American writer and editor, co-founder and co-editor with Harold Loeb (1891–1974) of *Broom*, an avant-garde magazine published 1921–1923.

though the rate of exchange was somewhat less favorable to the American dollar,[4] living was less expensive than in New York.

* * *

In his autobiography, *Being Geniuses Together* (1938), Robert McAlmon[5] describes his personal investigations of statements made in American newspapers and magazines about the "dissolute" and "wastrel" expatriates; he discovered that the men were writers or painters who worked hard, lived simply, and scarcely ever spent lavishly. There were parasites and drunks, of course; but these one could find anywhere, and "the hangers-on might as well go to hell in Paris as become equally spineless, futile, and distressing specimens in their home villages. A Parisian drunk is not nearly so sad to watch as the small-town down-and-outer. He isn't alone or lonely." McAlmon himself published his friends' books at the Contacts Editions Press. Pound, Mary Butts, Robert Coates, Gertrude Stein, Ernest Hemingway ("his first two books to appear anywhere"), H. D., Ford Madox Ford,[6] William Carlos Williams, and other writers were represented on his lists.

Americans in exile wrote, painted, composed, sculpted—or, as editors, sponsors, or select audience, encouraged those who did.

4. It is a mistake to overemphasize this fact in considering expatriation in the 1920s. The dollar was worth much more in Germany, Italy, Austria, and other European countries than in France. Yet, and in spite of the relatively high cost of living in Paris, the exchange rate did definitely favor those who had dollars to bring with them. Below are typical values during the 1920s (information given me by Professor Warren I. Susman of Rutgers University):

Date	*the dollar in francs*
September 14, 1919	7.98
September 16, 1920	15.18
September 5, 1922	12.84
July 1, 1923	16.395
July 1, 1924	18.94
July 1, 1925	22.16
July 1, 1926	35.84
July 1, 1927	25.545
July 1, 1928	25.40
July 1, 1929	25.5425
July 1, 1930	25.46
July 1, 1931	25.465
July 1, 1932	25.5125
July 1, 1933	20.02
July 1, 1934	15.1425

One might point out that, except for 1920 and 1926, the franc was relatively stable in the decade, with nothing like the inflationary fluctuations of some other European currencies [*Author*].

5. American writer and publisher (1895–1956), founding publisher of Contact Editions (Paris) and co-editor, with William Carlos Williams (1883–1963), of *Contact*, a literary magazine.

6. Mary Butts (1890–1937), English writer. Robert Coates (1897–1973), American art critic and writer. H. D. (Hilda Doolittle) (1886–1961), American poet.

Most of them were conscious of being quite at the center of important, exciting events. In small or large groups, they were to be seen at the home of Gertrude Stein, at 27 rue de Fleurus; in the offices of Ford's *transatlantic review* or Samuel Putnam's[7] *New Review*; in Joyce's apartment; and, perhaps most important of all, at 12 rue de l'Odéon, Sylvia Beach's shop. William Carlos Williams, in his *Autobiography*, speaks of her and of Adrienne Monnier's unfailing efforts to encourage and to help modern writers:

> At the slightest invitation from Sylvia she [Adrienne Monnier] would close her shop door, on the opposite side of the rue de l'Odéon, to see a writer from abroad. To conserve and to enrich the literary life of her time was her unfailing drive. They conspired to make that region of Paris back of the old theatre a sanctuary for all sorts of writers: Joyce, of course, and many of the younger Americans found it a veritable home.

* * *

MALCOLM COWLEY

Traveller's Cheque†

* * *

Transatlantic Review

There is a point beyond which historical parallels cannot be carried. The United States in 1921, unlike Russia in 1867, had ceased to be a colony of European capitalism. It exported not only raw materials but finished products, and the machinery with which to finish them, and the methods by which to distribute them, and the entire capital required in the process. In addition to wheat and automobiles, it had begun to export cultural goods, hot and sweet jazz bands, financial experts, movies and political ideals. There were even American myths, among others that of the hardheaded, softhearted businessman enslaved by his wife. Yet our literature had not registered the changed status of the nation. American intellectuals as a group

7. Samuel Putnam (1892–1950), American translator and editor who lived as an expatriate in Paris, founder and editor of *The New Review*, a literary magazine published 1931–32.

† From *Exile's Return: A Literary Odyssey of the 1920s* (New York: Viking, 1951), pp. 81–84; 93–97; 132–35. Notes are by the editor of this Norton Critical Edition.

continued to labor under a burden of provincialism as heavy and jagged as that which oppressed the compatriots of Dostoevski.[1]

Almost everywhere, after the war, one heard the intellectual life of America unfavorably compared with that of Europe. The critics often called for a great American novel or opera; they were doggedly enthusiastic, like cheer leaders urging Princeton to carry the ball over the line; but at heart they felt that Princeton was beaten, the game was in the bag for Oxford and the Sorbonne; at heart they were not convinced that even the subject matter of a great novel could be supplied by this country. American themes—so the older critics felt—were lacking in dignity. Art and ideas were products manufactured under a European patent; all we could furnish toward them was raw talent destined usually to be wasted. Everywhere, in every department of cultural life, Europe offered the models to imitate—in painting, composing, philosophy, folk music, folk drinking, the drama, sex, politics, national consciousness—indeed, some doubted that this country was even a nation; it had no traditions except the fatal tradition of the pioneer. As for our contemporary literature, thousands were willing to echo Van Wyck Brooks[2] when he said that in comparison with the literature of any European country, "it is indeed one long list of spiritual casualties. For it is not that the talent is wanting, but that somehow this talent fails to fulfill itself."

* * *

Indeed, there were several waves or successive groups of exiles, and their different points of view were reflected in a whole series of little exiled magazines. The myth of the Lost Generation was adopted by the second wave, by the friends of Ernest Hemingway who contributed in 1924 to the *Transatlantic Review*; this was also the magazine that showed the greatest interest in colloquial writing about American themes. *Transition*, which came later, was more international. It included among its contributors many of the dyed-in-the-wool expatriates, those who had deliberately cut every tie binding them to the homeland except one tie: their incomes still came from the United States.

* * *

1. Fyodor Dostoyevsky (1821–1881), Russian novelist.
2. American literary critic and historian (1886–1963).

On Bullfighting

When the novel's action shifts to Pamplona in Book II, the bullfight (or *corrida*) is especially important. Hemingway had become fascinated by the *corrida* upon first witnessing bullfights in Spain; several of the early prose pieces of *In Our Time* focused on the spectacle. Frederick J. Hoffman's selection here takes Hemingway at his word about the simplicity and fundamental character of "violent death" available, in the postwar world, only in the bullring, and discusses Jake's wound and his relationship with Brett in terms of the bullfight's ritual and its opportunity for the performance of "grace under pressure." Two of the "interchapters" from *In Our Time* (1925) are included. Chapter IX tells the story of a young matador who must fight five bulls in the *corrida* because two other matadors are incapacitated. Chapter XII narrates Villalta's killing of a bull, emphasizing his talent and bravery and the way bull and man become one at the moment of the kill. The two young matadors resemble Pedro Romero in their talent and dedication, and the vignettes capture the atmosphere of the *corrida* that Hemingway also pursues in the novel. Bullfighting continued to capture Hemingway's attention for the rest of his life. In 1932, he published a nonfiction study of the *corrida, Death in the Afternoon*. In that book, Hemingway describes the bullfight and argues for its specific values as an art form that is a performance of timeless concerns—the confrontation with mortality—even as it produces a time-bound and ephemeral occasion.

FREDERICK J. HOFFMAN

[On the Bullfight]†

* * *

With the feeling that he must understand and honestly account for this condition, Hemingway came to Paris early in the 1920s to learn how to write; he found that the greatest difficulty, "aside from know-

† From *The Twenties: American Writing in the Postwar Decade* (New York: Free Press, 1949), pp. 93–95.

ing truly what you really felt, rather than what you were supposed to feel, and had been taught to feel, was to put down what really happened in action. . . ." He wanted to begin with "the simplest things, and one of the simplest things of all and the most fundamental is violent death." The only place to see that happen, "now that the wars were over, was in the bullring."

The consequences of this interest are testified to both in *Death in the Afternoon* (1932) and in *The Sun Also Rises* (1926). In the total design of the bullfight, as in its details of risk, grace, danger, and death, Hemingway apparently found the perfect palliative to the bewilderment and terror felt by the victims of the "unreasonable wound." The key to Hemingway's interest in the bullfight seems to be the artificial nature of its design; quite aside from the very real danger of death that it poses for the matador, it is true that he creates, manipulates, and controls that danger. It is the only art, Hemingway said in *Death in the Afternoon*, "in which the artist is in danger of death and in which the degree of brilliance in the performance is left to the fighter's honor." Here there is nothing unreasonable; there are no surprises, no tragedies that cannot be explained as the result of fear, ignorance, or mere gracelessness. Within the limitations imposed by usage and circumstance (tradition and "present danger"), it is possible to evaluate courage and virtue, "purity of line" and "grace under pressure."

The bullfight had a simplified past and a continuous, ritualized present. It was above all possible to measure, to gauge, human emotions within a set of brilliantly formed "calculated risks." There is no doubt that Hemingway was attracted to the simplicity of the matador-hero, to his lack of sophistication, and to his constant preoccupation with the concrete details of his task and craft. This simplicity of dedication—that is, among those fighters who were "the real thing"—when circumstances were right and when acts of grace and courage were sympathetically seen and understood, became for Hemingway a meaningful ritual for his time, the most meaningful he was able to find during the first postwar decade.

The strength of his interest in Spain and in the bullfights is fully seen in *The Sun Also Rises*. This novel is a brilliant improvisation of a moral point of view, largely because of that interest. That the *corrida* was a specious resolution of postwar ills and that it could not, because of its artificiality, really take the place of religion or become a substitute tradition does not necessarily nullify its importance. The bullfight contributed both a criticism and a corrective to the persons involved in the atmosphere of postwar life. It is an ideal measure of that group's inadequacy; and it profoundly influenced certain persons and certain actions. The bullfight marked an ideal unity of specific detail with formal tradition, a unity lacking in the lives of the expatriates. The past had preserved the matador's naïveté, his purity and his "honor"; the requirements of the fight itself meant that with each new appearance in the ring he had to renew his caution, his skill, and his courage. While the procedures were largely fixed by tradition, there was nothing lifeless or mechanical or meaningless in them. The motion, the emotion, and the action formed a single figure that could be seen and shared by those who had understanding. In every detail this artificial pattern of behavior, this aesthetic ordering of human risk and emotion, contrasts sharply with the lives of Jake Barnes and his friends.

* * *

ERNEST HEMINGWAY

From In Our Time†

Chapter IX

The first matador got the horn through his sword hand and the crowd hooted him. The second matador slipped and the bull caught him through the belly and he hung on to the horn with one hand and held the other tight against the place, and the bull rammed him wham against the wall and the horn came out, and he lay in the sand, and then got up like crazy drunk and tried to slug the men carrying him away and yelled for his sword but he fainted. The kid came out and had to kill five bulls because you can't have more than three matadors, and the last bull he was so tired he couldn't get the sword in. He couldn't hardly lift his arm. He tried five times and the crowd was quiet because it was a good bull and it looked like him or the bull and then he finally made it. He sat down in the sand and puked and they held a cape over him while the crowd hollered and threw things down into the bull ring.

Chapter XII

If it happened right down close in front of you, you could see Villalta snarl at the bull and curse him, and when the bull charged he swung back firmly like an oak when the wind hits it, his legs tight together, the muleta[1] *trailing and the sword following the curve behind. Then he cursed the bull, flopped the muleta at him, and swung back from*

† From *In Our Time*, Chapter IX and Chapter XII (New York: Boni and Liveright, 1925), pp. 107, 138. Note is by the editor of this Norton Critical Edition.

1. A small red cape affixed to a stick or baton, used by a matador to guide the bull through turns during the bullfight.

the charge his feet firm, the muleta curving and at each swing the crowd roaring.

When he started to kill it was all in the same rush. The bull looking at him straight in front, hating. He drew out the sword from the folds of the muleta and sighted with the same movement and called to the bull, Toro! Toro! *and the bull charged and Villalta charged and just for a moment they became one. Villalta became one with the bull and then it was over. Villalta standing straight and the red hilt of the sword sticking out dully between the bull's shoulders. Villalta, his hand up at the crowd and the bull roaring blood, looking straight at Villalta and his legs caving.*

Literary Influences

The first two selections here are by early friends and mentors, Gertrude Stein and Sherwood Anderson. They illustrate stylistic influences legible in Hemingway's early work, including *The Sun Also Rises*. Michael Arlen's novel *The Green Hat* was named by several early reviewers as a source for the representation of Brett Ashley, and it provides a sense of the more dominant tone of fictions about such characters in the early 1920s.

GERTRUDE STEIN

From The Gentle Lena†

Lena was patient, gentle, sweet and german. She had been a servant for four years and had liked it very well.

Lena had been brought from Germany to Bridgepoint by a cousin and had been in the same place there for four years.

This place Lena had found very good. There was a pleasant, unexacting mistress and her children, and they all liked Lena very well.

There was a cook there who scolded Lena a great deal but Lena's german patience held no suffering and the good incessant woman really only scolded so for Lena's good.

Lena's german voice when she knocked and called the family in the morning was as awakening, as soothing, and as appealing, as a delicate soft breeze in midday, summer. She stood in the hallway every morning a long time in her unexpectant and unsuffering german patience calling to the young ones to get up. She would call and wait a long time and then call again, always even, gentle, patient, while the young ones fell back often into that precious, tense, last bit of sleeping that gives a strength of joyous vigor in the young, over them that have come to the readiness of middle age, in their awakening.

Lena had good hard work all morning, and on the pleasant, sunny afternoons she was sent out into the park to sit and watch the little two year old girl baby of the family.

† From *Three Lives: Stories of The Good Anna, Melanctha and the Gentle Lena* (New York: Grafton Press, 1909, rpt. in New York: Dover, 1994), pp. 142–44.

The other girls, all them that make the pleasant, lazy crowd, that watch the children in the sunny afternoons out in the park, all liked the simple, gentle, german Lena very well. They all, too, liked very well to tease her, for it was so easy to make her mixed and troubled, and all helpless, for she could never learn to know just what the other quicker girls meant by the queer things they said.

The two or three of these girls, the ones that Lena always sat with, always worked together to confuse her. Still it was pleasant, all this life for Lena.

The little girl fell down sometimes and cried, and then Lena had to soothe her. When the little girl would drop her hat, Lena had to pick it up and hold it. When the little girl was bad and threw away her playthings, Lena told her she could not have them and took them from her to hold until the little girl should need them.

It was all a peaceful life for Lena, almost as peaceful as a pleasant leisure. The other girls, of course, did tease her, but then that only made a gentle stir within her.

Lena was a brown and pleasant creature, brown as blonde races often have them brown, brown, not with the yellow or the red or the chocolate brown of sun burned countries, but brown with the clear color laid flat on the light toned skin beneath, the plain, spare brown that makes it right to have been made with hazel eyes, and not too abundant straight, brown hair, hair that only later deepens itself into brown from the straw yellow of a german childhood.

Lena had the flat chest, straight back and forward falling shoulders of the patient and enduring working woman, though her body was now still in its milder girlhood and work had not yet made these lines too clear.

The rarer feeling that there was with Lena, showed in all the even quiet of her body movements, but in all it was the strongest in the patient, old-world ignorance, and earth made pureness of her brown, flat, soft featured face. Lena had eyebrows that were a wondrous thickness. They were black, and spread, and very cool, with their dark color and their beauty, and beneath them were her hazel eyes, simple and human, with the earth patience of the working, gentle, german woman.

Yes it was all a peaceful life for Lena. The other girls, of course, did tease her, but then that only made a gentle stir within her.

"What you got on your finger Lena," Mary, one of the girls she always sat with, one day asked her. Mary was good natured, quick, intelligent and Irish.

Lena had just picked up the fancy paper made accordion that the little girl had dropped beside her, and was making it squeak sadly as she pulled it with her brown, strong, awkward finger.

"Why, what is it, Mary, paint?" said Lena, putting her finger to her mouth to taste the dirt spot.

"That's awful poison Lena, don't you know?" said Mary, "that green paint that you just tasted."

Lena had sucked a good deal of the green paint from her finger. She stopped and looked hard at the finger. She did not know just how much Mary meant by what she said.

"Ain't it poison, Nellie, that green paint, that Lena sucked just now," said Mary. "Sure it is Lena, its real poison, I ain't foolin' this time anyhow."

Lena was a little troubled. She looked hard at her finger where the paint was, and she wondered if she had really sucked it.

It was still a little wet on the edges and she rubbed it off a long time on the inside of her dress, and in between she wondered and looked at the finger and thought, was it really poison that she had just tasted.

"Ain't it too bad, Nellie, Lena should have sucked that," Mary said.

Nellie smiled and did not answer. Nellie was dark and thin, and looked Italian. She had a big mass of black hair that she wore high up on her head, and that made her face look very fine.

Nellie always smiled and did not say much, and then she would look at Lena to perplex her.

And so they all three sat with their little charges in the pleasant sunshine a long time. And Lena would often look at her finger and wonder if it was really poison that she had just tasted and then she would rub her finger on her dress a little harder.

Mary laughed at her and teased her and Nellie smiled a little and looked queerly at her.

Then it came time, for it was growing cooler, for them to drag together the little ones, who had begun to wander, and to take each one back to its own mother. And Lena never knew for certain whether it was really poison, that green stuff that she had tasted.

* * *

SHERWOOD ANDERSON

Hands†

Upon the half decayed veranda of a small frame house that stood near the edge of a ravine near the town of Winesburg. Ohio, a fat little old man walked nervously up and down. Across a long field that

† From *Winesburg, Ohio* (New York: B. W. Huebsche, 1919, rpt. in New York: W. W. Norton, 1995), pp. 9–13.

had been seeded for clover but that had produced only a dense crop of yellow mustard weeds, he could see the public highway along which went a wagon filled with berry pickers returning from the fields. The berry pickers, youths and maidens, laughed and shouted boisterously. A boy clad in a blue shirt leaped from the wagon and attempted to drag after him one of the maidens who screamed and protested shrilly. The feet of the boy in the road kicked up a cloud of dust that floated across the face of the departing sun. Over the long field came a thin girlish voice. "Oh, you Wing Biddlebaum, comb your hair, it's falling into your eyes," commanded the voice to the man, who was bald and whose nervous little hands fiddled about the bare white forehead as though arranging a mass of tangled locks.

Wing Biddlebaum, forever frightened and beset by a ghostly band of doubts, did not think of himself as in any way a part of the life of the town where he had lived for twenty years. Among all the people of Winesburg but one had come close to him. With George Willard, son of Tom Willard, the proprietor of the New Willard House, he had formed something like a friendship. George Willard was the reporter on the *Winesburg Eagle* and sometimes in the evenings he walked out along the highway to Wing Biddlebaum's house. Now as the old man walked up and down on the veranda, his hands moving nervously about, he was hoping that George Willard would come and spend the evening with him. After the wagon containing the berry pickers had passed, he went across the field through the tall mustard weeds and climbing a rail fence peered anxiously along the road to the town. For a moment he stood thus, rubbing his hands together and looking up and down the road, and then, fear overcoming him, ran back to walk again upon the porch on his own house.

In the presence of George Willard, Wing Biddlebaum, who for twenty years had been the town mystery, lost something of his timidity, and his shadowy personality, submerged in a sea of doubts, came forth to look at the world. With the young reporter at his side, he ventured in the light of day into Main Street or strode up and down on the rickety front porch of his own house, talking excitedly. The voice that had been low and trembling became shrill and loud. The bent figure straightened. With a kind of wriggle, like a fish returned to the brook by the fisherman, Biddlebaum the silent began to talk, striving to put into words the ideas that had been accumulated by his mind during long years of silence.

Wing Biddlebaum talked much with his hands. The slender expressive fingers, forever active, forever striving to conceal themselves in his pockets or behind his back, came forth and became the piston rods of his machinery of expression.

The story of Wing Biddlebaum is a story of hands. Their restless activity, like unto the beating of the wings of an imprisoned bird, had given him his name. Some obscure poet of the town had thought of it. The hands alarmed their owner. He wanted to keep them hidden away and looked with amazement at the quiet inexpressive hands of other men who worked beside him in the fields, or passed, driving sleepy teams on country roads.

When he talked to George Willard, Wing Biddlebaum closed his fists and beat with them upon a table or on the walls of his house. The action made him more comfortable. If the desire to talk came to him when the two were walking in the fields, he sought out a stump or the top board of a fence and with his hands pounding busily talked with renewed ease.

The story of Wing Biddlebaum's hands is worth a book in itself. Sympathetically set forth it would tap many strange, beautiful qualities in obscure men. It is a job for a poet. In Winesburg the hands had attracted attention merely because of their activity. With them Wing Biddlebaum had picked as high as a hundred and forty quarts of strawberries in a day. They became his distinguishing feature, the source of his fame. Also they made more grotesque an already grotesque and elusive individuality. Winesburg was proud of the hands of Wing Biddlebaum in the same spirit in which it was proud of Banker White's new stone house and Wesley Moyer's bay stallion, Tony Tip, that had won the two-fifteen trot at the fall races in Cleveland.

As for George Willard, he had many times wanted to ask about the hands. At times an almost overwhelming curiosity had taken hold of him. He felt that there must be a reason for their strange activity and their inclination to keep hidden away and only a growing respect for Wing Biddlebaum kept him from blurting out the questions that were often in his mind.

Once he had been on the point of asking. The two were walking in the fields on a summer afternoon and had stopped to sit upon a grassy bank. All afternoon Wing Biddlebaum had talked as one inspired. By a fence he had stopped and beating like a giant woodpecker upon the top board had shouted at George Willard, condemning his tendency to be too much influenced by the people about him. "You are destroying yourself." he cried. "You have the inclination to be alone and to dream and you are afraid of dreams. You want to be like others in town here. You hear them talk and you try to imitate them."

On the grassy bank Wing Biddlebaum had tried again to drive his point home. His voice became soft and reminiscent, and with a sigh of contentment he launched into a long rambling talk, speaking as one lost in a dream.

Out of the dream Wing Biddlebaum made a picture for George Willard. In the picture men lived again in a kind of pastoral golden age. Across a green open country came clean-limbed young men, some afoot, some mounted upon horses. In crowds the young men came to gather about the feet of an old man who sat beneath a tree in a tiny garden and who talked to them.

Wing Biddlebaum became wholly inspired. For once he forgot the hands. Slowly they stole forth and lay upon George Willard's shoulders. Something new and bold came into the voice that talked. "You must try to forget all you have learned," said the old man "You must begin to dream. From this time on you must shut your ears to the roaring of the voices."

Pausing in his speech, Wing Biddlebaum looked long and earnestly at George Willard. His eyes glowed. Again he raised the hands to caress the boy and then a look of horror swept over his face.

With a convulsive movement of his body. Wing Biddlebaum sprang to his feet and thrust his hands deep into his trousers pockets. Tears came to his eyes. "I must be getting along home. I can talk no more with you," he said nervously.

Without looking back, the old man had hurried down the hillside and across a meadow, leaving George Willard perplexed and frightened upon the grassy slope. With a shiver of dread the boy arose and went along the road toward town. "I'll not ask him about his hands," he thought, touched by the memory of the terror he had seen in the man's eyes. "There's something wrong, but I don't want to know what it is. His hands have something to do with his fear of me and of everyone."

And George Willard was right. Let us look briefly into the story of the hands. Perhaps our talking of them will arouse the poet who will tell the hidden wonder story of the influence for which the hands were but fluttering pennants of promise.

In his youth Wing Biddlebaum had been a school teacher in a town in Pennsylvania. He was not then known as Wing Biddlebaum, but went by the less euphonic name of Adolph Myers. As Adolph Myers he was much loved by the boys of his school.

Adolph Myers was meant by nature to be a teacher of youth. He was one of those rare, little-understood men who rule by a power so gentle that it passes as a lovable weakness. In their feeling for the boys under their charge such men are not unlike the finer sort of women in their love of men.

And yet that is but crudely stated. It needs the poet there. With the boys of his school, Adolph Myers had walked in the evening or had sat talking until dusk upon the schoolhouse steps lost in a kind of dream. Here and there went his hands, caressing the shoulders of the boys, playing about the tousled heads. As he talked his voice became soft and musical. There was a caress in that also. In a way the voice and the hands, the stroking of the shoulders and the touching of the hair was a part of the school-master's effort to carry a dream into the young minds. By the caress that was in his fingers he expressed himself. He was one of those men in whom the force that creates life is diffused, not centralized. Under the caress of his hands doubt and disbelief went out of the minds of the boys and they began also to dream.

And then the tragedy. A half-witted boy of the school became enamored of the young master. In his bed at night he imagined unspeakable things and in the morning went forth to tell his dreams as facts. Strange, hideous accusations fell from his loose-hung lips. Through the Pennsylvania town went a shiver. Hidden, shadowy doubts that had been in men's minds concerning Adolph Myers were galvanized into beliefs.

The tragedy did not linger. Trembling lads were jerked out of bed and questioned. "He put his arms about me," said one. "His fingers were always playing in my hair," said another.

One afternoon a man of the town, Henry Bradford, who kept a saloon, came to the schoolhouse door. Calling Adolph Myers into the school yard he began to beat him with his fists. As his hard knuckles beat down into the frightened face of the schoolmaster, his wrath became more and more terrible. Screaming with dismay, the children ran here and there like disturbed insects. "I'll teach you to put your hands on my boy, you beast," roared the saloon keeper, who, tired of beating the master, had begun to kick him about the yard.

Adolph Myers was driven from the Pennsylvania town in the night. With lanterns in their hands a dozen men came to the door of the house where he lived alone and commanded that he dress and come forth. It was raining and one of the men had a rope in his hands. They had intended to hang the schoolmaster, but something in his figure, so small, white, and pitiful, touched their hearts and they let him escape. As he ran away into the darkness they repented of their weakness and ran after him, swearing and throwing sticks and great balls of soft mud at the figure that screamed and ran faster and faster into the darkness.

For twenty years Adolph Myers had lived alone in Winesburg. He was but forty but looked sixty-five. The name of Biddlebaum he got from a box of goods seen at a freight station as he hurried through an eastern Ohio town. He had an aunt in Winesburg, a black-toothed old woman who raised chickens, and with her he lived until she died. He had been ill for a year after the experience in Pennsylvania, and after his recovery worked as a day laborer in the fields, going timidly about and striving to conceal his hands. Although he did not understand what had happened he felt that the hands must be to blame. Again and again the fathers of the boys had talked of the hands. "Keep your hands to yourself," the saloon keeper had roared, dancing with fury in the school house yard.

Upon the veranda of his house by the ravine, Wing Biddlebaum continued to walk up and down until the sun had disappeared and the road beyond the field was lost in the grey shadows. Going into his house he cut slices of bread and spread honey upon them. When the rumble of the evening train that took away the express cars loaded with the day's harvest of berries had passed and restored the silence of the summer night, he went again to walk upon the veranda. In the darkness he could not see the hands and they became quiet. Although he still hungered for the presence of the boy, who was the medium through which he expressed his love of man, the hunger became again a part of his loneliness and his waiting. Lighting a lamp, Wing Biddlebaum washed the few dishes soiled by his simple meal and, setting up a folding cot by the screen door that led to the porch, prepared to undress for the night. A few stray white bread crumbs lay on the cleanly washed floor by the table; putting the lamp upon a low stool he began to pick up the crumbs, carrying them to his mouth one by one with unbelievable rapidity. In the dense blotch of light beneath the table, the kneeling figure looked like a priest engaged in some service of his church. The nervous expressive fingers, flashing in and out of the light, might well have been mistaken for the fingers of the devotee going swiftly through decade after decade of his rosary.

MICHAEL ARLEN

From The Green Hat†

* * *

Now here is the difficult part of this history. Of the many gaps it will contain, this seems to me the most grave, the least excusable. One should write, if not well, at least plausibly, about the things that happen. And yet I cannot be plausible about this, because I do not know how it happened. I did not ask her. Did she want to? Mrs. Storm was a lady who gave you a sense of the conventions. Mrs. Storm was a . . . and yet . . . I do not know anything about her.

I am trying, you can see, to realise her, to add her together; and, of course, failing. She showed you first one side of her and then another, and each side seemed to have no relation with any other, each side might have belonged to a different woman; indeed, since

† From *The Green Hat* (New York: George H. Doran Company, 1924), pp. 26–30.

then I have found that each side did belong to a different woman. I have met a hundred pieces of Iris, quite vividly met them, since last I saw her. And sometimes I have thought of her—foolishly, of course, but shall a man be wise about a woman?—as some one who had by a mistake of the higher authorities strayed into our world from a land unknown to us, a land where lived a race of men and women who, the perfection of our imperfections, were awaiting their inheritance of this world of ours when we, with that marvellous indirectness of purpose which is called being human, shall have finally annihilated each other in our endless squabbles about honour, morality, nationality.

We have all of us a crude desire to "place" our fellows in this or that category or class: we like to more or less what they are, so that, maybe, we may know more or less what we shall be to them. But, even with the knowledge that she was Gerald's sister, that she was twenty-nine years old, that she was the niece of Lord Portairley, you could not, anyhow I couldn't, "place" Mrs. Storm. You had a conviction, a rather despairing one, that she didn't fit in anywhere, to any class, nay, to any nationality. She wasn't that ghastly thing called "Bohemian," she wasn't any of the ghastly things called "society," "country," upper, middle, and lower class. She was, you can see, some invention, ghastly or not, of her own. But she was so quiet about it, she didn't intrude it on you, she was just herself, and that was a very quiet self. You felt she had outlawed herself from somewhere, but where was that somewhere? You felt she was tremendously indifferent as to whether she was outlawed or not. In her eyes you saw the landscape of England, spacious and brave; but you felt unreasonably certain that she was as devoid of patriotism as Mary Stuart. She gave you a sense of the conventions; but she gave you—unaware always, impersonal always, and those cool, sensible eyes!—a much deeper sense that she was somehow outside the comic, squalid, sometimes, almost fine laws by which we judge as to what is and what is not conventional. That was why, I am trying to show, I felt so profoundly incapable with her. It was not as though one was nonexistent; it was as though, with her, one existed only in the most limited sense. And, I suppose, she affected me particularly in that way simply because I am a man of my time. For that is a limitation a man can't get beyond—to be of his time, completely. He may be successful, a man like that—indeed, should he not blow his brains out if he is not?—but he who is of this time may never rise above himself: he is the galley-slave working incessantly at the oars of his life, which reflects the lives of the multitude of his fellows. Yes, I am of my time. And so I had with this woman that profound sense of incapability, of defeat, which any limited man must feel with a woman whose limitations he cannot know. She was—in that phrase of Mr. Conrad's which can mean so little or so much—she was of all time. She was, when the first woman crawled out of the mud of the primeval world. She would be, when the last woman walks towards the unmentionable end.

"Good-bye," I said, and then, as I looked from the disordered room and my disenchanted life at her, the eyes in the shadow of the green hat were brilliant with laughter, so that I was stunned. "Why are you laughing?" I asked, or perhaps I did not ask that, perhaps she had not been laughing at all, for when I was recovered from my stupor her eyes were quite grave, and dark as in a crypt. I pushed open the door of my room.

"How I would like," she said, that husky voice, "a glass of cold water!" That was what she said, and so I let her go in alone into the sitting-room whilst I turned on the tap in the bathroom. Fiercely and long I let the water run, pleased with the way it was filling the little house with its clean roar, pleased with the clean scent of the rushing water, which is always like the scent of cool sunlight. Then she said: "You have had a quick bath," and so we became friends.

She stood among the littered books on the floor, looking round at the disorder, like a tulip with a green head. She sipped the water, looking round wisely over the rim of the tumbler. I explained that I was leaving to-morrow, and therefore the disorder.

We talked.

In that disordered room, so littered with books that you might hardly take a step without stumbling over one, it was not a difficult task. Indeed, is never so easy to talk about books as when they are about the floor, so that you may turn them over with your foot, see what they are, pick them up and drop them anywhere with no precious nonsense as to where they should exactly go.

She waved her glass of water about, sipping it. A drop of water clung like a gem to the corner of her painted mouth. It was not fair.

Talking with her in that room was like talking with her as we walked on a windy heath: she threw out things, you caught all you could of them, you missed what you liked, and you threw something back. Now and then something would turn up in a voice which was suddenly strong and clear, and every time her voice was strong and clear you were so surprised that you did not hear so well as when she spoke inaudibly. She had none of the organised, agonised grimaces of the young lady of fashion. But one knew she was not a young lady of fashion, for she hadn't a sulky mouth.

* * *

CRITICISM

Reviews and Early Criticism

This section illustrates the early reception of *The Sun Also Rises* both in periodical reviews and in the first generation of academic interpretation of the novel.

The *Times Literary Supplement* review is an exemplary English review of the novel (with its British title) that finds some merit in the bullfighting scenes but ultimately judges the novel "an unsuccessful experiment" because the narrative and characters are "frankly tedious." Hemingway had cultivated the attention of Edmund Wilson, a critic for the influential magazine *New Republic,* and Wilson had published an early, brief but positive, review of *In Our Time.* His review of *The Sun Also Rises,* also published in *New Republic,* exemplifies the positive reception of the novel, a reading by someone who had found Hemingway's stories impressive and is inclined to admire the novel. Allen Tate's review, on the other hand, illustrates the novel's more critical reception. Though he had been persuaded by the stories and had reviewed Hemingway positively in *The Nation* magazine before, Tate is impatient with the novel at both aesthetic and moral levels.

Edmund Wilson returned to the novel in his 1941 book, *The Wound and the Bow.* Here is one of the early substantial readings of the novel that set the terms for its reception over the next couple of generations. Wilson situates Hemingway in a tradition of nineteenth and twentieth century fiction exploring woundedness, and finds in this novel (as well as his other writing to date) the protagonist's wound to be both aesthetically and ethically generative. It is against the horizon of Wilson's powerful early reading (as well as those of Leslie Fiedler and Philip Young) that much of the best recent criticism has developed revisionist interpretations. Fiedler's is a classic treatment of Brett Ashley in terms of Hemingway's fondness "for women who seem as much boy as girl," insistent upon Brett's rejection of the typical role of castrating "bitch." Young is an early articulator of the idea of a "code" operative in Hemingway's fiction, a dedication to such virtues as reticence and "grace under pressure" modeled by the protagonists of the early fiction, including Jake Barnes.

TIMES LITERARY SUPPLEMENT

Fiesta†

In his first volume of short stories Mr. Ernest Hemingway got some very delicate and unusual effects by retranslating his impressions, as it were, into a primitive kind of imagery. He described his characters and their behaviour with deliberate naivety, identifying what they did and what they felt in an artful and extremely suggestive manner. Now comes a novel, FIESTA[1] . . . , which is more obviously an experiment in story-making, and in which he abandons his vivid impressionism for something much less interesting. There are moments of sudden illumination in the story, and throughout it displays a determined reticence; but it is frankly tedious after one has read the first hundred pages and ceased to hope for anything different. This is criticism we should not think of applying to the work of a less talented writer The crude, meaningless conversation which Mr. Hemingway gives us is best taken for granted, it may be true to life, as the saying is, but there is hardly any point in putting it into a novel. Besides, so much of it consists of offers of drink and the bald confession of drunkenness that what virtue it has is staled by repetition.

Drink, indeed, is an extraordinary bugbear for these Americans in Paris, almost more troublesome than sex. However, they are all artists, and it seems to be the artistic lot to be able to consume quantities of liquid which would send most human beings to the grave. Brett, the heroine, is scarcely ever sober; Jake, who loves her, but who has been smashed up in the war (it is terrible irony that Mr. Hemingway intends—and partly achieves—here), is a reserved, rather sardonic creature, and almost the only credible person in the story. His position lends some persuasiveness to Brett's nymphomania, although it does not make her less tiresome. The other men who love her or live with her are unexciting; Cohn is a caricature, Mike never comes to life, the young matador is a mixture of perversity and convention. The Spanish scenes give us something of the quality of Mr. Hemingway's earlier book, but they hardly qualify the general impression of an unsuccessful experiment.

† From *[London] Times Literary Supplement* (30 June 1927): 454. Reprinted in *Critical Essays on Ernest Hemingway's* The Sun Also Rises, ed. James Nagel (New York: G. K. Hall and Co., 1995), p. 45. Note is by the editor of this Norton Critical Edition.

1. The first British publication of *The Sun Also Rises* was entitled *Fiesta*.

EDMUND WILSON

The Sportsman's Tragedy†

The reputation of Ernest Hemingway has, in a very short time, reached such proportions that it has already become fashionable to disparage him. Yet it seems to me that he has received in America very little intelligent criticism. I find Lee Wilson Dodd, for example, in the 'Saturday Review of Literature,' with his usual gentle trepidation in the presence of contemporary life, deciding with a sigh of relief that, after all, Ernest Hemingway (a young man who has published only three books) is not Shakespeare or Tolstoy; and describing Hemingway's subjects as follows: 'The people he observes with fascinated fixation and then makes live before us are . . . all very much alike: bull-fighters, bruisers, touts, gunmen, professional soldiers, prostitutes, hard drinkers, dope fiends. . . . For what they may or may not be intellectually, esthetically or morally worth, he makes his facts ours. In the 'Nation,' Joseph Wood Krutch, whose review is more sympathetic than Mr. Dodd's, describes Hemingway as follows: 'Spiritually the distinguishing mark of Mr. Hemingway's work is a weariness too great to be aware of anything but sensations. . . . Mr. Hemingway tells us, both by his choice of subject and by the method which he employs, that life is an affair of mean tragedies. . . . In his hands the subject matter of literature becomes sordid little catastrophes in the lives of very vulgar people. (1) I do not know whether these reviewers of 'Men Without Women' have never read Hemingway's other two books, or whether they have simply forgotten them. Do the stories in 'In Our Time' and in 'The Sun Also Rises' actually answer to these descriptions? Does 'Men Without Women' answer to them? The hero of 'In Our Time' who appears in one or two stories in the new volume, and the hero of 'The Sun Also Rises,' are both highly civilized persons of rather complex temperament and extreme sensibility. In what way can they be said to be 'very vulgar people'? And can the adventures of even the old bull-fighter in "The Undefeated" be called a 'sordid little catastrophe'?

* * *

The barbarity of the world since the War is *** the theme of Hemingway's *** "The Sun Also Rises." By his title and by the

† From *New Republic* 53 (14 December 1927): 102–103. Reprinted in *Critical Essays on Ernest Hemingway's* The Sun Also Rises, edited by James Nagel (New York: G. K. Hall and Co., 1995), pp. 46–49.

quotations which he prefixes to this book, he makes it plain what moral judgment we are to pass on the events he describes: "You are all a lost generation." What gives the book its profound unity and its disquieting effectiveness is the intimate relation established between the Spanish fiesta with its processions, its revelry and its bull-fighting and the atrocious behavior of the group of Americans and English who have come down from Paris to enjoy it. In the heartlessness of these people in their treatment of one another, do we not find the same principle at work as in the pagan orgy of the festival? Is not the brutal persecution of the Jew as much a natural casualty of a barbarous world as the fate of the man who is accidentally gored by the bull on the way to the bull-ring? The whole interest of "The Sun Also Rises" lies in the attempts of the hero and the heroine to disengage themselves from this world, or rather to arrive at some method of living in it honorably. The real story is the story of their attempts to do this—attempts by which, in such a world, they are always bound to lose in everything except honor. I do not agree, as has sometimes been said, that the behavior of the people in "The Sun Also Rises" is typical of only a small and special class of American and English expatriates. I believe that it is more or less typical of certain phases of the whole western world today; and the title "In Our Time" would have applied to it with as much appropriateness as to its predecessor.

Hemingway's attitude, however, toward the cruelties and treacheries he describes is quite different from anything else which one remembers in a similar connection. * * * Yet, to speak of Hemingway in these terms is really to misrepresent him. He is not a moralist staging a melodrama, but an artist presenting a situation of which the moral values are complex. Hemingway thoroughly enjoys bull-fighting, as he enjoys skiing, racing and prize-fights, and he is unremittingly conscious of the fact that, from the point of view of life as a sport, all that seems to him most painful is somehow closely bound up with what seems to him most enjoyable. The peculiar conflicts of feeling which arise in a temperament of this kind, are the subject of his fiction. His most remarkable effects, effects unlike anything else one remembers, are those, as in the fishing trip in 'The Sun Also Rises,' where we are made to feel, behind the appetite for the physical world, the falsity or the tragedy of a moral situation. The inescapable consciousness of this discord does not arouse Hemingway to passionate violence; but it poisons him and makes him sick, and thus invests with a singular sinister quality—a quality perhaps new in fiction—the sunlight and the green summer landscapes of 'The Sun Also Rises.' Thus, if Hemingway is oppressive, as Mr. Dodd complains, it is because he himself is oppressed. And we may find in him—in the clairvoyant's crystal of that incomparable art—an image of the common oppression.

ALLEN TATE

Hard-Boiled†

The present novel by the author of "In Our Time" supports the recent prophecy that he will be the "big man in American letters." At the time the prophecy was delivered it was meaningless because it was equivocal. Many of the possible interpretations now being eliminated, we fear it has turned out to mean something which we shall all regret. Mr. Hemingway has written a book that will be talked about, praised, perhaps imitated; it has already been received in something of that cautiously critical spirit which the followers of Henry James so notoriously maintain toward the master. Mr. Hemingway has produced a successful novel, but not without returning some violence upon the integrity achieved in his first book. He decided for reasons of his own to write a popular novel, or he wrote the only novel which he could write.

To choose the latter conjecture is to clear his intentions, obviously at the cost of impugning his art. One infers moreover that although sentimentality appears explicitly for the first time in his prose, it must have always been there. Its history can be constructed. The method used in "In Our Time" was *pointilliste*,[1] and the sentimentality was submerged. With great skill he reversed the usual and most general formula of prose fiction, instead of selecting the details of physical background and of human behavior for the intensification of a dramatic situation, he employed the minimum of drama for the greatest possible intensification of the observed object. The reference of emphasis for the observed object was therefore not the action; rather, the reference of the action was the object, and the action could be impure or incomplete without risk of detection. It could be mixed and incoherent; it could be brought in when it was advantageous to observation, or left out. The exception, important as such, in Mr. Hemingway's work is the story Mr. and Mrs. Elliott. Here the definite dramatic conflict inherent in a sexual relation emerged as fantasy, and significantly; presumably he could not handle it otherwise without giving himself away.

In "The Sun Also Rises," a full-length novel, Mr. Hemingway could not escape such leading situations, and he had besides to approach

† From *The Nation* (15 December 1926): 624, 644. Reprinted in *Critical Essays on Ernest Hemingway*'s The Sun Also Rises, ed. James Nagel (New York: G. K. Hall and Co., 1995), pp. 42–43. All notes are by the editor of this Norton Critical Edition.

1. Pointillism, a technique in oil painting in which small dots of unmixed color are placed so that, blended by the viewer's eye, shapes and complex colors may be perceived.

them with a kind of seriousness. He fails. It is not that Mr. Hemingway is, in the term which he uses in fine contempt for the big word, hard-boiled; it is that he is not hard-boiled enough, in the artistic sense. No one can dispute with a writer the significance he derives from his subject-matter, one can only point out that the significance is mixed or incomplete. Brett is a nymphomaniac; Robert Cohn, a most offensive cad; both are puppets. For the emphasis is false; Hemingway doesn't fill out his characters and let them stand for themselves; he isolates one or two chief traits which reduce them to caricature. His perception of the physical object is direct and accurate; his vision of character, singularly oblique. And he actually betrays the interior machinery of his hard-boiled attitude: "It is awfully easy to be hard-boiled about everything in the daytime, but at night it is another thing," says Jake, the sexually impotent, musing on the futile accessibility of Brett. The history of his sentimentality is thus complete.

There are certain devices exploited in the book which do not improve it; they extend its appeal. Robert Cohn is not only a bounder, he is a Jewish bounder. The other bounders, like Mike, Mr. Hemingway for some reason spares. He also spares Brett—another device—for while her pleasant folly need not be flogged, it equally need not be condoned; she becomes the attractive wayward lady of Sir Arthur Pinero and Michael Arlen.[2] Petronius's Circe, the archetype of all the Bretts, was neither appealing nor deformed.[3]

Mr. Hemingway has for some time been in the habit of throwing pebbles at the great—which recalls Mr. Pope's couplet about his contemporary Mr. Dennis.[4] The habit was formed in "The Torrents of Spring," where it was amusing. It is disconcerting in the present novel; it strains the context; and one suspects that Mr. Hemingway protests too much. The point he seems to be making is that he is morally superior, for instance, to Mr. Mencken, but it is not yet clear just why.[5]

2. Sir Arthur Pinero (1855–1934), English playwright. Michael Arlen (1895–1956), British novelist.
3. Petronius (27–66 CE), Roman courtier during the reign of Nero and author of the *Satyricon,* in which the character Circe (named for the witch in Homer's *Odyssey*) appears.
4. John Dennis (1658–1734), English critic and playwright, was satirized by the English poet Alexander Pope (1688–1744), in his mock epic *The Dunciad* (1729).
5. H. L. Mencken (see Book I, chapter VI, p. 32, note 4).

EDMUND WILSON

From The Wound and the Bow: Seven Studies in Literature†

* * *

The next fishing trip is strikingly different [from "Big Two-Hearted River"]. Perhaps the first had been an idealization. Is it possible to attain to such sensuous bliss merely through going alone into the woods: smoking, fishing, and eating, with no thought about anyone else or about anything one has ever done or will ever be obliged to do? At any rate, today, in *The Sun Also Rises,* all the things that are wrong with human life are there on the holiday, too—though one tries to keep them back out of the foreground and to occupy one's mind with the trout, caught now in a stream of the Pyrenees, and with the kidding of the friend from the States. The feeling of insecurity has deepened. The young American now appears in a seriously damaged condition: he has somehow been incapacitated sexually through wounds received in the war. He is in love with one of those international sirens who flourished in the cafés of the post-war period and whose ruthless and uncontrollable infidelities, in such a circle as that depicted by Hemingway, have made any sort of security impossible for the relations between women and men. The lovers of such a woman turn upon and rend one another because they are powerless to make themselves felt by *her.*

The casualties of the bullfight at Pamplona, to which these young people have gone for the *fiesta*, only reflect the blows and betrayals of demoralized human beings out of hand. What is the tiresome lover with whom the lady has just been off on a casual escapade, and who is unable to understand that he has been discarded, but the man who, on his way to the bull ring, has been accidentally gored by the bull? The young American who tells the story is the only character who keeps up standards of conduct, and he is prevented by his disability from dominating and directing the woman, who otherwise, it is intimated, might love him. Here the membrane of the style has been stretched taut to convey the vibrations of these qualms. The dry sunlight and the green summer landscapes have been invested with a sinister quality which must be new in literature. One enjoys the sun and the green as one enjoys suckling pigs and Spanish wine, but the uneasiness and apprehension are undruggable.

† From *The Wound and the Bow: Seven Studies in Literature* (New York: Oxford UP, 1947), pp. 217–21.

Yet one can catch hold of a code in all the drunkenness and the social chaos. 'Perhaps as you went along you did learn something,' Jake, the hero, reflects at one point. 'I did not care what it was all about. All I wanted to know was how to live in it. Maybe if you found out how to live in it you learned from that what it was all about.' 'Everybody behaves badly. Give them the proper chance,' he says later to Lady Brett.

'"You wouldn't behave badly." Brett looked at me.' In the end, she sends for Jake, who finds her alone in a hotel. She has left her regular lover for a young bullfighter, and this boy has for the first time inspired her with a respect which has restrained her from 'ruining' him: 'You know it makes one feel rather good deciding not to be a bitch.' We suffer and we make suffer, and everybody loses out in the long run; but in the meantime we can lose with honor.

* * *

LESLIE FIEDLER

From Love and Death in the American Novel†

* * *

Hemingway is only really comfortable in dealing with "men without women." The relations of father to son, of battle-companions, friends on a fishing trip, fellow inmates in a hospital, a couple of waiters preparing to close up shop, a bullfighter and his manager, a boy and a gangster: these move him to simplicity and truth. Perhaps he is best of all with men who stand alone—in night-time scenes when the solitary individual sweats in his bed on the verge of nightmare, or arises to confront himself in the glass; though he is at home, too, with the Rip Van Winkle archetype, with men in flight from women. Certainly, he returns again and again to the fishing trip and the journey to the war—those two traditional evasions of domesticity and civil life. Yet he feels an obligation to introduce women into his more ambitious fictions, though he does not know what to do with them beyond taking them to bed.

* * *

In Hemingway the rejection of the sentimental happy ending of marriage involves the acceptance of the sentimental happy beginning

† From *Love and Death in the American Novel* (New York: Stein and Day, 1960, rpt. in 1975 and in Funks Grove, IL: Dalchey Archive Press, 1998), pp. 316–20. Reprinted with permission of Dalchey Archive Press. All notes are by the editor of this Norton Critical Edition.

of innocent and inconsequential sex, and camouflages the rejection of maturity and of fatherhood itself. The only story in which he portrays a major protagonist as having a child is the one in which he remembers with nostalgia his little Trudy of the "well holding arms, quick searching tongue," and looks forward to the time when his son will have a gun and they can pop off to the forest like two boys together. More typically he aspires to be not Father but "Papa," the Old Man of the girl-child with whom he is temporarily sleeping; and surely there is no writer to whom childbirth more customarily presents itself as the essential catastrophe. At best he portrays it as a plaguey sort of accident which forces a man to leave his buddies behind at the moment of greatest pleasure as in "Cross Country Snow"; at worst, it becomes in his fiction that horror which drives the tender-hearted husband of "Indian Camp" to suicide, or which takes Catherine away from Lieutenant Henry in *A Farewell to Arms.*

Poor things, all they wanted was innocent orgasm after orgasm on an island of peace in a world at war, love-making without end in a scarcely real country to which neither owed life or allegiance. But such a relationship can, of course, never last, as Hemingway-Nick Adams-Lieutenant Henry has always known: "They all ended the same. Long time ago good. Now no good." Only the dead woman becomes neither a bore nor a mother; and before Catherine can quite become either she must die, killed not by Hemingway, of course, but by childbirth! It is all quite sad and lovely at the end: the last kiss bestowed on what was a woman and is now a statue, the walk home through the rain. Poe himself could not have done better, though he was haunted not by the memory of a plump little Indian on the hemlock needles but a fantasy of a high-born maiden "loved with a love that was more than love" and carried away by death.

Had Catherine lived, she could only have turned into a bitch; for this is the fate in Hemingway's imagination of all Anglo-Saxon women. In him, the cliché of Dark Lady and Fair survives, but stood on its head, exactly reversed. The Dark Lady, who is neither wife nor mother, blends with the image of Fayaway, the exotic servant-consort reconstructed by Melville in *Typeé* out of memories of an eight-year-old Polynesian girl-child.[1] In Hemingway, such women are mindless, soft, subservient; painless devices for extracting seed without human engagement. The Fair Lady, on the other hand, who gets pregnant and wants a wedding, or uses her sexual allure to assert her power, is seen as a threat and a destroyer of men. But the seed-extractors are Indians or Latins, black-eyed and dusky in hue, while the castrators are at least Anglo-Saxon if not symbolically blond. Neither are permitted to be virgins; indeed, both are imagined

1. A novel published in 1846 by Herman Melville (1819–1891).

as having been often possessed, though in the case of the Fair Woman promiscuity is used as a device for humiliating and unmanning the male foolish enough to have entered into a marriage with her. Through the Dark anti-virgin, on the other hand, a new lover enters into a blameless communion with the other uncommitted males who have possessed her and departed, as well as with those yet to come. It is a kind of homosexuality once-removed, the appeal of the whorehouse (Eden of the world of men without women) embodied in a single figure.

When Hemingway's bitches are Americans, they are hopeless and unmitigated bitches; symbols of Home and Mother as remembered by the boy who could never forgive Mama for having wantonly destroyed Papa's Indian collection! Mrs. Macomber, who, in "The Short Happy Life of Francis Macomber," kills her husband for having alienated the affections of the guide with whom she is having one of her spiteful little affairs, is a prime example of the type. And "the woman," in "The Snows of Kilimanjaro" another, who with her wealth has weaned her husband from all that sustained his virility, betrayed him to aimlessness and humiliation. Like Fitzgerald's betrayed men, he can choose only to die, swoon to the death he desires at the climax of a dream of escape.

The British bitch is for Hemingway only a demi-bitch, however, as the English are only, as it were, demi-Americans. Catherine is delivered from her doom by death; Brett Ashley in *The Sun Also Rises* (1926) is permitted, once at least, the gesture of herself rejecting her mythical role. But it is quite a feat at that, and Brett cannot leave off congratulating herself: "You know it makes one feel rather good deciding not to be a bitch." Yet Brett never becomes a woman really; she is mythicized rather than redeemed. And if she is the most satisfactory female character in all of Hemingway, this is because for once she is presented not as an animal or as a nightmare but quite audaciously as a goddess, the bitch-goddess with a boyish bob (Hemingway is rather fond of women who seem as much boy as girl), the Lilith of the '20's. No man embraces her without being in some sense castrated, except for Jake Barnes who is unmanned to begin with; no man approaches her without *wanting* to be castrated, except for Romero, who thinks naïvely that she is—or can easily become—a woman. Indeed, when Brett leaves that nineteen-year-old bullfighter, one suspects that, though she avows it is because she will not be "one of those bitches who ruins children," she is really running away because she thinks he might *make* her a woman. Certainly, Romero's insistence that she let her hair grow out has something to do with it: "He wanted me to grow my hair out. Me, with long hair. I'd look so like hell. . . . He said it would make me more womanly. I'd look a fright."

To yield up her cropped head would be to yield up her emancipation from female servitude, to become feminine rather than phallic; and this Brett cannot do. She thinks of herself as a flapper, though the word perhaps would not have occurred to her, as a member of the "Lost Generation"; but the Spaniards know her immediately as a terrible goddess, the avatar of an ancient archetype. She tries in vain to enter into the circle of Christian communion, but is always turned aside at the door; she changes her mind, she has forgotten her hat—the apparent reason never matters; she belongs to a world alien and prior to that of the Christian churches in which Jake finds a kind of peace. In Pamplona, Brett is surrounded by a group of *riau-riau* dancers, who desert a religious procession to follow her, set her up as a rival to Saint Fermin: "Some dancers formed a circle around Brett and started to dance. They wore big wreaths of white garlic around their necks. . . . They were all chanting. Brett wanted to dance but they did not want her to. They wanted her as an image to dance around." Incapable of love except as a moment in bed, Brett can bestow on her worshipers nothing more than the brief joy of a drunken ecstasy—followed by suffering and deprivation and regret. In the end, not only are her physical lovers unmanned and degraded, but even Jake, who is her priest and is protected by his terrible wound, is humiliated. For her service is a betrayal not only of his Catholic faith but of his pure passion for bullfighting and trout-fishing; and the priest of the bitch-goddess is, on the purely human level, a pimp.

* * *

PHILIP YOUNG

From Ernest Hemingway†

* * *

The Sun Also Rises, which appeared later in 1926, reintroduces us to the hero. In Hemingway's novels this man is a slightly less personal hero than Nick was, and his adventures are to be less closely identified with Hemingway's, for more events are changed, or even "made up." But he still projects qualities of the man who created him, many of his experiences are still either literal or transformed autobiography, and his wound is still the crucial fact about him. Even when, as Robert Jordan of *For Whom the Bell Tolls*, he is somewhat disguised, we have little or no trouble in recognizing him.

† From *Ernest Hemingway* (New York: Rinehart and Co., 1952), pp. 54–60. Reprinted with permission of the author's estate. Notes are by the editor of this Norton Critical Edition.

Recognition is immediate and unmistakable in *The Sun Also Rises*. Here the wound, again with its literal and symbolic meanings, is transferred from the spine to the genitals. Jake Barnes was emasculated in the war. But he is the same man, a grown Nick Adams,[1] and again the actual injury functions as concrete evidence that the hero is a casualty. He is a writer living in Paris in the twenties as, for example, Harry was; he was, like Nick, transplanted from midwestern America to the Austro-Italian front; when things are at their worst for him, like Fraser he cries in the night. When he refuses the services of a prostitute, and she asks, "What's the matter? You sick?" he is not thinking of his impotence alone when he answers, "Yes." He is the insomniac as before, and for the same reasons: "I blew out the lamp. Perhaps I would be able to sleep. My head started to work. The old grievance." And later he remembers that time, which we witnessed, when "for six months I never slept with the light off." He is the man who is troubled in the night, who leaves Brett alone in his sitting room and lies face down on the bed, having "a bad time."

In addition, Jake like Nick is the protagonist who has broken with society and with the usual middle-class ways; and, again, he has made the break in connection with his wounding. He has very little use for most people. At times he has little use even for his friends; at times he has little use for himself. He exists on a fringe of the society he has renounced; as a newspaper reporter he works just enough to make enough money to eat and drink well on, and spends the rest of his time in cafés, or fishing, or watching bull-fights. Though it is not highly developed yet, he and those few he respects have a code, too. Jake complains very little, although he suffers a good deal; there are certain things that are "done" and many that are "not done." Lady Brett Ashley also knows the code, and distinguishes people according to it; a person is "one of us," as she puts it, or is not—and most are not. The whole trouble with Robert Cohn, the boxing, maladroit Jew of the novel, is that he is not. He points up the code most clearly by so lacking it: he will not go away when Brett is done with him; he is "messy" in every way. After he has severely beaten up Romero, the small young bullfighter, and Romero will not give in, Cohn cries wretchedly, proclaims his love for Brett in public, and tries to shake Romero's hand. He gets that hand in the face, an act which is approved as appropriate comment on his behavior.

Cohn does not like Romero because Brett does. She finally goes off with the bullfighter, and it is when she leave him too that she makes a particularly clear statement of what she and the other "right" people have salvaged from the wreck of their compromised lives. She

1. Nick Adams is the main character in a number of Hemingway's short stories.

has decided that she is ruining Romero's career, and besides she is too old for him. She walks out, and says to Jake:

> "It makes one feel rather good deciding not to be a bitch. . . . It's sort of what we have instead of God."

In early editions, *The Sun Also Rises* had on its title page, in addition to the passage on futility in *Ecclesiastes* from which the title is taken, Gertrude Stein's famous "You are all a lost generation." The novel provides an explanation for this observation, in addition to illustrating it in action. As in the story called "In Another Country," the picture of the hero wounded and embittered by his experience of violence is broadened to include other people. Brett Ashley, for example, and her fiancé Mike Campbell are both casualties from ordeals similar to those which damaged Jake. Brett has behind her the very unpleasant death of her first fiancé; Mike's whole character was shattered by the war. *A Farewell to Arms* can be read as background to the earlier novel: some of Brett's past is filled in by Catherine Barkley, whose fiancé had been blown to bits in the war, and most of Jake's by Frederic Henry.

The fact that characters in *The Sun Also Rises* are recognizable people, taken from "real life," does not contradict the fact that they are in this pattern. Various personages known to Paris of the twenties have thought that they recognized without difficulty the originals—Donald Ogden Stewart, Harold Stearns, Harold Loeb, Lady Duff Twysden, Ford Madox Ford, and Pat Guthrie—and even Jake had his counterpart in actuality. But Hemingway, like most authors, has changed the characters to suit his purposes, and it is clear that whatever his origins, Jake, for instance, owes most to the man who created him, and is the hero.

He is the hero emasculated, however, and this must primarily account for the fact that he does not always seem entirely real. As he feels befits his status, he is largely a passive arranger of things for others, who only wants to "play it along and just not make trouble for people." But as narrator, at least, he is convincing, and if there is something blurred about him it helps to bring the participants into a focus that is all the sharper. Hemingway has always been good with secondary characters, finding them in a bright flash that reveals all we need know. Here, as he somehow manages to make similar people easily distinguishable, the revelations are brilliant. One remembers Brett and Cohn longest, for they get the fullest development, but Count Mippipopolous is wonderful, and wonderful too—save for their anti-Semitism, largely missing from the twenty-five cent edition, which advertises that "Not one word has been changed or omitted"—are Mike and Bill.

Chiefly it is Hemingway's ear, a trap that catches every mannerism of speech, that is responsible for the fact that wastrels come so alive and distinct. That famous ear caught a great many "swells" and "grands" that have dated—for slang is one thing almost certain to go bad with the passage of time—and some of the dialogue of camaraderie ("Old Bill!" "You bum!") is also embarrassing. But taken as a whole the talk is superb and, as a whole, so is the rest of the writing in the book. Hemingway's wide-awake senses fully evoke an American's Paris, a vacationer's Spain. Jake moves through these places with the awareness of a professional soldier reconnoitering new terrain. The action is always foremost, but it is supported by real country and real city. The conversational style, which gives us the illusion that Jake is just telling us the story of what he has been doing lately, gracefully hides the fact that the pace is carefully calculated and swift, the sentences and scenes hard and clean. This is true of the over-all structure, too: the book is informal and relaxed only on the surface, and beneath it lies a scrupulous and satisfying orchestration. It is not until nearly the end, for example, when Cohn becomes the center of what there is of action, that opening with him seems anything but a simply random way of getting started. This discussion of Cohn has eased us into Jake's life in Paris, and especially his situation with Brett. Suddenly the lines are all drawn. An interlude of trout fishing moves us smoothly into Spain and the bullfights. At Pamplona the tension which all try to ignore builds up, slowly, and breaks finally as the events come to their climax simultaneous with the fiesta's. Then, in an intensely muted coda, a solitary Jake, rehabilitating himself, washes away his hangover in the ocean. Soon it is all gone, he is returned to Brett as before, and we discover that we have come full circle, like all the rivers, the winds, and the sun, to the place where we began.

This is motion which goes no place. Constant activity has brought us along with such pleasant, gentle insistence that not until the end do we realize that we have not been taken in, exactly, but taken nowhere; and that, finally, is the point. This is structure as meaning, organization as content. And, as the enormous effect the book had on its generation proved, such a meaning or content was important to 1926. The book touched with delicate accuracy on something big, on things other people were feeling, but too dimly for articulation. Hemingway had deeply felt and understood what was in the wind. Like Brett, who was the kind of woman who sets styles, the book itself was profoundly creative, and had the kind of power that is prototypal.

But for another generation, looking backward, this quality of the novel is largely gone out of it. The pessimism is based chiefly on the story of a hopeless love, and for Jake this is basis enough. But his situation with Brett sometimes seems forced—brought up periodically for air that it may be kept alive—as if Hemingway, who must have been through most of Jake's important experiences, but not exactly this one, had to keep reminding himself that it existed. And worse: though the rest of the pessimism rises eloquently out of the novel's structure, it does not seem to rise out of the day-to-day action at all. There is a gaping cleavage here between manner and message, between joy in life and a pronouncement of life's futility. Jake's disability excepted, always, the book now seems really the long *Fiesta* it was called in the English edition, and one's net impression today is of all the fun there is to be had in getting good and lost.

And yet *The Sun Also Rises* is still Hemingway's *Waste Land*, and Jake is Hemingway's Fisher King.[2] This may be just coincidence, though the novelist had read the poem, but once again here is the protagonist gone impotent, and his land gone sterile. Eliot's London is Hemingway's Paris, where spiritual life in general, and Jake's sexual life in particular, are alike impoverished. Prayer breaks down and fails, a knowledge of traditional distinctions between good and evil is largely lost, copulation is morally neutral and cut off from the past chiefly by the spiritual disaster of the war, life has become mostly meaningless. "What shall we do?" is the same constant question, to which the answer must be, again, "Nothing." To hide it, instead of playing chess one drinks, mechanically and always. Love is a possibility only for the two who cannot love; once again homosexuality intensifies this atmosphere of sterility; once more the Fisher King is also a man who fishes. And again the author plays with quotations from the great of the past, as when in reply to Jake's remark that he is a taxidermist. Bill objects, "That was in another country. And besides all the animals were dead."

To be sure, the liquor is good, and so are the food and the conversation. But in one way Hemingway's book is even more desperate than Eliot's. The lesson of an "asceticism" to control the aimless expression of lust would be to Jake Barnes only one more bad joke, and the fragments he has shored against his ruins are few, and quite inadequate. In the poem a message of salvation comes out of the life-giving rain which falls on western civilization. In Hemingway's waste land there is fun, but there is no hope. No rain falls on Europe this time, and when it does fall, in *A Farewell to Arms*, it brings not life but death.

* * *

2. T. S. Eliot (1888–1965), American poet, author of *The Waste Land* (1922). The Fisher King is a key figure in the poem, wounded and awaiting death so that the land may be healed.

Modern Criticism

I have arranged these critical essays to highlight areas of critical interest and to stage potential "debates" around those areas. There are, of course, other ways to approach them, whether chronologically or with an eye to method (beginning, perhaps, with Donaldson and Wagner, both of whom work in largely formalist modes and progressing through the theoretically inflected work of Baldwin or Moddelmog or Fore and/or the more thoroughly historically contextualized readings of Michaels or Spilka).

The section begins with readings that connect Hemingway's style in the novel with the literary and literal landscapes of Paris and Pamplona in which the novel's action plays out. Linda Wagner's essay reads the novel's style in terms of Ezra Pound's dictates for Imagism and focuses on passages of description in Paris and Spain that she argues are legible as imagist prose poetry, linking Hemingway's style and the places on which he focuses narrative attention. Where many readers have lumped the representation of Parisian life in the novel with Hemingway's later treatment of it in *A Moveable Feast*, and while some earlier critics read the novel's detailed explorations of Parisian geography in symbolic terms, Field uses the context of contemporaneous guidebooks to show how Hemingway produces something of a "tourist experience" in moments that function as modernist travelogue.

Gender has, from such early readings as Leslie Fiedler's, been a key area of focus for critics of *The Sun Also Rises.* Mark Spilka reads the novel in light of the posthumous publication of Hemingway's novel, *The Garden of Eden*, arguing for Jake's "vulnerability to pain through the essential feminization of his power to love." Debra A. Moddlemog traces the ways the novel stages conflicts among traditional significations of gender and sexuality to show how the novel "exposes the intellectual limitations that result when 'gender' and 'sexuality' are read as innocent acts of nature and as fixed binaries."

As Edmund Wilson and Philip Young suggest in their early responses to the novel, and as important passages such as Jake's conversation with Count Mippipopolous illustrate, questions of value are thematically central in *The Sun Also Rises.* Scott Donaldson's influential reading attends to the literal economies and the figurative language of exchange, earning, and compensation in the novel to derive a moral vision dependent on obligation and modeled by Jake, who insists on paying his own way and on paying for his pleasures, whether literally or emotionally/spiritually. Where Donaldson writes figuratively of transactions, exchange, and currency in his elaboration of an ethics in the novel, Marc D. Baldwin undertakes a straightforwardly Marxist analysis, construing Hemingway's stylistic emphases on the unsaid as an aesthetic management of ideologically obscured reductions of characters to exchange value.

Contemporary readers of *The Sun Also Rises* will be justifiably troubled by some of Hemingway's racially and ethnically derogatory language, as well as by the antisemitic prejudice of some characters (and, it may be argued, of the novel's fabric of assumption). This section offers two takes on the representation of Robert Cohn. Walter Benn Michaels situates Hemingway in the context of American nativist discourses of the 1910s and 1920s, reading the representation of Cohn, especially, as influenced by powerful and prejudiced understandings of the figure of the Jew in American culture. Jeremy Kaye offers a rejoinder to analyses like Michaels's, reading the novel's representation of Cohn against the grain to find in it not (or not simply) an antisemitic portrayal but also an "agent of Jewish manhood" who disrupts the novel's "privileged pairing of hegemonic and Hemingwayesque masculinity."

Masculinity is at stake not only in the treatment of Cohn but also, inescapably, in the character of Jake Barnes. Greg Forter reads the novel in the context of a crisis of masculinity he sees in American culture in the early twentieth century and argues that the novel's staging of a conflict between "autonomous and invulnerable masculinity" and "emotionally expressive and connected" masculinity through its fetishization of style works through that crisis. Ultimately, he argues, the novel falls into melancholy (rather than Freud's productive mourning) as it offers a series of failed substitutions for the loss of phallic potency that Jake has suffered. Masculinity is often equated with potency or able-bodiedness. Informed by contemporary disability studies, Dana Fore reads the novel as an implicit critique of the dominant "medical model" of disability. Jake's self-understanding throughout the novel and the ending that Fore characterizes as "downbeat" combine to suggest that "a philosophy that continually denies bodily realities can be as physically and mentally destructive as a literal wound."

PARIS AND PAMPLONA IN STYLE

LINDA W. WAGNER

The Sun Also Rises: One Debt to Imagism†

Ernest Hemingway's appreciation for Ezra Pound is widely known—his constant praise for Pound during a life marred by broken friend-

† From "*The Sun Also Rises*: One Debt to Imagism." *The Journal of Narrative Theory* (formerly *Journal of Narrative Technique*) 2.2 (May 1971): 88–98. Reprinted by permission of the publisher. Page numbers in brackets refer to this Norton Critical Edition. Notes are by the author of the original work.

ships and bitter words; his 1956 check for $1000, sent to Pound seemingly in lieu of the Nobel Prize medal. Yet Hemingway's fiction is rarely read as having benefited from his intense relationship with the older writer in the early 1920's. We know the legends of the young Hemingway in Paris, apprentice to Stein, Joyce, and Pound, but we have never known what happened to Hemingway's early work. John Peale Bishop remembers, however, that the early manuscripts went to Pound and "came back to him blue penciled, most of the adjectives gone. The comments were unsparing."[1] Whereas Stein's influence was mainly general, it would seem that Pound's dicta were substantiated with practical suggestions.

* * *

During the years following 1913, when [Pound's] essays about Imagism first appeared, the trademark of that poetic movement was concentration. One of the primary aims was "To use absolutely no word that does not contribute to the presentation,"[2] a directive aimed at eliminating from poetry its weak phrases and lines of filler. "Use either no ornament or good ornament," Pound warned; "Don't be descriptive. . . . Go in fear of abstractions." Such axioms demanded that the poet employ his craft consciously, a word at a time, and that he give his impressions the sharp focus of the image.

Pound also defined the image as "that which presents an intellectual and emotional complex in an instant of time." By stressing the wide inclusive powers of the image, he greatly strengthened the Imagist concept; and his emphasis on *speed* gave new life to the post-Victorian poem that was nearly buried in expected details. As he continued, "It is the presentation of such a 'complex' instantaneously which gives the sense of sudden liberation . . . that sense of sudden growth which we experience in the presence of the greatest works of art"—epiphany, if you will.

The Imagists usually worked in free verse forms because they could thus more easily attain organic form, a shape consistent with the mood and subject of the poem being written. Concentration, speed, and the use of the writer's own conversational language—these were the chief means the Imagists chose to present those objects or experiences which would convey the "white light" of full meaning. Concentration, speed, and the use of the writer's own conversational language—these are certainly trademarks of the famous Hemingway style.

Influence studies are impractical unless intrinsic evidence exists in quantity. The montage effect of the highly compressed stories and

1. Quoted by George Wickes in *Americans in Paris* (Garden City, New York, 1969), 162.
2. "Imagism" and "A Few Don'ts by an Imagiste," *Poetry,* I, No. 6 (March 1913), 199–201.

vignettes of Hemingway's 1924 *In Our Time* is the young writer's most obvious tribute to Imagism itself, and has been noted by several critics. But perhaps the most sustained example of the Imagist method transferred to prose is that maligned novel, *The Sun Also Rises,* 1926. In using the methods of suggestion, compression, and speed within the outlines of traditional novel form, Hemingway achieved a lyric evocation of one segment of life in the 1920's.

Perhaps we should remember that Hemingway was disappointed throughout his life because *SAR* was the novel most often misread; it was the "naturalistic" Hemingway, or at any rate, the "realistic" novel. As he recalled much later, "I sometimes think my style is suggestive rather than direct. The reader must often use his imagination or lose the most subtle part of my thought."[3]

* * *

When Pound directed writers to "Use absolutely no word that does not contribute to the presentation," he was implying a sharp selection of detail. Because Hemingway's selection of detail was so accurate, even skeletal presentations are usually convincing. Brett's bowed head as Mike and Robert argue shows well her tired submission to the present situation, just as Jake's drinking too much after Brett leaves with Romero tells us clearly his emotional state. The repetition of mealtime and drinking scenes in the novel is particularly good for showing the slight but telling changes in a few recurring details. It is of course these changes in the existing relationships that are the real center of the novel, rather than any linear plot.

Following the sometimes minute vacillations in a friendship, or the subtle shadings in a conversation, admittedly demands close attention from the reader. As T. S. Eliot was to point out, reading the modern novel requires concentration as intense as reading poetry—as well as training in that kind of skill. "A prose that is altogether alive demands something that the ordinary novel-reader is not prepared to give."[4]

Hemingway also used a somewhat oblique characterization of his protagonists. Jake and Brett are not always present. Jake as narrator usually speaks about others rather than himself, and when he does think about his own dilemma, it is again in the laconic phrases that leave much to the reader's own empathy. Even though Hemingway introduces Jake in the opening chapter, his focus seemingly falls on Robert Cohn. He tells us innocently enough that Cohn was a college boxing champ, although "he cared nothing for boxing, in fact he disliked it." Then Hemingway begins to accumulate related

3. "The Great Writer's Last Reflections on Himself, His Craft, Love, and Life," *Playboy,* X, No. 1 (January 1963), 120ff.
4. Introduction to *Nightwood, The Selected Works of Djuna Barnes* (New York, 1962), 228.

details: later we see that Romero loves his bullfighting, just as Bill and Jake love fishing. We must then be suspicious of a man who devotes himself to something he dislikes. Subsequent chapters continue the parallel descriptions of Jake and Cohn, and less apparently of Frances Clyne with Brett. It is a stroke of genius that Hemingway waits until we have clearly seen what Jake and Brett are not to present them for what they are—sad but honest people—together, in a would-be love scene.

The Sun Also Rises is also filled with passages that could easily be considered images if they were isolated from their context. * * * The brief moment when Brett enters the café in the company of homosexuals combines a good set of graphic details with the evocation of Jake's sad excitement and anger as he sees her:

> A crowd of young men, some in jerseys and some in their shirtsleeves, got out. I could see their hands and newly washed, wavy hair in the light from the door. The policeman standing by the door looked at me and smiled. They came in. As they went in, under the light I saw white hands, wavy hair, white faces, grimacing, gesturing, talking. With them was Brett. She looked very lovely and she was very much with them.
>
> One of them saw Georgette and said: "I do declare. There is an actual harlot. I'm going to dance with her, Lett. You watch me."
>
> The tall dark one, called Lett, said: "Don't you be rash."
>
> The wavy blond one answered: "Don't you worry, dear." And with them was Brett. [17]

The policeman's smile, the grimacing, the dancing—Hemingway often worked through actions to reveal character and specific mood. But the touchstone here, as often throughout the book, is Jake's own mood, his astonished sadness, caught in the simple refrain line, "And with them was Brett."

Not only does Hemingway use concentrated descriptive passages, he also moves quickly from one passage to another, sometimes without logical transition. This use of juxtaposition to achieve speed in impressions is another poetic technique, enabling a short piece of writing to encompass many disparate meanings. Near the end of the novel, when the reader's attention should be on Brett and Romero as lovers, or on Jake as sacrificial figure, Hemingway instead moves to the account of a young man killed in the morning bull run. "A big horn wound. All for fun. Just for fun," [145] says the surly bartender, picking up one of the repeated key words in the book—*fun, luck, values.* The bartender's emphasis on the unreasoning fun ends with Hemingway's objective report of the younger man's death, his funeral, and the subsequent death of the bull. . . . Hemingway follows this already wide-reaching image with the suggestion of Cohn's "death" as Brett leaves with Romero. This brief descriptive sequence, then, has established the deaths of man, bull, man—all at the whim of the fiesta and its larger-than-life hero, the matador.[5]

Another device used frequently in the book is Hemingway's re-creation of natural idiom—in both dialogue and introspective passages—and perhaps more importantly his use of prose rhythms appropriate to the effect of the writing desired. Although the Imagist axiom, "Compose in the sequence of the musical phrase, not that of the metronome," was more liberating to poetry than it was to prose, it also spoke for a kind of freedom in prose—sentences unrestricted in tone, diction, or length because of formal English standards. In passages like this opening to Part III, Hemingway arranges sentences of varying lengths and compositions to create the tone he wants (here, a melancholic nostalgia), a tone which may be at odds with the ostensible facts of such a passage.

> In the morning it was all over. The fiesta was finished. I woke about nine o'clock, had a bath, dressed, and went down-stairs. The square was empty and there were no people on the streets. A few children were picking up rocket-sticks in the square. The cafés were just opening and the waiters were carrying out the comfortable white wicker chairs and arranging them around the marble-topped tables in the shade of the arcade. They were sweeping the streets and sprinkling them with a hose.
>
> I sat in one of the wicker chairs and leaned back comfortably. The waiter was in no hurry to come. The white-paper announcements of the unloading of the bulls and the big schedules of special trains were still up on the pillars of the arcade. A waiter wearing a blue apron came out with a bucket of water and a cloth, and commenced to tear down the notices, pulling the paper off in strips and washing and rubbing away the paper that stuck to the stone. The fiesta was over. [165]

In these two paragraphs Hemingway moves from an emphasis on Jake's feelings and actions to the specific details of his locale, using those details to complete his sketch of Jake—alone, and now numbly realizing only that "it was all over." To open the second section with more description of Jake helps the reader keep his focus on the protagonist. The observable details are significant to the story (here and usually throughout the novel) primarily because they help identify an emotional state. Even the movement within this passage, building from the short rhythms of the opening to the longer phrases

5. As Hemingway's columns on bullfighting substantiate, the lure of the matador is irresistible, for both sexes. See pp. 90–108, *By-Line: Ernest Hemingway,* ed. William White (New York, 1967).

of the penultimate sentence, and coming back to the restrained "refrain," suggests a crescendo in feeling.

* * *

The passage describing the fiesta also provides a good example of Hemingway's failure to use overt symbols (a failure which troubled many critics enough that they began inventing parallels between bulls, steers, and men). In repeating "The fiesta was over," Hemingway suggests broader implications for "fiesta"—a natural expectation of gaiety and freedom, here ironically doomed because of the circumstances of the characters. Through the description, we easily feel Jake's nostalgia, but not because fiesta is a true symbol; it never assumes any existence other than its apparent one. As Pound, again, had phrased the definition, "the natural object is always the adequate symbol. . . . if a man use 'symbols' he must use them that their symbolic function does not obtrude."[6] In one sense, in *The Sun Also Rises,* the amount of liquor a person drinks is symbolic—of both the kind of person he is, and the emotional condition he is in. So too is anger, and various stages of it. But the purely literary symbol—which the unsuccessful fireworks exhibition might suggest—is rare. Even the fireworks sequence is used more to show various characters reaction to the failure than it is to represent another object or state of being *per se.* That Brett does not want to watch the failure is as significant for her character as the fact that she enjoys the artistry of the bullfights.

* * *

Even Jake's wound is given in a simple declarative sentence, the poignancy of its terseness aided by the opening modifier: "Undressing, I looked at myself in the mirror of the big armoire beside the bed." The only adjective in the sentence describes a piece of furniture; the situation itself needs no description. Hemingway is, graphically, and in mirror image, "presenting," as Pound had edicted. The mention of bed also adds pathos to the brief line. The concentration on the furniture offers a moment of deflection also, before Hemingway brings us back to more understatement:

> Undressing, I looked at myself in the mirror of the big armoire beside the bed. That was a typically French way to furnish a room. Practical, too, I suppose. Of all the ways to be wounded. I suppose it was funny. [25]

6. *Poetry,* 201. [Ed.] See also "A Retrospect" in *Pavannes and Divagations* (New York: Knopf, 1918), 97 and 103.

The climactic act of the novel, for Jake, his giving Brett to Romero, is another model of suggestive gesture instead of speech: "He looked at me. It was a final look to ask if it were understood. It was understood all right."

* * *

In his eagerness to present rather than to tell (to render rather than report), Hemingway erred only in following the Imagist doctrines perhaps too closely. *The Sun Also Rises* is a difficult book to read correctly, until the reader understands the way it works; then it becomes a masterpiece of concentration, with every detail conveying multiple impressions, and every speech creating both single character and complex interrelationships. It also takes us back to Pound's 1923 description of the best modern prose, which should "tell the truth about *moeurs contemporaines* without fake, melodrama, conventional ending."[7] There is nothing fake about anything in *The Sun Also Rises,* least of all the writing. And to read it as a masterpiece of suggestion makes one compliment Mark Schorer for his statement that Hemingway had in his career written "the very finest prose of our time. And most of it is poetry."[8]

ALLYSON NADIA FIELD

Expatriate Lifestyle as Tourist Destination: *The Sun Also Rises* and Experiential Travelogues of the Twenties[†]

> Ernest cared far less than I about aesthetics. What he cared about was the action and the emotional body of the traveler. He was a born traveler as he was a born novelist.
>
> —Janet Flanner

> What was the value of travel if it were not this—to discover all romance is not bound between the covers of novels?
>
> —Robert F. Wilson, *Paris on Parade*

When *The Sun Also Rises* was published in 1926, F. Scott Fitzgerald famously dubbed Ernest Hemingway's novel "a romance and a guidebook" (Aldridge 123). The novel was celebrated as a *roman à clef*

7. Pound, *Pavannes and Divagations* (Norfolk, Conn., 1958), 50–51.
8. "With Grace Under Pressure," *New Republic,* 127 (October 6, 1952), 19.
† From "Expatriate Lifestyle as Tourist Destination: *The Sun Also Rises* and Experiential Travelogues of the Twenties." *The Hemingway Review* 25.2 (Spring 2006): 29–43. Copyright 2006. The Ernest Hemingway Foundation. All Rights Reserved. Reprinted by permission of the publisher. Notes are by the author of the original work. Page numbers in brackets refer to this Norton Critical Edition.

that depicted an actual segment of Parisian expatriate society. By the time Hemingway began *The Sun Also Rises*, he was already a fixture in the Parisian expatriate literary community, and had garnered mention in Robert Forrest Wilson's 1924 guidebook *Paris on Parade*. Hemingway was reputedly disdainful of tourists, yet the novel's repetition of place names is organized into itineraries similar to those of travel guides contemporaneous to the novel. While not explicitly a guidebook, *The Sun Also Rises* can be considered as part of the tradition of travelogues such as *Pages from the Book of Paris, Paris with the Lid Lifted, How to be Happy in Paris (without being ruined)*, and *Paris on Parade* that offer experiential guides to a lifestyle, rather than to monuments or museums. With Jake Barnes's emphasis on his environment and recurrent references to the streets, bars, and cafés frequented by his expatriate companions, Hemingway contributes to a body of travel literature describing the places that constitute the geography of the infamous expatriate lifestyle. While *A Moveable Feast* presents a Paris of memory and nostalgia for Hemingway, *The Sun Also Rises* is a fictionalized depiction of the Left Bank that should be read against the contemporaneous travelogues promoting the *quartier* as a stylish destination; the expatriate artist lifestyle becomes a tourist experience as Hemingway depicts the fictional movements in *The Sun Also Rises* as experiential travelogue.[1]

In Search of Experience: "Gay Paree" Travelogues of the Twenties

In *Paris on Parade*, published in 1924, Robert Forrest Wilson presents a guidebook to Paris in the form of an exposé uncovering the lifestyle of the Americans who constitute a significant presence in the city: "only ten thousand of us; but, my, what a noise we make! How important we are to Paris!" (274).[2] Wilson is not interested in promoting an authentic French experience. Instead, he guides his reader through the "American village" of the Latin Quarter and Montparnasse on Paris's Left Bank. He writes, "Gay Paree, indeed, can scarcely be regarded as a French institution at all. It is a polyglot thing existing upon French tolerance, the gaiety being

1. J. Gerald Kennedy describes the Paris of *A Moveable Feast* as "an imaginary city, a mythical scene evoked to explain the magical transformation of an obscure, Midwestern journalist into a brilliant modern author" (128). Paris as an "imaginary city" is a function of Hemingway's nostalgia, a longing to return to a mythical past in a "fantastic place" (Kennedy 130).
2. Wilson remarks that the numbers seem larger because Americans are "so flattered and deferred to" and "so much in the fore in post-war Parisian life" (276). The police counted 30,000 Americans in Paris yet the Chamber of Commerce only unearthed 10,000. Wilson attributes this discrepancy to the failure of the police to accurately count foreigners entering and exiting the country (276–7). By 1927, there were 15,000 official American residents in Paris and 35,000 by the estimate of the Parisian police (Lynn 149).

contributed largely by the guests" (Wilson 279). The legend of "Gay Paree"—drinking, dancing, and other behavior unencumbered by puritan values—lured tourists who were more enamored with the lifestyle on display than with the monuments speckling the city.

Wilson devotes a chapter to the newly extended Latin Quarter (reaching to Montparnasse), an area "that has emerged from the war, a Parisian district which (so far as its American citizenry is concerned) has for its focus, community center, club and town-hall the Café du Dôme" (194). Wilson explains that the area is defined by the "American influence" of its large expatriate artist community (196):

> The new Latin Quarter is completely centralized around one spot—the corner of the Boulevards Raspail and Montparnasse. Here stand the Café du Dôme and the Café Rotonde; and you can no more know the present Latin Quarter without knowing these two cafés than you can know an Ohio county-seat without knowing its public square and court-house. They are half its life. (209–10)

The expatriates, Wilson explains, frequent only a few of the area cafés: "At the Raspail-Montparnasse corner on a summer evening, for instance, those two chief artists' cafés of the new Quarter, the Dôme and the Rotonde, will be jammed to the last chair inside and out, with dozens standing on the sidewalks waiting for places" (206). This is a Paris created by its American inhabitants and defined by main boulevards, particular cafés, and the mores of the expatriates. The result is a cosmopolitan American city unhindered by the restrictions of Prohibition.

Wilson encourages his readers to seek out "one of the last few genuine American barrooms remaining on earth" (113). Writing to an American audience, Wilson acknowledges that in Paris "Prohibition is three thousand miles away," yet "these law-abiding pages will afford no clue to the location of this exiled place beyond assertions that it is in plain sight from the entrance to Ciro's restaurant and that its owner's name is Harry" (113–4).[3] Wilson points to Harry's Bar, but guides his reader to engage in "a Parisian thing," to order *aperitifs* at a café off the tourist path (114).[4] After all, as the Gallic

3. By chapter thirteen, Wilson has forgone his earlier discretion and writes, "In the back room of Harry's New York Bar in Paris the expatriates hold forth on their grandiose schemes" (302).
4. Wilson tells his Prohibition-era readers, quite charmingly: "And among the French, at least, drinking in a café carries no obloquy with it. French women visit the neighborhood bars almost as much as men—honest virtuous women of the community—housewives, store keepers, and shop girls and stenographers pausing on their way to and from work to snatch hot coffee" (120). Despite implying that the primary draw of the cafés is "hot coffee," Wilson goes on for several pages to describe the various types of Parisian *aperitifs* unavailable, at least legally, in America, and includes a complete chapter on experiencing French wine. Anecdotally, some of Wilson's advice for his 1924 readers is as useful now as it was eighty years ago, such as his advice for catching

proverb professes, "the French cock is a wine-drinking cock" (168). Wilson's guide to Left Bank lifestyle was one of many such volumes published in the 1920s and purporting to provide the reader with an insider's view of "Gay Paree."

* * *

In *Paris on Parade*, Wilson reserves a chapter for "the bookshop crowd," referring to the writers and literary enthusiasts who frequent Sylvia Beach's famous Shakespeare and Company. Wilson identifies James Joyce as the "supreme modern master of English" in the eyes of the bookshop crowd, but he mentions "the outstanding personages of this interlocking directorate of the Continental advance movement in English letters" and names Robert McAlmon, Ford Madox Ford, Bill Bird, George Antheil, Ezra Pound, and Hemingway (244).[5] A favorite subject of Wilson's guide, Hemingway reputedly "mingles democratically with the artist-writer crowd at the Café du Dôme" (248). Wilson writes on the up-and-coming young writer:

> Mr. Bird has published a book by Ernest Hemingway and so has Mr. McAlmon. This fact and the further one that he is intimate with the bookshop circle seem to mark Mr. Hemingway for Young Intellectualism's own, but there are indications that his sojourn is to be only temporary. In other words, his work promises to remove him from the three-hundred-copy class of authorship. . . . He has recently finished a novel which is said to break new ground. (248)

This novel was not *The Sun Also Rises*, the first draft of which was written between July and September 1925 and published in October 1926.[6] Wilson is most likely referring to the thirty-page long *in our time*, completed in May 1923 and published in Paris by Bill Bird in April 1924 (Brenner 731–3). However, Hemingway fulfilled Wilson's prophecy with *The Sun Also Rises*, a novel that depicts travel as the permanent state of its expatriate protagonists.

Jake Barnes as Tour Guide to Hemingway's "Paris"

Hemingway's novel, with Jake's detailed itineraries, is indebted to the travelogues that represent the lifestyle of the "dilettantish Americans"

---

the attention of an evasive *garçon*: "Get up as if you were going to leave without paying. Then he will dart from his hiding, a model of smiling courtesy, and will add up your amount, give you your change, thank you for the tip, and bid you au revoir as if there had been no unpleasantness about it all" (134).

5. Ford Madox Ford's role, according to Wilson, is in the publication of "a terribly dull magazine," the *transatlantic review* (244).
6. For a detailed discussion of the first draft of the novel, see William Balassi, "The Trail to *The Sun Also Rises*: The First Week of Writing."

that Hemingway held in contempt (Lynn 160).[7] Yet the culture of drinking that Hemingway portrays in *The Sun Also Rises* is mirrored in the guidebooks as a major emphasis and the travelogues are strikingly resonant with Jake's repeated itineraries and references to the lifestyle of the expatriate community, including the importance of cafés and bars such as the Dôme, Select, Closerie des Lilas, Deux Magots, Zelli's, Café Napolitain, The Crillon, and The Ritz.[8]

* * *

* * *Hemingway literalizes rites of passage with Jake who wanders through Paris delineating points on an itinerary marking sites of experience, a geography of memory.

In chapter four, after leaving Brett with the Count, Jake describes his walk home: "I went out onto the sidewalk and walked down towards the Boulevard St. Michel, passed the tables of the Rotonde, still crowded, looked across the street at the Dome, its tables running out to the edge of the pavement" [24]. His path is defined by the cafés that align the boulevard and the activity still going on within them. In the morning, marked by the start of chapter five, Jake describes walking to work and passing tourists engrossed in street performances. In contrast to the stationary tourists, Jake is among the crowds of people going to work. Implicitly aligning himself with the bustling Parisians, he remarks "It felt pleasant to be going to work" [28]. Jake's methodical recounting of street names, cafés, and *quartiers* underscores his status as an *étranger.* Yet he is comfortably cosmopolitan in his "home town" of Paris and distinguishes himself from the tourists he passes (Griffin 173). Jake's walk to work recalls Claude Washburn's 1910 personal memoir/guidebook *Pages from the Book of Paris*, which juxtaposes "Americans with guidebooks" who serve to "heighten one's sense of the city's emptiness" and working Parisians, sequestered in their *bureaux* (159).

Yet for all of Jake's specificity, his Paris is not that of Hemingway. Hemingway constructs another Paris distilled from his own experience. Hemingway's "Paris" is an amalgam of brand names, recognizable by their accents and familiarity (Café Select, Café Napolitain, Montparnasse, The Ritz). In this respect, *The Sun Also Rises* shares with the guidebooks the notion that such names can be code for certain social mores. Hemingway's Paris also reflects his fictional style,

7. In the manuscript draft of the novel, Hemingway opens with a description of Montparnasse. J. Gerald Kennedy notes that "to suggest the torment of his characters, Hemingway created a nocturnal city, a nightmarish whirl of bars, cafés, taxis, restaurants, and dance halls" (97).

8. For a thorough discussion of Hemingway's "mental map of Paris," see J. Gerald Kennedy's *Imagining Paris,* chapter 3.

defined by Aldridge as "not a realistic reflection of a world but the literal manufacture of a world, piece by piece, out of the most meticulously chosen and crafted materials" (123). Hemingway manufactures an environment for his characters based on actual places, but those places become mere points on a decontextualized itinerary, creating a guidebook Paris without an overview map.[9]

Describing an itinerary through the city, Jake's narration takes on the tone of a travelogue: "The Boulevard Raspail always made dull riding" [32]. He also reflects the prejudices of the travel writers for certain cafés: "The taxi stopped in front of the Rotonde. No matter what café in Montparnasse you ask a taxi-driver to bring you to from the right bank of the river, they will always take you to the Rotonde" [33]. Jake walks "past the sad tables of the Rotonde" and chooses the Select [33]. In his guide to Paris, Wilson notes that the Rotonde (identified as a Russo-Scandinavian haunt) is a large, well-lit café with orchestra and nightly dancing and is "more pretentious in every way" than the Dôme, but it is a newer café "and the American Quarterites will have little to do with it" (210–11). Hemingway does not explain the Rotonde's stigma, but Jake's action is in keeping with Wilson's observation. In his 1927 *How to be Happy in Paris (without being ruined)*, John Chancellor also notes that the American residents of the Quarter frequent the Select or the Dôme rather than the Rotonde (161).

* * *

* * * The travelogues that appeared during Hemingway's tenure in Paris* * * guide their readers through the Paris enjoyed by Jake, Brett, and their fellow "club" members. Yet the novel does more than fictionalize a moment in Paris's social history. With *The Sun Also Rises*, Hemingway not only contributes to the body of travel literature that offers an insider's perspective on the lifestyle of the self-exiled writers, artists, and bon vivants who made Paris in the 1920s legendary, but also mythologizes the historic moment.

Writing on Hemingway in Paris, Carlos Baker explains: "One trouble was that tourists in the Latin Quarter, gazing raptly into the Rotonde in search of atmosphere, naturally supposed that what they saw were real Parisian artists" (6). Baker notes that Hemingway was put off by the "congregation of poseurs" milling idly at the corner of the Boulevard Montparnasse and the Boulevard Raspail (6).[1] Yet, the cafés of the area—the Select, Rotonde, and the Dôme—feature

9. Neither Reynolds nor Wilson provides maps of Paris in his guidebook.
1. Baker notes, however, that the two supposedly opposing camps, the serious artists and the "wastrels and adventurers" did commingle in the Left Bank cafés (20).

prominently in Hemingway's novel. While he might not have been one of the "barflyblown bohemians" that Baker distinguishes from the serious artists working in the Left Bank, Hemingway collapses the distinction between the authentic and the imitative in his fictionalizing of expatriate lifestyle in *The Sun Also Rises* (Baker 29).

Baker portrays a Left Bank divided between true artists and "poseurs." Yet this distinction is curiously absent from Hemingway's novel. Biographers such as Baker and Griffin point to Hemingway's concern over authenticity, the desire to portray the *real* underscored by F. Scott Fitzgerald when he famously asserted that Hemingway is "the real thing" (Kuehl and Jackson 78). Hemingway does little to defend the authenticity of his artist characters, implying, for example, that the literary skills of Cohn are less than brilliant. Charles Fenton remarks that Hemingway's familiarity with Europe gave "authenticity of atmosphere" to his early works. Yet his characters are concerned with a different kind of authenticity, one that rewrites the aristocratic expression "people like us" into Brett's clubby "one of us."

* * *

Conclusion: Experiential Travel

The relationship between Hemingway and tourism makes it fitting that Hemingway himself has become a destination of sorts for literary critics and curiosity seekers. John Leland's *A Guide to Hemingway's Paris with Walking Tours* offers the literary-minded traveler a Hemingway-inspired introduction to the city. For Leland, Hemingway's appeal to the American traveler is that "he was only and always a visitor there, and gave us, exclusively and passionately, an outsider's view" (viii). Unlike the "insider's" guides of the 1920s, Leland's guide is predicated on the shared outsider status of Americans in Paris.

It is also fitting that the *bal musette* located on the ground floor of Hemingway's first home in Paris at 74, rue du Cardinal Lemoine was transformed into a pornographic theatre in 1975 (Gajdusek 9).[2] If the guide-books discussed above and *The Sun Also Rises* can be understood as examples of experiential travel writing, then they can also be considered in the context of sex tourism in modern literature. From Flaubert's 1849 licentious journey through the Middle East to Michel Houellebecq's 2001 novel *Platforme*, travel provides an environment for sexual behavior unthinkable at home. Away from Prohibition and puritan prudishness, expatriate Paris becomes the city for experience, with tourists seeking such experience turning

2. More recently, the space has become an avant-garde cinema (Gajdusek 62).

to lifestyle guides like Reynolds's and Wilson's, complete with the "naughty places" of Paris. But as in *The Sun Also Rises*, both sexual excess and tourism's frantic insistence on perpetual experience have the unavoidable consequence of making sex seem banal and travel boring. Tourists, expatriates, and Hemingway's fictionalized comrades alike are iterations of Emma Bovary and Léon, seeking the sheltering space of foreign streets.

On the other side of "Gay Paree" is the alcoholic self-destructiveness of Hemingway's haunted expatriates, their lifestyle rationed by the banality of rote itinerary. Like a Parisian prophetess, Gertrude Stein had the last word before Hemingway became an icon when she observed that Hemingway "looks like a modern and . . . smells of the museums" (qtd. in Aldridge 121). Hemingway wrote of experience and contributed to the experiential travelogue, but has himself become a monument.

WORKS CITED

Aldridge, John W. "Afterthoughts on the Twenties and *The Sun Also Rises*." In *New Essays on* The Sun Also Rises. Ed. Linda Wagner-Martin. Cambridge: Cambridge UP, 1987. 109–129.

Atherton, John. "The Itinerary and the Postcard: Minimal Strategies in *The Sun Also Rises*." *ELH* 53.1 (Spring 1986): 199–218.

Baker, Carlos. *Hemingway: The Writer as Artist*. Princeton: Princeton UP, 1956.

Balassi, William. "The Trail to *The Sun Also Rises*: The First Week of Writing." In *Hemingway: Essays of Reassessment*. Ed. Frank Scafella. New York and Oxford: Oxford UP, 1991. 33–51.

Brenner, Gerry. *A Comprehensive Companion to Hemingway's A Moveable Feast; Annotation to Interpretation*. Lewiston: Edwin Mellen, 2000.

Chancellor, John. *How to Be Happy in Paris Without Being Ruined*. New York: Henry Holt, 1927.

Fenton, Charles A. *The Apprenticeship of Ernest Hemingway: The Early Years*. New York: Farrar, Straus, and Young, 1954.

Flaubert, Gustave. *Madame Bovary: A Story of Provincial Life*. 1857. Trans. Alan Russell. London: Penguin Books, 1950.

Gajdusek, Robert E. *Hemingway's Paris*. New York: Scribner's, 1978.

Griffin, Peter. *Less Than a Treason: Hemingway in Paris*. New York and Oxford: Oxford UP, 1990.

Hemingway, Ernest. *Green Hills of Africa*. 1935. New York: Scribner's, 1963.

———. *A Moveable Feast*. 1964. New York: Scribner's, 2003.

———. *The Sun Also Rises*. 1926. New York: Scribner's, 2003.

Kennedy, J. Gerald. *Imagining Paris: Exile, Writing, and American Identity*. New Haven: Yale UP, 1993.
Kuehl, John and Jackson Bryer, eds. *Dear Scott / Dear Max: The Fitzgerald-Perkins Correspondence*. New York: Scribner's, 1971.
Leland, John. *A Guide to Hemingway's Paris with Walking Tours*. Chapel Hill, NC: Algonquin, 1989.
Lynn, Kenneth S. *Hemingway*. New York: Simon and Schuster, 1987.
Maurice, Arthur Bartlett. *The Paris of the Novelists*. New York: Doubleday, Page, 1919.
Reynolds, Bruce. *Paris with the Lid Lifted*. New York: George Sully, 1927.
Wall, Cheryl A. "Paris and Harlem: Two Culture Capitals." *Phylon* 35.1 (1st Qtr., 1974): 64–73.
Washburn, Claude C. *Pages from the Book of Paris*. Boston and New York: Houghton Mifflin, 1910.
Wilson, Robert Forrest. *Paris on Parade*. Indianapolis: Bobbs-Merrill, 1924, 1925.

GENDER AND SEXUALITY

MARK SPILKA

Three Wounded Warriors†

In late September 1929, when Ernest Hemingway first met Allen Tate in Sylvia Beach's Paris bookshop, there was more on his mind than Tate's indirect discovery, through Defoe, of Marryat's strong influence on his work; he was, in fact, far more deeply troubled by Tate's discovery, in his review of *The Sun Also Rises*, of his penchant for sentimentalizing his own weaknesses through fictional personas like Jake Barnes. Thus, in a letter to Carlos Baker dated April 2, 1963, Tate recalls not only how Hemingway had accosted him "without preliminary" about wrongly attributed influences, but had also accosted him about the Barnes-like impotence of their mutual friend, Ford Madox Ford:

> We walked up the street to the Place de l'Odeon and had an aperitif at the old Cafe Voltaire. . . . The next subject he intro-

† From *Hemingway's Quarrel with Androgyny* (Lincoln, NE: U of Nebraska P, 1990), pp. 197–208. Copyright © 1990 by the University of Nebraska Press. Reprinted by permission of the University of Nebraska Press. Notes are by the author of the original work. Page numbers in brackets refer to this Norton Critical Edition.

> duced I can repeat almost in his words; "Ford's a friend of yours. You know he's impotent, don't you?" . . . I listened, but finally said that his impotence didn't concern me, even if it were true that he was impotent, since I was not a woman. I learned soon in the local gossip of the *petit cercle Americain* that Ford had been one of the first persons to help Ernest, and as you know Ernest couldn't bear being grateful to anybody.[1]

Tate may be making another indirect discovery here, for not only had Ford befriended Ernest and made him subeditor of his literary journal, the *transatlantic review;* he had also written a "tale of passion," *The Good Soldier* (1915), which like *The Sun Also Rises* is narrated by an "impotent" man and may well have served as another hidden source of influence! At any rate, Tate's response to Ernest—that he was not a woman, and so untroubled by Ford's presumed impotence—was exactly right, and seems to have sealed the fast friendship which from then on held between them. It was the assurance Ernest needed of a common toughness of outlook, a common stake in that hard-boiled modern sensibility that each of them—as novelist and critic—was now serving, and (not least among these assurances) a common witty maleness.

Actually Tate had challenged such assurances in his harsh review of *The Sun Also Rises.* As we have seen, in his two previous reviews of Hemingway's work for *The Nation*, he had welcomed him for the seriousness and integrity of his prose in *In Our Time*—"the most completely realized naturalistic fiction of the age"—and had praised his "indirect irony" and satiric bent in *The Torrents of Spring*, deeming the book itself "a small masterpiece of American fiction."[2] But in reviewing *The Sun Also Rises* he had sharply registered his disappointment at Hemingway's lapse from the achievement of *In Our Time.*

* * *

Understandably enough, Hemingway was stung by this treatment from a previously strong admirer. In a letter to Maxwell Perkins written on December 21, 1926, a week after the appearance of Tate's review in *The Nation*, he begins with news of Edmund Wilson's enthusiasm for the novel ("best . . . by any one of my generation"), then praises the editor of *Scribner's Magazine* for proposing to run together three complementary stories that "would make a fine group. And perhaps cheer up Dos, Allen Tate, and the other boys who fear

1. Allen Tate to Carlos Baker, 2 April 1963, Firestone Library, Princeton.
2. Tate, "Good Prose" and "The Spirituality of Roughnecks," as quoted in Stephens, *Ernest Hemingway,* 14, 26.

I'm on the toboggan." Then, in a long postscript, he begins with his friend Dos Passos's criticism of the Pamplona scenes in the novel, and ends, significantly, with Tate's several criticisms of his characters and, above all, his toughness:

> Critics, this is still Mr. Tate—have a habit of hanging attributes on you themselves—and then when they find you're not that way accusing you of sailing under false colours—Mr. Tate feels so badly that I'm not as hard-boiled as he had publicly announced. As a matter of fact I have not been at all hard-boiled since July 8, 1918—on the night of which I discovered that that also was Vanity.[3]

The title of Tate's review for *The Nation* had been "Hard-Boiled." July 8, 1918, was, of course, the night on which Hemingway was wounded by shell fire and machine-gun fire while serving canteen supplies in the Italian trenches at Fossalta. It would not be the last time he would use the authority of being wounded as an answer to unwounded critics. But the interesting point, in view of the later public hardening of his personal attitudes, is his insistence on his own vulnerability, his own stake in his character's nightly fears. Indeed, he shares in the kind of self-pity to which Tate objects in his fiction, as to a sentimental indulgence unworthy of true art, a disclosure of personal impotence.

Jake and Brett

What are we to make, then, of Jake Barnes's sexual wound? Hemingway was certainly not an impotent man when he created that curious condition—a lost portion of the penis—for his first-person narrator. His own wounds had been to the legs and scrotum, the latter a mere infection suggesting perhaps that worse had been barely avoided. In a late letter (December 9, 1951) he explained to a Rinehart editor, as an example of the complications of a writer's involvement in his own fictions, "the whole genesis of The Sun Also Rises":

> It came from a personal experience in that when I had been wounded at one time there had been an infection from pieces of wool cloth being driven into the scrotum. Because of this I got to know other kids who had genito urinary wounds and I wondered what a man's life would have been like after that if his penis had been lost and his testicles and spermatic cord remained intact. I had known a boy that had happened to. So I took him and made him into a foreign correspondent in Paris, and, inventing, tried to find out what his problems would be

3. Hemingway, *Selected Letters*, 239–40.

> when he was in love with someone who was in love with him and there was nothing that they could do about it. . . . But I was not Jake Barnes. My own wound had healed rapidly and well and I was quit for a short session with the catheter.[4]

The last point is interesting in that there is nothing in the novel to indicate if or when Jake was quit with the catheter, or how he urinates now. But more interesting still is the choice of war wounds for an unmarried foreign correspondent in Paris otherwise much like himself. We know that Hemingway's close relations with his friend Duff Twysden, the ostensible model for Jake's beloved Brett Ashley, had much to do with the choice. As Scott Fitzgerald (who knew something about that relation) opined, Jake seems more like a man trapped in a "moral chastity belt" than a sexually wounded warrior: and indeed, it was Hemingway's marital fidelity to Hadley that apparently kept him from having an affair with Duff; so too, Fitzgerald implies, Jake Barnes with Brett, though there is no Hadley in the novel.[5]

There may, however, be an Agnes Von Kurowsky. Barnes and Lady Ashley had met each other in a British hospital where Brett worked as a nurse's aide, just as Ernest had met Agnes at a Milan hospital where she worked as an American Red Cross nurse. This prefiguring of the plot of *A Farewell to Arms* is no more than a background notation in *The Sun Also Rises*; but it does remind us of the emotional damage Ernest had sustained from his rejection after the war by Agnes Von Kurowsky and his complicity in that rejection. If Jake's sexual wound can be read as an instance of the way in which war undermines the possibilities of "true love," then we begin to understand to some extent why Hemingway chose that curious condition as an index to the postwar malaise, the barrenness of waste-land relations among the expatriates he knew in Paris—and brought with him to Pamplona. It was in a way a self-inflicted wound he was dealing with which had the war's connivance.

Lawrence's Clifford Chatterley, paralyzed from the waist down by a war wound, is a good example of such projected impotence since he functions obviously enough as the bearer of Lawrence's condition while he was writing the novel, the victim by that point in his life of tubercular dysfunction. But Hemingway was there before him with Jake Barnes, as of course Joyce had been there before Hemingway with Leopold Bloom, his imagined Jewish alter ego in *Ulysses*,

4. Hemingway, *Selected Letters*, 745.
5. See Fitzgerald's long letter to Hemingway on cutting the early chapters, in Frederic Joseph Svoboda's *Hemingway and* The Sun Also Rises: *The Crafting of a Style*, 140: "He isn't *like an impotent man. He's like a man in a sort of moral chastity belt*" (italics mine). See also Baker, *Ernest Hemingway*, 203: "The situation between Barnes and Brett Ashley, as Ernest imagined it, could very well be a projection of his own inhibitions about sleeping with Duff."

and Henry James with Strether in *The Ambassadors*, and Ford Madox Ford with Dowell in *The Good Soldier*; and much farther back, Laurence Sterne with *Tristram Shandy*. The tradition of impotent narration or of impotent heroes, whether comic, serious, or tragic, is an old and honorable one; and our only question is what went into Hemingway's decision to employ it.

Our most recent clue comes from the posthumously published edition of *The Garden of Eden* (1986), the hero of which engages in androgynous forms of lovemaking with his adventurous young wife in the south of postwar France, and at one point in the original manuscript imagines himself as one of the lesbian lovers in a mysterious statue by Rodin, called variously *Ovid's Metamorphoses, Daphnis and Chloe*, and *Volupté*, and deriving from a group called *The Damned Women* from *The Gates of Hell.*[6] Since the hero also changes sex roles at night with his beloved, we have one interesting explanation for Hemingway's postwar choice of a symbol for his own unmanning by war wounds and the American nurses who tend them: for if Jake remains "capable of all normal feelings as a *man* but incapable of consummating them," as Hemingway told George Plimpton in a famous interview, his physical wound suggests also the female genitals as men erroneously imagine them, at least according to Freud.[7] The exact nature of the wound, moreover, is literally nowhere spelled out or explained in the novel; we have only Hemingway's word for the intended condition. It becomes clear nonetheless from the type of mannish heroine he imagines, after Lady Duff Twysden's British example, that an exchange of sexual roles has indeed occurred, prefiguring that of *The Garden of Eden*, and that it is Jake and not Brett who wears that traditionally female protection, the chastity belt.

What are we to make, then, of Brett Ashley's British mannishness? * * *

* * * In *The Sun Also Rises*, of course, it is Jake Barnes who is the lenient Catholic, Brett Ashley the licensed European; but the combination is striking, especially if we consider Jake for a moment as an aspect of his beloved British lady, or her lesbian lover:

> Brett was damned good-looking. She wore a slipover jersey sweater and a tweed skirt, and her hair was brushed back like a boy's. She started all that. She was built with curves like the hull of a racing yacht, and you missed none of it with that wool jersey. . . .

6. *The Garden of Eden* manuscript, bk. 1, chap. 1, pp. 17, 23–24, in Hemingway Collection, Kennedy Library, Boston, Mass. For reproductions of bronze and plaster versions of the statues in question, see especially *The Sculptures of Auguste Rodin,* ed. John Tancock.
7. Plimpton, "Ernest Hemingway," in *Writers at Work.*

I told the driver to go to the Parc Monsouris, and got in, and slammed the door. Brett was leaning back in the corner, her eyes closed. I got in and sat beside her. The cab started with a jerk.

"Oh darling, I've been so miserable," Brett said. . . .

The taxi went up the hill. . . . We were sitting apart and we jolted close together going down the old street. Brett's hat was off. Her head was back. I saw her face in the lights from the open shops, then it was dark . . . and I kissed her. Our lips were tight together and then she turned away. . . .

"Don't touch me" she said, "please don't touch me." . . .

"Don't you love me?"

"Love you? I simply turn all to jelly when you touch me."

"Isn't there anything we can do about it? . . .

"I don't know," she said. "I don't want to go through that hell again." . . .

On the Boulevard Raspail . . . Brett said: "Would you mind very much if I asked you to do something?

"Don't be silly."

"Kiss me just once more before we get there."

When the taxi stopped I got out and paid. Brett came out putting on her hat. She gave me her hand as she stepped down. Her hand was shaky. "I say, do I look too much of a mess?" She pulled her man's felt hat down and started in for the bar. . . .

"Hello, you chaps," Brett said. "I'm going to have a drink. [18–22]

The cab ride is a setup for the ending, when Jake and Brett are in another such cab in Madrid, pressed together as the cab slows down, with Brett saying, "Oh, Jake. . . . We could have had such a damned good time together," and Jake replying: "Yes. Isn't it pretty to think so"[180]. A hard-boiled ending, but those early kisses tell us otherwise. For through them Jake's vulnerability to pain through the essential feminization of his power to love has been established; like a woman, he cannot penetrate his beloved but can only rouse and be roused by her through fervent kisses; nor is he ready, at this early stage of the sexual revolution, for those oral-genital solutions which recent critics have been willing to impose upon him. His maleness then is like Brett's, who with her boy's haircut and man's felt hat may be said to remind us of the more active lesbian lover in the Rodin statue, named playfully Daphnis in one version to an obvious Chloe. Which again makes us wonder if Jake is not in some sense an aspect of his beloved—not really her chivalric admirer, like Robert Cohn, but rather her masculine girlfriend, her admiring Catherine from the novel years ahead who similarly stops her car on the return from

Nice to kiss her lesbian lover, then tells her androgynous husband about it and makes him kiss her too—or, in Jake's more abject moments, her selfless Catherine from the novel next in line.

True enough, we see Jake enduring a form of love about which nothing can be done, working out what could be called a peculiarly male predicament, a sad form of a common wartime joke, in accord with Hemingway's stated plan; and in his struggles against his own self-pity we see a standard of male conduct against which we are asked to measure Robert Cohn's more abject slavishness to his beloved lady, and Mike Campbell's, and even (more to its favor) young Pedro Romero's manly devotion. And truer still, we are asked to judge Brett's liberation as a displacement of male privilege and power in matters of the heart and loins, a sterile wasteland consequence of postwar change. But what if the secret agenda is to admire and emulate Brett Ashley? What if Brett is the woman Jake would in some sense like to be?

"She started all that," he tells us admiringly, and perhaps even predictively. Brett's style-setting creativity becomes, in *The Garden of Eden*, the leading characteristic of Catherine Bourne, whose smart boyish haircuts, blond hairdyes and matching fisherman's shirts and pants—all shared with her androgynous husband David—are plainly expressions of the new postwar mannishness, the new rivalry with men for attention and power, for a larger stake in the socio-sexual pie: new sexual freedoms and privileges, then, new license. They are also forms of artistry, like Catherine's unexpected talent for talk; and if Brett's talent is less for talk than for putting chaps through hell, she is oddly also the same risk-taking character, the same sexual adventurer we ultimately meet in Catherine Bourne, though strictly heterosexual in her conquests—except perhaps with Jacob Barnes. "I suppose she only wanted what she couldn't have," muses the latter, not seeing as yet how well those words describe himself [25].

I do not mean to imply here that Jacob, a soulful wrestler with his own physical condition, would also like to make it with bullfighters and other males—that seems to me misleading—but rather that—in accord with the oddly common attraction for men of lesbian lovemaking, the imagining into it that exercises suppressed femininity, and indeed the need for such imagining, such identification with the original nurturing sources of love—he wants Brett in a womanly way. Hemingway's childhood twinning with his older sister Marcelline may have made him more sensitive to such desires and more strongly liable first to suppress and then ultimately to express them; but he was in fact expressing something common, difficult, and quite possibly crucial to coming of age as a man in this century's white bourgeois circles. His admiration for the liberated ladies of the 1920s was widely shared, and his ultimate enslavement by their androgynous powers may tell us more about ourselves and our times than we care to know.

Certainly Jake is enslaved by Brett as are Robert Cohn and Mike Campbell and even Pedro Romero, who escapes her only through her charitable withdrawal of her devastating love. That is the Ulyssean predicament, the Circean circle. * * *

Still another "romantic lady" would figure in the making of Brett Ashley. Critics have long noted the influence of Michael Arlen's heroine Iris March, in *The Green Hat*, possibly because of the fetish made of Brett's man's hat but also because of the modern twist on an old tradition. As Allen Tate observed in criticizing Hemingway for sparing certain characters in *The Sun Also Rises* from equitable judgment, Brett "becomes the attractive wayward lady of Sir Arthur Pinero and Michael Arlen"; whereas "Petronius's Circe, the archetype of all the Bretts, was neither appealing nor deformed" [234]. Such observations are useful in that Brett is indeed given special treatment, early on, as "one of us"—that is to say, "one of us" stoical and perhaps Conradian survivors—and is granted a certain nobility at the end for her refusal to destroy the worthy Pedro, to say nothing of her repeated returns to Jake Barnes for support and reassurance, as to the novel's touchstone for stoic endurance. Similarly Arlen's attractively wayward heroine in *The Green Hat* is given more than the usual share of male honor as she protects her suicidal first husband's good name at the expense of her own, assuming to herself the "impurity" (i.e., syphilis) that killed him, and then, in another grand gesture of self-denial, sending her true love back to his wife before roaring off in her yellow Hispano-Suiza to a fiery and quite melodramatic death; and Iris too is characterized as "one of us" and is said to "meet men on their own ground always."[8] Even so, Brett is probably based on still another Arlen heroine in more important ways. Thus, as Carlos Baker reports, Scott Fitzgerald had passed the time on a motor trip with Hemingway in May 1925 "by providing detailed summaries of the plots of the novels of Michael Arlen," one of which—a tale called "The Romantic Lady"—seems to have moved him (though he denied it) to go and do likewise.[9]

* * *

8. Michael Arlen, *The Green Hat,* 95, 229, 231.
9. Baker, *Ernest Hemingway,* 189. See also *Selected Letters,* 238. For Fitzgerald's acute observation that the original opening chapters are indeed written in the effusive style of Michael Arlen (to which Fitzgerald strongly objected), see Svoboda, *Hemingway,* 138: "You've done a lot of writing that *honestly* reminded me of Michael Arlen." See also chapter 14 of *The Torrents of Spring,* where Yogi Johnson tells a version of Arlen's "The Romantic Lady" in which a beautiful woman uses him for voyeuristic purposes (79–81). In *Along with Youth,* 65, Peter Griffin mistakes this obvious borrowing for autobiographical truth.

One thinks of Brett surrounded by wreathed dancers when the fiesta at Pamplona explodes [151]; or "coming through the crowd in the square, walking, her head up, as though the fiesta were being staged in her honor" [151]; or of the book's epigraph from Ecclesiastes—"the earth abideth forever"—and Hemingway's odd assertion that "the abiding earth" is the novel's hero.[1] If Arlen's romantic lady is any evidence, "abiding heroine" might be more to the point—"earthy" ladies who make their own laws, confine sex to adventurous one-night stands which, in Hemingway's more cynical world, do not mean anything, but which are in fact cynical enough in Arlen's formulation—his Marlovian narrator having been divorced six months before, he now reminds us, for having himself gone back for the punishment of marriage. "Be very gentle with me" indeed: those oddly passive, now androgynous remarks remind us all too tellingly that it was Pauline who pursued and won Ernest away from Hadley in 1926, the year in which *The Sun Also Rises* was first published.

DEBRA A. MODDELMOG

Contradictory Bodies in *The Sun Also Rises*[†]

With its attention to male bonding and rituals such as fishing, drinking, and bullfighting, *The Sun Also Rises* has become known as "classic Hemingway." Co-existing with these rituals is a thwarted heterosexual relationship—Jake and Brett's—a romantic situation that is also characteristic of Hemingway's fiction. The repetition of this pattern throughout Hemingway's work (e.g., *A Farewell to Arms, For Whom the Bell Tolls, Across the River and Into the Trees, Islands in the Stream*) suggests that Hemingway felt that the intense homosociality of his fiction demanded equally intense heterosexuality to deflect suspicions that either his male characters or he had homosexual tendencies.[1] Yet a closer look at *The Sun Also Rises* reveals that Hemingway's depiction of gender and sexuality is more complex than this description allows. Ironically, in mapping out this territory of interrogation, I will draw upon the very concepts that I

1. Hemingway to Maxwell Perkins, 19 November 1926, in *Selected Letters*, 229.

† From *Reading Desire: In Pursuit of Ernest Hemingway* (Ithaca: Cornell UP, 1999), pp. 92–100. Page numbers in brackets refer to this Norton Critical Edition. Notes are by the authors of the original work. Some of the notes have been omitted.

1. Peter F. Cohen has recently presented an argument regarding the intense male bonds in *A Farewell to Arms* that coincides with the one I make in this chapter regarding *The Sun Also Rises*. Although my argument posits a more comprehensive circulation of desire among the characters, Cohen has recognized that a Hemingway heroine might serve as an erotic go-between for two Hemingway heroes.

claim Hemingway's work problematizes (masculinity/femininity, homosexuality/heterosexuality). As Gayatri Spivak observes, "There is no way that a deconstructive philosopher can say 'something is not something' when the word is being used as a concept to enable his discourse."[2] Despite this paradox, by tracing how Hemingway's texts bring traditional significations of gender and sexuality into conflict, I hope to illustrate that Hemingway's first novel (like one of his last, *The Garden of Eden*) exposes the intellectual limitations that result when "gender" and "sexuality" are read as innocent acts of nature and as fixed binaries.

Early in *The Sun Also Rises*, a scene occurs that seems to establish the gender and sexual ideologies upon which the story will turn: Jake Barnes and Brett Ashley's meeting at a dance club in which Jake is accompanied by a prostitute, Georgette Hobin, and Brett is accompanied by a group of homosexual men. In a poststructuralist reading that provides the starting point for mine, Cathy and Arnold Davidson observe that by switching dancing partners, these characters arrange themselves in different pairings: Jake and Georgette, Jake and Brett, the young men and Brett, the young men and Georgette. These partner exchanges initially suggest "the fundamental equivalence" of the women as well as of the men. Georgette and Brett are conjoined under the pairing of prostitution/promiscuity, just as Jake and the young men are linked under the pairing of sexually maimed/homosexual. Consequently, this episode reveals the contradictions in Jake's own life. Jake relies upon the homosexuality of the young men to define his manhood (at least his desire is the right kind), but that definition is tested by the joint presence of Georgette and Brett, neither of whom Jake has sex with.[3] As the Davidsons conclude, "The terrifying ambiguity of [Jake's] own sexual limitations and gender preferences may well be one source of his anger (it usually is) with Brett's companions, and another reason why he articulates his anger and hatred for them before he reveals his love for her" (92).

But this perceptive reading illuminates only one of the "fundamental equivalences" set up in this scene; further, it fails to recognize that as these equivalences multiply, the glue connecting the descriptive pair loses its adhesive power. Through a series of interchanges, Jake and Brett are equated differently; established relations dissolve and are rearranged into new relations. What began as an inseparable unit

2. Gayatri Spivak, "A Response to 'The Difference Within': Feminism and Critical Theory," in *The Difference Within: Feminism and Critical Theory*, ed. Elizabeth Meese and Alice Parker (Philadelphia: John Benjamin, 1989), 213.
3. Arnold Davidson and Cathy Davidson, "Decoding the Hemingway Hero in *The Sun Also Rises*," in *New Essays on* The Sun Also Rises, ed. Linda Wagner-Martin (Cambridge: Cambridge University Press, 1987), 89–92.

(sexually maimed-homosexual) ends up as free-floating terms (sexually maimed, homosexual), and the characters, particularly Jake and Brett, are revealed as bodies of contradictions. Ultimately these pairings challenge the validity of defining gender and sexuality in terms of binarisms—masculine/feminine, heterosexual/homosexual.

For instance, the pairing of Brett and Georgette, like the pairing of Jake and the homosexual men, is complex and multifaceted. The resemblance between the two women is underscored when Jake, half-asleep, thinks that Brett, who has come to visit him, is Georgette [26]. Obviously such a correspondence reveals that both women sleep around, one because she believes it's the way she is made [42], the other because it's the way she makes a living. Yet this explanation of motives reminds us that women's outlets for their desires were closely intertwined with economic necessity in the years following World War I, even in the liberated Left Bank of Paris. As a white, heterosexually identified, upper-class woman, Brett still must depend, both financially and socially, on hooking up with one man or another. As Wendy Martin observes, "If Brett has gained a measure of freedom in leaving the traditional household, she is still very much dependent on men, who provide an arena in which she can be attractive and socially active as well as financially secure."[4]

Brett's self-destructive drinking and her attempts to distance herself from sexual role stereotyping—for example, her short hair is "brushed back like a boy's" [18] and she wears a "man's felt hat"[22]—indicate her resentment of this prescribed arrangement. Susan Gubar reminds us that many women artists of the modernist period escaped the strictures of socially defined femininity by appropriating male clothing, which they identified with freedom.[5] For such women, cross-dressing became "a way of ad-dressing and re-dressing the inequities of culturally-defined categories of masculinity and femininity" (Gubar, 479). Like Catherine Bourne of *The Garden of Eden*, Brett Ashley fits this category of women who were crossing gender lines by cross-dressing and behaving in "masculine ways." Although Brett's wool jersey sweater reveals her to be a woman, the exposure is not enough to counter the effect of her masculine apparel and appearance on the men around her. Pedro Romero's urge to both make her look more "womanly" [176] and marry her might be explained as the response of a man raised to demand clear distinctions between the gender roles of men and women. But the attempt of the more carefree Mike Campbell to convince Brett to buy a new

4. Wendy Martin, "Brett Ashley as New Woman in *The Sun Also Rises*," in *New Essays on* The Sun Also Rises, ed. Linda Wagner-Martin (Cambridge: Cambridge University Press, 1987), 71.
5. Susan Gubar, "Blessings in Disguise: Cross-Dress as Re-Dressing for Female Modernists," *Massachusetts Review* 22 (1981): 478.

hat [58] and to marry him suggests that Brett is dangerously close to overturning the categories upon which male and female identity, and patriarchal power, depend. The "new woman" must not venture too far outside the old boundaries.

Brett's cross-dressing conveys more than just a social statement about gender. It also evokes suggestions of the transvestism practiced by and associated with lesbians of the time (and since). * * * Sexologists such as Havelock Ellis recognized the so-called mannish woman as only one kind of lesbian; nonetheless, the wearing of men's clothing by women was often viewed as sexual coding. Certainly many lesbians chose to cross-dress in order to announce their sexual preference.[6] One hint that we might read Brett's cross-dressing within this context comes in the parallel set up between her and Georgette. When Jake introduces Georgette to a group seated in the restaurant, he identifies her as his fiancée, Georgette Leblanc. As several scholars have pointed out, Georgette Leblanc was a contemporary singer and actress in Paris—and an acknowledged lesbian.[7] This association consequently deepens the symbolic relationship of Brett to Georgette, linking them in a new equation: independent/lesbian. Brett's transvestism crosses over from gender inversion to sexual sign: not only does Brett desire the lesbian's economic and social autonomy but she also possesses same-sex desire.

In fact, Brett's alcoholism and inability to sustain a relationship might be indications not of nymphomania, with which the critics have often charged her, but of a dissatisfaction with the strictures of the male-female relationship. Brett's announcement, for example, that she can drink safely among homosexual men [19] can be taken to mean that she cannot control her own heterosexual desire, though it could also reveal underlying anxiety toward the heterosexual desire of men. Such an anxiety might be related to her abusive marriage, but that experience need not be its only source. As Brett tells Jake after the break-up with Pedro Romero, "I can't even marry Mike" [177]. Of course, soon after this, she declares, "I'm going back to Mike. . . . He's so damned nice and he's so awful. He's my sort of thing" [177]. Yet even in giving her reasons for returning to Mike,

6. George Chauncey observes that Havelock Ellis, like other contemporary sexologists, attempted to differentiate sexual object choice from sexual roles and gender characteristics, an attempt reflected in the distinguishing of the sexual invert from the homosexual. Chauncey also notes, however, that the sexologists were less willing to apply this distinction to women. Hence, whereas Ellis could claim that male homosexuals were not necessarily effeminate or transvestites, he was less capable of separating a woman's behavior in sexual relations from other aspects of her gender role. See Chauncey, "Sexual Inversion," 124–25.

7. Apparently, Hemingway did not feel kindly toward Georgette Leblanc. In a letter to Ezra Pound (c. 2 May 1924), Hemingway noted that Margaret Anderson was in Paris with "Georgette Mangeuse [man-eater] le Blanc," *Ernest Hemingway: Selected Letters, 1917–1961*, ed. Carlos Baker (New York: Charles Scribner's Sons, 1981), 115. But whether he knew her personally is uncertain.

Brett reveals her inner turmoil and ambivalence. Like Mike, she is both "nice" and "awful," and the novel ends before this promised reunion occurs.

We should be careful not to equate Brett's anxiety about male heterosexual desire with lesbian desire nor to presume that unhappy heterosexual relations are a necessary condition for lesbian desire. In fact, Brett's same-sex desire is hinted at in other ways than her cross-dressing and her frustrations with heterosexual men, namely, through her association with her homosexual companions. As Jake states three times, she is "with them," she is "very much with them" [17]. This homosexual identification helps to explain Brett's attraction to Jake who, according to Hemingway in a letter written in 1951, has lost his penis but not his testicles and spermatic cord (*Ernest Hemingway: Selected Letters*, 745). If we accept this explanation, Jake lacks the physical feature that has traditionally been the most important in distinguishing sex as well as male sexual desire. He is a sexual invalid and, as a consequence, sexually in-valid.[8] Jake's maleness, masculinity, and heterosexuality, lined up and linked under the law of compulsory heterosexuality, are separated and problematized. Like a woman, Jake has no penis with which to make love with Brett. Instead, Brett ministers to him, "strok[ing] his head" as he lies on the bed [24], and recognizes that the absent male sex organ makes Jake different from other suitors.[9] In this context, Jake's notion that Brett "only wanted what she couldn't have" [25] takes on added meaning. Besides non-penile sex, she wants to find some way to accommodate the fluidity of sexual desire and gender identification that characterizes her condition.

Brett's affiliation with homosexual men and her transgendering complicate, in turn, Jake's relationship with her. Jake calls Brett "damned good-looking" and describes her hair as being "brushed back like a boy's" [18], two attributions that dissolve into one in Jake's later identification of Pedro Romero as "a damned good-looking boy" [124]. Jake's attraction to Brett can be partially attributed to his homosexual desire, a desire that seems about to break through the surface of Jake's narrative at any time.[1] As the Davidsons observe

8. Peter Messent's essay on *The Sun Also Rises* suggested this play on words, *New Readings of the American Novel* (London: Macmillan Education, 1990), 92. Although he does not state the matter as I have, he also seems to have borrowed this idea from Sandra M. Gilbert, "Costumes of the Mind: Transvestism as Metaphor in Modern Literature," *Critical Inquiry* 7 (1980): 409.

9. Peter Messent has also recently explored gender fluidity in *The Sun Also Rises*, and his reading lends support to many of the suppositions I set forth here. Messent states, "In *The Sun Also Rises*, gender roles have lost all stability," 112. Among other things, he points to Georgette's sexual forwardness with Jake, Brett's pre-dawn visit to Jake's room after he retired there with a "headache," the count's bringing of roses to Jake, and Jake's crying, 114.

1. As support for this argument, consider Susan Gubar's suggestion that seductive cross-dressers "can function as sex symbols for men, reflecting masculine attitudes that range

and as I mentioned earlier, this desire can be seen in Jake's conflicted response to Brett's homosexual companions. It can also be seen in Jake's possession of *afición*, which must be confirmed by the touch of other men [98]. To quote the Davidsons, there is something "suspect" in the aficionados vesting so much of their manhood in a boylike matador who woos a bull to death through "girlish flirtation and enticement." As a consequence, "the whole ethos of *afición* resembles a sublimation of sexual desire, and the aficionados—serving, guiding, surrounding the matador out of the ring and applauding him in it—seem all, in a sense, steers."

Jake's descriptions of the meeting of the bull and bullfighter imply more than flirtation; the encounter evokes images of sexual foreplay and consummation. He states, "The bull wanted it again, and Romero's cape filled again, this time on the other side. Each time he let the bull pass so close that the man and the bull and the cape that filled and pivoted ahead of the bull were all one sharply etched mass" [159]. Later Jake expresses the climax of the bullfight, the bull's death, in terms reminiscent of sexual climax:

> [F]or just an instant [Romero] and the bull were one, Romero way out over the bull, the right arm extended high up to where the hilt of the sword had gone in between the bull's shoulders. Then the figure was broken. There was a little jolt as Romero came clear, and then he was standing, one hand up, facing the bull, his shirt ripped out from under his sleeve, the white blowing in the wind, and the bull, the red sword hilt tight between his shoulders, his head going down and his legs settling. [160]

Jake's relationships with Bill Gorton and Pedro Romero constitute two of the more important sources of sublimated homosexual desire. During their fishing trip to the Irati River, Bill tells Jake, "Listen. You're a hell of a good guy, and I'm fonder of you than anybody on earth. I couldn't tell you that in New York. It'd mean I was a faggot" [85]. In expressing his fondness for Jake, Bill realizes the risk he takes in declaring strong feelings for another man. His words might be construed, by himself as well as by others, as an admission of homosexual love. To avoid being interpreted in that way, Bill must declare homosexual desire an impossibility. However, Bill's phrasing in this passage and his subsequent focus on homosexuality suggest that such desire is a very real possibility. For one, his statement "I'm fonder of you than anybody on earth" can be read as "I'm fonder of you than I am of anybody else on earth" or as "I'm fonder of you than anybody else is." Either reading elevates Bill and Jake's

from an attempt to eroticize (and thereby possess) the independent woman to only slightly submerged homosexual fantasies," 483. While I do not discount the first possibility (eroticism in the service of possession), here I am tracing the latter function.

relationship to a primary position. It is a connection more binding and important than any other relationship Bill has formed.

In addition, Bill's worry that disclosing his affection for Jake would, in New York, mean that he is "a faggot" indicates Bill's awareness of the instability of the line separating homosocial and homosexual behavior and desire. Outside the geographic and psychological boundaries of New York and its taxonomy of deviance, Bill's feelings are platonic; inside those boundaries, they are homosexual.[2] Bill's concern about the boundaries for same-sex relationships indicates that he cannot be sure about the "purity" of his feelings for Jake or of Jake's for him. In an early draft of the novel, Bill's obsession and concern are even more apparent. Bill tells Jake that New York circles have marked him (Bill) as "crazy." "Also I'm supposed to be crazy to get married. Would marry anybody at any time. . . . Since Charley Gordon and I had an apartment together last winter, I suppose I'm a fairy. That probably explains everything." Bill also reinforces his awareness, and fear, of the instability of sexual identity when he attacks the literary world of New York by claiming that "every literary bastard" there "never goes to bed at night not knowing but that he'll wake up in the morning and find himself a fairy. There are plenty of real ones too" (quoted in Mellow, 312–13).

Even though Hemingway eventually cut this passage about fairies and the unstable sexual identities of "literary bastards," the anxieties it expresses remain in the published text. Having stated his fondness for Jake, Bill moves the discussion away from their relationship, but he cannot drop the subject of homosexuality: "That [homosexual love] was what the Civil War was about. Abraham Lincoln was a faggot. He was in love with General Grant. So was Jefferson Davis. . . . Sex explains it all. The Colonel's Lady and Judy O'Grady are Lesbians under their skin" [85–86]. By identifying homosexual desire as the cause of all private and public action, a supposedly absurd exaggeration, Bill defuses the tension that expressing his affection for Jake creates. Yet homosexuality is still very much in the air—and "under their skin."

2. In *Gay New York*, George Chauncey argues that only in the 1930s, 1940s, and 1950s "did the now-conventional division of men into 'homosexuals' and 'heterosexuals,' based on the sex of their sexual partners, replace the division of men into 'fairies' and 'normal men' on the basis of their imaginary gender status as the hegemonic way of understanding sexuality," 13. But Chauncey also notes that "exclusive heterosexuality became a precondition for a man's identification as 'normal' in middle-class culture at least two generations before it did so in much of Euro-American and African-American working class culture," 14. To outside observers of the homosexual subculture, "faggot," in the 1930s, would have been the equivalent of "queer" and "fairy." However, to insiders, "queer" was reserved for men who had a homosexual interest, whereas "fairy" and "faggot" referred only to those men "who dressed or behaved in what they considered to be a flamboyantly effeminate manner," *Gay New York*, 15–16. Bill's comment about how his words and feelings might be interpreted in New York seem to indicate an awareness that he would be seen as inverting norms of both gender and sexuality.

This homosexual current flowing through the text reaches its crisis at the same time that the heterosexuality of the text is also at its highest tension: during the liaison that Jake arranges between Brett and Pedro. As we have seen, Jake describes Pedro in terms that repeat his descriptions of Brett. Further, his first impression of the bullfighter is a physical one—"He was the best-looking boy I have ever seen" [121]—and his later observations continue this focus on Pedro's body. Jake tells Brett that Pedro is "nice to look at" [136], notices his clear, smooth, and very brown skin [136], and describes Pedro's hand as being "very fine" and his wrist as being small [137]. Considering the way Jake gazes upon Pedro's body (a body that, like Brett's, blends male and female, masculine and feminine), the moment when Jake brings together Pedro and Brett is also the moment when the text reveals its inability to separate heterosexual from homosexual desire within the desiring body.

This scene has typically been read as the tragic fulfillment of a traditional love triangle in which two men want the same woman and desire moves heterosexually: Jake wants Brett who wants Pedro who wants Brett. Yet given the similarity in the way Jake describes Brett and Pedro, given Jake's homoerotic depictions of the bullfighter's meeting with the bull, and given the sexual ambiguities embodied by Brett and Jake, it seems more accurate to view this relationship not as a triangle but as a web in which desire flows in many directions. When Brett and Pedro consummate their desire for each other, Pedro also becomes Jake's surrogate, fulfilling his desire for Brett and hers for him, while Brett becomes Jake's "extension" for satisfying his infatuation with Pedro. Although Jake is physically and phallically absent from Pedro and Brett's "honeymoon" [140], his desire is multiply and symbolically present. Of course, the inadequacy of a figurative presence is disclosed when Brett persists in telling Jake the details of her relationship with Pedro, a verbal reenactment that drives him to overeat and overdrink.

The final scene of the novel situates Jake between the raised baton of the policeman, an obvious phallic symbol and representative of the Law, and the pressure of Brett's body. Such a situation suggests that the novel does not stop trying to bridge the multiple desires of its characters. However, Brett's wishful statement—"we could have had such a damned good time together"—and Jake's ironic question—"Isn't it pretty to think so?"[180]—reveal that at least part of the failure, part of the "lostness," conveyed in the novel is that such a bridge cannot be built. The prescriptions for masculinity and femininity and for heterosexuality and homosexuality are too strong to be destroyed or evaded, even in a time and place of sexual and gender experimentation.

As my analysis suggests, to explore the fundamental equivalences implied in the dancing club scene and their reverberations throughout

The Sun Also Rises leads to constructing a network of ambiguities and contradictions pertaining to sexuality and gender. As I admitted earlier, in creating such a construction, I have had to draw upon the very concepts that I claim Hemingway's novel calls into question (masculinity/femininity, homosexuality/heterosexuality). But by refusing to qualify or resolve the contradictions surrounding these categories and by focusing attention upon the points at which they conflict, we see that Hemingway's novel puts gender and sexuality into constant motion. Although modern society attempts to stabilize conduct and appearance as masculine or feminine, and desire as homosexual, heterosexual, or bisexual, it is still not easy to contain and categorize desire and behavior. Actions, appearance, and desire in *The Sun Also Rises* spill over the "normal" boundaries of identity and identification so that categories become destabilized and merge with one another.

This is not to say that Brett and Jake have discarded society's scripts for femininity and masculinity, or for heterosexuality and homosexuality, in favor of more contemporary concepts such as transgendered or queer. Their actions, particularly Brett's flirtations and Jake's homophobia, show that they know these scripts well. Nevertheless, as we see by following the several parallels suggested in the club scene, both Jake and Brett continually stray from the lines the scripts demand. The text asks us to suspect, and finally to critique, those systems of representation that are insufficient and hence disabling to efforts to comprehend the human body and its desires.

KINDS OF CAPITAL AND CURRENCY

SCOTT DONALDSON

Hemingway's Morality of Compensation†

> Books should be about the people you know, that you love and hate, not about the people you study up about. If you write them truly they will have all the economic implications a book can hold.[1]
>
> Ernest Hemingway

† From *American Literature* 43.3 (1971): 399–420. Republished by permission of the copyright holder, Duke University Press. Notes are by the author of the original work. Page numbers in brackets refer to this Norton Critical Edition.

1. Quoted in Carlos Baker, *Hemingway: The Writer as Artist* (Princeton, N.J., 1963), p. 197.

I

* * *

Ernest Hemingway, throughout his fiction but especially in *The Sun Also Rises,* * * * expressed his view of compensation in the metaphor of finance—a metaphor which runs through the fabric of his first novel like a fine, essential thread, a thread so fine, indeed, that it has not before been perceived. * * *

It is Jake Barnes who explicitly states the code of Hemingway's "very moral" novel. Lying awake at Pamplona, Jake reflects that in having Brett for a friend, he "had been getting something for nothing" and that sooner or later he would have to pay the bill, which always came:

> I thought I had paid for everything. Not like the woman pays and pays. No idea of retributions or punishment. Just exchange of values. You gave up something and got something else. Or you worked for something. You paid some way for everything that was any good. I paid my way into enough things that I liked, so that I had a good time. Either you paid by learning about them, or by experience, or by taking chances, or by money. Enjoying living was learning to get your money's worth and knowing when you had it. You could get your money's worth. The world was a good place to buy in. [109]

It is understandable that Jake, sexually crippled in the war, should think that he has already paid for everything; and it is an index of his maturity, as a man "fully grown up," that he comes to realize that he may still have debts outstanding, to be paid, most often and most insistently, in francs and pesetas and pounds and dollars.

For Jake's philosophical musing is illustrated time and again in the profuse monetary transactions of *The Sun Also Rises*. On the second page of the novel, one discovers that Robert Cohn has squandered most of the $50,000 that his father, from "one of the richest Jewish families in New York," has left him; on the last page of the book, that Jake has tipped the waiter (the amount is unspecified) who has called a taxi for him and Brett in Madrid [6, 180]. Between the beginning and the end, Hemingway specifically mentions sums of money, and what they have been able to purchase, a total of thirty times. The money dispensed runs up from a franc to a waiter to the fifty francs that Jake leaves for his *poule*, Georgette, at the dancings, to the two hundred francs which Count Mippipopolous gives to Jake's concierge, to the $10,000 the count offers Brett for a weekend in her company. Mostly, though, the monetary amounts are small, and pay for the food, drink, travel, and entertainment that represent the good things in life available to Jake.

Hemingway reveals much more about his characters' financial condition and spending habits than about their appearance: the book would be far more useful to the loan officer of a bank than, say, to the missing person's bureau, which would have little more physical information to go on, with respect to height, weight, hair and eye color, than that Brett had short hair and "was built with curves like the hull of a racing yacht" [18] and that Robert Cohn, with his broken nose, looked as if "perhaps a horse had stepped on his face" [5]. When Hemingway cut 40,000 words out of the first draft of *The Sun Also Rises* but retained these ubiquitous references to the cost of things, he must have kept them for some perceptible and important artistic purpose.

II

In fact, he had several good reasons to note with scrupulous detail the exact nature of financial transactions. Such a practice contributed to the verisimilitude of the novel, denoting the way it was; it fitted nicely with Jake's—and his creator's—obsession with the proper way of doing things; and mainly, it illustrated in action the moral conviction that you must pay for what you get, that you must earn in order to be able to buy, and that only then will it be possible, if you are careful, to buy your money's worth in the world.

In the early 1920's exchange rates in postwar Europe fluctuated wildly. Only the dollar remained stable, to the benefit of the expatriated artists, writers, dilettantes, and party-goers who found they could live for next to nothing in Paris. Malcolm Cowley and his wife lived there the year of 1921 in modest comfort on a grant of $1,000, twelve thousand francs by that year's rate.[1] By the summer of 1924, when Barnes and his companions left for the fiesta at Pamplona, the rate was still more favorable, almost 19 francs to the dollar.[2] And you could get breakfast coffee and a brioche for a franc or less at the cafés where Hemingway, expatriated with the rest, wrote when the weather turned cold.[3] There were even better bargains elsewhere, and the Hemingways, somewhat strapped once Ernest decided to abandon journalism for serious fiction, found one of the best of them in the winter of 1924–1925, at Schruns in the Austrian Voralberg, where food, lodging, snow and skiing for the young writer, his wife, and son came to but $28.50 a week.[4] Europe was overflowing with (mostly temporary) American expatriates, living on the cheap.

1. Malcolm Cowley, *Exile's Return* (New York, 1951), pp. 79–81.
2. For information on the rate of exchange as of June 30, 1924, I am indebted to Murray Weiss, editor of the *International Herald Tribune*.
3. Carlos, Baker, *Hemingway: The Writer as Artist*. (Princeton, N.J, 1963), p. 18.
4. Carlos Baker, *Ernest Hemingway: A Life Story* (New York, 1969), p. 174.

Any novel faithful to that time and that place was going to have to take cognizance of what it cost to live and eat and drink.

Hemingway regarded most of his fellow Americans on the left bank as poseurs pretending to be artists, but "nearly all loafers expending the energy that an artist puts into his creative work in talking about what they are going to do and condemning the work of all artists who have gained any degree of recognition." The tone of moral indignation in this dispatch, one of the first that Hemingway sent the *Toronto Star Weekly* from Paris in 1922, is emphasized by the anecdote he includes about "a big, light-haired woman sitting at a table with three young men." She pays the bill, and the young men laugh whenever she does: "Three years ago she came to Paris with her husband from a little town in Connecticut, where they had lived and he had painted with increasing success for ten years. Last year he went back to America alone."[5]

To the writer, single-minded in his dedication to his craft, the time-wasting of café habitués represented the greatest sin of all. It was the work that counted, and talking about art was hardly a satisfactory substitute. As Jake remarks, setting forth an axiom of Hemingway's creed, "You'll lose it if you talk about it" [178].[6] In the posthumously published *A Moveable Feast*, Hemingway laments having accompanied the hypochondriacal Scott Fitzgerald on an unnecessarily drawnout trip to Lyon. Nursing his traveling companion, he "missed not working and . . . felt the death loneliness that comes at the end of every day that is wasted in your life."[7] Observing the playboys and playgirls of Paris waste their lives on one long hazy binge, Hemingway as foreign correspondent felt much the same disgust that visits Jake after the revels at Pamplona, when he plunges deep into the waters off San Sebastian in an attempt to cleanse himself.

What distinguishes Jake Barnes from Mike and Brett, who at least make no pretenses toward artistic (or any other kind of) endeavor, and from Robert Cohn, a writer who is blocked throughout the novel, is that he works steadily at his regular job as a newspaperman. He is, presumably, unsupported by money from home, and he spends his money, as he eats and drinks, with conspicuous control. Above all, he is thoughtful and conscientious in his spending. Sharing a taxi with two fellow American reporters who also work regularly and well at their jobs but at least one of whom is burdened, as he is not,

5. Baker, *Writer*, p. 6. Charles A. Fenton, *The Apprenticeship of Ernest Hemingway* (New York, 1958), pp. 124–125.
6. Hemingway said much the same thing to Mary Lowry, a fellow reporter on the *Toronto Star*, in the fall of 1923. See Fenton, p. 253.
7. For the full account of the trip to Lyon, see Ernest Hemingway, *A Moveable Feast* (New York, 1964), pp. 128–160.

by "a wife and kids," Jake insists on paying the two-franc fare [29]. He does the right thing, too, by Georgette, the streetwalker he picks up at the Napolitain. Not only does he buy her dinner as a preliminary to the sexual encounter she has bargained for, but upon deserting her for Brett, he leaves fifty francs with the patronne—compensation for her wasted evening—to be delivered to Georgette if she goes home alone. The patronne is supposed to hold the money for Jake if Georgette secures another male customer, but this being France, he will, Brett assures him, lose his fifty francs. "Oh, yes," Jake responds, but he has at least behaved properly [20], and Jake, like his creator, was "always intensely interested in how to do a thing," from tying flies to fighting bulls to compensating a prostitute.[8] Besides, he shares a double kinship with Georgette: she too is sick, a sexual cripple, and she pursues her trade openly and honestly.

The case is different with Lady Ashley, who acquires and casts off her lovers nearly as casually as Georgette, but does so without thought of the consequences to others. There is a certain irony in Brett's telling Jake that it was wrong of him to bring Georgette to the dance, "in restraint of trade" [19]. Surely this is a case of the pot and kettle, for she has arrived in the company of a covey of homosexuals. More to the point, it is women like Brett—and even, to a lesser degree, Cohn's companion Frances Clyne—who provide unfair competition to the streetwalkers of Paris.

After an unsatisfactory time with Brett, Jake Barnes returns to his room, where he immediately goes over his bank statement: "It showed a balance of $2,432.60. I got out my checkbook and deducted four checks drawn since the first of the month, and discovered I had a balance of $1,832.60. I wrote this on the back of the statement" [24]. This is make-work, an attempt to delay thinking about the love for Brett that he cannot consummate. But it is also characteristic of Jake's meticulousness about money. The surprising thing, in fact, is that Jake should have spent as much as $600 in any given month, for he is a man who tries very hard always to get his money's worth. He knows whom to write to secure good bullfight tickets, and he reserves the best rooms in the best hotels at the best price. In Bayonne, he helps Bill buy "a pretty good rod cheap, and two landing-nets," and checks with the tourist-office "to find what we ought to pay for a motor-car to Pamplona": 400 francs [67]. At Burguete, he bargains to have the wine included in the twelve-pesetas-a-day hotel room he and Bill share, and they make certain at dinner that they do "not lose money on the wine" [82]. He is annoyed when Cohn sends a wire of only three words for the price of ten ("I come

8. Fenton, pp. 150–151.

Thursday"), and takes revenge by answering with an even shorter telegram ("Arriving to-night") [95]. After the fiesta, when a driver tries to overcharge Jake for a ride from Bayonne to San Sebastian, he first works the price down from fifty to thirty-five pesetas and then rejects that price too, as "not worth it" [169]. Jake is careful to fulfill his obligations, but he will not be taken advantage of. Once, in church, regretting that he is such a rotten Catholic, he even prays that he will "make a lot of money" [72], but here the verb is important, for he next begins thinking about how he might make the money. He does not pray or even hope to *have* a lot of money, or for it to descend upon him from the trees or the deaths of relatives. Robert Cohn and Mike Campbell remind him, often and painfully, of what inherited money, or the promise of it, can do to undermine a man.

III

Though physically impotent and mentally tortured, Jake Barnes remains morally sound, while Mike Campbell, Robert Cohn, and Brett Ashley, who are physically whole, have become morally decadent. As Baker observes, *The Sun Also Rises* has "a sturdy moral backbone," deriving much of its power from the contrast between Barnes-Gorton-Romero, who constitute the "moral norm" of the book, and the morally aberrant trio of Ashley-Campbell-Cohn.[9] What has not been observed is that money and its uses form the metaphor by which the moral responsibility of Jake, Bill, and Pedro is measured against the carelessness of Brett, Mike, and Robert. Financial soundness mirrors moral strength.

Bill Gorton is the most likable of the crew at the fiesta. Modeled upon the humorist Donald Ogden Stewart, Bill regales Jake with topical gags about Mencken, the Scopes trial, literary fashions, and middle-class mores. An enthusiast, he finds every place he visits equally "wonderful" [51]. The adjective is a private joke between Barnes and Gorton, for Bill knows as well as Jake that when things are really wonderful, it is neither necessary nor desirable to say so. Thus, hiking through the magnificent woods at Burguete, Bill remarks simply, "This is country" [86]. The five days they share at Burguete stand in idyllic contrast to the sickness and drunkenness which characterize both Paris and Pamplona. It is not that Bill and Jake do not drink together on the fishing trip; they drink prodigious quantities of wine. But it is drinking for the pleasure they have earned, both through hard work (in contrast to Cohn, Gorton is a producing writer) and through the rigors of the outdoor life they

9. Baker, *Writer*, pp. 82–83, 92.

choose to pursue on vacation. Furthermore, Bill knows when not to drink. After dinner at Madame Lecomte's and a long walk through Paris, Jake proposes a drink. "No," says Bill. "I don't need it" [57].

* * *

Bill's comic determination to purchase stuffed animals foreshadows Jake's serious reflections on compensation. Passing a Paris taxidermist's, Bill appeals to Jake to buy

> "Just one stuffed dog. I can take 'em or leave 'em alone. But listen, Jake. Just one stuffed dog."
>
> "Come on."
>
> "Mean everything in the world to you after you bought it. Simple exchange of values. You give them money. They give you a stuffed dog." [54]

His affinity for spending money on the ridiculous emerges again at Pamplona, when he buys Mike eleven shoeshines in a row. "Bill's a yell of laughter," Mike says, but Jake, who unlike them has not had much to drink, "felt a little uncomfortable about all this shoeshining" [127]. Still, Bill's expenditures buy amusement for himself and others (including, of course, the reader), and these otherwise merely amusing incidents serve to illustrate the principle of exchange of values: to obtain stuffed dogs, shoeshines, or drinks, you must deliver payment.

IV

Robert Cohn, for whom Gorton conceives an immediate dislike, does not belong with the party at Pamplona. A romantic, he is understandably unable at first to conceive that his weekend with Brett at San Sebastian has meant nothing to her, but he forfeits any claim to sympathy by his subsequent stubborn and violent unwillingness to accept that obvious fact. Terribly insecure, he takes insult after insult from Frances and Mike without retaliation, though he is ready enough, anachronistically, to fight with his "best friend" Jake over what he construes as insults to Brett. A Jew in the company of Gentiles, he is a bore who takes himself—and his illusions—far too seriously. Unlike Jake, he has not "learned about" things. He does not know how to eat or drink or love. It is no wonder that Harold Loeb, unmistakably recognizing himself in Hemingway's portrait of Cohn, "felt as if he had developed an ulcer" and, decades later, attempted to vindicate himself in his autobiography.[1]

1. Baker, *Life*, p. 223. Loeb's autobiography was entitled *The Way It Was* (New York, 1959).

Still, it would be possible to pity Cohn for his dominant malady (is not romantic egotism a less unlovely illness than nymphomania or dipsomania?) were it not for his callous and opportunistic use of the money he has not earned. His allowance ($300 a month, from his mother) comfortably stakes him to his period of expatriation. He has written a novel which has been "accepted by a fairly good publisher," but it is not, clearly, a very good novel, and now the well has run dry. In his idleness, he hangs around Jake's office, disturbing his work, and even proposes to pay Jake's way as his companion on a trip to South America, a continent he invests with an aura of romance [9]. How Hemingway felt about such proposals was later made clear in *A Moveable Feast*, when he reflected, in connection with the trip to Lyon with Fitzgerald, that he "had been a damned fool to accept an invitation for a trip that was to be paid for by someone else."[2] But biographical evidence is hardly necessary to make the point that Cohn, whose money comes to him through no effort of his own but fortuitously because of the accident of his birth, does not understand the proper way of spending it: the point is made implicitly by a number of incidents in *The Sun Also Rises*.

Having inherited a great deal of money, he has wasted nearly all of it on a little magazine—and in maintaining the prestige that came to him as its editor. He is consistently lucky in gambling, but that does him more harm than good. What comes too easily has a pernicious effect on him as a person. While he was in New York to see his publisher, for example, several women had been nice to him as a budding novelist.

> This changed him so that he was not so pleasant to have around. Also, playing for higher stakes than he could afford in some rather steep bridge games with his New York connections he had held cards and won several hundred dollars. It made him rather vain of his bridge game, and he talked several times of how a man could always make a living at bridge if he were ever forced to. [9]

Cohn wins a 100-peseta bet with Gorton that Mike and Brett will not arrive as scheduled at Pamplona, but the bet costs him any possibility of friendship with Bill. Gorton wagers, in fact, only because Cohn's arrogance in parading inside knowledge of Brett's and Mike's habits makes him angry. Furthermore, when the wager has been agreed on, Cohn first does Bill the indignity of asking Jake to remember it, and then, to make amends after he has won, pretends that it really does not matter [70–71].

2. Hemingway, *Feast*, p. 138.

What most damns Cohn, however, is his habit of buying his way out of obligations to women. Frances Clyne, one of the bitchiest women in Hemingway's fiction, reveals this practice of Cohn's in a devastating scene. Flat broke and not so young or attractive as she once was, Frances is being packed off to England so that her paramour may see more of the world—and, he surely hopes, of Lady Ashley:

> "Robert's sending me. He's going to give me two hundred pounds [about a thousand dollars] and then I'm going to visit friends. Won't it be lovely? The friends don't know about it, yet."
>
> She turned to Cohn and smiled at him. He was not smiling now.
>
> "You were only going to give me a hundred pounds, weren't you, Robert? But I made him give me two hundred. You're really very generous. Aren't you, Robert?" [38]

"I do not know," Jake reflects, "how people could say such terrible things to Robert Cohn." But Frances can say them, and get away with it, because they are absolutely true. Cohn, in fact, has disposed of another girl, his "little secretary on the magazine," in just the same way, except cheaper [38]. It is in his attempt to buy his way out of entanglements, without expending anything of himself, that Robert Cohn most viciously breaks the moral code of compensation.

Furthermore, there are suggestions in the book that Cohn is tight-fisted with his money. He has, apparently, tried to bargain with Frances. He directs Jake to buy him a double-tapered fishing line, but says he will pay later instead of now [60]. After unleashing a stream of insults against Cohn ("Don't you know you're not wanted?"), Mike Campbell tells Bill Gorton, who is about to remove Cohn from the slaughter, to stay. "Don't go," Mike said. "Robert Cohn's about to buy a drink." The clear implication is that Robert Cohn rarely buys drinks [105].

Mike, on the other hand, is more than willing to buy drinks, whenever—which means rarely—he has any money. As is true of all the other major characters in the book, Hemingway reveals a good deal about Mike's financial condition and habits. Brett, Jake tells Robert, is going to marry Mike Campbell. "He's going to be rich as hell some day" [30]. Cohn refuses to believe that Brett will marry Mike—and indeed, the matter remains in doubt at the end of the novel—but there is no question about Mike's potential wealth. He is trying, Brett says, to get his mother to pay for her divorce so they can be married. "Michael's people have loads of money" [48]. But for the moment, he makes do on a rather skimpy allowance, and is not even allowed to write checks. When he needs funds, he must "send a wire to the keeper" [60].

Mike Campbell is held under strict financial control for the best of reasons: he is totally irresponsible about money. With his anticipated future wealth serving as a promissory note, he sponges off everyone in sight and simply does not pay his debts. After suffering a business collapse, he has had to resort to bankruptcy, an ungentlemanly if legal way of evading creditors. It is, as Brett realizes when she introduces him, one of the two most important and typical things about the man she intends to marry. The other is that he drinks far too much: "This is Bill Gorton. This drunkard is Mike Campbell. Mr. Campbell is an undischarged bankrupt" [58].

Mike is no more conscientious about settling his debts to friends than to his former business "connections." Yet he possesses a certain self-deprecatory wit, and Bill Gorton, especially, is drawn to him. Bill likes Mike so much, in fact, that is very difficult for him to admit that Mike does not meet his obligations. One night in Pamplona, Mike, Bill, and Bill's girl Edna are thrown out of a bar by the police. "I don't know what happened," Bill says, "but some one had the police called to keep Mike out of the back room. There were some people that had known Mike at Cannes. What's the matter with Mike?" "Probably he owes them money," Jake says. "That's what people usually get bitter about." The next morning, Bill remembers the incident more clearly: "There was a fellow there that had helped pay Brett and Mike out of Cannes, once. He was damned nasty." The night before, Bill had emphatically defended his friend: "They can't say things like that about Mike." But in the light of dawn, he modifies the statement: "Nobody ought to have a right to say things about Mike. . . . They oughtn't to have any right. I wish to hell they didn't have any right" [149, 150]. Bill's own loyalty to Mike finally crumbles when, after the fiesta, another incident makes it clear *why* they have the right.

Jake, Bill, and Mike have hired a car together, and stop at "a very Ritz place" in Biarritz where they roll dice to see who will pay for the drinks. Mike loses three times in a row, but cannot pay for the third round:

> "I'm so sorry," Mike said. "I can't get it."
> "What's the matter?"
> "I've no money," Mike said. "I'm stony. I've just twenty francs. Here, take twenty francs."
> Bill's face sort of changed. [166]

He had had just enough money for his hotel bill in Pamplona, Mike explains, though it turns out that Brett has given him all of her cash to pay his bill. Neither can Mike help pay for their car, and his promise to send Jake what he owes is hardly reassuring.

* * *

Brett shares with Mike a carelessness of personal behavior which stems from a lifetime of having had things done for her. Her room in Madrid, for example, "was in that disorder produced only by those who have always had servants" [176]. She makes appointments and does not keep them. She accepts the generosity of others as if it were her due. The Paris homosexuals, one feels certain, were paying her way. Count Mippipopolous finances her champagne binge. "Come on," she says at Pamplona. "Are these poisonous things paid for?" [107]. In the bar of the Palace Hotel in Madrid, she asks Jake, "*Would* you buy a lady a drink?" [178]. She has been given, she admits, "hell's own amount of credit" on her title [144]. And, of course, she and Mike had jointly run up the bills they could not settle at Cannes. Moreover, she satisfies her demanding sexual appetites at the expense of others, effectively turning Robert into a steer, Mike into a swine, and Jake into a pimp. She is clearly not what Madame Duzinell, Jake's concierge, calls her after the bribe of 200 francs from the count, "très, très gentille" [40].

Oddly, though, Brett observes a strict code in connection with her sexual activity. She will not accept money for her favors. Thus she rejects the count's offer of "ten thousand dollars to go to Biarritz [or Cannes, or Monte Carlo] with him" [26]. She pays Mike's way, not vice versa, out of the Hotel Montoya. Though Romero pays the hotel bill in Madrid, she will take nothing else from him. "He tried to give me a lot of money, you know. I told him I had scads of it. He knew that was a lie. I couldn't take his money, you know" [176]. In sending Romero away, against the urgings of the flesh, she has done the right thing at the cost of real personal anguish. She will be neither a whore nor "one of those bitches that ruins children" [177].

Furthermore, Brett's apparent nymphomania can be at least partly excused by the unhappy circumstances of her past life. She has lost one man she loved in the war, and married another ("Ashley, chap she got the title from") who has returned quite mad from serving as a sailor. "When he came home," Mike explains, "he wouldn't sleep in a bed. Always made Brett sleep on the floor. Finally, when he got really bad, he used to tell her he'd kill her. Always slept with a loaded service revolver. Brett used to take the shells out when he'd gone to sleep. She hasn't had an absolutely happy life" [149]. Like Jake, she still suffers from war wounds. Like him, too, she articulates her awareness of the law of compensation. If she has put chaps through hell, she's paying for it all now. "Don't we pay for all the things we do, though?" [21].

Brett's case is far more ambiguous than that of Robert Cohn or Mike Campbell. If she recklessly imposes nearly insupportable burdens on others, she carries an even heavier burden herself. Morally, she is neither angel nor devil, but somewhere, rather fascinatingly, in between. It is almost as if Hemingway himself were alternately attracted to and repelled by Brett. In Carlos Baker's biography there is a strong implication that Hemingway either had, or wanted to have, an affair with Duff Twysden, the prototype for Brett. In the fall of 1925, Duff sent Hemingway a note asking for a loan: "Ernest my dear, forgive me for this effort but can you possibly lend me some money? I am in a stinking fix but for once only temporary and can pay you back for *sure*. I want 3,000 francs—but for Gods sake lend me as much as you can."[3] In the novel, as if to protect Duff, Hemingway transfers her behavior to Mike Campbell: it is he and not Brett who asks, repeatedly, for loans.

V

Hemingway's insistence on the need to earn, and to pay for, what you get is in no way a statement in support of materialism, for it is accompanied by disgust with the crooked and corrupting values of the commercial world. Eager to line their pockets, the merchants of Pamplona double prices during the fiesta [113]. Away go the café's marble-topped tables and comfortable white wicker chairs, to be replaced by cast-iron tables and severe folding chairs: "The café was like a battleship stripped for action." The warship's objective, of course, is to relieve peasants and tourists alike of their cash. At the start of the fiesta, the peasants confine their drinking to the outlying shops, where wine sells for 30 centimes a liter. "They had come in so recently from the plains and the hills that it was necessary that they make their shifting in values gradually. . . . Money still had a definite value in hours worked and bushels of grain sold. Late in the fiesta it would not matter what they paid, nor where they bought." When the peasants reach the stage of heedlessness (epitomized by the futile death of one of them during the running of the bulls), they will have lost any sense of the dignity of labor, of hours worked and bushels sold [113].

The cancer of commercialism also threatens to infect bullfighting. Romero is forced to face a dangerously bad bull, who cannot see well the lure of the cape, because the promoters have paid for the bull and "don't want to lose their money" [159]. The crowd sends a volley of cushions, bread, and vegetables into the ring where Belmonte, ill and more cautious than he once had been, is performing his art. "Belmonte was very good. But because he got thirty thousand pesetas and people had stayed in line all night to buy tickets to see him, the crowd demanded that he should be more than very good." His greatness had been "discounted and sold in advance," and nothing he could do would satisfy those who watched him do it [156, 158].

3. Baker, *Life*, p. 196.

Montoya, an *aficionado* who represents bullfighting's conscience, puts up all the good toreros at his hotel, and keeps in his room framed photographs of the bullfighters he "really believed in." The pictures of the commercial bullfighters, though, are consigned first to a desk drawer and then to the waste basket [97]. Montoya welcomes Jake, a fellow *aficionado*, and is grateful for his advice not to deliver to Romero his invitation from the American ambassador. "People take a boy like that," the hotel-keeper explains. "They don't know what he's worth. . . . They start this Grand Hotel business, and in one year they're through" [127]. Montoya is even inclined to forgive Jake his friends, but that tolerance dissolves when he sees "Pedro Romero with a big glass of cognac in his hand, sitting laughing between me [Jake] and a woman with bare shoulders, at a table full of drunks. He did not even nod" [130]. When Jake and his companions check out, Montoya does "not come near" them [160].

Romero, however, remains immune to the disease of commercialism—and the caution unto cowardice it is likely to breed. He wants and expects to make money as a bullfighter: when Brett reads in his hand that there are thousands of bulls in his future, "Good," he replies, and in an aside to Jake in Spanish, "At a thousand duros apiece." But he has not yet begun to compromise his bullfighting, as Belmonte has, by insisting on manageable bulls with smallish horns [158]. And Hemingway invokes the metaphor of profit and loss in comparing Pedro's afternoon of triumph to the jeers that had greeted Belmonte: "Pedro Romero had the greatness. He loved bull-fighting, and I think he loved the bulls, and I think he loved Brett. Everything of which he could control the locality he did in front of her all that afternoon. . . . But he did not do it for her at any loss to himself. He gained by it all through the afternoon" [158]. His willingness to take chances, one of the ways, as Jake has reflected, in which you could pay "for everything that was any good," gives the bullfight, his relationship with Brett, and the fiesta itself a kind of dignity.

It hardly matters that "the Biarritz crowd" does not appreciate what he has accomplished, with either his bad bull or his good one [159–60]. Hemingway obviously regards the rich English and American tourists from Biarritz, come for one day of the quaint fiesta at Pamplona, with undisguised scorn. Those who buy false wares, like the secretly manipulated boxer toys hawked on the streets of Paris, deserve no more than they get [28].

The depth of this contempt can be measured against the sympathetic portrayal of Wilson-Harris, the Englishman who fishes and plays three-handed bridge with Jake and Bill at Burguete. When his companions must leave, Harris (as the Americans call him) insists on buying them a bottle of wine apiece. The atmosphere is one of warm camaraderie, punctuated by Harris's regret that Bill and Jake must leave. As they board the bus for Pamplona, Harris presses still another gift upon each of them: a dozen flies that he has tied himself. "They're not first-rate flies at all," he insists. "I only thought if you fished them some time it might remind you of what a good time we had." It has been a good time indeed, so that Jake first wishes Harris were coming along to Pamplona but then reflects that "You couldn't tell how English would mix with each other, anyway" [96]. But you can tell: a man who spends his holiday trout fishing in the Pyrenees and who behaves so generously would not have mixed at all well with the perpetually carousing crew at the fiesta.

* * *

A teacher in Oak Park, Illinois, an upper-middle-class suburb noted for nothing so much as its respectability, once wondered "how a boy brought up in Christian and Puritan nurture should know and write so well of the devil and the underworld."[4] But Ernest Hemingway carried with him always an inheritance from the community where he grew up, a faith in the efficacy and staying power of certain moral values. Strongest among these was the axiom that you had to earn your happiness, though the price might come exceedingly high, with its corollary that easy money could ruin a man. In his first novel, Hemingway imposed this standard on the expatriate world of the early 1920's. At the end of the last book he wrote, looking back on those years as an idyl when he had worked hard and loved well and taken nothing without making full payment, his nostalgia found expression in the same metaphor which runs through *The Sun Also Rises:* "Paris was always worth it and you received return for whatever you brought to it. But this is how it was in the early days when we were very poor and very happy."[5]

MARC D. BALDWIN

"To Make It into a Novel . . . Don't Talk About It": Hemingway's Political Unconscious†

The vanguard of contemporary social criticism agrees with Georg Lukacs that the "truly social element of literature is the form."[1]

4. Fenton, p. 2.
5. Hemingway, *Feast*, p. 192.

† From *The Journal of Narrative Theory* (formerly *Journal of Narrative Technique*) 23.3 (Fall 1993): 170–87. Reprinted by permission of the publisher. Notes are by the author of the original work. Page numbers in brackets refer to this Norton Critical Edition.

1. Quoted in Terry Eagleton, *Marxism and Literary Criticism*, 20.

Frank Lentricchia argues that the "literary act is a social act" (19). Rosalind Coward and John Ellis observe that "Language at any historical moment is riddled with styles, rhetorics, 'ways of speaking' which impose a specific social position, a definite view of the world. These ideological discourses are the product of the articulation of ideology in language" (79). Terry Eagleton insists that the "true bearers of ideology in art are the very forms, rather than the abstractable content" (*Marxism* 24). Catherine Belsey asserts that the critic, by "analyzing the discourses which are its raw material and the process of production which makes it a text, recognizes in the text not 'knowledge' but ideology itself in all its inconsistency and partiality" (128). Or, as Fredric Jameson puts it, "formal realizations, as well as formal defects, are taken as the signs of some deeper corresponding social and historical configuration which it is the task of criticism to explore" (*Marxism* 331).

Ernest Hemingway once said that his challenge in writing *The Sun Also Rises*[2] was "to make it into a novel" (*Feast* 202). For Hemingway, "make" connotes the distinctively material and socially conscious work of a professional journalist/artist. He "made" (read *dominated* or *forced*) his material into an acceptable artistic form by appropriating such strategies as suggestion and omission expressly to obscure his political content. Since these methods are not only literary but comprise the behavioral "code" of the narrator, they act as a governor upon Jake's way of seeing and saying the world. That is, having decided to be suggestive, impressionistic, repressive, ironic, and apolitical, Jake will not—and, at times, perhaps, cannot—give utterance to a wide variety of potential thoughts or conclusions. For example, at various times in the story Jake battles with himself, Brett, Cohn, Bill, and Montoya over his code of silence, over not talking about certain things. This en/forced repression stymies both communication and understanding. Such an ideologically informed restriction upon expression constitutes the text's "problematic," which Louis Althusser defines as "the particular unity of a theoretical formation . . . an ideological field . . . a determinate unitary structure" (*Marx* 32, 66, 67) that governs what is said and not-said. Jameson ratifies Althusser's conception, agreeing that the problematic "'determines' the thinking done . . . in the sense in which it serves as an ultimate limitation on thought" (*Language* 135). In *The Political Unconscious: Narrative as a Socially Symbolic Act,* Jameson develops the notion that narrative itself is, as his subtitle implies, a mechanism employed by the collective consciousness to repress historical contradictions. In fact, through its unified, ideologically informed, determinate structure, Jake's "problematic" narrative

2. Hereafter referred to as *SAR*.

method represses the text's production. Hemingway's celebrated techniques are the formal means that not only transform the raw materials of experience into politically palatable art but also expose the contradictions within the very society that produced them.

* * * Hemingway's impressionistic techniques[3] serve to suggest and evoke the obverse of their shiny face, reflecting the clashing contradictions within his method and ideology: from a distance (on the surface) all seems reliable, objective, equal, and harmonious; yet the close-up view (beneath the surface) reveals an unreliable, subjective, unequal, and clashing "reality." Tony Tanner calls this surface *democratic* side of Hemingway's practice "his faith" (152). Curiously, any *faith*, as modern epistemology holds and as Hemingway's (and Jake's) own stance on belief structures implies, is definitively subjective and subject to refutation, contradiction, and disavowal. Hemingway does have a *faith* in the "operating senses," but that faith does not occlude the obverse belief that one's senses have been known to deceive. Even as Jake has philosophies "now" that he knows will seem "silly" five years from "now" [109], even as he admits that he has "not shown Robert Cohn clearly" [35], and even as he describes Brett's way "of looking that made you wonder whether she really saw out of her own eyes" [21], he is the scene of the clash between one's subjective impressions and both the re/presentation of those impressions and the variant impressions of other eyes and minds. Thus, perhaps *colorist* is a better term for Jake's selective way of seeing and recording his impressions: although an impressionist who sees reality as necessarily fragmented, Jake's psychological biases indelibly highlight what he wants us to see, and blur what he does not want us to see.

Frederick R. Karl argues that impressionism

> made a strong political and social statement. It brought down large events to forms of language. . . . Seemingly so harmless, . . . [it] was a devastating attack on realistic values. Its breakdown of formal scene into areas of color patterns expressed social and political breakdown and, at the same time, challenged realistic versions of that dissolution of social forms. (110)

Hemingway did appear to create "realistic" landscapes, attempting, as Emily Stipes Watts argues, "to describe a landscape so that any reader or viewer might recognize it, . . . [yet he] abstracted, that [is,] his landscapes are carefully contrived rather than wholly real" (38). He made the land as he made the novel, by separating the assembled objects in space and re/forming them with deliberate attention to the forms themselves, foregrounding the artistic devices.

3. For discussions of Hemingway and impressionism see James Nagel, 17–26; and Emily Stipes Watts.

With his geometrical forms and his careful delineation of even distant objects, Hemingway "asserted the existence or presence of form and organization in nature." These forms suggest a permanence in nature which is "unrelated to man" (Watts 40–41). Watts comments on the "metaphysical" significance of the enduring, orderly, solid land" (47) yet ignores the material significance implied by the absence of its counterpart, civilization. James Nagel ventures further into the material with his conclusion that Hemingway's impressionistic scenes, "by implication, express something of the empirical and metaphysical condition of mankind, one devoid of sympathy, benevolence, justice, a condition Hemingway was about to suggest was the very nature of modern life" (22). One wonders *why* "modern life" is "devoid" of such things. Although he may perhaps be overstating the case, attributing a conscious political motive to impressionism, Karl argues that "the impressionists had discovered nothing less than a language more significant than matter. Each painter in his own way was transforming 'content' (state, ideologies, politics, social thought) into intangibles such as light, shade, color, ambivalent forms that blurred representation"(107). Ernst Fischer also perceives political forces at work in impressionism:

> dissolving the world in light, breaking it up into colours, recording it as a sequence of sensory perceptions, became more and more the expression of a very complex, very short-term subject-object relationship. The individual, reduced to loneliness, concentrating upon himself, experiences the world as a set of nerve stimuli, impressions, moods, as a 'shimmering chaos,' as 'my' experience, 'my' sensation. (75)

The following passage almost eerily exemplifies what both Karl and Fischer have described as a writer's (Jake's) appropriation of impressionism to transform political and social content into light, color, and nerve stimuli. Jake is one lonely man "concentrating upon himself":

> Two taxis were coming down the steep street. They both stopped in front of the Bal. A crowd of young men, some in jerseys and some in their shirt sleeves, got out. I could see their hands and newly washed, wavy hair in the light from the door. The policeman standing by the door looked at me and smiled. They came in. As they went in, under the light I saw white hands, wavy hair, white faces, grimacing, gesturing, talking. With them was Brett. She looked very lovely and she was very much with them. [17]

As Jake describes the "crowd of young men," he prefaces his observations with "I could see. . . ." Clearly, as Fischer formulates social impressionism, Jake's is an "expression of a very complex, very short-term subject-object relationship." What he sees—or what he chooses to see—are disembodied fragments of people, "hands and newly washed, wavy hair in the light from the door." Jake is the subject and the "young men" are the objects in this "complex . . . short-term . . . relationship." Jake is "dissolving the world in light, breaking it up into colours, recording it as a sequence of sensory perceptions. . . ." Note that although "the light from the door" was insufficient to see the colors of the hands and the hair, Jake and the policeman can already tell that these young men are of a different social and sexual sphere. Although Jake, too, has been fragmented (having lost his sexual ability in the war), by all appearances he is "normal," so the policeman (symbol of state authority) smiles at him, a non-verbal sign of their common bond.

"As they went in, under the light I saw white hands, wavy hair, white faces. . . ." The light, according to Jake, has been shed upon this procession of the self-pampered, effeminate Others who have invaded his society, his circle. With their "white hands, wavy hair, white faces" signifying their unmanly attitude, Jake thoroughly dehumanizes "them" by compartmentalizing their behavior into "grimacing, gesturing, talking." This "crowd of young men" is a group of homosexuals, another form of "they," the significant Others who represent the changing face of society and politics.

"With them was Brett." Only after both taxis have emptied, after the "crowd" has disembarked and passed by him, after he has dissected "them" into white body parts under the light, does Jake mention that Brett is with them. Was she trailing the crowd and he didn't notice her until now? Not likely. Rather, ever the colorist, Jake sketches the parts before the whole. Paradoxically, however, he does not fragment Brett, even though she is one of the fragmented and decadent ones: "She looked very lovely. . . ." Her entire body remains intact "and she was very much with them." "Very much" carries an enormous emotional weight, suggesting that Brett has betrayed a confidence or a trust, that she has defected to the other side, so to speak. The juxtaposition (as a painter brushes blue and yellow strokes side by side to suggest green) of Jake, the "young men," and Brett, implies a breakdown in social and sexual politics. This decomposition of elements into a newly suggested whole continues when "One of them saw Georgette and said: 'I do declare. There is an actual harlot.'" Georgette *is* an "actual harlot," whom Jake picked up out of loneliness. "One of them" characterizing Georgette as an "actual harlot" in combination with Brett being "very much with them," suggests that Jake's beloved is no model of virtue. "Somehow they always made me angry," continues Jake. ". . . [Brett] had been taken up by them. I knew then that they would all dance with her. They are like that" [17].

* * *

The cumulative effect of this impressionistic breaking down and fragmenting, this reduction and repetition of expression, is to transform individuals into abstractions or mere things. Lukacs refers to this process by which the socio-economic system breaks a whole (whether an individual or the production and distribution system) down into ever smaller and more manageable units, as reification. Jameson warns that this reification of workers has become, in some quarters, a mode of experiencing the world. Jake's fragmenting the gays into body parts and reassembling them into a "crowd" of "they" and "them" is certainly a reifying mode of experiencing *his* world. Jake's penchant for separating and compartmentalizing, for agglutinating and generalizing, leads me to suspect Hemingway of creating a character who commits what he (Hemingway himself) has declared to be a cardinal sin of politicians: the use of abstractions to further self-serving causes and promote his own world view.

* * *

As material society, "they" (the other, the absent cause of History, the hegemonic forces of economics and politics) clash with Jake's ideal culture of "us" and toreo (bullfighting). Through this process of foregrounding the concentric rings of the fiesta (within the walled city) and the bullring and their attendant "circle" of humanity (aficionados such as "us"), Jake embraces a new idealism, a condition where culture and humanity are supposedly split from their material history. This separation both distances Jake from and ties him to his own ideology: he would renounce and expose abstractions, seemingly seeking the concrete, yet he promotes in "they," "us," and toreo three highly codified and linguistically constructed master abstractions that are, as literary abstractions tend to be, "actively ideological."[4] Like the outer society Jake ostensibly abhors and rejects, both "us" and toreo thrive on the violent domination and effacement of their origins—obscuring the historical past—and opposition by "them." Furthermore, Jake's obsessive notation throughout *SAR* of cash transactions and monetary value makes it abundantly clear that both "us" and toreo depend upon economic considerations for their transformation from abstractions into concrete material existence.

Marx argues that all seemingly concrete "populations," or any "living whole," are abstractions and cannot be accurately represented until evaluated according to their relationship to the basic categories "such as division of labour, money, value . . ." (188). In fact, according to Jameson, "the emergence of the economic . . . is simply

4. See Raymond Williams, 45.

the sign of the approach of the concrete" (*Marxism* 322). This entire process of production and consumption is *overdetermined*,[5] for the economic cause relies upon the cultural effect to cover its paper trail. Similar to Romero, who conceals his devices, and Jake who omits his motivations, toreo and "us" exist in their ritualized and glorified forms in order to suppress the real reason for their necessity: profit for their promoters. Like the larger system that they replicate and reproduce, even as they are advertised as pristine alternatives, both "us" and toreo determine and hail their aficionados largely in terms of money. Thus, Jake's beloved abstractions are a method of laundering the spoils of dominance: by abstracting group characteristics, Jake washes them clean of all but a trace of their historical origins.

Terry Eagleton posits that through this process of literary abstraction,

> as history is distantiated, becoming, so to speak, more 'abstract,' the signifying process assumes greater dominance, becoming more 'concrete.' The literary work appears free-producing and self-determining—because it is unconstrained by the necessity to produce any particular 'real'; but this freedom simply conceals its more fundamental determination by the constituents of its matrix (*Ideology* 74).

The literary method of abstraction, by "distantiating" the history of its figures, acts, in effect, as an apparatus of ideology. By extension, then, Hemingway's ultimate "distantiation" of history—by which his "signifying process assumes greater dominance"—is his abstraction of time into an absolute, ever-present, perpetual now.

Many critics claim that Hemingway writes in the "perpetual now," or what Ihab Hassan calls "the huge and abrupt present" (90). * * *

I define this narrative mode of the perpetual present as that realm between consciousness and the raw material of experience, where the intensity of the moment seems to hold time in suspended animation. As a reporter, Jake observes both his surroundings and his reaction to them, seemingly capable of measuring the distance and difference between this "now" and yesterday and tomorrow. He should, in other words, be able to perceive historical change. Thoroughly ahistorical, the perpetual now depends upon both the Catholic Church's advice "not to think about it" [25] and what is ostensibly Jake's own policy, not to talk about it. Thinking and talking about experience cobbles consciousness with experience and jettisons the individual out of the perpetual present into the stream of time. The

5. Overdetermination, a concept which Althusser borrowed from psychoanalysis, stresses the interrelationship among the economic, ideological, cultural, and political elements of society. None is dominant; they all influence one another.

very process of internalizing experience, of saying what you feel, shatters the safe illusion of now-and-forever that ideology would perpetuate. Ideology needs its subjects to reside in the perpetual now.

We need look no further than George Orwell and Aldous Huxley for these themes: they who obliterate the past control the present, so long as the present that they provide is full of immediate sensual pleasures. Orwell's Big Brother allows their proles "films, football, beer, and, above all, gambling" (61–62); Huxley's Ford provides the people with "Solidarity Service . . . a circular rite" (53, 55), soma, and sex. In *SAR*, the people enjoy bullfighting, drinking, and sex. Football, the Solidarity Service, and bullfighting are all rituals played out in a ring of community involvement. The intoxicants, sex, and gambling are common pleasures, repetitive sedatives to please and numb, illusions of reality.

Richard Lehan calls this realistic element of Hemingway's style "a way of seeing" (210). In explicating the following passage—on the bus ride to Pamplona Jake and Bill are observing the scenery while Cohn sleeps—Lehan points out that many of the nouns are immediately modified by descriptions:

> there was a big river off on the right shining in the sun from between the lines of trees, and away off you could see the plateau of Pamplona rising out of the plain, and the walls of the city, and the great brown cathedral, and the broken skyline of the other churches. . . . We passed the bull ring, high and white and concrete-looking in the sun. . . . There was a crowd of kids watching the car, and the square was hot, and the trees were green, and the flags hung on their staffs, and it was good to get out of the sun and under the shade of the arcade that runs all the way around the square. [70]

Lehan notices that Jake first records "the thing and then the response to the thing," concluding that "it is impossible to think abstractly in this language; one is rooted to the concrete, to the elemental, to the here and now . . ." (210). Lehan does not note, however, that although this passage appears photographic, with little overt subjective description, Jake's selection of details speaks silent volumes: the city (civilization) rises over the plains (nature); civilization is walled and its "skyline" (horizons) are dominated by churches, those apparatuses of the state which advise Jake (the wounded victim) "not to think about it [his wound]"; the abstract ritual of toreo is performed in a "concrete-looking" bullring; children form an admiring "crowd"; flags, more abstract symbols of the state, "hung on their staffs." The city, the churches, the bullring, the children, and the flags are all productions of humanity that, in turn, reproduce the state. Jake may be physically in the "now" but his "way of seeing," as Lehan puts it, is historically informed and acutely categorical and hierarchical. The town dominates nature and dominating the town are the church, the state, and their centralizing ritual, the bullring. Furthermore, with the democratic power of parataxis, every "and" attributes equal importance to the town and its churches and the crowd of kids and the square and the trees and the flags. Humanity, its walled town, nature, the church, and the state are all represented as equals. The bullring, however, is accorded its own sentence. No "and" links toreo, the central abstraction, with anything else. The bullring stands in the center of the town and serves as the center of the fiesta, itself "the creator of time," says Octavio Paz, "the absolute present, endlessly re-creating itself" (210–11).

* * *

In *Anatomy of Criticism*, Northrup Frye attributes the emergence of the modern novel and its obsession with alienation, disintegration, and decay to the historical mode of irony. Maurice Beebe contends that "Modernism is characterized by an attitude of detachment and non-commitment which I would put under the general heading of 'irony'" (1073). According to Lukacs in *The Theory of the Novel*, the form of the modern novel is ironic because the artist reflects the disparity between material reality and the ideal world that God gave up on. Although Frye, Beebe, and Lukacs were not referring to Hemingway, their broad formulations certainly could be applied to *SAR*. E. M. Halliday *is* referring specifically to Hemingway when he calls this disparity between the ideal and the real "the ironic gap between expectation and fulfillment, pretense and fact, intention and action, the message sent and the message received, the way things are thought or ought to be and the way things are" (15).[6]

In *SAR*, irony operates "as resistances to the oppression of material and historical forces, as safeguards of inner freedom . . ." (Ahearn 27). Through irony, Jake is able to distance himself from the pain of his wound, able to conceal his suffering from the world. At once a

6. Such "unresolved ambiguities," says Earl Rovit, are produced by Hemingway's "use of irony and the withholding of explanatory information." He further notes that irony "work[s] to hold the reader at bay in the same way that Jake establishes a measured distance between himself and Brett." Concluding that Hemingway uses irony (and the iceberg principle) as "strategic devices that exclude the reader," Rovit wonders "why Hemingway would come to harbour such powerful, if somewhat concealed attitudes of defensive hostility . . . [and] why we would [as] a culture of supposedly democratic ideals and aspirations embrace . . ." such a vision (184). In identifying irony as a strategy of excluding and distancing Others, Rovit is flirting with marxist criticism. To his credit, Rovit later offers class consciousness as a possible reason for Hemingway's "defensive hostility," but as I have noted, like most Western critics he simply cannot bring himself to accuse capitalism itself—the brains, bankers, and bodyguards behind those "democratic ideals and aspirations"—of any crimes.

strategy of containment and a rejection of idealism, irony announces the silent engagement of the artist with ideology. Hayden White best explains its relevance:

> Irony thus represents a stage of consciousness in which the problematical nature of language itself has become recognized. . . . [It] provides a linguistic paradigm of a mode of thought which is radically self-critical with respect not only to a given characterization of the world of experience but also to the very effort to capture adequately the truth of things in language. It is, in short, a model of the linguistic protocol in which skepticism in thought and relativism in ethics are conventionally expressed. (37–38)

This "linguistic protocol" sounds a great deal like Hemingway's professional demeanor of artistic "purity." As a front to maintain his apolitical facade, irony effectively taxonomizes any and all material 'not-saids' under the ideal rubric "skepticism in thought." A work of art may be skeptical, as long as it is not specific about the nature of its skepticism. An artist's hands should not be soiled, as it were, by subjects such as "that dirty war." An artist, by implicit fiat, cannot overtly indict the state, but he can express through irony the pervasive "relativism of ethics" inherent within the affairs of capitalism.

Suckled on the expansionist fervor of America's rise to world economic power at the turn of the twentieth century, William James' and Charles Sanders Pierce's pragmatism bestowed upon capitalism the sanctifying sanction of a high-minded philosophy. Pragmatism posits that ethics are relative to conditions and that if something works, it is right and good. If ever a system gave birth to a philosophy that in turn became its apologist, this was it. And the trope mediating the contractual arrangements between capitalism and pragmatism was/is Irony with a capital "I." Irony operates like money, the motivating force behind the pragmatic rationalization of capitalism: they are both forms of value that disguise the nature of their production. As money hides the labor of specific historical individuals, Irony is Hemingway's linguistic currency, his means of exchanging his knowledge and opinions (earned by his specific life's labor) for the shiny coins (such as "wonderful," "nice," "I suppose it was funny," and "Isn't it pretty to think so?") more readily accepted by the general public. The majority of the population will not pay much money for journalism, for ideas contrary to their received notions. A little knowledge might jeopardize their apathy and passivity, and thus their ostensibly safe and secure position within society. Hemingway knew that and since he wanted to be known as a writer of novels (which would sell) he concealed in irony (and in the other devices), as does money itself, the labor that went into the production of his currency, his work. Effectively homogenized, he avoided classification as a political writer and remained a "purely" commercial artist, bankable, and thus publishable (read bankrollable).

In *SAR*, Hemingway created an ironic commercial masterpiece: the narrator, wounded/sterilized in a war waged by the same profiteering class for whom he now writes/works, loves but cannot reproduce with a woman who is so psychically wounded by the war that she too cannot attain sexual/reproductive satisfaction. As the pragmatic system has taught (by its thoroughly economic and political war), ethics are relative, so intercourse, sexual or otherwise, becomes just another self-serving proposition, whereby if boyfriends are bankrupt (either sexually as is Jake or financially as is Mike) what's a poor liberated woman to do but deal with a man who has money (Cohn) or tight pants (Romero)? The ultimate irony in *SAR*, as Marx and Hegel taught and as White so succinctly restates, is that society is "the instrument of man's liberation from nature and the cause of man's estrangement from one another. Society both unified and divided, liberated and oppressed, at one and the same time" (282).

WORKS CITED

Ahearn, Edward J. *Marx and Modern Fiction*. New Haven: Yale University Press, 1989.

Althusser, Louis. *For Marx*. Trans. Ben Brewster. London: Allen Lane, Penguin Press, 1969.

———. "Ideology and Ideological State Apparatuses." *Critical Theory Since 1965*. Eds. Hazard Adams and Leroy Searle. Tallahassee: Florida State University Press, 1986: 239–251.

Baudrillard, Jean. *The Mirror of Production*. Trans. Mark Poster. St. Louis: Telos Press, 1975.

Beebe, Maurice. "What Modernism Was." *Journal of Modern Literature* 3 (July 1974).

Belsey, Catherine. *Critical Practice*. London: Methuen, 1980.

Coward, Rosalind and John Ellis. *Language and Materialism*. London: Routledge & Kegan Paul, 1977.

Eagleton, Terry. *Criticism and Ideology*. London: Verso, 1978.

———. *Marxism and Literary Criticism*. Berkeley: University of California Press, 1976.

Fischer, Ernst. *The Necessity of Art*. New York: Penguin Books, 1959.

Halliday, E. M. "Hemingway's Ambiguity: Symbolism and Irony." *American Literature* 28 (1956).

Hemingway, Ernest. *A Moveable Feast*. New York: Charles Scribner's Sons, 1964.

———. *The Sun Also Rises*. New York: Charles Scribner's Sons, 1926.

Huxley, Aldous. *Brave New World*. New York: Harper Row, 1932.

Jameson, Fredric. *Marxism & Form*. Princeton, NJ: Princeton University Press, 1971.

———. *The Prison-House of Language*. Princeton: Princeton University Press, 1972.

Karl, Frederick R. *Modern and Modernism: The Sovereignty of the Artist 1885–1925*. New York: Atheneum, 1985.

Lehan, Richard. "Hemingway Among the Moderns." *Hemingway: In Our Time*. Ed. Richard Astro and Jackson J. Benson. Corvallis: Oregon State University Press, 1974.

Lentricchia, Frank. *Criticism and Social Change*. Chicago: University of Chicago Press, 1983.

Lukacs, Georg. *History & Class Consciousness*. Trans. Rodney Livingstone. Cambridge, MA: MIT Press, 1968.

Marx, Karl. *The Grundrisse*. Ed. David McLellan. New York: Harper Torchbooks, 1971.

Nagel, James. "Literary Impressionism." *Hemingway Review* (Spring 87): 17–26.

Orwell, George. *1984*. New York: Harcourt Brace Jovanovich, 1949.

Paz, Octavio. *The Labyrinth of Solitude*. Trans. Lysander Kemp. New York: Grove, 1961.

Rovit, Earl. "On Psychic Retrenchment in Hemingway." *Hemingway: Essays of Reassessment*. Ed. Frank Scafella. New York: Oxford University Press, 1991.

Tanner, Tony. "Ernest Hemingway's Unhurried Sensations." *Ernest Hemingway: A Study of the Short Fiction*. Ed. J. M. Flora. Boston: Twayne, 1989.

Wagner-Martin, Linda. "*The Sun Also Rises*: One Debt to Imagism." *Modern Critical Interpretations of* The Sun Also Rises. Ed. Harold Bloom. New York: Chelsea House Publishers, 1987.

Watts, Emily Stipes. *Ernest Hemingway & the Arts*. Chicago: University of Illinois Press, 1971.

White, Hayden. *Metahistory*. Baltimore: Johns Hopkins University Press, 1973.

Williams, Raymond. *Marxism and Literature*. Oxford: Oxford University Press, 1977.

Nativism, Antisemitism, and Race

WALTER BENN MICHAELS

From Our America: Nativism, Modernism, and Pluralism†

* * * Hemingway's Robert Cohn * * * says in *The Sun Also Rises* that Lady Ashley has "breeding" [30]. Jake Barnes says in response to Cohn that she is "very nice." "Breeding" is the term used by people who don't really have any; "nice" is the term used by people who do.

Cohn thinks that Brett has "a certain quality, a certain fineness"; "nice" is deployed by Hemingway against descriptions like that and, more generally, against the "abstract words" famously condemned in *A Farewell to Arms* (1929). "There were many words that you could not stand to hear," Hemingway writes, "and finally only the names of places had dignity."[1] "Nice" isn't the name of a place, but it is a name for people who come from a place as opposed to, say, Gatsby who—despite the family history designed to show that he is not "just some nobody"—really is "Mr. Nobody from Nowhere" (130).[2] Removing Fitzgerald's quotation marks, Hemingway installs "nice"—along with words like "good" and "true"—at the heart of a prose style that no longer needs the explicit vocabulary of race (e.g., "Nordic") to distinguish those who have breeding from those who don't, in the way that, say, Jake's concierge distinguishes between visitors who are not to be allowed up and visitors like Brett, who is "very nice," which is to say, "très, très gentille," which is to say, "of very good family" [40]. "Nice" has its pedigree; indeed, pedigree is its pedigree. As a character in Fitzgerald's *The Beautiful and Damned* (1922) puts it, "if a person comes from a good family, they're always nice people.[3]

Robert Cohn, not a very good writer, doesn't "know how to describe" [30] the "quality" that Jake Barnes so easily finds a word for.

† From *Our America: Nativism, Modernism, and Pluralism* (Durham: Duke University Press, 1995), pp. 26–29, 72–74, 150–51, 163–64. Notes are by the author of the original work. Some notes have been omitted. Page numbers in brackets refer to this Norton Critical Edition.

1. Ernest Hemingway. *A Farewell to Arms* (New York, 1969), 185.
2. The contrast with Nick, "growing up in the Carraway house in a city where dwellings are still called through decades by a family's name" (177), is especially sharp.
3. F. Scott Fitzgerald, *The Beautiful and Damned* (New York, 1950), 408.

To be nice—even better, to be able to *say* nice—is to identify yourself as neither Gatsby nor Cohn; the social point of Hemingway's prose style was relentlessly to enforce such distinctions: "Cohn made some remark about it being a very good example of something or other, I forget what. It seemed like a nice cathedral, nice and dim, like Spanish churches" [67]. Racial inferiority is reproduced here as aesthetic failure. To be insufficiently "race-conscious," as Cohn had been before going to Princeton, was to be insufficiently alert to the difference between people who really were nice and people who just looked or acted nice. The war had encouraged such inattentiveness: Tom can't understand how Gatsby "got within a mile" of Daisy unless "he brought the groceries to the back door" (132); the answer, of course, is that Gatsby was wearing the "invisible cloak of his uniform" (149) so that Daisy couldn't see he was just Jimmy Gatz. Tom has to make what he calls a "small investigation" to clear up the confusion. Even Cohn "can be . . . nice" (101); in fact, Hemingway's obsessive commitment to distinguishing between Cohn and Jake only makes sense in the light of their being in some sense indistinguishable, a fact that the novel makes particularly vivid in their relations to Brett. But such similarities are definitively disrupted by the taxonomies of the bullfight and by the "oral spiritual examination" [98] Jake has to pass to prove that he has *aficion*. "Aficion is passion," Jake says: the difference between a bullfighter with it and a bullfighter without it is that the one gives "real emotion" while the other gives "a fake emotional feeling" [125]. The bullfighter with *aficion* in *The Sun Also Rises* is Romero, who is to an "imitation" like Marcial as Nick is to Gatsby or as Jake is to Robert Cohn: "He knew everything when he started. The others can't ever learn what he was born with" [124].

Aficion thus takes its place alongside niceness as another name for breeding. It may be "spiritual" but, like breeding, it is manifest in bodies; when aficionados see that Jake has it too, they put a hand on his shoulder: "It seemed as though they wanted to touch you to make it certain" [98]. But this doesn't exactly mean that *aficion* can be reduced to breeding. For one thing, as we have already seen, the term "breeding," when applied to people, isn't itself very nice; Robert Cohn is reproved for using it to describe Brett, and when Brett herself urges Mike Campbell to "show a little breeding" [105] and behave better to Cohn, Mike answers her, "Breeding be damned. Who has any breeding anyway, except the bulls?" And, for another thing, even the bulls' breeding can't exactly be reduced to breeding. Only bulls have breeding, as Mike says, but as Mike also says, "bulls have no balls" [105, 130]. Mike is drunk and he means to be insulting the bullfighter Brett is so attracted to, but there is an important sense in which Hemingway's identification of breeding with a literal inability to breed should be taken seriously, as should indeed the converse identification of literal breeding prowess with a lack of breeding.

"One thing's sure and nothing's surer," someone sings at Gatsby's house, "The rich get richer and the poor get—children" (96). Or, as the author of *The Passing of the Great Race*, Madison Grant, put it, "If we continue to allow [immigrants] to enter they will in time drive us out of our own land by mere force of breeding.[4] Grant and Stoddard both worried that, compared to the other races, whites were the "slowest breeders" (7), and Stoddard focused in particular on the sterilizing effect of immigration on whites: "There can be no question," he wrote later in the decade (after the Immigration Act of 1924 had ostensibly put an end to mass immigration), "that every low-grade alien who landed prevented a native American baby or a North European baby from ever being born" (*Re-Forging*, 167).[5] This contraceptive effect finds a weirdly literal echo in *The Sun Also Rises*, where the alien Cohn is the only one with children and where, more tellingly, he has an appropriately sterilizing impact on Nordic types like his girlfriend Frances who, having "wasted two and a half years" [37] on Cohn, imagines that her childbearing opportunities have passed: "I never liked children much," she says, "but I don't want to think I'll never have them."

Frances, however, is hardly the most spectacular example in *The Sun Also Rises* of the inability to reproduce. Jake Barnes is. The Great War, according to Stoddard, was a breeding disaster for the white race since, in killing millions of Nordic soldiers at an age when they were "best adapted to fecundity," it had (like immigration) "prevented millions more from being born or conceived" (*Rising Tide*, 185, 184). Jake's war wound is often understood as a symbol for the Lost Generation's disillusion, but the testimony of writers like Stoddard and Grant gives new meaning to the wound and to the very term Lost Generation. War tends to "induce sterility," Stoddard writes (184); "You . . . have given more than your life," the Italian colonel

4. Madison Grant, introduction to Stoddard, *The Rising Tide of Color*, xxx.

5. The rationale for this claim is provided in *The Rising Tide* in a long quotation from the racist writer Prescott Hall who, appealing to what he describes as a racial Gresham's law, insists that the "poorer" of two races "in the same place tends to supplant the better. Mark you, *supplant*, not drive out . . ." (257); some members of the superior race migrate. Hall says, "*but most are prevented from coming into existence at all.*" Hence, according to Stoddard, "The whole white race is exposed . . . to the possibility of social sterilization and final replacement or absorption by the teeming colored races" (298). Similar observations were commonplace. In *America Comes of Age, A French Analysis* (New York, 1927), for example, Andre Siegfried remarked that in "certain classes of Americans" (he instanced "intellectuals and university graduates"), "reproduction seems almost to have ceased," and he cited "figures" "published and quoted all over the country" showing that "On the basis of the present ratio, 1,000 Harvard graduates . . . will have only fifty descendants at the end of two centuries, whereas 1,000 Rumanians [*sic*] in Boston will have 100,000" (111).

tells Jake [25]. The Great War, the "White Civil War," had induced sterility above all in members of the "Nordic race" since it was Nordic men who "went forth eagerly to battle" (Stoddard, *Rising Tide*, 183) while "the little brunet Mediterranean either stayed home or even when at the front showed less fighting spirit, took fewer chances, and oftener saved their skins"; "You, a *foreigner*, an *Englishman* . . . have given more than your life," the Italian colonel says. The war had thus "unquestionably left Europe much poorer in Nordic blood," or, as Madison Grant put it, "As in all wars since Roman times, from the breeding point of view, the little dark man is the winner" (quoted in *The Rising Tide*, 183). In *The Sun Also Rises* the little dark man is Robert Cohn (during the war he "stayed home" [Grant] and "had three children" [Hemingway]), and one might say that Jake's war wound is simultaneously a consequence of the war and of unrestricted immigration since, as interpreted by the racial discourse of the '20s, immigration and the war were simply two aspects of the same phenomenon, the rising tide of color.

* * *

My Country, Right or Wrong

"Robert Cohn was once middleweight boxing champion of Princeton. Do not think that I am very much impressed by that as a boxing title, but it meant a lot to Cohn" [5]. The first two sentences of *The Sun Also Rises* are devoted to enforcing the distinction between Jake and Cohn, and its third sentence makes sure that the distinction be understood as something more than a question of sophistication about sports: the reason that his boxing prowess meant so much to Cohn is that it helped to "counteract the feeling of inferiority and shyness he had felt at being treated as a Jew at Princeton." Cohn's failure to appreciate the true meaning of his title is thus identified with his being made "race-conscious," and both the failure and the new consciousness, as I have noted earlier, are connected to the many failures of appreciation that mark Cohn's relations with Jake, from his inability to respond appropriately to cathedrals to his turning "green" at the bullfight when he'd only worried about being "bored"—"Does Cohn look bored?" Jake asks his friend Bill Gorton; "That kike!" Bill replies [121]. Hemingway's insistence on these distinctions would seem like ludicrous overkill if it weren't made necessary by the fact that, as noted earlier, Jake and Cohn are in certain respects so much alike, a fact that the novel makes particularly vivid in their relations to Brett—if, after all, Cohn follows Brett around "like a poor bloody steer" [105], it's Jake's footsteps he's treading in.

What attracts Cohn to Brett is "a certain quality, a certain fineness" that Jake dispatches with the same response he makes to the pedantry about cathedrals: "She's very nice" [30]. But the deployment here of "nice" against "fine" and "straight" is complicated by the fact that words like "fine" (e.g., "The pastureland was green and there were fine trees . . ." [64]) and especially "straight" play a crucial role in Jake's own vocabulary; it's the fact that Romero's work is "straight and pure and natural in line" [124] that distinguishes it from the "false aesthetics" of the "commercial" bullfighters. Romero's bullfighting gives "real emotion," as opposed to the "fake emotional feeling" given by his competitors, even by Belmonte, who is now nothing but "an imitation of himself." Jake's prose, the prose of "nice," "straight," and "pure," is "real"; Cohn's appropriation of that vocabulary establishes the way in which we are to understand his similarity to Jake: it is the similarity of the "imitation" to the real thing. (It's as if Cohn's real point in following Brett around like a steer is to become more like Jake.)

In bullfighting, this reality is called *aficion*, and, even though Americans are thought at best to be able to "simulate" [98] it, Jake has it. In writing, it is the vocabulary of experience, of words which serve not to represent the experience but to testify to its authenticity. (Hugh Kenner describes Hemingway as the "recorder of authenticities.")[6] Thus, although the usual procedure of *The Sun Also Rises* is to translate French dialogue into idiomatic English, it is sometimes translated with a bizarre literality (as in the concierge's reference to Brett as "a species of woman" [26]) and sometimes not translated at all (as in the concierge's later description of Brett as "gentille" [40]). These strategies have differently disruptive impacts on the realism of the representation—one by making her say what she *really* said, the other by making her say something that nobody has *ever* said—but they both bear witness to the reality of Jake's having heard her, to the authenticity of his experience of her French.[7]

But the point here is not simply that the impulse toward realism pushes Hemingway beyond realism, or even that the commitment to authenticity turns out to conflict with the conventions of realistic

6. Hugh Kenner, *A Homemade World* (New York, 1975), 145.
7. The thematic point of these disruptions is characteristically articulated by reference to Cohn; when Cohn decides he doesn't like Paris and wants to go to South America, Jake dismisses both ideas as having come "out of a book." (Indeed, Jake thinks that "all of Paris" [32] is experienced by Cohn through books, and through Mencken in particular.) Paris, Jake tells him, "is a good town" [11] that's "nice at night" [11]. "Good" and "nice" don't come out of a book, they come out of an experience of Paris as direct as the experience of the concierge's French.

representation. For the effort to achieve phenomenological authenticity goes beyond both realism and the critique of realism. What I mean by this is just that phenomenological authenticity finds its semiotic parallel in linguistic untranslatability: the literality of "species of woman" speaks to the failure of translation; "très très gentille" simply refuses translation. The meaning of these signs is understood as essentially linked to the particular form of their signifiers. From this standpoint, an idiomatic translation of "*espèce de femme*" could only be understood as seeking to disguise this fact, whereas the insistence on "très très gentille" unabashedly proclaims it. Thus the claim of authenticity for the writer's experience asserts at the same time the primacy of the sign's materiality.

This movement recapitulates two familiar (if often opposed) accounts of modernism, one emphasizing the primacy of experience, the other the primacy of language. But my point here is not just to emphasize the compatibility of the commitments to experience and to the materiality of the sign. For in Hemingway, both these commitments are put to work in the effort to separate the "imitation" from the "real," Cohn from Jake. "There is no Spanish word for bullfight" [128], Jake remarks, which is to say that the aesthetic of sincerity embodied in the bullfight is simultaneously an aesthetic of untranslatability. What we call a bullfight cannot properly be translated into Spanish, and what Spaniards call what we call a bullfight is not properly translated by "bullfight." The meaning of this link between experience and language is made explicit by the contemptuous response to Cohn's telegram informing Jake and Bill Gorton of his plans: "The telegram was in Spanish: 'Vengo Jueves Cohn.' I handed it to Bill. 'What does the word Cohn mean?' he asked?" [94]. The joke is precipitated by Cohn's writing in Spanish when everyone else writes in English and when, by contrast to Jake, he can't really speak Spanish. But its point depends upon the fact that names are like bullfights: there are no words for them in other languages. So Cohn's writing in Spanish is treated as an attempt to translate what cannot be translated, by speaking Spanish to try to make himself "one of us" and by treating his name as if it could be translated to try to disguise who he really is. Bill's response ends up, in other words, presenting the telegram as if it were an effort of assimilation—as if Cohn's speaking Spanish were to be understood on the model of Jews' speaking English and as if his identifying himself as the author of a Spanish sentence were to be understood as his attempt to anglicize a Jewish name.[8]

8. In connection with Cohn's efforts to speak Spanish, it is worth remembering something of the history of the Jews in Spain, not because Hemingway was interested in it but because of the difference that history made to the institution of the bullfight,

JEREMY KAYE

The "Whine" of Jewish Manhood: Re-reading Hemingway's Anti-Semitism, Reimagining Robert Cohn†

Introduction

Even though Hemingway wrote several Jewish characters in his career, debates surrounding his anti-Semitism predominantly hinge on his portrait of Robert Cohn.[1] The scholarly archive on Hemingway's negative, if conflicted, characterization of Cohn is virtually unified in its belief that *The Sun Also Rises*'s infamous Jewish boxer conforms to anti-Semitic stereotype. After all, critics reason, he is the novel's "primary whipping boy" (Traber 238), and he is also Jewish; these two things cannot be coincidental.

Allen Tate inaugurated this critical castigation of Cohn with a devastating 1926 review of Hemingway's novel in *The Nation*. Tate calls Cohn a "most offensive cad," a "puppet," and a "Jewish bounder" (43). Without significant exception, Cohn's marginalized status has gone unchallenged ever since. Nearly four decades later, in 1964,

---

which is, of course, central both to the Hemingway aesthetic in general and to *The Sun Also Rises* in particular.

The bullfight emerged as the great Spanish national festival in the sixteenth century, which is to say, in the wake of the Christian reconquest, which, "culminating in the expulsion of the Jews in 1492 and of the Muslims in 1502," was, as Marc Shell has put it, "*the* nationalist event in Spanish history" (*Children of the Earth*, 26). At the heart of this reconquest were the Statutes of the Purity of the Blood, which enacted distinctions not merely between Christians on the one hand and Jews and Muslims on the other but between "original Christians and conversos." The statutes changed the difference between Christians and non-Christians from a difference of religious practice into a difference of blood, and not only converts but even those whose ancestors had converted to Christianity emerged, by the standard of blood purity, as insufficiently Spanish. Shell identifies this transformation with what he regards as the underside of Christianity's universalist understanding of all humans as brothers—those who are not my brothers are not human. The bullfight, in his view, "helps to fix ideologically the difference between national and non-national" (30); it commemorates the emergence of Spain as a nation of "brothers." Whether or not one wishes to follow Shell in his reading of Christian intolerance, the identification of the bullfight as an element in an essentially racial nationalism is obviously suggestive for a reading of *The Sun Also Rises*. In Hemingway, *aficion* plays the role of pure blood, defining the group to which the Jew Robert Cohn cannot belong and structuring his attempts to join it (by sleeping with Brett, by imitating Jake) as inevitably failed efforts of conversion. The attraction of the bullfight, then, is its utility in the construction of a race—not, to be sure, a Spanish race but rather one that is nativist American in structure and international Nordic in personnel.

† From *The Hemingway Review* 25.2 (Spring 2006): 44–60. Reprinted by permission of the publisher. Notes are by the author of the original work. Page numbers in brackets refer to this Norton Critical Edition.

1. Hemingway's other Jewish characters are minor in comparison to Cohn. Two well-known examples are Al from "The Killers," whom Robert E. Meyerson calls "[t]he most sinister Jew Hemingway ever portrayed" (99), and the more sympathetic Doc Fischer from "God Rest You Merry, Gentlemen."

Leslie Fiedler was still echoing Tate's negative sentiments, describing Cohn as "the despised Robert Cohen [*sic*], Jewish butt of *The Sun Also Rises*" (64). Jonathan Freedman, in a 2003 essay investigating modernism and anti-Semitism, describes the novel in these terms:

> Jake Barnes, the castrated, war-wounded narrator, is shadowed by Robert Cohn, the alcoholic, former boxing champion at Princeton, now besotted with Lady Brett Ashley, with whom he has a brief affair about which he *whines* for most of the novel and whose new boyfriend, a matador, he savagely beats at the end of the novel. ("Lessons" 423, emphasis added)

Freedman contends that this negative portrait of Cohn typifies a "remarkably consistent pattern of response with respect to the figure of the Jew" within American modernism (423). This remarkable consistency, in Freedman's estimation, has caused many critics to place Cohn with other anti-Semitic representations of Jews in the modernist canon: Meyer Wolfsheim, criminal Jewish financier and fixer of the World Series in F. Scott Fitzgerald's *The Great Gatsby*; Simon Rosedale, the wealthy Jew who cannot seem to assimilate fully into the social elite in Edith Wharton's *The House of Mirth*; and even "those damned jews" or "yitts" in Ezra Pound's *Cantos*. Yet, unlike Freedman and other critics, I am not so sure that the characterization of Robert Cohn is an open-and-shut case of anti-Semitism.

In titling this essay "the whine of Jewish manhood," I have used the word "whine" to suggest two important aspects of my approach toward Cohn. The word first pays homage to several generations of Hemingway's readers and critics who have condemned Cohn as a "whiner"—unable to "take it like a man" the way that Jake Barnes can, unable to live up to a model of Hemingwayesque masculinity that prides itself on suffering or "emotional restraint."[2] Secondly, I use the word whine to draw attention to its long association with Jewish men. When critics such as Freedman refer to Cohn as a "whiner,"[3] they are tapping into an anti-Semitic tradition relegating Jewish men to a feminized, less-than-male status. As Daniel Boyarin has recently shown, "In the antisemitic [*sic*] imaginary of Europe (and perhaps Africa and Asia as well) Jews have been represented traditionally as female" (69). Such discourse seeks to pathologize the Jewish man as feminine within a tradition that privileges an idealized masculinity based on Western ideals of manhood such as strength, stoicism, adequacy, heterosexuality, and, most importantly, figurative possession of the phallus (see Silverman 15–51).

2. For more on suffering as foundational to Hemingway's vision of manhood, or on his aesthetic of "emotional restraint," see Fantina 89–92 and Strychacz 14–52, respectively.
3. Sanford Pinsker in *The Schlemiel as Metaphor* regards Cohn as a "whiner par excellence" (40).

Largely represented in the Western cultural imagination through such anti-Semitic tropes as the wimp, sissy, bookworm, or whiner, the Jew in obvious contrast to an idealized masculinity, is symbolically castrated, lacks the phallus. We see this conventional scripting of race and gender drawn upon repeatedly in critical readings of *The Sun Also Rises*: Jake Barnes as the figure of "white" or phallic masculinity, and Cohn, the Jew, as the figure of a deviant, less-than-white masculinity.[4] Yet the majority of criticism concerning Cohn fails to consider the transgressive possibilities deployed by his Jewishness. As the work of Daniel Boyarin and others in the "new Jewish cultural studies" so clearly demonstrates, theories about the construction and deployment of white masculinity rely on the abjected status of Jewish masculinity (see, e.g., Boyarin and Boyarin). While previous critics treated the feminized Jewish male character as "anti-Semitic [*sic*] fantasy," Boyarin instead calls for scholarship reclaiming the subversive possibilities of a figure belonging to a "culture of men . . . resisting, renouncing, and disowning the phallus" (69, 68).

My reading of Cohn explores a critical engagement between such work on Jewish masculinity and work exploring what Thomas Strychacz has called "Hemingway's theaters of masculinity." Recent path-breaking criticism has explored the construction and deployment of masculinity in Hemingway's work through issues of performativity, masochism, and fetishism.[5] Taking my cue from such scholarship, I ask several questions: How can we use the Jewish male's disruption of hegemonic masculinity to rethink one of modernism's most infamous and most vilified Jewish characters? How can we talk about Cohn's Jewishness without treating it as a stereotype of Jewish inferiority? Moreover, how can we talk about the "whiteness" of Hemingway and Jake Barnes without viewing it as the source of racist/subjugating/anti-Semitic practices? How can we reimagine

4. Here and throughout I deploy the term "white" to oppose Jew—rather than the more commonly invoked "WASP" or "Gentile"—in the interest of an accurate historical rendering of race in the modernist era. In the decades prior to World War II, Jewishness was not only characterized by religious and cultural difference, but, significantly, took on a racial character as well. While Jews would almost certainly be considered "white" in today's America, in the 1920s Jews bore the mark of the racialized subject, considered "off-white" or "not-quite-white" (Brodkin). Anthropologist Karen Brodkin narrates this historical transformation in *How Jews Became White Folks*, explaining the processes and discursive contexts that "made Jews a race and that assigned them first to the not-white side of the American racial binary, and then to its white side" (22). It was not until the post-WWII (and post-Holocaust) era, explains Brodkin, that American Jews would be considered "just as white as the next white person" (35). For a similar account of how Jews have "been both white and Other" (176) within a larger argument about the historical constructedness of whiteness as a racial formation, see Jacobson 171–99.

5. Gender studies have long been a staple of Hemingway scholarship (see Comley and Scholes), with important books by Strychacz, Fantina, and Eby exemplifying the best recent [as of 1994—*Ed.*] work on masculinity.

Cohn, not as an *object* of anti-Semitism as critics have cast him, but rather as an *agent* of Jewish manhood, disrupting the novel's privileged pairing of hegemonic and Hemingwayesque masculinity?

Whereas many critics have relegated Cohn's Jewishness to the margins of the novel (either as pure anti-Semitic stereotype, or as unimportant to a reading),[6] I would argue instead for its centrality. The fact that critics abide so willingly by the conventional racial scripting of Robert Cohn is ironic, not least because Cohn literally has the penis Jake lacks. Cohn is the novel's figure of hypermasculinity. He, not Jake, has an affair with Lady Brett and boxes his way through both Jake and Pedro Romero. Jake's narration may be obsessed with Cohn in part because Cohn possesses the penis that Jake desperately wants and needs. This obsession manifests itself in the novel's first ten pages, filled not with Jake Barnes's exploits, but with Robert Cohn's. At times an object of Jake's affection ("I rather liked him" [8]), at other times an object for Jake's rage and anxieties ("I certainly did hate him" [73]), Cohn is easily the most talked-about character in *The Sun Also Rises*, inspiring feelings of love, desire, envy, or revulsion in almost every character in the novel. We might even say that Cohn exerts a certain control over the narrative, that his energy makes the novel more interesting and alive when he is present.

Critics are not wrong in characterizing Hemingway's representation of Cohn as anti-Semitic, yet why is Jake's animosity toward Cohn so often reconstituted in critical readings? Many of Hemingway's critics and biographers are quick to apologize for the author, deeming his use of anti-Semitic slurs "regrettable," but equally quick to add, as Carlos Baker does, that "like Frost, Pound, and Eliot, to name a few—[Hemingway] was born into a time when such epithets were regrettably commonplace on most levels of American society" (xvii).[7] Biographer Jeffrey Meyers lists twenty-two Jewish friends and acquaintances of Hemingway, implying that even if the author's portrait of Cohn was anti-Semitic, Hemingway himself could not have been because he kept Jewish company (72, 586). "Jewish jokes were part of Hemingway's heritage," rationalizes Scott Donaldson, before drawing our attention to the strange biographical fact that

6. As Robert E. Meyerson puts it, "[I]f Cohn's function in Hemingway's tale is clear, what is not so clear is the purpose of rendering Cohn a Jew. . . . For the most part, references to Cohn's Jewishness or to Jews in general are just the mindless pot shots of trigger-happy loose tongues. The impetus behind them is not specific" (97, 100). Michael Reynolds posits that the novel's anti-Semitism is "irrelevant to the reading of the novel" (54). Carlos Baker adds, "Hemingway's anti-Semitism was no more than skin deep; it was mainly a verbal habit rather than a persistent theme like that of Pound" (xvii).

7. See also Reynolds ("Hemingway is a historical result, no better or worse than the America in which he was raised" [54]); Gross; and Rudat.

schoolmates had nicknamed Hemingway "Hemingstein" (20). Hemingway himself, in a 1926 letter to his publisher Maxwell Perkins, felt compelled to defend his portrait of Cohn against charges of anti-Semitism, defiantly asking, "Why not make a Jew a bounder in literature as well as in life? Do jews always have to be so splendid in writing?" (*SL* 240). In 1949, Bantam Press got into the act when, in a post-Holocaust edition of *The Sun Also Rises*, their editors expurgated the novel's one use of the slur "kike," all six uses of the adjective "Jewish," and six out of eleven appearances of "Jew" and "Jews" (Gross 149).

Much of this critical predicament is built into Hemingway studies as a discipline which, for better or worse, often privileges biography as a tool for interpreting the fiction. Debra A. Moddelmog, in her book *Reading Desire*, articulates how scholarship ostensibly about Hemingway's writing has worked instead to construct and reconstruct his persona. She notes that "the attention he has received is so clearly overdetermined and thus makes visible what is often hard to see: that critics' desires play an integral role in the construction of authors and the interpretation of their works" (2). Following Moddelmog, we can begin to see that the desire of scholars for the "real" or "true" Hemingway not to be anti-Semitic actually informs how they have read and interpreted the novel's anti-Semitism.[8]

This interrogation of anti-Semitism from the site of production—was Hemingway anti-Semitic or wasn't he?[9]—is necessarily limited. Once Hemingway has been either *outed* as anti-Semitic or *defended* from charges of anti-Semitism, the only thing left for the critic to do is articulate exactly how the portrait of Cohn is or is not anti-Semitic, how it does or does not deploy Jewish stereotypes. But the novel's central racial hierarchy remains intact: Hemingway/Jake's white masculinity on top, and Cohn's feminized, less-than-white Jewishness below. In attempting to rectify anti-Semitism, such critics explain anti-Semitism, but they never explain Cohn's Jewishness as a possible source of identification and agency. Because critics have most often explored Cohn from the site of Hemingway's *production*, they overlook the site of *reception*. Here the question "Was he or

8. Ironically, Moddelmog's point is best exemplified in what is to my knowledge the only article that defends (rather than demonizes) Cohn. In his little-cited 1957 essay, "In Defense of Robert Cohn," Arthur L. Scott argues that Cohn is "worth saving" (309); however, his defense of Cohn is really a defense of Hemingway, agreeing with the latter's statement that, "'If you think the book is anti-Semitic you must be out of your mind'" (310). See also Kenneth S. Lynn, who after juxtaposing Hemingway's real-life "insensate desire to 'get' Harold Loeb" with Jake Barnes's "ambivalently sympathetic" (296) portrait of Robert Cohn, interprets this disparity in terms of Hemingway's persona: "A complicated man, Ernest Hemingway" (295).

9. I am indebted to Jonathan Freedman for this formulation. See "Lessons" 421.

wasn't he anti-Semitic?" can be reformulated as "Can a new reading of Cohn's Jewishness emerge that neither Hemingway nor his critics account for?"

* * *

Historicism, Anti-Semitism, and the Difference of the Jew's Body

Historical context is crucial for understanding the function of Jewishness in *The Sun Also Rises*, although not only as a way, as most critics would have us believe, to excuse Hemingway's anti-Semitism as symptomatic of the rampant racism-cum-nativism permeating the modernist period. Whereas apologetic commentators depict Hemingway and other modernist writers as merely *reflecting* the era's dominant racial ideologies, it is crucial to see that such writers also took part in *creating* such ideologies. Walter Benn Michaels's important rereading of modernism, *Our America*, argues that "the great American modernist texts of the '20s must be understood as deeply committed to the nativist project of racializing the American" (13). For Michaels, "Americanness" must always be understood as "whiteness," not as a biological-scientific category, but as a socially constructed and historically changing marker of racial and cultural identity. *The Sun Also Rises*, as an exemplary model of what Michaels calls "nativist modernism," fosters a hegemonic version of "white" Americanness in a context where immigrant groups such as Jews, Italians, and Irish, among others, are racialized as non-white.[1]

Hidden Threat: Muscle Jews, White Male Fetishism, and the Construction of Cohn

The trouble with Robert Cohn in Hemingway's novel, and the reason why Jake's narration is obsessed with containing him, is that if Jake Barnes did not repeatedly *call* Cohn a "Jew," we would never know that Cohn was Jewish. Certainly, Hemingway's narrator is guilty of pointing out the "Jewishness" of Cohn's body,[2] but more often Jake performs rather envious appraisals of Cohn's body. For

1. Although both Irish and Jews would be considered white later in the century, it is crucial to understand both groups as non-white in the period under investigation (see Brodkin on Jews; see Ignatiev for a similar argument regarding the Irish in America).
2. One of Jake's first descriptions of Cohn is that he "read too much and took to wearing spectacles" (*SAR* 3), evoking images of the Jewish bookworm. Moreover, at several points in the text, Jake describes Cohn's skin as "sallow," possibly alluding to a stereotypic yellowness or sickliness of the Jew's skin (see Gilman 194–209). Examples include: "Cohn's face was sallow" [105]; "[Cohn's] face had the sallow, yellow look it got when he was insulted . . ." [131] "[Cohn's] face was sallow under the light" [139].

every reference to Cohn's "flattened" nose or "sallow" skin, we have many more references to his having a tennis player's body, a boxer's body, a body that turns Jake into a "human punching-bag" and "massacre[s]" Pedro Romero [146, 147]. Cohn's body seems quite healthy compared to Jake's war-wounded, impotent body. In fact, readers are never given a very good sense of Jake's body. When Jake does look at his "wound," he quickly turns away, too ashamed to look for longer than a moment: "Undressing, I looked at myself in the mirror. . . . Of all the ways to be wounded. I suppose it was funny. I put on my pajamas and got into bed" [25]. In comparison, Jake's narration often appears obsessed with gazing upon Cohn's body: "He was nice to watch on the tennis-court, he had a good body, and he kept it in shape" [35].

Cohn is not the weak and sickly caricature of anti-Semitic fantasy. Rather, he embodies Max Nordau's idea of the "Muscle Jew." Nineteenth-century Zionist Nordau called for a "new Jewish body" produced through "sport" and "exercise" in order to combat the "inherent neurological weaknesses of the Jew" (Gilman 53–4). This discourse allowed the Jewish subject to shed physical stereotypes of Jewishness (such as a sick and feeble body) and identify instead with the dominant category of "white" masculinity (a muscular body). Cohn, for instance, becomes a boxer to "counteract the feeling of inferiority and shyness he had felt on being treated as a Jew at Princeton" [5]. Through boxing, the "painful self-consciousness" he feels at being made "race-conscious" [6] turns into a "certain inner comfort" that comes with "knowing he could knock down anybody who was snooty to him" [5]. Boxing allows Cohn a sort of psychical assimilation, a sense that he is no more different than anyone else. Boxing also affords him physical assimilation, as his transformation into a Muscle Jew rids him of the stereotypes of Jewish embodiment exemplified by his hook nose, "permanently flattened" in a boxing accident which Jake describes as "certainly improv[ing] [his nose]" [5]. Rather than the hyper-visibility attendant on having a non-white racial body, Cohn's rebuilt, muscular body gives him invisibility. As a boxer, Cohn is absorbed into the hegemonic body of 1920s American whiteness. He becomes simply another member of the crowd, unmemorable and invisible: "I never met any one of his class who remembered him," writes Jake [5]. "If he were in a crowd nothing he said stood out" [35].

Some critics have tried to account for the fact that Cohn's Jewish body is not very different from Jake's white body. For instance, Walter Benn Michaels suggests that "Hemingway's obsessive commitment to distinguishing between Cohn and Jake only makes sense in the light of their being in some sense indistinguishable" (27).

Although he takes us part of the way in deconstructing the binary that separates the white Jake from the Jewish Cohn, Michaels is clear to distinguish their indistinguishability, noting, "[I]t is the similarity of the 'imitation' to the real thing" (73). As a Jew, Cohn can only "imitate" masculinity, while Jake embodies the "real thing." I would suggest, however, that Cohn's function in the novel is far more radical than merely to imitate Jake's white masculinity. Cohn performs white masculinity so well, in fact, that he exposes its very nature as a construct rather than an essential identity.

* * * Cohn often embodies [the] ideal [of white masculinity] better than Hemingway's surrogate, Jake Barnes. For instance, Cohn has been educated at Princeton, an Ivy League bastion of genteel white male culture, while we never know where or if Jake went to college. Cohn is a member of one of the richest and oldest families in New York, whereas Jake, the rootless expatriate, must work and does not have a family, or at least never mentions one. Furthermore, Cohn performs hyper-masculinity in the novel with his tendencies toward sexuality, aggression, and violence. Because Cohn is so close to the white masculine ideal, his Jewishness becomes even more threatening to Jake. The Jewish Cohn as a "threat" to whiteness registers with Daniel Itzkovitz's notion of "Jewish difference [being] all the more threatening because it [is] lurking somewhere behind an apparent bodily sameness" (181). It is precisely because the racial boundary between the two men is so thin that Jake must continually reiterate with verbal insults Cohn's status as a Jew, labeling him a "Jew" and a "kike" at various points in the novel. Jake's own failure to live up to the white masculine ideal means that he must compensate for his lack with repeated denigrations of Cohn's Jewishness.

Cohn's Jewishness, then, is an almost wholly imaginary creation on the part of Hemingway/Jake, situated equally within his/their masculine pose and narrative desire. For Jake, Cohn's Jewishness operates along the lines of the psychoanalytic notion of the fetish, the unsuitable substitute object of desire with its commonly invoked formula: "I know very well, but still. . . ."[3] If we follow this formula, we can recast this statement for Jake as, "I know very well that I must reject Cohn because he is Jewish, but still I need him all the same." Paradoxically, Cohn is not only the hated object of racial "difference" in the novel, the Jewish scapegoat onto whom Jake projects his worst fears and anxieties, but also the object Jake *needs* for his (and Hemingway's) versions of white identity to remain stable. Jake cannot be white—where whiteness is defined by the possession of the phallus—without the Jewish Cohn. Cohn is the fetish object holding

3. For this construction of fetishistic disavowal, see Žižek 18–9.

in place the "dominant fiction" (Silverman 15–51) that structures masculinity in the novel.

The usefulness of Cohn's Jewishness as a fetish giving integrity to Jake's masculinity corresponds with the notion of "Hemingway's fetishism" theorized by Carl P. Eby in his recent book bearing the same title. Eby successfully demonstrates how Hemingway's "fetishization of race" works so that he can define himself as "white" and "male" in relation to an insistent and ever-present racial and sexual otherness" (157). This structure of fetishistic disavowal and masculine consolidation with regard to racial bodies becomes particularly problematic, and even takes on a homoerotic character, when we remember what Jake is lacking, what he needs from Cohn in order to maintain a white masculine subject position. As Jake is missing the necessary object for the coherence of phallic masculinity—the penis itself—we can extrapolate that he sees Cohn as a symbol for his lost penis. Thus Cohn makes Jake "whole" again. It is as if Jake says, "I know very well that Cohn cannot have my lost penis, but still. . . ." Cohn's presence—indeed, his penis—allows Jake to deny his own castration (symbolic and literal) and project that lack onto Cohn's Jewishness. In order for this denial to function, however, Jake must first identify with Cohn, because Cohn has the penis he needs, before he can reject him as a Jew, thereby disavowing Cohn's importance in the making of his manhood.

This dialectical relationship of identification and disavowal structures the novel's tropes of whiteness and masculinity. It also proves that Jake cannot be the sole point of identification in the novel, as he would have to be in order for us successfully to "read" Cohn as a purely anti-Semitic stereotype. Because Jake must identify with Cohn (and his Jewish penis) in order to cover up his own lack, Jake's narration creates a chain of identification leading readers to identify with Cohn as well, even though the novel seems programmatic in its efforts to prevent such identification. In order to disavow this "perverse," unwanted identification with Cohn, Hemingway's readers must become complicit in his subjugation. Acknowledging Cohn's performative function in *The Sun Also Rises* would open up a field of racial disavowal and desire that would challenge the novel's myth of masculine wholeness. Instead, most readers accept Hemingway's scapegoating of Cohn in order that the novel's powerful figuration of Hemingwayesque masculinity can endure unscathed.

Cohn's importance to the novel's racial structure is perhaps best understood after he leaves the narrative in Pamplona. Unlike most critics who reason that Cohn's exit from the novel "marks the dismissal of the Jewish question" (Meyerson 104), I would argue that his Jewishness becomes most important to the novel at exactly this juncture. After Cohn's departure, everything falls apart for Jake: the sacred art of bullfighting is profaned; the fiesta ends with Jake feeling "[l]ow as hell" [163]; and his and Brett's idealized love for one another is lost. Cohn's absence from this last quarter of the text exacerbates Jake's masculine dissolution because he no longer has the fetish object that has consolidated his identity. Yet Cohn's psychological presence persists even after he is physically gone, becoming a sort of structuring absence that drives (if not disrupts) the narrative. A great deal of dialogue in the last chapters of the novel concerns Cohn: "'Is Cohn gone?'" [150]; "But her Jew has gone away" [153]; "I feel sorry about Cohn," [162]; "Oh, to hell with Cohn" [162]. "What do you suppose he'll do?" [162]; "that damned Cohn" [177]. Cohn's stubborn refusal to be forgotten constitutes his subversive potential.

* * *

WORKS CITED

Baker, Carlos. "Introduction." *Ernest Hemingway: Selected Letters, 1917–1961*. Ed. Carlos Baker. New York: Scribner's, 1981. ix–xxi.

Berman, Ron. "Protestant, Catholic, Jew: *The Sun Also Rises*." *The Hemingway Review* 18.1 (Fall 1998): 33–48.

Boyarin, Daniel. "Homotopia: The Feminized Jewish Man and the Lives of Women in Late Antiquity." *Differences* 7.2 (Summer 1995): 41–81.

Boyarin, Jonathan and Daniel Boyarin, eds. *Jews and Other Differences: The New Jewish Cultural Studies*. Minneapolis, MN: U of Minnesota P, 1997.

Brodkin, Karen. *How Jews Became White Folks and What That Says About Race in America*. New Brunswick, NJ: Rutgers UP, 1998.

Comley, Nancy and Robert Scholes. *Hemingway's Genders: Rereading the Hemingway Text*. New Haven, CT: Yale UP, 1994.

Donaldson, Scott. "Humor in *The Sun Also Rises*." In *New Essays on* The Sun Also Rises. Ed. Linda Wagner-Martin. Cambridge: Cambridge UP, 1987. 19–42.

Eby, Carl P. *Hemingway's Fetishism: Psychoanalysis and the Mirror of Manhood*. Albany, NY: SUNY Press, 1999.

Fantina, Richard. "Hemingway's Masochism, Sodomy, and the Dominant Woman." *The Hemingway Review* 23.1 (Fall 2003): 84–105.

Fiedler, Leslie. *Waiting for the End*. New York: Stein and Day, 1964.

Fitzgerald, F. Scott. *The Great Gatsby*. New York: Scribner's, 1953.

Freedman, Jonathan. "Lessons Out of School: T. S. Eliot's Jewish Problem and the Making of Modernism." *Modernism/Modernity* 10.3 (September 2003): 419–29.

Gilman, Sander. *The Jew's Body*. New York: Routledge, 1991.
Gross, Barry. "Dealing with Robert Cohn." In *Hemingway in Italy and Other Essays*. Ed. Robert W. Lewis. New York: Praeger, 1990. 123–30.
Hemingway, Ernest. "God Rest You Merry, Gentlemen." *Winner Take Nothing*. New York: Scribner's, 1933. 41–50.
———. "The Killers." *Men Without Women*. New York: Scribner's, 1927. 78–96.
———. Letter to Maxwell Perkins. 21 December 1926. *Ernest Hemingway: Selected Letters, 1917–1961*. Ed. Carlos Baker. New York: Scribner's, 1981. 239–40.
———. *The Sun Also Rises*. New York: Scribner's, 1926.
———. *The Sun Also Rises*. New York: Bantam, 1949.
Ignatiev, Noel. *How the Irish Became White*. New York: Routledge, 1995.
Itzkovitz, Daniel. "Secret Temples." In *Jews and Other Differences: The New Jewish Cultural Studies*. Eds. Jonathan Boyarin and Daniel Boyarin. Minneapolis, MN: U of Minnesota P, 1997. 176–202.
Jacobson, Matthew Frye. *Whiteness of a Different Color: European Immigrants and the Alchemy of Race*. Cambridge, MA: Harvard UP, 1998.
Knopf, Josephine Z. "Meyer Wolfsheim and Robert Cohn: A Study of a Jewish Type and Stereotype." In *Ernest Hemingway's* The Sun Also Rises. Ed. Harold Bloom. New York: Chelsea House, 1987. 61–70.
Loeb, Harold. "Hemingway's Bitterness." *Connecticut Review* 1.1 (October 1967): 7–24.
Lynn, Kenneth S. *Hemingway*. New York: Simon and Schuster, 1987.
Meyers, Jeffrey. *Hemingway: A Biography*. New York: Harper and Row, 1985.
Meyerson, Robert E. "Why Robert Cohn? An Analysis of Hemingway's *The Sun Also Rises*." In *Critical Essays on Ernest's Hemingway's* The Sun Also Rises. Ed. James Nagel. New York: G.K. Hall, 1995. 95–105.
Michaels, Walter Benn. *Our America: Nativism, Modernism, and Pluralism*. Durham, NC: Duke UP, 1995.
Moddelmog, Debra A. *Reading Desire: In Pursuit of Ernest Hemingway*. Ithaca, NY: Cornell UP, 1999.
Pinsker, Sanford. *The Schlemiel as Metaphor: Studies in Yiddish and American Jewish Fiction*. Carbondale, IL: Southern Illinois UP, 1991.
Reynolds, Michael S. The Sun Also Rises: *A Novel of the Twenties*. Boston: Twayne, 1988.

Rudat, Wolfgang E. H. "Anti-Semitism in *The Sun Also Rises*: Traumas, Jealousies, and the Genesis of Cohn." In *Hemingway: Up in Michigan Perspectives*. Ed. Frederic J. Svoboda and Joseph J. Waldmeir. East Lansing, MI: Michigan State UP, 1995. 137–47.

Scott, Arthur L. "In Defense of Robert Cohn." *College English* 18.6 (March 1957): 309–14.

Silverman, Kaja. *Male Subjectivity at the Margins*. New York: Routledge, 1992.

Strychacz, Thomas. *Hemingway's Theaters of Masculinity*. Baton Rouge: Louisiana State UP, 2003.

Tate, Allen. "Hard Boiled." In *Critical Essays on Ernest Hemingway's* The Sun Also Rises. Ed. James Nagel. New York: G. K. Hall, 1995. 42–3.

Traber, Daniel S. "Whiteness and the Rejected Other in *The Sun Also Rises*." *Studies in American Fiction* 28.2 (Fall 2000): 235–53.

Žižek, Slavoj. *The Sublime Object of Ideology*. London: Verso, 1989.

MASCULINITY AND (DIS)ABILITY

GREG FORTER

Melancholy Modernism: Gender and the Politics of Mourning in *The Sun Also Rises*†

The turn toward gender issues in Hemingway studies has made the author exciting and pressingly urgent once more.[1] This work has freed us from the myth of Hemingway as "He-Man of American literature";[2] it has made it possible to see in his writing more than the stylistic and representational embodiment of invulnerable manhood—a masculinity courageously asserting itself in the face of unmanning and life-threatening dangers. Instead, we have become attuned to the cracks in Hemingway's masculine armor. We have learned that manhood was for him a fraught and always fragile aspiration rather than an accomplished fact. For many of us, this has meant that what seems most moving in Hemingway now is his persis-

† From *The Hemingway Review* 21.1 (Fall 2001): 22–37. Copyright 2001. The Ernest Hemingway Foundation. All Rights Reserved. Notes are by the author of the original work. Reprinted by permission of the publisher. Page numbers in brackets refer to this Norton Critical Edition.

1. The key texts here are Comley and Scholes, Eby, Lynn, Moddelmog, and Spilka.
2. From a Barnes and Noble catalogue, quoted in Moddelmog 2.

tent struggle, against enormous psychic odds, to resist his ossification into a man whose gynophobic self-loathing leads him to despise all feminine "softness"—both within and without him.

My essay contributes to an understanding of this struggle in several related ways. I argue that *The Sun Also Rises* records the battle with special intensity; it stages Hemingway's conflict between an autonomous and invulnerable masculinity on one hand, and an emotionally expressive and connected one on the other—a battle he resolves through the fetishization of style. This conflict is linked to the larger problem of loss in the novel. My broadest contention is that this loss records an external crisis that was not simply personal but social in character. I want, accordingly, to start by describing the social origins of the loss inscribed by the novel as Jake's wound, before moving on to theorize Hemingway's response to this loss, to link this response to American modernism more generally, and to offer a reading of *The Sun Also Rises* within the context thus elaborated.

The loss in question resulted from the crisis in masculinity that took place in the United States at the turn of the last century. Sociologist Michael Kimmel has chronicled this crisis with particular acuity. He suggests that the period from 1890 to 1920 witnessed the decline of a style of manhood by which men proved themselves as men in the volatile space of the market; to do so, they had to exert an almost obsessive control over the vagaries of their bodies, but could in the process wrestle a degree of autonomy, self-mastery, and power. According to Kimmel, the explosive spread of monopoly capitalism undermined this style of manhood. The opportunities for self-making afforded by small-scale capitalism began to disappear; men became increasingly reduced to parts in a bureaucratic machine, unable to achieve the sense of autonomy so central to the meaning of manhood they inherited. This transformation went hand in hand with challenges by women and ethnic minorities to middle-class male social power. And it gave rise to a widespread panic about the feminizing effects of modern urban living—a panic about the "feminization of American culture" produced by the shifts I've described. The result, according to Kimmel, was an intense nostalgia for the rugged autonomy—the physical potency and virile self-mastery—being eclipsed by structural transformations in American life (81–188).

American modernism, at least in one of its most dominant strands, represents a relatively cohesive set of expressive responses to this crisis. Modernists as diverse as Eliot, Cather, Fitzgerald, Faulkner, and Hemingway responded to the loss of autonomous manhood in a melancholic manner. That is, they were unable to mourn or fully "work through" the loss, in part because of the nature of their attachment to the masculinity whose loss they lamented—an attachment that the psychoanalytic distinction between mourning and melancholia can help us describe.

The distinction was first proposed by Freud in "Mourning and Melancholia," whose title names two ways of responding to personal or social loss. Mourning is the process of a healthy grieving. In it, the person experiencing loss comes gradually to relinquish his or her attachment to the lost object, and so to accept the necessity of remedial substitution: the need to displace desire and attachment from the dead onto the living, in the form of "good enough" replacements for what the self has lost. The condition of this capacity to mourn is a specific kind of object-relatedness. The mourner is able to relinquish lost objects because he or she has experienced them as separate all along. The ego has already come to grips with the painful reality of separateness—the experience of borders and edges, of an interval between "me" and "you," with all the dangers of loss, abandonment, and betrayal that this entails. Because the other exists in this way as a genuinely external object, its loss can be felt as real and fully integrated by the mourner, without a catastrophic confrontation with the limits to infantile narcissism.

Melancholia, by contrast, is a reaction to loss from within an attachment to objects that does not acknowledge their difference from the self. In one sense, the object here is not an "object" at all, but a kind of narcissistic extension or prolongation of the ego. Freud writes that the melancholic's "object-choice has been effected on a narcissistic basis, so that the object-cathexis, when obstacles come in its way, can regress to narcissism" (43). In other words, melancholia can result only when the attachment to an object is psychically archaic—when one loves in the other the image of oneself, because one has not learned to experience the other as having an independent existence outside of omnipotent fantasy. The melancholic responds to loss not by gradually relinquishing the dead in the name of substitutes, but, as Freud says, by "regress[ing] to narcissism": by identifying the self with the other, incorporating the other into the self, and keeping him or her alive as an internally differentiated part of the ego. "The shadow of the object [has fallen] on the ego," Freud writes (43). Entombing within itself the only "object" it deems worth having, the ego becomes existentially impoverished, unable to open up to new love, structurally inhibited and unresponsive.

* * *

In addition to biographical relevance, melancholia has here a cultural significance. At moments of profound social crisis, the melancholic process can become a general, collective condition, and this is what happened in American modernism's reaction to the loss of masculine authority and potency. It's crucial that this loss entails an ideal rather than a person. For ideals are, in some basic way, cathected narcissistically; they have to do with one's sense of self as much as one's relation to others. They speak to the self's constitution through incorporations of what a culture defines as valuable. The historical loss of a masculine ideal would seem almost inevitably to produce in men a narcissistic injury: a rupture between their actual selves and the exalted image from which history has severed them. The response to such loss would therefore be likely to develop along melancholic lines.

Such an injury *could*, of course, be grieved and fully worked through. But the modernists who interest me did not pursue this opportunity. In response to social trauma, they sought neither to renounce nor to rescue a disappearing ideal of male autonomy and power, but rather to insist on its enormous value and its inevitable loss. These writers pay homage to a type of virility that they argue is at once the best version of manhood *and* something that can no longer be socially incarnated—that cannot withstand the onslaught of a destructive and emasculating modernity. These modernists could be said to remain melancholically fixated on a lost masculine ideal that is fundamentally toxic, and that they themselves show to be unlivable. This fixation makes it impossible to mourn or fully work through their losses—or to see in those losses an opportunity for reinventing masculinity in a less rigidly constrained, less psychically defensive, and less socially destructive fashion.[3]

I

The Sun Also Rises offers an especially fruitful illustration of this process. It traces a *doubly* melancholic pattern, staging Hemingway's paralyzing identification with two different, lost, and incompatible forms of manhood, neither of which he is able to relinquish. These forms of manhood are the sentimental and the hard. The loss of each, paradoxically enough, is figured by the phallic wound at the book's center. The novel responds to their loss by celebrating highly fetishized codes of speech and ritualized modes of behavior—*styles*—which seek at once to memorialize and to deny the amputation around which the novel turns.

The war wound clearly stands as the psychic yet physical sign of a lost masculine potency. Precisely because he was once "whole," and

3. Work on modernism in relation to mourning is just beginning. I'm particularly indebted to Seth Moglen's *An Other Modernism*, which, though not centrally concerned with masculinity, argues that modernism in the U.S. contains two distinct strands—one fixating melancholically on loss, and one seeking more progressively to mourn and project lost aspirations into the future. Other significant contributions to the field include Breitwieser and Ramazani.

precisely because he has lost that wholeness in a war dividing the old world from the new, Jake bears an emblematically modern male consciousness, haunted by the memory of a potency and plenitude it cannot recover. The wound defines him as fundamentally lacking, devoid of authentic substance; it suggests that the thing which once gave content to identity by differentiating men hierarchically from women—the penis—is now both literally and structurally inaccessible. This state of affairs makes it extremely difficult for modern men to *be* men; the wound cuts them off from the anatomical source of their own undoubted virility—a source that, in our cultural imaginary, is the root of male social power as well. It reconfigures masculine identity in terms of a restless and unfulfillable desire, with satisfaction definitively deferred in the absence of an enabling organ. And the wound leads to an experience of love as a kind of "hell on earth" [22], remaking even the city of romance—Paris—as a "pestilential" place [55] where the plague of unfulfillment plays itself out without mercy.

But the wound also carries an opposite meaning: the loss of a genteel, sentimental, and implicitly feminine masculinity. Jake's amputation and his knowledge of its consequences in this sense differentiate him from Robert Cohn, at once a kind of premodern anachronism and a "steer" who doesn't know he's a steer [105]. The problem with Cohn, in other words, is that he *has not himself been wounded*. There are other characters in the novel of whom this is literally true—Mike, Bill, and Brett, for example. But they at least "know about" the wound; they have been metaphorically, if not literally, damaged, and have suffered the kind of disillusionment the novel in part approves.

Cohn, in contrast, continues to behave as if a host of values that the wound renders hollow are still in fact live possibilities. Most significantly, he continues to *believe*—that's what makes him so distasteful and embarrassing to those who at least struggle to believe only in the impossibility of belief. He believes in "Literature" with a capital "L", substituting books for lived experience [9, 11], comparing Brett at one point to Circe [106], and seeking even to live what he thinks of as the writer's life of narcissistic unattachment [39]. He believes in romance—the romance of faraway and exotic places, romantically described in turgidly romantic prose [9]—as well as the romance of mutually fulfilling love. He believes in outdated notions of chivalry, in a way that leads him to defend his "lady love" (Brett) against the corruption of her own promiscuity [131]. And he believes, finally, perhaps above all, in traditional forms of meaningfulness, remaining oblivious to the wound that renders meaning something to be *made*, not inherited. This blindness makes Cohn unable to embrace the casual brutalities of modern sex, to see that his sexual encounter with Brett "didn't mean anything" [133].

Such a portrayal is clearly meant to convict Cohn of sentimentality. To be both sentimental and a man is to be at least implicitly feminized. So Cohn is caustically said to have been "moulded by the two women who trained him" [35]. He's repeatedly shown to cry when he gets mad [39, 142, 148], to be incapable of drinking with the big boys [117–18], and to be essentially emasculated by both his evident pining for Brett and his willingness to "take" the verbal punishment dished out by the woman he's trying to abandon (Frances). Far from guaranteeing his manly success, then, the absence of a wound works to castrate Cohn.[4] The actual loss of a penis, in contrast, functions paradoxically as the sign of real manliness,[5] saving Jake from the related perils of sexual pleasure and affective connections, from the risk of a sentimental softening that would render him, in Hemingway's eyes, insufficiently "hard," insufficiently modern—and therefore, insufficiently manly.

The wound thus carries the contradictory burden of two complex histories of loss—the loss of male power and potency on one hand, and the apparently more beneficent rupture with sentimental manhood on the other. This contradiction results from Hemingway's inability to relinquish either male sentiment *or* male power, an incapacity intimately connected with the meaning of his modernism. As previous suggested, Hemingway's work responds not just to a personal, but to a social crisis in masculinity. That crisis led many we've come to call modernists to engage in an intense masculinization of artistic production, consolidating the borders between art and not-art along explicitly gendered lines, and rejecting direct expressions of emotion as flabby, artistically unauthentic, insufficiently ironic—in short, feminine.[6] Hemingway of course participated in this modernist cauterization of affect. His style of affective omission and *The Sun*'s repeated injunction against talking about "it" are both good examples of this proclivity.

* * *

II

But the danger of even this unexpressed affect is apparently danger enough. Hemingway therefore seeks to resuscitate the phallic masculinity whose loss ought to be guaranteed by the fact of Jake's

4. This view of Cohn's unmanliness in part reflects Jake's need to disparage a potent rival. But the fact that Hemingway lets us see this in no way undermines Jake's judgments. The novel engages in strategies, particularly modes of second-person address, that construct readers as privileged insiders, seducing us into accepting both Jake's relatively benign evaluations and his more pernicious ones. See Wyatt 56–57.
5. See Moddelmog (129) and Schwartz (53–56).
6. Huyssen's essay is the classic statement concerning the modernist equation of sentimentality with a debased mass culture, and of mass culture with femininity. See also Clark, esp. 1–41.

wound. That masculinity is not simply mourned as a lost illusion of the past. Nor is it openly celebrated as an authentic content for modern men—a move forbidden by the modernist redefinition of manhood in relation to lack and loss. Instead, phallic manhood is melancholically idealized *as lost*, enlisted in an endless battle against the longed for disturbance of affect, but only once it has been displaced from a psychic content or meaning to a style. *The Sun Also Rises* celebrates such style, not only by lauding the aesthetically formalizing tendencies of Romero's matadorial technique, but also by insisting repeatedly on the "how" as against the "what" ("I did not care what it was all about," says Jake. "All I wanted to know was how to live in it" [109]). The novel celebrates codes of speech and forms of ritualized behavior which compensate for the lack of content or meaning in modern life, while also protecting their adherents from the dangers of unfettered intimacy.

This dual function—compensation and protection—is crucial to the workings of style in the novel. For example, to be a "good drunk" [109] is to cultivate a "style" of drunkenness that avoids excessively emotional outbursts of an affectionate or violent kind, even while courting the alcoholic pressure to *succumb* to emotional expression.[7] Similarly, in the fishing episode, Bill and Jake both acknowledge the wound that ought to undermine at least Jake's professions of masculine prowess, and set about asserting that prowess by conquering the feminine waters and producing an aesthetic order from their chaos [85–88].[8]

The linguistic style of the novel and of its characters' speech likewise works to compensate for the emotion it omits yet continues to yearn for. Perhaps the most central example of this strategy is the book's refusal to specify the nature of Jake's injury:

> Undressing, I looked at myself in the mirror of the big armoire beside the bed. . . . Of all the ways to be wounded. . . . I put on my pajamas and got into bed. . . . I read [*Le Toril*] all the way through, including the Petite Correspondance and the Cornigrams. I blew out the lamp. Perhaps I would be able to sleep.
>
> My head started to work. The old grievance. Well, it was a rotten way to be wounded and flying on a joke front like the Italian. In the Italian hospital . . . the liaison colonel came to visit me. . . . I was all bandaged up. But they had told him about it. Then he made that wonderful speech: "You, a foreigner, an

7. Mike is a "bad drunk" not only because alcohol makes him behave aggressively toward Cohn, but because it brings out his excessively affectionate behavior toward Brett [109].
8. Blackmore offers an interesting account of how the fishing sequence at once destabilizes gender binaries and reconsolidates them in homophobic fashion (63–65).

> Englishman" (any foreigner was an Englishman) "have given more than your life." What a speech! I would like to have it illuminated to hang in the office. He never laughed. He was putting himself in my place, I guess. "Che mala fortuna! Che mala fortuna!"
>
> . . . I lay awake thinking and my mind jumping round. Then I couldn't keep away from it, and I started to think about Brett and all the rest of it went away. I was thinking about Brett and my mind stopped jumping around and started to go in sort of smooth waves. Then all of a sudden I started to cry. Then after a while it was better and I lay in bed and listened to the heavy trains go by . . . and then I went to sleep. [25]

This is a justly celebrated passage, one at the center of debates over whether Hemingway's depiction remains ironically detached or succumbs to sentimentality. What strikes me about such debates is that critics rarely question the *value* of ironic detachment or of the omissions that enable it. The power of the scene derives in part from the fact that Jake declines to name the wound, as well as from his refusal to tell us what exactly he's feeling. Such omissions and understatements load his crying with an emotional intensity that resides in its very lack of specificity. He cries because of "it," and the Church tells him "Not to think about it," but the compulsively repetitive character of trauma requires him to return to "it," again and again. Attempts to name the wound, meanwhile, are rendered ridiculous by the Italian colonel's stumbling efforts to glorify it in words—efforts whose failure suggests that to name the injury is at once to trivialize and sentimentalize the unspeakable horrors of Jake's unmanning.

But at the same time, it is important to note the costs of this omission. There is a kind of gentility in the refusal to give the wound its name—a delicacy that Hemingway would seem to want explicitly to reject. This delicacy is less an expression of courage than a symptom of fear. To name the wound would be to give it a frightening psychic and physical specificity, raising the challenge of what it felt like to receive the wound, and what it feels like to have it. This would mean giving emotional content to Jake's illegible tears as well. Rather than linking those tears to Brett in some unspecified way ("I was thinking about Brett. . . . Then all of a sudden I started to cry"), naming would require Jake to specify exactly what the wound has made impossible for him.

* * *

In each of the cases I have described—drinking, fishing, speaking—a highly codified or stylized form of mastery invokes a knowledge it also disavows: knowledge of a phallic wound, knowledge of sentiment. The valorization of style thus functions precisely as a fetish, seeking to resolve the dilemmas of lost manhood by melancholically perpetuating what it pretends to grieve. Style defends against yet keeps alive the dual loss of sentiment and potency by serving as a kind of monument that ceaselessly speaks of the losses its erection seeks to silence. Style allows Hemingway and his characters neither openly to embrace lost affect nor to do without it, neither to lay claims to a hard masculinity nor really to renounce it.

In the case of phallic potency, the very irreparable character of loss bespeaks Hemingway's melancholic fixation. Because Jake is the victim of an amputation, his desire is *literally* unfulfillable. What he seeks but can never attain is less sexual satisfaction itself than a restoration of the penile object that cannot be recovered. The loss figured by his wound, therefore, can neither be forgotten nor mourned. It can't be forgotten because the penis remains absolutely constitutive of Jake's identity; the ultimate object of his desire is unforgettably inscribed as lost on his living body. And it can't be mourned because that would require the sober imperfection of displaced substitutes, and the *ideal* of phallic potency admits of no substitution.

Ideals by definition cannot be mourned—cannot be replaced with something like but different. Ambivalence is the prerequisite for productive grieving.[9] Although *The Sun Also Rises* offers a series of stylistic "substitutes" for the lost and idealized penis, the novel's fundamentally melancholic character results from the fact that these must fail. Style alone cannot fill the hole that constitutes modern masculinity, while filling that hole is, on *The Sun's* own terms, both the only way to set the world right and an unacceptably sentimental denial of historical and psychic reality.

* * *

WORKS CITED

Baker, Houston A. *Modernism and the Harlem Renaissance*. Chicago: U of Chicago P, 1987.

Benstock, Shari. *Women of the Left Bank: Paris, 1900–1940*. Austin: U of Texas P, 1986.

Blackmore, David. "'In New York It'd Mean I Was A . . .': Masculinity Anxiety and Period Discourses of Sexuality in *The Sun Also Rises*." *The Hemingway Review* 18.1 (Fall 1998): 49–67.

9. This statement attempts to complicate Freud's assertion that, unlike melancholia, mourning springs from a relatively unambivalent relation to the lost object. Such claims need to be supplemented by Klein's insistence on the *centrality* of ambivalence to successful grieving (152, 156–158).

Boone, Joseph Allen. *Libidinal Currents: Sexuality and the Shaping of Modernism*. Chicago: U of Chicago P, 1998.

Breitwieser, Mitchell. "*The Great Gatsby*: Grief, Jazz and the Eye-Witness." *Arizona Quarterly* 47.3 (1991): 17–70.

Clark, Suzanne. *Sentimental Modernism: Women Writers and the Revolution of the Word*. Bloomington: Indiana UP, 1991.

Comley, Nancy R., and Robert Scholes. *Hemingway's Genders: Rereading the Hemingway Text*. New Haven: Yale UP, 1994.

Davidson, Arnold E., and Cathy N. Davidson. "Decoding the Hemingway Hero in *The Sun Also Rises*." *New Essays on* The Sun Also Rises. Ed. Linda Wagner-Martin. Cambridge: Cambridge UP, 1987. 83–107.

Eby, Carl P. *Hemingway's Fetishism: Psychoanalysis and the Mirror of Manhood*. Albany, NY: SUNY P, 1999.

Freud, Sigmund. "Mourning and Melancholia." 1917. *Essential Papers on Object Loss*. Ed. Rita V. Frankiel. New York: New York UP, 1994. 38–51.

Hemingway, Ernest. *The Sun Also Rises*. 1926. New York: Scribner's, 1954.

Huyssen, Andreas. "Mass Culture as Woman: Modernism's Other." *After the Great Divide: Modernism, Mass Culture, Postmodernism*. Bloomington: Indiana UP, 1986. 44–62.

Kimmel, Michael S. *Manhood in America: A Cultural History*. New York: Free Press, 1996.

Klein, Melanie. "Mourning and Its Relation to Manic-Depressive States." 1940. *The Selected Melame Klein*. Ed. Juliet Mitchell. New York: Free Press, 1986. 146–174.

Lynn, Kenneth. *Hemingway*. New York: Simon and Schuster, 1987.

Moddelmog, Debra A. *Reading Desire: In Pursuit of Ernest Hemingway*. Ithaca, NY: Cornell UP, 1999.

Moglen, Seth. "An Other Modernism: John Dos Passos and the Politics of Literary Form." Diss. UC Berkeley, 1999.

Ramazani, Jahan. *Poetry of Mourning: The Modern Elegy from Hardy to Heaney*. Chicago: U of Chicago P, 1994.

Schwartz, Nina. "Lovers' Discourse in *The Sun Also Rises*: A Cock and Bull Story." *Criticism* 26.1 (1984): 49–69.

Spilka, Mark. *Hemingway's Quarrel with Androgyny*. Lincoln: U of Nebraska P, 1990.

Wyatt, David. *Prodigal Sons: A Study of Authorship and Authority*. Baltimore, MD: Johns Hopkins UP, 1980.

DANA FORE

Life Unworthy of Life?: Masculinity, Disability, and Guilt in *The Sun Also Rises* †

As Michael S. Reynolds and others have noted, the intense campaign of persona-building that Hemingway engaged in after being wounded in World War I makes it difficult to assess his level of anxiety over degeneration through disability. Even so, the cultural research of Joanna Bourke and Betsy L. Nies suggests that this fear would have been more than "in the air" for a wounded man returning from Europe. Bourke, for instance, notes that an increase of pension claims sensitized Britain to the literal costs of war-related disability and helped to re-energize debates over which veterans "deserved" charity and which did not (63–75). Nies, in turn, describes how similar financial concerns and the popularization of eugenic theories in the United States combined to make the war-wounded body a site for particularly intense fears about "degeneration."[1]

* * *

The *Sun Also Rises* articulates ideas currently debated within the field of disability studies, especially those related to the concept of the "disabled identity" (Linton 8–32). An examination of these new concepts, in turn, allows a re-evaluation of Hemingway's attitudes toward wounds and masculinity. Specifically, the experiences of emasculated war hero Jake Barnes reflect Hemingway's awareness of what researchers call a "medical model" of disability—a worldview that equates disability with pathology and that forces disabled people continually to "prove" to the world at large that they are completely "cured" and therefore "normal."[2] The novel's downbeat ending suggests that a philosophy that continually denies bodily realities can be as physically and mentally destructive as a literal wound. In the end, Jake will never achieve the psychological stability he craves

† From *The Hemingway Review* 26.2 (Spring 2007): 74–88. Notes are by the author of the original work. Page numbers in brackets refer to this Norton Critical Edition.

1. Discussing how racist stereotypes from the 19th century carried over into the 20th, Nies describes how the growing presence of wounded veterans in postwar America engendered a paradoxical glorification of the "fighting Nordic male" even as it fostered a widespread "collapse in the belief in the sanctity of physical borders of white soldiers" (23). According to the Lamarckian logic behind this worldview, a wounded soldier had the potential to weaken the "national health" by transmitting his "defects" into the gene pool.
2. Simi Linton defines the "medical model" as a worldview that "casts human variation as deviance from the norm, as pathological condition, as deficit, and, significantly, as an individual burden and personal tragedy." This philosophy allows non-disabled people to ignore "the social processes and policies that constrict disabled people's lives" (11).

because he finally accepts prevailing social and medical philosophies about his injury—and these ideas, in turn, will always leave him vulnerable to the fear that he will "degenerate" into an invalid or a "pervert." * * *

The specters of the eunuch and the "queer" haunt Jake Barnes and drive his search for a viable identity. In the novel, Jake's struggle to define himself as a disabled man plays out in what Thomas Strychacz calls "theatrical representations," in which he exists on a continuum of behavior "between" male characters (8, 74–80). These are men whose behavior and physical characteristics seem like exaggerated aspects of Jake's own, at least potentially. Specifically, Jake occupies a psychological middle-ground between the disabled characters Count Mippipopolous and the bullfighter Belmonte—and as he accepts or rejects these characters, we are meant to understand that he is embracing or discarding the stereotypes of able-bodiedness or disability they represent.

Generally speaking, critics have glossed over the complexity of the relationship between Jake's identity and the stereotypes linking wounds, physical power, and masculine degeneration. This oversight is due largely to the influence of Freudian thinking even within more "modern" readings of the novel that move away from the older, blatantly "heroic" and masculinist interpretations of Philip Young, Carlos Baker, and Jeffrey Meyers.[3] And so while recent interpretations have established Hemingway's awareness of gender construction and varieties of erotic desire, they consider disability primarily as a catalyst alerting Jake in a general way to the existence of a "polymorphous" sexuality. The Freudian school either aligns Jake with the stereotypical figure of the disabled man who receives a compensatory "gift" of artistic or emotional sensitivity because of his impairment, or uncritically accepts the notion that he is "turning" gay because of his injuries.

Wolfgang Rudat's essay on the Count deserves a second look at this point. Rudat identifies Mippipopolous as the only psychologically healthy disabled man in the novel, situating him within an "inspirational" discourse crafted to show how a man with injuries

3. Young arguably provides the most sustained examination of disabled men in Hemingway's works, as well as the most influential material for defining the nature of disability issues in *The Sun Also Rises*. Young's analysis goes beyond subsequent critics in its clarification of the disability experience, insofar as it resists the temptation to view Jake's mutilated penis as a metaphor for societal malaise. He recognizes that physical disabilities are never completely "overcome," and that they force individuals to view the world in different ways for a lifetime. Yet even Young falls back into the absolutist thinking that characterizes much Freudian thought regarding disability, suggesting that the disabled can never adapt to physical impairment that cannot be completely cured. Rather, disability becomes a totalizing flaw that causes the "primitivization" of personality (169), the core of an *idée fixe* that fuels a never-ending sense of "dis-grace" (41) and a dangerous "ambivalence" toward life.

arguably similar to Jake's might achieve a greater sense of mental stability. Rudat explains that Brett Ashley introduces the Count as a pawn in her quasi-sadomasochistic relationship with Jake, as yet another substitute for Jake himself, and as a target for her repressed frustration:

> [When] Brett turns to Jake to assure him that the Count is one of them, that is, that the Count is also wounded, and then makes a show of telling the Count that she loves him and that he is a "darling," she is telling Jake that the Count too is sexually "wounded". . . . The Count, whom according to her own statement Brett has told that she was in love with Jake . . . knows . . . that Brett has now communicated to Jake that he, the Count, is sexually disabled. Not only does the Count take in stride the communication to another man of his own sexual status, but he actually confirms it in order to be able to explain to the other man his philosophy of life, that is, that he "can enjoy everything so well," including relations with women. (Rudat 7)

This is a persuasive analysis of the sadomasochistic elements in Brett and Jake's relationship, but because it assumes without question that the Count is literally the best-adjusted disabled man in the novel, Rudat's reading gives a distorted picture of the disability experience that Hemingway wants to articulate.

Rudat does not recognize, for instance, that the strategies for psychic healing suggested by the Count's performance—the "subduing" of sexual desire and the transference of erotic energy into "symbolic gratification" (7)—amount to little more than a passive acceptance of the asexual status that non-disabled society considers proper for the disabled. Jake knows that the Count's solution amounts to a renunciation of his sexuality. He is familiar with this kind of "cure," and he has declared it useless; alone in his hotel room, he remembers that "the Catholic Church had an awfully good way of handling [his disability.] Good advice, anyway. Not to think about it. Oh, it was swell advice. Try and take it" [26].

Contrary to Rudat's reading, wherein Jake realizes the larger significance of the Count's advice only gradually, Jake is instantly aware that the Count is being presented to him as a "role" model, and he resents it for reasons that would be clear to a man like Hemingway, who had had a real brush with catastrophic injury. Jake's almost complete silence during this "playful" interlude between Brett and the Count may indicate his anger over having the Count paraded in front of him as a version of what Leonard Kriegel calls "the charity cripple"—a figurehead whose injuries are assumed by the non-disabled to represent the effects of all injuries, and whose typically devil-may-care attitude is held out as worthy of emulation by other "cripples" (36–37).

Jake is silent when Brett forces the Count to undress and expose his wounds, and when she declares, "I told you [he] was one of us" [46], Jake recognizes her condescension toward both the Count and himself. He knows that what Brett really wants to say is, "Look, the Count is like *you*" because he has suffered severe injury and survived; by implication, the Count's boundless ebullience is something Brett hopes Jake will adopt as well, simply because she cannot stand to be around depressing or gloomy people.

The Count, in turn, is also aware of what Brett is doing, and embraces the role of "supercrip" she has offered him. He parrots the inspirational drivel she wants to hear: "You see, Mr. Barnes, it is because I have lived very much that now I can enjoy everything so well. Don't you find it is like that?" To this utopian assessment of post-disability living, Jake responds curtly, "Yes. Absolutely" [46]. Anger and embarrassment clip his sentences, and the affect is flat and mechanical because Jake wants to limit his participation in what is essentially Brett's own private freak show.

The banter ends with a significant exchange between Brett and the Count. During a discussion of the Count's values, Brett declares, "You haven't any values. You're dead, that's all." To which the Count responds, "No, my dear. You're not right. I'm not dead at all" [46]. The concept of death here is more than a metaphor for *fin de siècle* malaise and ennui among the wealthy (Gaggin 95–99): it serves to expose the liminal nature of existence for the disabled male in this society. On the one hand, the fact that Brett can so glibly declare the Count "dead" shows how close her thinking is to the eugenic/Social Darwinist stereotypes of the period. The Count's insistent and unequivocal response, in turn, gives the lie to his studied joviality and shows his own awareness of his marginalized status, revealing how desperately a disabled man must prove to others and himself that he is "worthy" to live. Hemingway's sensitivity to stereotypes of disability, rather than Jake's inability to interpret the Count's advice correctly, helps explain why the novel quickly casts such a "positive" role model into obscurity.

* * *

How then might Jake Barnes achieve happiness in a world shaped by the limitations of his sexually mutilated body and by cultural narratives that stigmatize deformity? The novel suggests, at least initially, that Jake might achieve a sense of wholeness if he can correctly interpret the veiled truths conveyed by Brett Ashley and Bill

Gorton. These are characters who, by virtue of their unconventional worldviews, serve not so much as role models but rather as guides to show Jake how he might thrive in his otherwise oppressive and limited environment.

* * *

Some of these hints come from Bill Gorton, who emerges as a mentor for Jake during an odd shopping trip in Paris. During this interlude, Bill's eccentric banter makes connections between dead bodies and ethics in ways designed to establish that Bill, like Brett, is someone comfortable with non-standard bodies and perhaps able to help Jake on his journey toward psychological wholeness. When Bill and Jake are out walking in Paris, Bill stops by a taxidermist's shop and becomes strangely insistent that Jake buy something. "Want to buy anything?" he asks. "Nice stuffed dog?" [54].

Jake declines, but Bill will not relent. "Mean everything in the world to you after you bought it," he says. "Simple exchange of values. . . . Road to hell paved with unbought stuffed dogs" [54]. This odd joking appeals to Jake, who remembers it later when he introduces Bill to Brett as a "taxi-dermist." To which Bill replies, "That was in another country. And besides all the animals were dead" [56]. Bill's words have struck a chord with Jake, as well they might—by linking the notions of compromised (or "ex-changed") values with "dead" bodies from "another country," Bill resurrects memories of the affable "supercrip" Count Mippipopolous and draws attention yet again to the question of how one can "overcome" or adapt to a catastrophic physical injury.

Bill's praise of out-of-place, nonstandard bodies and his certainty about their value seem to constitute a metaphorical expression of the same open-mindedness that led him to rescue a black Viennese boxer from a lynch mob earlier in the novel—a scene which Bill describes in similarly nonchalant, playful terms in order to downplay the mob's potential for violence [52]. Taken together, these scenes establish Bill's importance to Jake's quest for wholeness as a disabled man. Specifically, these incidents show that Bill Gorton, like Brett Ashley, is committed to a nontraditional code of behavior allowing him to see value in bodies that the larger society would declare worthless or "dead." He seems eminently suitable as a friend for Jake: as a self-styled philosopher about what makes life worth living, Bill may be able to help Jake formulate his own principles for survival as a wounded man.

* * *

To see the full range of ideas Hemingway presents here, it is necessary to reevaluate the psychoanalytical play that occurs between

Jake and Bill in the woods. Analyses of Gorton's highly symbolic banter by both Blackmore and Buckley confirm, in essence, that Bill copies the tactics of a skilled psychotherapist, verbally creating a "safe" space for Jake to express hidden or taboo feelings without fear of censure. Thus, Bill's graphic admission that his "fond[ness]" for Jake would make him a "faggot" in New York [85] is an invitation for Jake to express similar feelings as part of the "talking cure" being constructed here.

What such analyses of this psychoanalytical session fail to see, however, is that Jake's same-sex desires may not be the only cause of his problems. For instance, the war-centered double entendres that initiate Bill's well-known repartee suggest the plight of disabled veterans. Even the famous scene where Bill teases Jake with the idea of "[getting it] up for fun" (Blackmore 60) is peppered with loaded questions that echo the standard phrases of a military recruiter: "Been working for the common good?" "Work for the good of all" [83]. Thus the text introduces a narrative thread about military service/disability that parallels the homoerotic subtext and intensifies as the joking continues between the two men.

Bill's persistent invocation of "irony and pity" further enhances this disability subtext: the phrase is a poetic crystallization of the attitudes and experiences that shaped the lives of disabled veterans during this era. Joanna Bourke, for instance, describes an "early sentimentalization" of the war-wounded that lasted until the 1920s (56). She explains that the most bathetic public responses were reserved for men with obvious deformities and amputations: in this early period, "public rhetoric judged soldiers' mutilations to be 'badges of their courage, the hall-mark of their glorious service, their proof of patriotism'" (56). According to the popular mythology of the times, a severe wound inspired more than just intense patriotism: women were supposed to be especially attracted to men with obvious injuries; these men, in turn, "were not beneath bargaining pity for love" (Bourke 56). For a time, a distinction was made between men wounded in war and those born with birth defects: the former were "broken warriors," and poems singing their praises "adopted the ironic, passive tone of the newly-styled, modern poetry" (Bourke 57).

The decline of national fascination with the war-wounded was foreshadowed by the concurrent stigmatization of veterans like Jake, whose disabilities were invisible to the public eye. Bourke reports: "The absent parts of men's bodies came to exert a special patriotic power. In the struggle for status and resources, absence could be more powerful than presence. The less visible or invisible diseases that disabled many servicemen . . . could not compete with limblessness" (59). This bias in favor of amputees translated into a pervasive resentment against men who were "merely" diseased or invisibly injured: such men were more often considered to be of inferior stock, or literally less "important" than men with obvious wounds (Bourke 59–60). During the postwar years, as the novelty of wounded men wore off and disabled veterans began to compete for resources with the civilian unemployed, this kind of resentment would even be directed against "heroic" amputees (Bourke 63–75.)

Given this historical context, there is a double irony at work in the novel. According to the new rules of this modern world, Jake could "pass" as one of the most heroic of heroes. He has suffered the all-important amputation of a "part"—one which most men would probably consider the most vital "limb" of all. And yet the injury cannot be paraded in front of the public for acclaim. Because his wound must remain hidden and unknown, it must also remain "shameful."

The other resonant moment of irony and pity occurs at the point where Bill's humorous play falters. The way Bill's lighthearted tone is broken intensifies the novel's focus on disability, revealing that Freudian therapy is ill-equipped to deal with the many problems associated with a physical impairment. In the midst of "defining" Jake, Bill explains,

> You're an expatriate. You've lost touch with the soil. You get precious. Fake European standards have ruined you. You drink yourself to death. You become obsessed by sex. You spend all your time talking, not working. You're an expatriate, see? You hang around cafes. . . . You don't work. One group claims women support you. Another group claims you're impotent. [85]

On one level, this chatter reinforces the novel's well-known destabilization of sexual stereotypes by lampooning the traditionally gay or bisexual figure of the Wildean "Decadent." However, if we employ the psychoanalytical perspective established by Blackmore, Rudat, and Buckley, this babble becomes "empty speech"—the Freudian term for symbolic discourse designed to mask unpleasant truths. Seen in this light, it becomes apparent that what Bill is desperately trying—and trying *not*—to talk about is Jake's wound.

Consider first how the passage develops the character of the *expatriate*. He or she is defined, ultimately, as someone who is "impotent." This seems like an odd conclusion if one adheres to the literal definition of an *expatriate* as someone who has left his or her homeland. However, the characterization makes sense if one scratches the surface of the word to reveal the homonym beneath—"ex-patriot," a euphemism for a discharged soldier. This hidden concept exposes the wound-related anxiety here, because Jake's mutilated penis is the reason he has become an "ex-patriot" and an impotent *expatriate*. All the flaws ascribed to this decadent character—alcoholism, laziness, unemployment, sexual obsessiveness, and dependence on women—are also weaknesses stereotypically ascribed to wounded men whose injuries have supposedly destroyed all positive aspects of their former personalities (Pernick 49–52).[4]

Jake's response to Bill's prompting is simple, yet significant: countering the charge of impotence, he says, "No . . . I just had an accident" [85]. The matter-of-fact tone here suggests that Jake may finally be able to accept his disability. He is on the on the verge of catharsis, of "coming out" as a disabled man (Shakespeare 50–55).

Any potential recovery is thwarted, however, by Bill's response: "Never mention that. . . . That's the sort of thing that can't be spoken of. That's what you ought to work up into a mystery. Like Henry's bicycle" [85]. The joking is only half-hearted here: to some degree, Bill really *doesn't* want Jake to talk about his wound explicitly because his amateur therapy session (and by extension, Freudian theory in general) cannot address the range of problems associated with physical impairment. Thus Bill, the advocate of irony and pity, becomes an ironic figure—a therapist asking his patient to repress inconvenient problems.

For his part, Jake intuits the opportunity for healing presented to him here, and wants to exploit it. He notes that Bill "had been going splendidly," and wants to "start him again" on a more in-depth discussion of Jake's wound [85]. But the task is too daunting for Bill. After a brief discussion of the nature of Henry's wound, Bill declares, "Let's lay off that" [85], and the conversation turns to repressed homosexuality—a more familiar (and less threatening) realm for amateur psychoanalysts.

Interpreting *The Sun Also Rises* from a disability perspective leads to a dark view of human existence, but not for the reasons most critics have discussed. Jake's struggles to find a place for himself in the postwar world help Hemingway to show that a wide and unacknowledged range of social ideas attach to physical impairment, and these cultural narratives work unobtrusively and insistently to make disability into a "master trope for human disqualification" (Mitchell and Snyder 3). A disability reading of the novel centers the work in Bill Gorton's refrain, "Oh, Give them Irony and Give them Pity" [83–84]. Hemingway gives us a novel where the failed romance between the hero and his lady represents the day-to-day

4. Martin S. Pernick explains the basis for this totalizing view of disability in his analysis of eugenics and euthanasia. Specifically, he discusses the widespread belief in core genetic material known as "germ plasm" which, according to the science of the time, could be altered by environmental factors encountered after birth, such as poisons, illness, psychological shock, and wounds. Damaged germ plasm could drive a previously healthy organism into a state of physiological degeneration or "atavism" and transmit a variety of dangerous personality traits through a family bloodline (Pernick 49–52).

struggle for (and with) "normality" for a generation of severely wounded survivors.[5]

The final, terrible irony of the novel is that it supports the idea that Brett and Jake *can* end their torment and be together in all senses of the word: sex is not impossible between them. However, neither Jake nor any of his well-meaning friends can rid themselves of their ingrained prejudices about disability, and these social constraints become the real obstacles to Jake's rehabilitation. The furtive sexual pleasures that Brett gives Jake are few and far between, and expressed in the classic Hemingway modes of elision, understatement, and silence indicative of guilt; for his part, Jake has internalized the stereotype of the sexually mutilated man who would be better off dead—he finally believes that "there's not a damn thing [he can] do" [21].

Thus, at the novel's conclusion, when Brett declares "Oh, Jake . . . we could have such a damned good time together," he can only respond, "Yes . . . Isn't it pretty to think so?" [180]. Although the use of "pretty" here is a "feminine" affectation, it is hardly, as Rudat has suggested (in "Hemingway on Sexual Otherness" and "Sexual Dilemmas"), the sign of Jake's life-affirming liberation from heterosexist prejudice. Rather, it is a sign that—despite occasional glimpses of his sexual potential—Jake has finally accepted the life society has mapped out for him as a disabled man. Jake will join Count Mippipopolous as a caricature of life and a toy for Brett's amusement, like one of the "pretty nice stuffed dogs" that stare at Bill Gorton from the window of a Paris taxidermy shop [54].

WORKS CITED

Baker, Carlos. *Ernest Hemingway: A Life Story*. New York: Scribner's, 1969.

———. "The Wastelanders." In *Modern Critical Interpretations:* The Sun Also Rises. Ed. Harold Bloom. New York: Chelsea House, 1987. 9–24.

Blackmore, David. "'In New York It'd Mean I Was A . . .' Masculinity Anxiety and Period Discourses of Sexuality in *The Sun Also Rises*." *The Hemingway Review* 18.1 (Fall 1998): 49–67.

5. Tom Shakespeare (1996) eloquently summarizes the most common stereotypes of disabled sexuality:

> Stereotypes of disability often focus on asexuality, or lack of sexual potential or potency. Disabled people are subject to infantilization, especially disabled people who are perceived as being 'dependent.' Just as children are assumed to have no sexuality, so disabled people are similarly denied the capacity for sexual feeling. Where disabled people are seen as sexual, this is in terms of deviant sexuality, for example, inappropriate sexual display or masturbation. (10)

Bourke, Joanna. *Dismembering the Male: Men's Bodies, Britain and the Great War*. Chicago: U of Chicago P, 1996.

Brown, Steven E. "Movie Stars and Sensuous Scars." In *Male Lust: Pleasure, Power, and Transformation*. Eds. Kay and Nagle, et al. New York: Harrington Park, 2000. 37–43.

Bruno, Richard L. "Devotees, Pretenders and Wannabes: Two Cases of Factitious Disability Disorder." *Journal of Sexuality and Disability* 15 (1997): 243–260.

Buckley, J. F. "Echoes of Closeted Desire(s): The Narrator and Character Voices of Jake Barnes." *The Hemingway Review* 19.2 (Spring 2000): 73–87.

Callahan, John. *Don't Worry, He Won't Get Far on Foot*. New York: Vintage Books, 1990.

Comley, Nancy R. and Robert Scholes. *Hemingway's Genders*. New Haven: Yale UP, 1994.

Eby, Carl P. *Hemingway's Fetishism: Psychoanalysis and the Mirror of Manhood*. New York: State U of New York P, 1999.

Elliot, Ira. "Performance Art: Jake Barnes and 'Masculine' Signification in *The Sun Also Rises*." *American Literature* 67 (March 1995): 77–94.

Gaggin, John. *Hemingway and Nineteenth-Century Aestheticism*. Ann Arbor: UMI Research, 1988.

Hemingway, Ernest. *The Sun Also Rises*. 1926. New York: Scribner's, 2003.

Kriegel, Leonard. "The Cripple in Literature." In *Images of the Disabled, Disabling Images*. Eds. Alan Gartner and Tom Joe. New York: Praeger, 1987. 31–46.

Linton, Simi. *Claiming Disability: Knowledge and Identity*. New York: New York UP, 1998.

Mellow, James R. *Hemingway: A Life Without Consequences*. New York: Houghton Mifflin, 1992.

Milam, Lorenzo. *The Cripple Liberation Front Marching Band Blues*. San Diego: MHO, 1984.

Mitchell, David T. and Sharon L. Snyder. *Narrative Prosthesis: Disability and the Dependencies of Discourse*. Ann Arbor: U of Michigan P, 2001.

Moddelmog, Debra A. *Reading Desire: In Pursuit of Ernest Hemingway*. Ithaca: Cornell UP, 1999.

Meyers, Jeffrey. *Hemingway: A Biography*. New York: Harper and Row, 1985.

Nies, Betsy L. *Eugenic Fantasies: Racial Ideology in the Literature and Popular Culture of the 1920s*. New York: Routledge, 2002.

Pernick, Martin S. *The Black Stork: Eugenics and the Death of "Defective" Babies in American Medicine and Motion Pictures Since 1915*. New York: Oxford UP, 1996.

Reynolds, Michael S. *Young Hemingway*. New York: Basil Blackwell, 1986.

Rudat, Wolfgang E.H. "Hemingway on Sexual Otherness: What's Really Funny in *The Sun Also Rises*." *Hemingway Repossessed*. Ed. Kenneth Rosen. Westport, CT: Praeger, 1994. 169–179.

———. "Sexual Dilemmas in *The Sun Also Rises:* Hemingway's Count and the Education of Jacob Barnes." *The Hemingway Review* 8.2 (Spring 1989): 2–13.

Shakespeare, Tom. *Untold Desires: The Sexual Politics of Disability*. London: Cassell, 1996.

Spilka, Mark. *Hemingway's Quarrel with Androgyny*. Lincoln: U of Nebraska P, 1990.

Strychacz, Thomas. *Hemingway's Theaters of Masculinity*. Baton Rouge: Louisiana State UP, 2003.

Vernon, Alex. "War, Gender, and Ernest Hemingway." *The Hemingway Review* 22.1 (Fall 2002): 34–55.

Young, Philip. *Ernest Hemingway: A Reconsideration*. University Park, PA: Pennsylvania State UP, 1966.

Ernest Hemingway: A Chronology

1899	Born Ernest Miller Hemingway on July 21 in Oak Park, Illinois, son of Clarence Edmonds Hemingway, a medical doctor, and Grace Hall Hemingway, a musician.
1913–17	Attends Oak Park and River Forest High School, where he performs especially well in English and participates in various sports including football, track and field, and boxing. Takes a journalism course as a junior and publishes his first article in January 1916. Edits the high school yearbook.
1917	Works for six months as a reporter for the *Kansas City Star* newspaper.
1918	Attempts to enlist in United States armed services (Army, Navy, and Marines), but is rejected due to poor eyesight. Recruited as a volunteer ambulance driver for the Red Cross. Arrives at the Italian Front in June. Participates in rescue and recovery of bodies after explosion at munitions factory in Milan, an incident he describes in *Death in the Afternoon* (1931). Stationed at Fossalta di Piave, where he is seriously wounded in the legs by machine gun fire and mortar shrapnel on July 8. Receives Italian Silver Medal for Bravery. While in hospital in Milan, meets and falls in love with Agnes von Kurowsky, a Red Cross nurse seven years older than he is. Meets and befriends Eric Edward ("Chink") Dorman-Smith, a British officer.
1919	Returns to the United States in January, planning to marry Agnes von Kurowsky, but receives a letter in March in which she informs him that she has married an Italian military officer. Takes a long camping and fishing trip in Michigan's Upper Peninsula in September, and later in the autumn accepts a job with the *Toronto Star*.
1920	Takes another summer trip to Michigan, after which he moves to Chicago (in September), where he writes and works as associate editor for *Cooperative Commonwealth*. Meets Sherwood Anderson, an American short story writer by whose themes and style Hemingway is heavily

influenced in his own early fiction. Meets Hadley Richardson, a young woman from St. Louis eight years his senior.

1921 Marries Hadley Richardson on September 3. In November, the couple move to Paris, where Hemingway takes a job as foreign correspondent for the *Toronto Star*.

1921–23 Lives with Hadley Richardson in Paris, first in a small apartment at 74, rue du Cardinal Lemoine, in the Latin Quarter. Meets Gertrude Stein, whose salon was decorated with work by Picasso, Miro, Cézanne, and others, and was a gathering place for expatriate American writers. Meets American poet Ezra Pound at Sylvia Beach's Shakespeare and Company bookshop; teaches Pound to box, receives advice on modern writing from Pound, and travels in Italy with the poet. Files over eighty stories for the *Toronto Star*, including articles covering the Greco-Turkish War of 1920–22, which provided material for several short prose sketches. In April 1923, publishes "In Our Time," a collection of six of those sketches, in the *Little Review*, an influential modernist "little magazine." Later that year publishes *Three Stories and Ten Poems* with Contact Editions, a small press run by the American writer Robert McAlmon (the volume includes "My Old Man," "Out of Season," and "Up in Michigan"). Travels to Spain for the first time and experiences the San Fermin festival in Pamplona, including the bullfights (about which he writes several sketches). Returns to Toronto in September 1923.

1924 Bored in Canada, returns to Paris in January, living now on the rue Notre-Dame des Champs. Co-edits *Transatlantic Review* with Ford Madox Ford, publishing "Indian Camp" in the magazine. At Pound's invitation, publishes *in our time*, a collection of eighteen prose sketches, with the Three Mountains Press, a small press in Paris operated by the American expatriate William Bird. Attends the San Fermin festival in July. Meets F. Scott Fitzgerald, whose *The Great Gatsby* leads him to think that he should write a novel.

1925 Hemingway's first full-length fiction collection, *In Our Time*, published by New York's Boni & Liveright. After visiting Pamplona again for San Fermin (with Lady Duff Twysden, Pat Guthrie, Donald Ogden Stewart, and Harold Loeb), begins writing a novel based on the week's events (the first draft of what will become *The Sun Also Rises*). Finishes the draft in eight weeks.

1926 Revises the manuscript extensively during a winter ski trip in Schruns, Austria. Begins an affair with Pauline Pfeiffer, who urges him to abandon his contract with Boni & Liveright and sign with Scribner's, a larger company. Sends the manuscript to Scribner's, who agree to publish it. Revises the novel in galleys, cutting the opening two chapters (at Fitzgerald's advice), in August 1926. *The Sun Also Rises* published by Scribner's in October.

1927 Divorced from Hadley Richardson in January. Converts to Catholicism; marries Pauline Pfeiffer in May. Publishes story collection, *Men Without Women* in October.

1928 Moves with Pauline Pfeiffer to Key West, Florida (at the suggestion of his friend, the writer John Dos Passos). Father commits suicide. Hemingway works on a new novel, *A Farewell to Arms*.

1929 Publishes *A Farewell to Arms* in September.

1932 Publishes *Death in the Afternoon*, a nonfiction book about the history, ritual, and artistry of the bullfight. A film version of *A Farewell to Arms* (starring Helen Hayes and Gary Cooper) is released.

1933 Publishes story collection, *Winner Take Nothing*. Travels with Pauline Pfeiffer for ten-week safari in East Africa. During this trip, which provided material and inspiration for *Green Hills of Africa* and for such stories as "The Brief Happy Life of Francis Macomber," contracts amoebic dysentery and is evacuated by airplane to Nairobi, Kenya (an incident that is fictionalized in "The Snows of Kilimanjaro").

1934 Buys a boat, the *Pilar*, and spends time sailing and fishing in the Caribbean.

1935 Publishes *Green Hills of Africa*.

1936 Meets journalist and writer Martha Gellhorn in Key West.

1937 Publishes novel, *To Have and Have Not*. Travels to Spain as a correspondent for the North American Newspaper Alliance (NANA) to cover the Spanish Civil War. Collaborates with filmmaker Joris Ivens on *The Spanish Earth*, a film promoting the Spanish Republic. Begins an affair with Martha Gellhorn, who is also covering the Civil War.

1938 Publishes *The Fifth Column and the First Forty-Nine Stories*, which incorporates the earlier collections, *In Our Time* and *Men Without Women*, along with the title play, set during the siege of Madrid. Spends several months in Key West and travels twice to Spain; witnesses the conclusive Battle of the Ebro, the final stand of Republican forces and International Brigades fighting on behalf of the Republic before they retreated across the river, defeated by the forces of General Francisco Franco.

1939 Separates from Pauline Pfeiffer. Moves to Cuba, where he rents "Finca Vigia" ("Lookout Farm") and is joined by Martha Gellhorn.

1940 Divorced from Pauline Pfeiffer; marries Martha Gellhorn. Establishes summer residence in Ketchum, Idaho, near Sun Valley, while maintaining winter residence in Cuba. Publishes novel, *For Whom the Bell Tolls*, which is nominated for the Pulitzer Prize.

1941 Travels to China with Martha Gellhorn, who is covering war in the country for *Collier's* magazine. Returns to Cuba before American declaration of war on Japan in December.

1943 Film of *For Whom the Bell Tolls* (starring Gary Cooper and Ingrid Bergman) released.

1944 Travels to London, where he meets Mary Welsh, a correspondent for *Time* magazine. Relationship with Martha Gellhorn falls apart. Witnesses the Normandy landings from a ship near Omaha Beach, but (like other correspondents) is not allowed to land. Spends summer, fall, and winter with American troops and French Resistance fighters in Europe. Upon the liberation of Paris by Allied forces, he visits Sylvia Beach and Pablo Picasso, and he is joined in Paris by Mary Welsh. Hospitalized for pneumonia after witnessing combat in the Hürtgen Forest. Film version of *To Have and Have Not* (loosely based on the novel, starring Humphrey Bogart and Lauren Bacall and directed by Howard Hawks) released.

1945 Divorces Martha Gellhorn. Suffers knee and head injuries in automobile accident.

1946 Marries Mary Welsh and they live together in Cuba and Idaho. Film of *The Killers* (loosely based on Hemingway's story, starring Burt Lancaster and Ava Gardner and directed by Robert Siodmak) released. Begins work on novel, *The Garden of Eden* (published posthumously in 1986).

1948 Travels with Mary Welsh in Europe, including several months' stay in Venice, where Hemingway becomes infatuated with Adriana Ivancich, a nineteen-year-old. Begins *Across the River and Into the Trees*, partially based on his relationship with Adriana Ivancich.

1950	Publishes novel, *Across the River and Into the Trees*. The novel receives mostly negative reviews.
1951	Publishes *The Old Man and the Sea*, which becomes a Book-of-the-Month Club selection and a bestseller.
1952	Wins Pulitzer Prize for *The Old Man and the Sea*. Film *The Snows of Kilimanjaro* (loosely based on Hemingway's story, starring Gregory Peck and Ava Gardner) released.
1954	Injured in two plane crashes in January while in Africa on safari. Receives the Nobel Prize for Literature. Unable to travel to Stockholm due to injuries suffered in the African plane crashes, he sends his prize address to be read at the ceremony, which includes the famous sentence, "Writing, at its best, is a lonely life."
1956	In Paris, retrieves trunks he had stored at the Ritz Hotel in 1928 and discovers in them notebooks from his years living in Paris. Drawing on these, he writes *A Moveable Feast*, a memoir of those years (posthumously published in 1964).
1957–59	During a period of productive writing, makes progress on *True at First Light* (published in 1999), *The Garden of Eden*, and *Islands in the Stream* (published 1970). Travels to Spain in 1959 to work on a series of articles about bullfighting for *Life* magazine; these become both a 40,000-word article published in *Life* in 1960 and a book, *The Dangerous Summer*, (published 1985). In July 1959, Fidel Castro deposes Fulgencio Batista and takes power in Cuba. Hemingway buys new home in Ketchum, Idaho.
1960	Leaves Cuba with Mary Welsh for the last time, depositing manuscripts and artworks in a Havana bank vault. Travels to Spain, where he becomes seriously ill (news reports claim that he is near death). Returns to New York in October and travels with Mary Welsh to Idaho. Checks into Mayo Clinic in Minnesota in November, where he is treated for depression with electroconvulsive therapy through December.
1961	Publishes *The Snows of Kilimanjaro and Other Stories*. Returns to Ketchum after being released in January from Mayo, but still suffering severe depression and suicidal ideation, returns to Mayo for further treatment. Released in late June, goes back to Ketchum. Dies by self-inflicted shotgun wound on July 2.

Selected Bibliography

• indicates work excerpted in this Norton Critical Edition.

Biographical and Historical

Baker, Carlos. *Ernest Hemingway: A Life Story*. New York: Scribner, 1969.

• Beach, Sylvia. *Shakespeare and Company*. New York: Harcourt, Brace and Company, 1956.

Bruccoli, Matthew J., ed. *Conversations with Ernest Hemingway*. Jackson: U of Mississippi P, 1986.

———, ed. *Hemingway and the Mechanism of Fame: Statements, Public Letters, Introductions, Forewords, Prefaces, Blurbs, Reviews, and Endorsements*. Columbia: U of South Carolina P, 2006.

Dearborn, Mary V. *Ernest Hemingway: A Biography*. New York: Knopf, 2017.

Fitch, Noel Riley. *Sylvia Beach and the Lost Generation*. New York: Norton, 1993.

Gajdusek, Robert E. *Hemingway's Paris*. New York: Scribner, 1978.

• Hemingway, Ernest. *The Letters of Ernest Hemingway. Volume 2: 1923–1925*. Edited by Sandra Spanier, Alfred J. DeFazio III, Robert Trogdon. Cambridge: Cambridge UP, 2013.

• Hoffman, Frederick J. *The Twenties: American Writing in the Postwar Decade*. New York: Free Press, 1962.

Lynn, Kenneth S. *Hemingway*. New York: Simon and Schuster, 1987.

Reynolds, Michael S. *Hemingway: An Annotated Chronology*. Detroit: Omnigraphics, 1991.

———. *Hemingway: The Paris Years*. New York: Blackwell, 1989.

———. *The Young Hemingway*. New York: Blackwell, 1986.

Wagner-Martin, Linda, ed. *A Historical Guide to Ernest Hemingway*. New York: Oxford UP, 2000.

———. *Ernest Hemingway: A Literary Life*. New York: Palgrave Macmillan, 2010.

Reference and Collections

Donaldson, Scott, ed. *The Cambridge Companion to Ernest Hemingway*. Cambridge: Cambridge UP, 1996.

Grissom, C. Edgar. *Ernest Hemingway: A Descriptive Bibliography*. New Castle, DE: Oak Knoll Press, 2011.

Holcomb, Gary E., and Charles Scruggs, eds. *Hemingway and the Black Renaissance*. Columbus: Ohio State UP, 2012.

Moddelmog, Debra A., and Suzanne Del Gizzo, eds. *Ernest Hemingway in Context*. Cambridge: Cambridge UP, 2013.

Nagel, James, ed. *Critical Essays on Ernest Hemingway's* The Sun Also Rises. New York: G. K. Hall, 1995.

Scafella, Frank, ed. *Hemingway: Essays of Reassessment*. New York: Oxford UP, 1991.

Stoneback, H. R. *Reading Hemingway's* The Sun Also Rises: *Glossary and Commentary*. Kent, OH: Kent State UP, 2007.

Wagner, Linda. *Ernest Hemingway: A Reference Guide*. Boston: G. K. Hall, 1977.

Wagner-Martin, Linda, ed. *Ernest Hemingway: Seven Decades of Criticism*. East Lansing: Michigan State UP, 1998.

———, ed. *Ernest Hemingway's* The Sun Also Rises: *A Casebook*. New York: Oxford UP, 2002.

———, ed. *New Essays on* The Sun Also Rises. New York: Cambridge UP, 1987.

Waldhorn, Arthur. *A Reader's Guide to Ernest Hemingway*. New York: Noonday, 1972.

Books about Hemingway

• Baldwin, Marc D. *Reading* The Sun Also Rises: *Hemingway's Political Unconscious*. New York: Peter Lang, 1997.

Berman, Ronald. *Fitzgerald, Hemingway, and the Twenties*. Tuscaloosa: U of Alabama P, 2001.

Donaldson, Scott. *By Force of Will: The Life and Art of Ernest Hemingway*. New York: Viking, 1977.

Griffin, Peter. *Less Than a Treason: Hemingway in Paris*. New York: Oxford UP, 1990.

Hays, Peter L. *The Critical Reception of Hemingway's* The Sun Also Rises. Rochester: Camden House, 2011.

• Moddelmog, Debra A. *Reading Desire: In Pursuit of Ernest Hemingway*. Ithaca: Cornell UP, 1999.

Reynolds, Michael S. *Hemingway's Reading 1910–1940: An Inventory*. Princeton: Princeton UP, 1981.

———. The Sun Also Rises: *A Novel of the Twenties*. Boston: Twayne, 1988.

Rudat, Wolfgang E. H. *A Rotten Way To Be Wounded: The Tragicomedy of* The Sun Also Rises. New York: Peter Lang, 1990.

Sarason, Bertram D. *Hemingway and the Sun Set*. Washington, DC: NCR Microcard, 1972.

• Spilka, Mark. *Hemingway's Quarrel with Androgyny*. Lincoln: U of Nebraska P, 1990.

• Svoboda, Frederic J. *Hemingway and* The Sun Also Rises. Lawrence: U of Kansas P, 1983.

Wyatt, David. *Hemingway, Style, and the Art of Emotion*. Cambridge: Cambridge UP, 2015.

Articles

Adair, William. "Cafes and Food: Allusions to the Great War in *The Sun Also Rises*." *Journal of Modern Literature* 25.1 (2001): 127–33.

———. "*The Sun Also Rises*: Mother Brett." *Journal of Narrative Theory* 40.2 (2010): 189–208.

Annesko, Michael. "The Torments of Spring: Jake Barnes's Phantom Limb in *The Sun Also Rises*." *Literature and Medicine* 33.1 (2015): 52–69.

Balassi, William V. "The Writing of the Manuscript of *The Sun Also Rises*, with a Chart of Its Session-by-Session Development." *Hemingway Review* 6.1 (1986): 65–78.

Bosse, Walter. "'Aggravatin' Papa': Race, Omission, and Discursive Liminality in Ernest Hemingway's *The Sun Also Rises*." *Pivot: A Journal of Interdisciplinary Studies and Thought* 3.1 (2014): 6–33.

Cain, William E. "Going Nowhere: Desire and Love in *The Sun Also Rises*." *South Carolina Review* 48.2 (2016): 154–67.

Cheatham, George. "'Sign the Wire with Love': The Morality of Surplus in *The Sun Also Rises*." *Hemingway Review* 11.2. (1992): 25–30.

Cohen, Milton. "Circe and Her Swine: Domination and Debasement in *The Sun Also Rises*." *Arizona Quarterly* 41.4 (1985): 293–305.

Curtis, Mary Ann C. "*The Sun Also Rises*: Its Relation to *The Song of Roland*." *American Literature* 60.2 (1988): 274–80.

Elliot, Ira. "Performance Art: Jake Barnes and 'Masculine' Signification in *The Sun Also Rises*." *American Literature* 67.1 (1995): 77–94.

• Field, Allyson Nadia. "Expatriate Lifestyle as Tourist Destination: *The Sun Also Rises* and Experiential Travelogues of the Twenties." *The Hemingway Review* 25.2 (Spring 2006): 29–43.

• Fore, Dana. "Life Unworthy of Life?: Masculinity, Disability, and Guilt in *The Sun Also Rises*." *The Hemingway Review* 26.2 (Spring 2007): 74–88.

• Forter, Greg. "Melancholy Modernism: Gender and the Politics of Mourning in *The Sun Also Rises*." *The Hemingway Review* 21.1 (Fall 2001): 22–37.

Holcomb, Gary Edward. "*The Sun Also Rises* in Queer Black Harlem: Hemingway and McKay's Modernist Intertext." *Journal of Modern Literature* 30.4 (2007): 61–81.

Josephs, Allen. "Toreo: The Moral Axis of *The Sun Also Rises*." *Hemingway Review* 6.1 (1986): 88–99.

• Kaye, Jeremy. "The 'Whine' of Jewish Manhood: Re-reading Hemingway's Anti-Semitism, Reimagining Robert Cohn." *The Hemingway Review*: 25.2 (Spring 2006): 44–60.

Kent, Jessica. "Baldwin's Hemingway: *The Sun Also Rises* in *Giovanni's Room*." *Twentieth Century Literature* 63.1 (2017): 75–93.

Kerrigan, William. "Something Funny about Hemingway's Count." *American Literature* 46.1 (1974): 87–93.

Morgan, Kathleen. "Between Two Worlds: Hemingway's Brett Ashley and Homer's Helen of Troy." *Classical and Modern Literature* 11.2 (1991): 169–80.

Muller, Timo. "The Uses of Authenticity: Hemingway and the Literary Field, 1926–1936." *Journal of Modern Literature* 33.1 (2009): 28–42.

Rudat, Wolfgang E. H. "Cohn and Romero in the Ring: Sports and Religion in *The Sun Also Rises*." *Arizona Quarterly*: 41.4 (1985): 311–18.

Schmigalle, Gunther. "How People Go to Hell: Pessimism, Tragedy, and Affinity to Schopenhauer in *The Sun Also Rises*." *Hemingway Review* 25.1 (2005): 7–21.

Schwarz, Jeffrey A. "'The Saloon Must Go, and I Will Take It with Me': American Prohibition, Nationalism, and Expatriation in *The Sun Also Rises*." *Studies in the Novel* 33.2 (2001): 180–201.

Scott, Arthur L. "In Defense of Robert Cohn." *College English* 18.6 (1957): 309–14.

See, Sam. "Fast Books Read Slow: The Shapes of Speed in *Manhattan Transfer* and *The Sun Also Rises*." *Journal of Narrative Theory* 38.3 (2008): 342–77.

Strychacz, Thomas. "Dramatizations of Manhood in Hemingway's *In Our Time* and *The Sun Also Rises*." *American Literature* 61.2 (1989): 245–60.

Tomkins, David. "The 'Lost Generation' and the Generation of Loss: Ernest Hemingway's Materiality of Absence in *The Sun Also Rises*." *MFS: Modern Fiction Studies* 54.4 (2008): 744–65.

Tompkins, Jane. "Criticism and Feeling." *College English* 39.2 (1977): 169–78.

Vernon, Alex. "The Rites of War and Hemingway's *The Sun Also Rises*." *Hemingway Review* 35.1 (2015): 13–34.

• Wagner, Linda W. "*The Sun Also Rises*: One Debt to Imagism." *The Journal of Narrative Technique* 2.2 (May 1971): 88–98.

Wagner-Martin, Linda. "Racial and Sexual Coding in Hemingway's *The Sun Also Rises*." *Hemingway Review* 10.2 (1991): 39–41.

Willis, Rachel. "Defusing Violence: Maneuvering Confrontation in *The Sun Also Rises*." *James Dickey Review* 29.1 (2012): 47–57.